REVIVED

SARAH NOFFKE

One-Twenty-Six Press.
Revived
Sarah Noffke

Published in the United States by One-Twenty-Six Press
ISBN: 978-0-9862080-4-1

Praise for Works:

Praise for Works:

"There are so many layers, so many twists and turns, betrayals and reveals. Loves and losses. And they are orchestrated beautifully, coming when you least expected and yet in just the right place. Leaving you a little breathless and a lot anxious. There were quite a few moments throughout where I found myself thinking that was not what I was expecting at all. And loving that."
-Mike, Amazon

"The writing in this story was some of the best I've read in a long time because the story was so well-crafted, all the little pieces fitting together perfectly."
-The Tale Temptress

"There are no words. Like literally. NO WORDS. This book killed me and then revived me and then killed me some more. But in the end I was born anew, better."
-Catalina, Goodreads

"Love this series! Perfect ending to an incredible series! The author has done this series right."
-Kelly at Nerd Girl

"What has really made these books stand out is how much emotion they evoke from me as a reader, and I love how it comes from a combination of both characters and plot together. Everything is so intricately woven that I have to commend Sarah Noffke on her skills as a writer."
-Anna at Enchanted by YA

For Colleen. Wasn't sure if you knew how much I appreciated your friendship so I did this.

Chapter One

If there were any windows in the Institute, I'd shatter them all. Assaulting stainless steel walls isn't just unsatisfying, it's ridiculously stupid. As evidenced by my bruised knuckles, steel is unrelenting to attacks. When glass shatters, it releases pain, numbs ache, dissipates anger. Steel mirrors me, amplifying the negative emotions. Encouraging them. I loathe metal. I'd tear my silver and copper bracelet off and chuck it across the Institute except it's the only thing keeping Zhuang from boring into my head and making me insane.

For the rest of my life, I will never forget the moments that followed Trey telling my brother and me that he was our lost father. Joseph's face paled; there was this weird mix of hope and pain in his eyes. Silence filled the room. I imagined a sound like sandpaper on tile as Trey's eyes shifted between Joseph and me. His fingers flexed as he braced himself, waiting for a response. Trey was already accustomed to my bad temper and tendency to explode, like when I learned that Joseph and I were twins. This time, I remained silent. Stunned.

Now I'm sitting in a remote corner of the Institute's five-story library. I have surrounded myself with fifty-eight books like a shield-wall. Hopefully this serves well enough to tell anyone who happens to find me that I want to be left alone. If it doesn't, then I'll rip pages out of the books and make a banner that reads "Stay Away!" I'm hoping it doesn't come to that. I love books and these are all of my favorites. Having them around me brings an ounce of comfort as I review the conversation from the night before.

Trey's words were like jagged pieces of stale bread that I was forced to swallow. After his confession, he explained in broken sentences that he had to split Joseph and me apart and have us raised by strangers. To protect us from Zhuang, he insisted. If we'd spent our childhood at the Institute, there would have been other problems. His eyes didn't look directly at us when he said, "It was difficult to make that decision, but that's the one I made. I know

1

you're already wondering why I've kept this secret from you. I don't see what benefit you'll gain by knowing I'm your father. You'll just be consumed with resentment and frustration now—exactly what I wanted to avoid. The moment I split you up and sent you away from the Institute, I made the decision that you'd never know the truth. In light of the severity of our current situation, however, honesty is the only remedy."

He was deflecting his mistakes onto Joseph. Also, he'd already played that "difficult decision" card on me in the past. This was manipulation and I wasn't buying it.

Surprisingly, it was Joseph who asked the first question as I sat frozen. "Who was our mother?"

"Her name was Eloise. She was a Middling," he said, meaning that she couldn't dream travel. Even the description of our mother as a Middling stuck in my throat. I thought that soon I'd be gagging from all the new information.

"What happened to her?" Joseph asked, not meeting Trey's eyes.

"There was an accident on a ship with no way to save her." His voice was cold, businesslike, and it made me hate him even more.

When I finally spoke there was nothing "businesslike" in my tone. I had questions and I wanted answers. No more deceptions. "Who else knows?"

"Only Ren," Trey said, staring directly at me. "No one else knows I'm your father."

"Why him?" I asked, disgusted immediately.

"That's not relevant," Trey answered.

"You realize this is complete bullshit!" I yelled.

"I figured you'd see it that way," he said flatly.

"Roya," Joseph tried to caution me.

"Shut up, Joseph!" I roared, feeling heavy and motivated. "You know whose fault it is that Zhuang has been revived? It's yours!" I said, pointing a shaking finger at Trey. "If you hadn't kept everything from us then this never would have happened."

"Roya, I really wish I could take the blame for Joseph's mistakes, but I can't," Trey said, staring at me, eyes red.

"Well, Trey, I really *wish* you'd take your lies and Institute and shove them all up your ass!"

Needless to say, that was the end of that conversation.

2

♦

Somehow, by breakfast the next day, most of the Institute knew about the latest scandal. Sitting at my table, I stirred my oatmeal until it turned to sludge. I tried to make sense of something that was never going to compute, even if I owned all the greatest minds in the entire world—like my father.

"You don't have to be a mind reader to know you're about to murder someone of high status," Samara said, easing into the seat next to me.

"Oh, well, I'll work on altering my thoughts a bit. I don't want to get arrested." I gave a ridiculously fake laugh, then added, "Do the Lucidites have a police force?"

Samara shook her head.

"So do you know?" I asked, letting the question hang in the air like smoke after a fire.

She nodded and stared at my oatmeal, unable to make eye contact with me.

"And is it because the information is sitting on the top of my head?" I asked.

"Well, yes, and also because Patrick told me when I was having my omelet made."

"Oh, that's fabulous," I said without a hint of enthusiasm. "Just how you want your closest friends to find out the news." The Institute suddenly felt small, although it was huge and went on for miles. Everyone would know within the hour. No one would hear the news from me.

I looked up right then to find George framed in the entryway to the main hall. He scanned the room, then his eyes seized mine, a whirl of concern in them. Hurried steps brought him over to me. He blinked, like trying to clear suddenly blurred vision. "Roya, what is it?" he asked, taking the seat on the other side of me.

Undulant pressure rose to the surface at the sound of his voice. I shrugged in response to his question. It wasn't a good response, but it was the only one I could manage without turning into a blubbering idiot, which wasn't an option. His presence piqued every emotion—making them impossible to easily handle. Unable to meet his eyes, which were no doubt leaking with desperate concern, I shot Samara a look and nodded. She returned the gesture.

3

"Roya and Joseph just learned Trey is their father," she said too loudly, an excitement in her voice she failed to suppress. "As you can probably tell by scanning the main hall, most of the Institute has just learned this too. I found out in the breakfast line," she added in a conspiratorial whisper.

George turned to me, went to grab for my hand, but paused an inch away. "Oh, Roya, I'm sorry. This is so unfair."

Unfair. George overuses that word the same way people overuse the word *awesome.* Most things aren't awesome. The Milky Way is awesome. Niagara Falls is awesome. But a pair of shoes isn't awesome. A side of fries isn't awesome. Neither is a new hairdo or most other things that are described using *that* word. And most things aren't unfair. Fairness isn't something that even exists in the world I live in. Things just are. Trying to equate them using a scale of justice is ridiculous and only leads to frustration and defeat.

"It's okay, George," I said, sounding oddly like I was trying to console him in this awkward situation. "I'm not fine, but I will be. Just need time to process."

He leaned down low, his breath smelling minty. "I'm here if you need anything."

"You didn't know, did you?" I accused, suddenly gripped by the idea. "You didn't know Trey was my father, the way you knew Joseph was my brother? You said you could feel the connection between us and that's how you knew before I did."

He shook his head, a roughness in his eyes like he was appalled that I'd even consider the notion. "No. I hardly feel any emotions from Trey," he said.

"I'm not sure he has any," I said, looking up from the table and immediately regretting it. Most people in the main hall were staring at me like I was wearing a plate of spaghetti on my head. And one person's expression in particular was enough to snap my sanity like a twig. Aiden's eyes grew wide as the white coat next to him leaned over and whispered the news in his ear. His chin jerked to the side and down, repulsion written on his face.

I expected him to bring his eyes back up to find mine, to offer me comfort in a look. I expected him to raise his head and finish his toast. I even half expected him to come over to me and say something, anything. But he didn't. Aiden stayed, eyes pinned on the table, stress furrowing his brow, for too long. I lost track of how

long he stayed frozen. Then I left, unable to bear how his paralysis threw my heart into a fit of wild tics.

Now I'm cuddled up on a couch in the library surrounded by books and not able to make sense of any of this. Volumes written by Poe, Emerson, Thoreau and their contemporaries aren't doing their jobs anymore. I'm starting to feel the doom push in on me.

Joseph strides up to my fortress of books and swiftly knocks it down with a single kick. "Enough!"

I turn over on my side, pull a book up next to me, and pretend to read it.

"Stark, this is worthless behavior," he reprimands.

"Who says?" I say, stretching out my feet on the coffee table in front of me.

"Face this *with* me," Joseph says, looking defenseless.

"Why'd you blab to everyone?" I ask, not hiding my disdain.

"It was an accident actually," Joseph says, pushing his hands through his short blond hair. "I told Trent when we were standin' in line at the buffet table this morning. I guess one of the kitchen people overheard it. By the time I'd gotten through the line and sat down it appeared a fair amount of people already knew. People love a scandal, what can I say."

"It shouldn't have come out," I say bitterly. "You were sloppy."

"Well, it's too late now, so get over it."

"That's what I was trying to do. You're interrupting my 'get-over-it' ritual."

"No I'm not. You're just using this as another excuse to sulk."

"I don't really need any more excuses, thank you very much." I pull a few of the closest books to me, hoping they'll provide the comfort and salvation I'm seeking through osmosis.

"I just need you to wake up," Joseph pleads with an exasperated tone. "You think I can face this without you right now?" Apparently he forgot how much he made me face alone while he was off resurrecting Zhuang, but this is probably not the right time to throw it in his face.

Joseph ignores my obvious body language that warns him to stay away, shoves a dozen books on the ground loudly, and sits down on the sofa next to me. "Please, just this once don't run away.

I need your help. This isn't somethin' I want to deal with on my own."

Suddenly something new enters my heart; it isn't my own self-pity, it's Joseph's suffering. I pull at the string attached to his emotion and a series of thoughts follow. They aren't my thoughts though, they're his. For some reason now I can pick up on his thoughts and emotions the way he's always done with me. I stay silent as I listen to him. *Why does she have to be so difficult? She's so selfish.*

I swiftly punch him in the arm.

"Ow!" he yelps. "What was that for?" he says, rubbing his arm.

"Selfish? Really? Well, you haven't seen anything yet."

Realization falls on his face after a brief moment of confusion. "Oh, well it's about time, Stark. Welcome to the sibling mind reading club."

Joseph has been able to pick up my thoughts since the beginning. However, I've had more difficulty with it. I suspect this is because I was too overwhelmed with facing Zhuang and dying. After that whole mess was over, Zhuang was apparently in Joseph's head, blocking our connection. Now is the first time I'm able to truly feel and know his thoughts. The experience is foreign, like I've just put on a pair of gloves that are too big but soon conform to my hands. It feels all wrong and also, completely right. And it creates an obligation to him I haven't felt before.

"All right," I finally say, "you're not alone in this, Joseph. We're a team. I'm here for you."

"Thank you," he says. "It hurts, doesn't it? It hurts to know that whatever his reasons were, he let us go. He put us each in a stranger's home believing that was somehow better for us than being here…together." Joseph stares off in the distance at nothing in particular.

"It doesn't make sense," I say.

With a shake of his head he continues, "He's so distanced from this whole thing. There are a million things he should be telling us, but instead he sums up everything in a few words."

"My thoughts exactly," I say.

"Like something about our mother. More than just her name would be nice."

"And why is it that Ren is the only other person who knew?" I ask, the question suddenly occurring to me.

"Yeah, that makes no sense whatsoever," Joseph says, then laughs unexpectedly. "Bet Trey is being bombarded with questions now."

"Good, I hope it's terribly difficult for him." My words feel rough as they come out of my mouth.

"Nah, I doubt it. He appears to be pretty good at deflecting these things."

"Isn't it weird that he's spoken to us so many times and not shown the least bit of sentiment?" I ask, twirling my hair rapidly around my finger.

"You think that's weird?" Joseph gawks at me. "That's you! That's totally your behavior."

I narrow my eyes. "I resent that statement."

"Sorry, but that's the truth."

"That's your opinion," I say, but silently I know there's some truth to what he says.

"Trey is really the least of my problems at this point. I'm actually grateful that people are busy gossiping about this conspiracy." Joseph tugs on his shirtsleeve, yanking it down by his wrist like he's suddenly cold.

"Because it takes the attention off the fact that you brought Zhuang back," I state abruptly.

"Yeah, as I said, sensitivity really isn't your strong suit."

"I can understand the guilt and frustration; however, it could have happened to anyone. Zhuang picked you because you fit the criteria, but it just as easily could have been me or someone else," I say.

"It wouldn't have been you. There's no way you would have fallen for it. If you can spot Chase's projections then you'd spot Zhuang's for sure."

"It was going to happen one way or another. You can probably appreciate Samara's position more than ever. She was in a similar predicament when she killed Pearl. What's done is done. Zhuang is alive because he was never dead. This just means that this time we have to kill him for good." I sound much more triumphant than I feel.

"We?" Joseph looks at me weakly.

7

"Yeah, this time we're a team," I say. "We have to act that way. For starters, we need to figure out how we're going to confront this whole Trey mess when we face the Institute."

Chapter Two

The decorations from last night's party are still hanging in Aiden's lab. A song I've never heard plays softly from the speakers overhead. And the Head Scientist looks like he's seen a ghost when I stroll in and lean against his door frame.

"Get in here," he says, rushing over to me. His arm extends. I expect it to wrap around my waist, wrenching me into him. Instead he holds down the button next to his lab door, sending it shut. The button, which is always highlighted blue, now turns red.

"What are you doing?" I ask as he paces back over to his main workstation and pins his worried eyes on the table.

"Locking the door."

I didn't know the doors in the Institute locked.

"Why?" I ask, cautiously making my way closer to him.

"Because we need to talk. Uninterrupted." His eyes look like they're trying to saw the table in front of him in two.

"Aiden," I say at his side.

He turns and faces me, but his eyes don't find mine, only stare off to the right. "I can't..."

"What?" I lose all the air in my chest suddenly.

He shakes his head. "I can't tell Trey about us. Not now."

"Why? Because he's my father?"

"Yes, because he's your father. And also because the timing is all wrong."

"Aiden, why won't you look at me?"

His blue eyes dart to mine, a rare sadness in them. "Roya, this is difficult. Everything has changed. I love you, but—"

"Nothing has changed," I interrupt.

"Yes it has. Before it was a professional issue. Now it's personal. Trey wasn't going to like the idea of me dating his greatest asset at the Institute. He's going to hate the idea of me dating his daughter."

"I don't care what Trey thinks!"

"I do. He's my boss!"

"He's a freaking liar!"

"Roya, please stop making this harder."

9

"Me? It's Trey. He literally, literally ruined my life. Put me in a stranger's home. Embedded them to raise me. Hid my twin. Hid my identity. Hid his identity. Refused to let me live where I wanted. Forced me to lead deadly missions. And puppeteered how everyone here interacts with me!" I'm screaming now. Waving my hands in the air. I step forward and consider beating my fists against Aiden's chest. The pain is about to engulf me—take over. Wrapping his arms around me, he pins me into him. My heart is a half skip from unleashing a torrent of tears. I thrash in his tightly grasping arms, until he squeezes me so firmly my heart feels flattened by the pressure.

"Roya, I'm sorry. I'm so sorry," he whispers into my hair.

My chest convulses with angry tears, but I win the battle, keeping them imprisoned inside me. Surrendering to his embrace, I wiggle an inch back, untucking my arms and sliding them around him. I tilt my chin back until I find his eyes staring down at me fiercely. His breath rolls onto my cheeks. Then suddenly his hands grip my arms, pushing me back away from him. Flustered, he retreats several steps.

"Aiden, please don't do this. I need you right now. Don't run from away this."

He shakes his head roughly. "I have to. The timing isn't right. Maybe in a while things will settle down—in a year or so."

"A year?! Are you serious?"

"Roya, this *is* serious. I can't risk it. Not right now."

"I thought you wanted this." I motion between the two of us. "I thought you wanted me."

"I do. It's just—"

"We deserve to be together."

His eyes close for a half beat. When he opens them I'm impaled by his pain. "People don't always get what they deserve. Things sometimes don't work out like they're supposed to."

Unable to accept this turn of fate my mind launches into a full search for a solution. "Look, I'm Trey's daughter. I can go to him, tell him about our relationship. I'll make sure he doesn't use it as a reason to fire you or take away your funding or do whatever it is that you're worried about."

"You don't get it. Trey will go to any length to protect you. My projects have mostly centered on you. I know the other head officials are also charged with guarding and watching you. It's their job too, to ensure everything necessary is discovered, invented, and innovated in order to secure your development and future. I knew he was slightly obsessed with you, but I always thought it was because you were Zhuang's challenger. Now I realize the full extent. And I know firsthand that Trey will go to any length to continue to protect you. Even if that means terminating an employee who compromised the integrity of the Institute by getting too close to its greatest asset."

"Why do you keep calling me that? Greatest asset?"

A harsh laugh falls out of his mouth. "Because that's how Trey refers to you in meetings."

"That's kind of sick."

He half shrugs.

"I can still talk to Trey," I plead. "I'll threaten him. Tell him I'll hate his guts if he punishes you."

"You already hate him. And Trey doesn't care if you like him or not. That's not his priority."

"Right, I get it. My protection is all he cares about."

"Roya, I was willing—excited—to expose our relationship yesterday, before all this came out. I thought I could convince Trey that our relationship wouldn't interfere with my work. But you're his daughter. I don't know how to face him with this. It isn't right. If it doesn't go well then I have so much I stand to lose."

"Well, I'm not keeping secrets anymore."

"I know."

"Which means..."

"No matter what, this has to be over anyways. Even in secret I can't risk it."

A wild force sprints forward in my mind. It's unleashed by my scorned heart, which has recently learned it has new depths it can sink to. "Aiden, you didn't tell me about Joseph. You embedded my fake family. And you've worked on demonic projects. I can get over all that and love you despite the lies and secrets. But what I can't overlook is that you're a coward."

11

Chapter Three

"What we both need is a distraction," I say as the elevator descends to the fifth level.

"Cable television works for that kind of thing," Joseph says.

"TV rots your brain."

"I'm all right with that. I'll just rely on my dashin' looks."

"I've got something we can do which is way better than watching mind-numbing TV," I say, pausing in front of the Panther room.

"Is there a zoo in the Institute that I'm unaware of?" Joseph says, reading the sign by the door.

"Who knows, but through this door is Shuman's department. No panthers...that I know of."

"I thought her spirit animal was a rattlesnake," Joseph says, scratching his head.

"It is. I have no idea why it's named that. Hell, I hardly understand half of what she says."

Unexpectedly, the door slides back. Shuman stands staring at us, her amethyst eyes rimmed with annoyance.

"We were just coming to see you," I say in a nervous rush.

"I know," she says, stepping back and permitting us to enter.

My eyes take a little while to adjust to the purplish light of the Panther room. It isn't until we're standing in front of the conference table that I can see without squinting.

"The department room is named after a Panther because this animal symbolizes the ability to see the unseen, which is much of what news reporters are expected to do," Shuman says, as though reciting something from a textbook.

"Oh, did you hear us in the hallway earlier?" I ask, embarrassment flushing my face red.

"No," she says at once. "I sensed the question."

Oh, right. That's not weird.

"Well, I brought Joseph with me because before you were interested in both of us reporting for you," I say, watching satisfied surprise fall on Joseph's face.

"Far out! Yeah, I'd love to news report," he says.

12

"I did express this interest," Shuman says, pushing her long, black ponytail off her shoulder like it's a nuisance. "I believe that if you, Joseph, pass the news reporting tests and trainings you will be incredibly good."

My face screws up in confusion. "Why would he have to go through the qualification and training process? I didn't have to."

"Your situation is quite different than your brother's. He has been weakened. It is important to determine that he is worthy of the task of news reporting. There is much at stake when you lie down to report and it is unwise to compromise his and the Institute's safety by putting him in that chair unprepared. I would—"

"I made a mistake," Joseph interrupts.

"That is clear enough." Shuman focuses on him. "But those problems do not need to become mine. Going through the process that all others have to follow is the best way to confirm this will not be an issue for you again in a different vein."

"He's been beside me through all the missions. He's proven that he's worthy of news reporting," I say.

"Joseph has also proven that he compromises his own safety and that of others when emotionally charged," Shuman says in an airy voice.

"People who make mistakes are in the best position to make better choices," I say, standing tall, trying to match Shuman's demeanor. "Just give him a chance. I'll be working with him. If there's a hint of a problem then he can go through 'the process.'"

Shuman stands stoically considering me and my words. After a quick deliberation she takes a step backwards. "Joseph, you will give your report directly to me when you are done today. Then we will decide if you will news reports or not." She glances at me. "Roya, give him a tour before you begin."

"Yes," I reply, feeling suddenly jittery with adrenaline.

She pivots and strides off like a soldier. I turn to Joseph with a suppressed smile of victory. He returns it.

"I like this idea for distraction, especially 'cause I was worried you were takin' me to the library to read books," Joseph says.

"That would have been a waste of my time. We both know you can't read."

"Yeah, yeah. Just go ahead and show me what happens in this voodoo shop."

I lead him down the same path I took when I first toured the News Reporting department. Joseph listens, looking eager and also anxious. When we arrive at my familiar reporting station I point to an adjacent, empty chair.

"So I just lie down and find something to report?" Joseph asks skeptically.

"Well, you've got to focus and meditate, but yes. It's pretty straightforward. There's something about the way they've constructed the environment here that helps," I explain, lying back in my own chair. "Clap on those headphones when you're ready."

"That's it? That's all of the explanation I get?"

"It's way longer than the one I got. Don't overthink it. You were born for this kind of stuff."

He smiles weakly at me. "All right, here goes nothing."

For the very first time I have an agenda while news reporting: to find information on Zhuang. Sadly, after a half an hour of meditating and focusing I admit defeat. It's been impossible in the past for any reporters to find information on Zhuang. I'm not sure why I thought I'd have different luck. However, I did receive a multitude of other stories. Unlike any times before when I've reported, I'm given a few flashes of different upcoming events. It must be Joseph's close proximity that's heightening my clairvoyance. The flashes include a natural disaster that will strike Indonesia within the hour, tonight's lottery numbers for the state of Illinois, a plane crash for flight 2347, a terrorist attack planned for two days from now, and a few other stories of national interest. Not only do I receive more than one story, which is unusual, but the timing of the events is hours or days from now—instead of minutes.

I awake from my vision and charge off to the computer terminal. With gentle keystrokes I detail the various events I witnessed. As usual the information is deemed "unverifiable."

Joseph's sitting at the large oval table in the main quarters of the department room. Shuman sits directly across from him, unblinking as she listens to his report. From my position, ten feet away, I'm unable to hear anything and too nervous to step any closer. After another minute Joseph stands up from the table and leans across it looking fluid and relaxed. He extends a hand to Shuman. She shakes it, but with a reluctant ambivalence.

"See you tomorrow," he sings, waving for me to follow as he charges to the exit.

"Were you able to see anything?" I ask, having trouble keeping up with his excited steps as we head to the elevator.

"Oh yeah," he says with a confident smirk. "I saw somethin' all right."

"Is it relevant enough?"

"I'd say so." He turns to me, his chest swelling with unmistakable pride. "I just told Shuman how she's gonna die."

Chapter Four

"Wow! Nice necklace, Stark," Joseph says, taking the seat next to me in the main hall. He leans in closer, eyeing the ruby beaded necklace that now holds the frequency adjuster.

"Thanks," I say, running my fingers over the cool faceted ruby beads. "It's our birthstone, you know."

"I didn't. Is it from Harvey and Harvey?"

"Yes, it's from Bob and Steve. For my birthday."

"I remember having a birthday as well. Where's my gift?"

I ignore him by turning to George. "The last time I saw them, Bob had a fit because the adjuster was tied around my neck with a piece of twine. He said if I had to wear equipment full-time that it deserved to be displayed with class."

A slow smile spreads across George's face. "It is classy. Makes the adjuster look more like an ancient artifact."

"I'm glad you like it," I say, clasping the adjuster between my fingers and turning to Joseph. "Anyway, if you want some fancy jewelry then go get your own pseudo parents."

"Nah, I'm good," Joseph sings, then gives a sudden laugh. "Hey, you reckon Trey owes our fake families money for back child support or somethin'?"

"Actually, you want to know what's weird?" I say, having a host of memories rush to the surface suddenly.

"Besides your fashion sense? Do tell," Joseph says.

I roll my eyes. "Well, every year or so my parents would get unexpected money. It was always for different reasons: an overpayment on the insurance policy, a class action settlement they didn't remember being a part of, different things like that. They actually began joking over the years about what long-lost aunt was going to die that year, leaving us unexpected money. Guess that was Trey, huh?"

"Just proves you've always been the favored child," Joseph says with a huff. "I can't ever remember my fake dad getting money."

"Or he hid it from you and spent it on booze," I say, remembering Joseph's fake father had problems when it came to drinking.

"Yeah, that's probably the truth. Still, I think Pops favors you."

"Oh, because he elects me for dangerous missions? More like he wants me dead."

"Whatever. Well, I've got to go see a guy about a thing," Joseph says, waving to George and me.

"Fine, just don't go resurrecting some zombie, would you?"

"Ha-ha, Stark. Not funny," he says over his shoulder.

"One day, we'll laugh about this whole Zhuang thing," I say to George, the only person I've confided in about the drama. "Well, we'll laugh if Zhuang doesn't kill us first."

"On another note, and hopefully less morbid," he says, sweeping crumbs back closer to his plate, "at your party you said there was something you wanted to talk to me about. Is now a good time?"

My mind flashes on that moment. Hard to believe, less than forty-eight hours ago I thought I had a future with Aiden. I was going to tell George about it, let him down easy. What was the point now? Aiden and I are history. "It's not important anymore," I say, dismissing the idea with a wave of my hand.

He eyes me cautiously. "Well, do you want to talk about the Trey situation?"

"Not really. Thanks though."

"You know, I didn't know my father," he says, then bites down on the corner of his bottom lip.

"Really?" I ask, more surprised by the disclosure than the information. George only goes into "sharing mode" when he's trying, senses he can make up ground with me.

"My mother is definitely a Middling, so he must be a Dream Traveler," he says.

"How do you figure?"

"Well, the trait has to come from somewhere, like a gene or something. Dream Travelers are a race, right? That's what Shuman says."

"True," I say, ruminating on the idea. "So what happened to him? Your father?"

"My mother says he was abusive. She ran away from him when I was a baby in order to protect us."

"That's sad. Were you ever curious about him?" I ask, thinking how the last couple of months my own curiosity regarding my real parents had been trumped by all the deadly missions.

"All the time for a while, but then I developed my empathesis and experienced the emotions of abusive people. They're toxic. I'm better off not knowing him."

"Maybe your dad is Ren," I say with a laugh. "He's verbally abusive and who knows what else he's capable of. Wouldn't that be weird if he was your secret father, like Trey is mine?"

George pretend scowls at me. It's kind of endearing. "My father was from Chicago, not London. And do I look the least bit like Ren?"

A sudden chuckle falls out of my mouth. "No, thank God. You're attractive and Ren looks like a giant leprechaun."

"Attractive, huh?"

"Well, yes." I blush. "Did you want me to elaborate on that description?"

He leans in close. "Very much so."

Just then from across the room Aiden's eyes collide with mine. I turn back to George in a rush.

"Well, the part I like about you most is your brown eyes—they're subtly intense." I laugh. "Does that combination even sound possible? Subtly intense?'"

"It does," he says evenly.

"And I love your hair," I say, skirting a bit of it off his forehead. "It's neither straight nor curly, brown nor blond. It's a mixture of all of it."

He smiles. "It's working."

"What? What is?" I say, pulling my hand back to the table.

"This is making Aiden jealous."

"George," I reprimand. "That's not—"

"Don't worry, I don't mind because I know you're not acting. I feel that you're sincerely attracted to me. You just have a double agenda."

Shocked by his unusually casual attitude I slide down an inch in my seat.

"However, *sooner* rather than later, this is going to have to be solely about us and not him," George says in a surprisingly smooth voice.

"You deserve that, George. I'm sorry. He's just had me confused in the past, but that's all changing. I see the truth now and realize I was being stupid before."

"He was leading you on. You're not stupid. I totally get it."

"You do?"

"Yes, because sadly if you lead me on then I'm going to trail behind you. I know that with absolute certainty. I'd willingly stick my heart into a fire if I knew it would get me closer to you."

"George, I haven't tried to lead you on. I've been honest with you."

"As have I."

"I'm not using you to make him jealous."

"Well, if you were then I could think of much bolder ways than just stroking my face," he says.

My face flushes hot. The usually reserved George is transforming into someone new. Maybe he senses the opportunity, but whatever the reason I like this side of him. I like all sides of him, but this one is exciting.

"Care to continue listing all the things you love about me?" he says, cutting into my thoughts.

I resist the urge to smile, but it no doubt still surfaces in my eyes. "Oh, I will, but you're going to have to earn your compliments."

"I'm more than willing to do that."

Chapter Five

Bob, Steve, and I are meeting in a place that's 1,783,510 square miles of nothing but sand. The odds of getting lost and never finding each other are too great. There's no way we can meet by the Starbucks or red fire hydrant because there's nothing. No landmarks, just sand for as far as my green eyes can see.

I close those eyes now and focus on the coordinates. Instantly I'm soaring through the silver tunnel like a comet plummeting to the earth, or so I imagine. Three sharp turns are followed by more charging. I enjoy the wind sweeping through my hair more than usual since I haven't dream traveled in a few days. Typically I do at least every other night, but Trey's ordered me not to dream travel alone since he fears Chase will stalk me.

When I land, the arid heat of the desert is rising fast. The sun peeks up over the horizon, which appears a million miles away. Bob and Steve aren't here yet. Incredible unending blankets of sand stretch out in all directions. The eco-region of the Sahara desert is not a place where you want to go with only half a tank of gas and a Snickers bar. Hell, you won't even get there on that. It's vast. Now as I stand looking at this place of nothingness I totally get it. Everything here is dead or hardened by the heat and the wind and the sand. From my perspective that's all that's here anyway.

The sun, a huge ball of fire in a pale blue sky, pierces my eyes as it lights up the landscape. Immediately, a presence presses up against my consciousness like it's right behind me tapping on my shoulder. Tentatively, I turn around. In the distance, maybe a mile, maybe twenty, it's hard to tell in a place like this, there's a figure. Unmistakably a person, but who? And why here?

I blink, trying to clear the mirage from my vision when a warm voice says, "What made you pick the desert as our meeting place?"

I pivot to find Bob standing five feet from me. His grayish-brown hair looks slightly red from the reflection of the sun and sand. A second later Steve appears beside him. He's taller than Bob by about four inches and when he scans our location he reminds me of a lighthouse on the coast. Suddenly remembering the figure behind me, I shoot around, but instantly know he's gone. Or she. Steve gives me a puzzled look. Since he's prone to worrying I redirect his attention at once. "Bob just asked me why I chose this place to meet."

"Indeed, that's a good question." Steve smiles easily.

"Excuse me for sounding melodramatic," I say, "but I wanted to visit a place that's somehow more dismal than how I currently feel. I'm hoping to be outdone by the Sahara, isn't that pathetic?"

Remorse clings to Bob's eyes as he shakes his head. Almost losing his footing, he takes a few awkward steps through the sand to get to me. When he manages the three treacherous steps he pulls me in for a soft hug. They know Trey's my father. Every Lucidite on Earth probably knows by this point. Bob hugs me until I'm uncomfortable, then he pulls back, and grips my arms and gently squeezes. "These emotions will pass, but only with time and reflection."

Steve stands beside him now and pats me on the shoulder. "How about we take a seat and try and help you work through some of these dismal thoughts and emotions? I'd say we could walk, but I fear Bob wouldn't make it far before falling."

I smile and take a seat, facing away from the sun. We're on the bank of a sand dune just before it sharply plunges toward another hill. The soft mounds of earth look like rolling orange clouds. And we're sitting on top of them.

"Maybe I should be happy I have a father, but he doesn't really seem like 'dad' material. He seems like a huge jerk without a conscience."

"I don't know," Bob says softly. "I think if you give him half a chance he might surprise you. Trey's actually considered to be a pretty sensitive guy, but maybe that's just in comparison to his father."

"What does his father have to do with any of this?" I ask blankly.

Bob and Steve exchange nervous glances.

"Oh, right," Bob says a bit hesitantly. "It sounds as if you don't know. Not sure it really matters at this point, but the reason that I mention Trey's father is because he was Flynn, the founder of the Lucidites. He would have been your grandfather."

Silence envelops the space around us as I plunge my hand into the sand, pulling up a fistful and letting it slide through my fingers. I do it again and again and again.

"Anyway, I only relate this to you because Trey has always been considered the soft, sensitive one of the two," Bob says, like he's speaking to a bomb which is about to explode. "Flynn was an exceedingly respected man. Incredibly tolerant of others, but he wasn't known for his patience or listening skills. Furthermore, when something needed to be said he'd cut right to the point. Most people considered him to be a bit harsh."

"From my dealings with Trey," Steve chimes in, trying to sound casual, "he at least tries to dress things up a bit. He has some tact. His father didn't have time for that kind of stuff. Two different styles, neither wrong though."

Flynn was my grandfather? The same guy who was held up in the infirmary for the first month I lived at the Institute? Did he know about Joseph and me? I guess he didn't much care, since he was off battling Zhuang. None of this computes. And that infuriates me. It isn't like this is an actual mathematical equation or anything. It's just people and lives and connections.

The sand runs through my hand again and I enjoy the soft release. "So how do other Lucidites feel about this whole mess?"

"There's an uprising," Steve says after giving Bob a cautious look.

"What? Really!? Why?" I say.

"First off," Steve begins, watching the sand pour through my fingers, "people don't like a liar. Although Trey never lied about being your father, it appears as though he kept the truth from you and Joseph as well as everyone else. Secondly, they've mostly jumped to the worst conclusions, saying he's a deadbeat for avoiding responsibility." Steve shrugs. "I admit it doesn't look good, but who are we to judge? It's obvious that he had his reasons. We'll know more when Trey releases his public statement."

"What?!" I yell, hearing my voice carry through the sand and nothingness for miles. "A public statement? Where? When?"

"Through the Lucidite news feed on the website," Steve says matter-of-factly. "He's been promising one for most of the day. I expect it will be posted tomorrow."

Why have I never been to this website? I bet my news reports sometimes show up there. Is it possible that there's information on me? Probably. That's how Steve had known I was in trouble so many months ago and rescued me. Then there's also the news after I battled Zhuang and my trek in the Grotte. It's weird to know my life is being published on this website. Now my family secrets are sitting there for all of the Lucidite world to read, and the only reason anyone cares is because the person who turned out to be my father is everyone else's leader. My life's undeniably strange.

Bob wraps his arm around my shoulder, pulls me in for a hug. With his head leaning on mine he says, "I know it feels like he abandoned you. I can't even imagine how confusing this whole mess is for you and Joseph to deal with. Just don't rush trying to understand all of this. These things usually take time to work through."

This is the reason I love these two men. They're more level-headed than anybody else I've ever met. Their advice never feels directional. It's always straightforward and honest, never seeking another agenda. And they're different enough that they balance each other out, which is entertaining as well as constructive. Steve draws in a long breath. "If it makes you feel better, a bunch of other Lucidites also think he's a big jerk without a conscience."

We laugh and watch the wind make designs in the sand. I change the subject, being sure to ask them how their current affairs are going. We spend the next couple of hours exchanging stories. By the time I'm ready to return to the Institute I'm feeling lighter than I have in days. This is always the way I feel after our long and thoughtful conversations.

"I'm really lucky to have the two of you," I say, hugging them, one arm around each of their necks. "I don't know why you ever took me in under your proverbial wing, but I'm sure glad you did."

"Bob, you're right." Steve looks at him with a sideways smile. "She doesn't get it."

Bob nods and puts his hand on the side of my head in a sentimental type way. "Ms. Roya Stark, what you don't get is that the honor has always been ours. Thank *you*."

I smile, not having the right words to respond. I wave and disappear, returning easily to my own bed inside the Institute.

♦

"So guess what?" I say to Joseph as he smothers his toast in egg yolk.

"You've decided to get a real hobby like BMX biking or rock climbing," he says, stuffing the bite in his mouth.

"Reading and running are hobbies."

"For boring people."

"Well, boring is my middle name."

"Hey, what's your middle name, since we're on the subject and all?"

"Actually, it's Elle." I'm struck by an epiphany, which is as clear as the waters of Maldives. I slap my hand to my forehead, a little giddy from the rush. "Of course! My name is an homage to our mother. Eloise. Trey, that sly bastard."

"Mmm…" Joseph's brow knits with confusion. "Well, I'm not sure what to make of mine then. It's Lynn. And if you say one thing about how it's a girl's na—"

"You were named after our grandfather!" I say triumphantly, proud to finally find some clues I can unravel on my own. "That's what I was just about to tell you. Flynn, the founder of the Institute, was our grandfather."

Joseph thrusts his plate away and goes limp like wilted lettuce, laying his forehead on the table. "What?" he says with quiet disbelief. "Just when I thought this couldn't get worse."

Confusion blankets my thoughts. Sure, this is another unexpected piece of the puzzle, but I'm unsure why Joseph is acting like it's bad news. After a minute I pat him on the back, staring around the main hall at curious spectators. "Hey, people are starting to look. Straighten up."

"Thanks for the empathy, Stark."

"Oh, did you mistake me for George?" I say bluntly. "Why does it matter to you who our grandfather was? I mean, you knew it had to be someone, right? I realize that it's weird that it's someone we knew of, but why is it such bad news to you?"

Joseph sits up, surveying our surroundings. He leans down low, a new ferocity in his eyes. "It matters because I killed him. I killed Flynn."

Chapter Six

Ice water feels like it's being forced down my throat. Words freeze in my mouth. The last thing I expected to hear come out of Joseph was those words. *I killed Flynn.* He's right, things just got worse…by about 633 percent, and that's a rough estimate.

For too long I stare wildly at Joseph's dark eyes, mine wide with disbelief. "What?" I finally say in one long croak.

"Zhuang m-m-made me do it," Joseph stutters. "Well, he didn't make me. He asked me. It's when he was pretendin' to be our father. You have to believe me when I tell you I really thought he was our father and really wanted him to love us. I wanted to love him. He told me that his suffering was being perpetuated by a man, and if I could go back and kill that person it would end his pain. Our father could heal and return to us. Zhuang convinced me this man was evil and needed to be stopped. That this would be better for all of humanity." Sinking down he lays his head on his arms on the table. Everything about him reeks of defeat.

My world tilts as I make room for this bizarre turn of events. "Joseph," I say cautiously, "what did you do?"

He pulls his head up and whispers just above his forearms. "I guess it was always meant to happen, 'cause Flynn did die a few months ago."

"True," I say, drowning in the implications of the weird assorted effects of time travel. Flynn had been murdered when I was preparing to be Zhuang's challenger. At the time we thought it was Zhuang who had done it, since they'd been battling in the dreamscape. But it was Joseph. Future Joseph. Not the innocent boy who I'd just learned was my twin brother, but the one who's staring back at me now with haunted eyes.

"Zhuang told me I had to time travel back to a few months ago, find this man and kill him," Joseph says. "When he explained the situation to me I was convinced that this was the only way to stop the torment he was suffering. I believed this man was an awful person who was devastating our father, although I never asked why. I realize now I should have, but it probably wouldn't have mattered.

I'd have done anythin' our father asked me to. Once he sucked out most of my energy I felt owned by him in multiple ways."

I seriously hope other people aren't watching us right now, but I don't dare look away from Joseph's distraught face. "When did this happen?"

"On our birthday. That morning. The same day we found out Trey was our father. Timing's a bitch, huh?" Joseph shivers like he's suddenly cold. "I'd never killed a man before. It changes you, sucks away a part of your spirit. Since that moment I stabbed him I've been sleepwalking. If it hadn't been for this Trey mess I'd be consumed with thinkin' about that moment, but somehow I've been able to shove it away. Fat chance I'll be able to do that again," he says with a cold chuckle. Pain, sharp like broken glass, fractures my heart for my brother. The imprint of his scars presses against my own heart.

"Roya, you wouldn't have believed what I did even if you saw it," he says in a distant voice. "In a dreamscape I walked straight up to him—this man I believed was evil and huntin' our father. I was surprised that he appeared to recognize me, was welcomin'. He asked me what I was doin' there. I didn't answer. Instead I pulled out a knife and rammed it into his chest. It was awful. Actually that word hardly describes what it was. Chests aren't meant to be stabbed. People aren't supposed to stop hearts from beating. That can't be our job." Joseph stares off in the distance silently. I don't interrupt him, knowing instinctively he's gathering himself to tell the rest. "I realize now," he says, his voice sounding dead, "that Flynn didn't see me as a threat. He'd been chasing Zhuang, and was weakened, having been stuck in the dreamscape for so long. It was easy to kill him."

"Zhuang must have figured out that you were the one who had to kill Flynn a few months ago," I say in an urgent whisper. "That's another reason he chose you to restore him." The implications of all of these events, strung together by a wobbly backwards timeline, sends a searing pain to my head.

"When it was over," Joseph says, sounding brutally haunted, "I knew I'd done something major, but I actually had no idea that guy was Flynn. How was I supposed to? Then yesterday I was walkin' through the lobby and was struck by a picture of a man in the display case. I'd never noticed it before. The caption said it was Flynn. I recognized him immediately as the man I'd been asked to kill. That was bad then, knowin' I'd killed the founder of the Institute, but now to know he was also our grandfather? What have I done?"

It's crystal clear now. Joseph has been used as a pawn to checkmate the Institute. This has all been orchestrated by Zhuang.

Seizing Joseph's trembling hand I say, "This is Zhuang's fault. This is Trey's fault. This is not something you need to blame yourself for."

His eyes are edged in a pain so terrifying it makes the hair on my skin rise when he looks up at me. "You don't think I'm a monster? For killing a man? For being so casual after the fact? Pretendin' nothing happened?"

"I think you've been hurt too much from an early age. You were trying to fix the world that broke you. When that didn't work you pretended you weren't broken. But you don't have to pretend with me, because no matter what you do I'll always accept you." I swallow, forcing the aching lump in my throat away.

Samara and George are making their way to our table with their breakfast plates. I pull Joseph up and wave to them as I steer him toward the exit. Although I know he's the master of charades, he's still in no shape to face anyone. He might have been able to put on a happy face this morning after realizing the implications of who he murdered, but now that the whole truth has been revealed I can see his mask slipping.

When I have him back to his room I help him into bed. He feels fragile suddenly, like he's battling the flu. "We'll get through this, Joseph, but let's try and take it one day at a time."

"Each passing day is feeling like enough to kill me at this point," Joseph says, staring at the ceiling. "I've restored Zhuang to full strength and killed our grandfather—the founder of our society. No more. I can't take any more," he says, sounding like a small child.

I feel his emptiness erupt into a wave of pain, so vicious I fear it will tear his insides into pieces. Feeling someone else's emotions is too much. It's mind-splitting agony. "Everything's going to be all right, Joseph. We're in this together."

♦

27

I can't fix what Joseph has done since events touched by time travel can't be changed. There's no way to go back and prevent what's happened. All I can do moving forward is lessen the pain. There's multiple ways I can do that, and the first involves using money to bandage Joseph's wounds. I grab my iPad off my desk and pull up the first clothing website that comes to mind. I buy him three shirts, a sweater, two pair of jeans, a belt, and a pair of sunglasses. All Armani. None of it's on sale. All of it outrageously expensive. I would have bought him a suit and shoes, but I don't think guessing on those sizes is a good idea. When choosing styles and colors I pick the boldest, stuff I'd never wear—that he'll no doubt love.

Much like me, Joseph never had new clothes. His father provided him with the bare minimum. I suspect in some cases Joseph went without, having to make do with things that he'd outgrown or were tattered. He's never talked about it, but the part of me that's somehow connected to his memories like they're my own, thinks he went without more than just clothes. If the glimpses I've seen of his childhood are correct, then he also went without food and medicine at times.

The total for the new wardrobe doesn't even dent my bank account. Since Joseph and I have been news reporting together I'm receiving several stories at once. The last three times I've reported, I've logged eight stories. At four hundred a pop my bank account is quickly growing. Since I don't have bills and Bob and Steve buy everything else for me, I haven't had a reason to spend any of it. Now I can't think of a better one than this.

In the beginning it felt weird to accept such a ridiculous amount of money for stories that came to me so effortlessly. However, it's getting easier. The 453 people who didn't get on a 747 destined to have engine failure over the Atlantic probably don't think I'm being overpaid. Now I just wish I knew where all this money came from. Another of Trey's secrets, I'm sure.

Chapter Seven

Aiden stands beside his workstation, banging his head to the music as he solders a tiny wire onto a board. For a few seconds I watch him from the doorway. Briefly I forget he isn't mine, never will be. The urge to walk up behind him and wrap my arms around his waist is too strong. An affliction. One I have to purge myself of before it tangles my heart until it's unusable. Just to see how he moves when no one's watching is enough to split me. His passion is there in every moment, his brain working faster than a million computers. After this short time as a voyeur, I know his brilliance and zeal is not an act, which breaks my heart even more. I kept hoping that everything about him was a façade, that I hadn't really fallen for a real person. But he's perfectly real, and I'm undeniably still in love with him in every way. In order not to obliterate my entire heart I stuff this realization down into the depths of my spirit. *All business, Roya.*

I knock on the door frame.

Without looking up he says, "Just take the parts to the back of my lab, please."

I knock again.

"Oh fine, if it's too heavy for you just put them on the floor next to this table," he says, fidgeting with what looks to be a stubborn wire.

Another knock. Aiden sighs loudly. "Gosh, just leave it at the door." He spins around and his face drops with surprise.

"Oh, it's you," Aiden says, sounding both relieved and nervous. "Sorry about that. I thought you were someone else. I didn't expect you so soon."

"I figured I'd get whatever this is about out of the way as quickly as possible," I say, depositing his meeting request into the trash bin.

He stares at me, a lovely pain in his eyes. In that one look I spy regret, longing, and despair. I shudder, too easily remembering the way he pushed me away the last time. Rejected me because of who I'm related to. He can feel all that negative emotion and more. Cowards deserve to suffer.

"Look, we have to work together," I say, keeping my voice unaffected. "I know you aren't accustomed to speaking freely, so I will. Let's just put all this crazy business behind us and be friends."

"Friends?" He says like it's a new word. A foreign one.

"Yes, you've had one of those, right? Or is science your only friend?"

He glares at me, pushing his black-rimmed glasses up on his nose. "You know, when you want to be, you're more catty than a whole slew of debutantes competing over the same beau."

"I'll take that as a compliment, although we both know I wouldn't compete for anyone."

An angry silence fills the space between us. I can almost feel us volley quiet complaints back and forth.

"Well, I didn't ask you down here so we could make friendship bracelets and braid each other's hair. Next time maybe," Aiden says, no smile in his voice or on his face. "As you know, Trey wants alterations made to the adjuster so that it doesn't change your natural frequency as much. Actually, he's assigned me to innovate a totally different solution that buffers your frequency from George without affecting you at all. However, that's still a little ways off. Anyway, I think I have a new patch that might satisfy his first request. It will take a few days of readings for me to know if it's worked to Trey's liking. How does that all sound?"

"Fine, I guess. Do I need to do anything different to test it out?"

"Well, you don't have to spend any extra time with George, if that's what you mean. You don't *have* to spend any time with him at all," he says, undeniable jealousy in his tone. "Since you're both occupying the Institute, the adjuster works the same whether you're close or levels apart."

"Thanks for the heads-up," I say dully. "What I meant was do I need to report on any changes to my abilities, which I realize can sometimes be linked to my frequency level? That's what Trey's worried about being affected, right? My abilities? Since I'm an asset and all."

"You never forget a thing, do you?"

"Consider me Ms. Memory Banks."

"Well, Ms. Banks, may I see the famed adjuster? The tweaks will only take a minute, maybe two," he says, eyeing me with a tamed desire.

30

My fingers hesitate halfway to my neck, a sudden concern stopping me. Aiden doesn't read minds, but he's intuitive enough to understand my reluctance. He shakes his head. "Don't worry, George will be fine. Mostly," he adds, a new bitterness in his tone. "And I'll be as quick as possible."

I untuck the necklace from under my shirt, unfasten it, and hand it over.

"Well, looky here," Aiden says, holding up the ruby necklace. "It's been blinged up. Nice."

"Bob and Steve's doing," I say.

"You know," Aiden says, unlatching the adjuster from the ruby-beaded necklace, "I told Trey the best and safest option for you was just have George leave the Institute. He hasn't been assigned to a department yet, so it makes perfect sense."

He looks up from the adjuster in time to catch my glare.

"Oh, you don't have to worry about George getting kicked out of here," Aiden says, disassembling the adjuster. "Trey wouldn't go for it. He thinks George is good for the Institute." He puts down the tiny pieces of the device and flicks a nearby screw across the room. It ricochets several times before finding a resting place. His angry eyes swivel up from the table, finding mine. "Sadly, Trey thinks George is good for you."

"So since you can't be with me, I'm not allowed to be with anyone else, is that right?" I say, voicing what he's just hovering above. "That's real mature."

"How would you feel in my position?"

"I wouldn't be in your position. I wouldn't work for a deceptive, autocratic asshole."

"That's funny, because you do. You're news reporting, right?"

"Technically, I work for Shuman."

"And who does she work for?"

"Well, I'm only working until I make enough money to open my own place where people don't lie and manipulate lives. I'm going to call it the Anti-Institute." *That's actually not a bad idea. I'm going to have to stop buying expensive clothes though.*

"Hope it goes well. Flynn would be proud."

"Thanks," I say, devoid of any real gratitude. Aiden returns to working on the adjuster. I find a spot on the floor that desperately needs my eyes' attention. "Hey, did you know Flynn was Trey's father?"

"Yeah," Aiden says instantly. "That was common knowledge."

"Hmmm," I say, looking back at the floor. "He would have been my grandfather."

"I realize that now. He was my mentor. I...I owe my position to him," Aiden says, his voice panged with grief.

The newest debacle with Joseph rises to my consciousness. Instantly my brain launches into strategic mode. "Do we know how Flynn died?"

"Yes, he was murdered." My pulse races in my head. "By Zhuang," Aiden adds a few seconds later.

"But do we know how?"

Aiden gives me a curious look. "Well, he was stabbed. We know that. We don't know where or when, though. Flynn was chasing Zhuang and was a few dozen layers deep in the dreamscape; that's what we suspect anyway. Zhuang must have finally confronted him. Or trapped his consciousness. Whatever happened, it killed Flynn pretty quickly."

"Is it possible to find out how exactly he was murdered?"

Aiden scratches his head. "I don't think so. Why?"

"I'm just interested, now that I know he was my grandfather."

"Do you want me to look into it?"

"No," I say too fast.

Another curious stare. "Well, if you change your mind—"

"It's okay. Don't worry about it." *Seriously, don't worry about it.*

"All right, well, I believe that should do it," Aiden says, snapping the front back onto the adjuster. He hands it to me, our eyes meeting briefly.

"So you'll know in a few days if this has worked well enough?" I say, trying to fasten the adjuster around my neck.

"Indeed I will."

The slippery clasp keeps closing before I have the other side locked through it. This is a problem I never had when the adjuster was on twine and I could tie it around my neck. I bring the catch around to my face so I can get a better look at it while I try and fasten it. From the corner of my vision I notice Aiden eye me cautiously.

"Having trouble there?" he asks.

"No, it's just the damn clasp on this new necklace is tricky," I say, the silver notch slipping through my fingers again.

"Here," Aiden says, stepping up close and taking the necklace from my fingers. "Let me help." My eyes stay pinned on the ruby beads in front of my face. Twice he fails to latch the loop through the hook.

"See, I told you it was tricky," I say with a small laugh.

"You weren't lying, but I won't be defeated," he says and shuts the clasps at precisely the right moment, fastening the necklace in place.

"Thanks," I say, looking up, finding his sapphire eyes. Instantly I know I should have kept my gaze low, away from his. He's too close, only a few inches away. He lays the necklace down on my chest, his fingers finding a place on my shoulders. The pause is long enough to bring a rush of desire and fear and pain to my mouth. Aiden leans in closer, tilts his head, his fingers still resting on my shoulders. My lips part. Words I hadn't rehearsed whisper across the space. "Go ahead," I urge him. "Go ahead, kiss me. And if you do, then you have just silently signed an agreement that you'll go to Trey and tell him about us." I lean in another inch, our mouths almost touching. "So what's it going to be? Are you going to kiss me?"

His fingers tighten on my shoulders. His breath sighs against my skin. Then he pushes me away in one swift movement, taking several steps backwards. "God, Roya, you know I can't."

A satisfied smile uncurls on my lips. *That's what I thought. Coward.* "Well, if you *can't,* then stop leading me on. Teasing me. Torturing the both of us," I say, my voice a thousand times cooler than how I actually feel.

"I'm not trying to do anything to hurt you. I can't help the way I feel or that my job prevents me from acting on those feelings. Roya—"

"Stop," I interrupt, injecting a casual note in my tone. "You've heard my request. Now honor it. Okay?"

Aiden shakes his head, distraught, torn emotions written on his face. "I wish things could be different."

"Hey, don't worry about it. Friends don't kiss each other anyway, right?" I say and turn and leave.

Chapter Eight

Trey releases his statement that evening. From my iPad I read it to Joseph as he paces his room:

It has recently surfaced that I am the father to Roya Stark and Joseph Jordan. These two individuals were brought to the Institute as potential challengers to face Zhuang. Ms. Stark was later chosen as the Challenger. Mr. Jordan served on the team that assisted her in the battle against Zhuang on June 13th. Later, Ms. Stark led the team, which included Mr. Jordan, that rescued Dr. Aiden Livingston from the Grotte on July 3rd.

Seventeen years ago I made the decision that my twins would be separated and sent to live in Middling homes. This decision was based on two important factors. The first is that it was immediately obvious they created a highly detectable energy current when together. I knew they must be separated if they were going to be kept safe from Zhuang, since the list of names of potential challengers had already been released. Secondly, as many of you know, the Institute does not provide a suitable environment for raising children, since they are unable to dream travel and are therefore confined within these walls.

They're now both residents of the Institute. It's my hope that they stay here long-term. I recognize there's a long road we must face in order to repair the distrust my secrecy has caused. My decisions may never be understood, but please know these choices were made to protect the Lucidite people, as well as my children.

Lastly, I'm more than proud that they have been instrumental in deteriorating Zhuang and rescuing the Head Scientist for the Institute. Although I can take zero credit for the accomplishments of these two people, I'm still proud to say I'm their father.

Trey Underwood,
Head of the Lucidite Institute

The knot in my throat has grown larger as I read. I'm thoroughly glad when the statement is over. I take a long sip of water, hoping that will loosen the constriction.

"Glad to know he didn't mention I restored Zhuang to full strength," Joseph says, still pacing.

"No one needs to know about that," I say. "I bet only the Head Officials know."

And George.

"That would be nice."

"It's hard to know what's real in this statement and what he's saying in order to repair his reputation," I say, tossing the iPad on the bed.

"Honestly, for him, he sounds down right sentimental," Joseph huffs, taking a seat.

"Yeah, what's this business about being proud to be our father? He didn't say anything remotely close to that in his office."

"Well, there was kind of a lot goin' on right then, if you remember correctly." Joseph rubs his eyes as he speaks.

"I remember."

"Maybe he really will try to earn our trust." Joseph gives me a misty-eyed expression.

I roll my eyes and let out an abrupt laugh. "Oh, who cares? Do you really think he's going to take us for ice cream on the weekends in hopes that we'll have some functional relationship? Don't you get it? Trey is the head of the Institute. Before that he was second-in-command to his father. He never had any interest in having children. We're a burden." I point at the iPad. "That was just some cleverly written crap in order to cover his ass. He's a politician fighting to maintain his power over the people. That's all."

"I think you're being kind of cynical," Joseph says bitterly.

"Don't delude yourself, Jordan." I laugh. "How did I never know your last name before now?"

Joseph doesn't laugh. He slouches, like his shoulders suddenly weigh a ton. "You don't pay attention."

"Well, I pay attention enough to know that Trey is playing a political game and we're just pawns." I give Joseph a long, hard look—dissecting him. "Don't be misled. He doesn't really care about us."

With a shrug he looks at the door. "We'll see."

I worry that Joseph is holding on to some fantasy about Trey being a good father to us, but I shouldn't push him right now. He's had a rough day. I don't really feel like lecturing him anymore at the moment. He's looking a little better than this morning, although he skipped meals and tormented himself for most of the day over killing our grandfather. I wish he could get the same kind of therapy that Samara received after she killed Pearl. It appeared to really have helped her to process the events and her emotions. However, Joseph and I can never tell anyone else what happened. There's way too much blame on Joseph at the current moment and it all needs to be deflected somehow. If he can just get a break, he might have a chance to rise up from this darkness, because more than anyone I know Joseph is a pure optimist. He makes the best of everything, even a childhood of abuse and neglect.

"Hey, will you dream travel with me tonight?" I ask, recapturing his lost attention.

"Yeah, sure," he says automatically. "Where you wanna go?"

"Hmmm…" I think for a minute. "How about Glasgow?"

"Scotland?"

"Yeah."

"I haven't been there yet. Sure. What's it known for?"

"Rain," I say with a smile.

"Hell, if it has weather period I'll take it. I, for one, get pretty tired of stainless steel walls," Joseph says, sounding uncharacteristically annoyed.

"I'm with you."

I pull my iPad off the bed and find an interesting place to meet. We decide on a time and I leave Joseph to sulk and process, which is the best thing for him at this point. It's decided that we won't news report today. Shuman will probably figure that with the public statement being released we decided to take the day off. She can fire us, but that's about as likely as her breaking into a scene from *Footloose*.

◆

Mossy air wraps around my body, giving me a sudden chill. The smell of wet grass springs up from the earth, instantly sending me back to my childhood. As soon as I land in the Necropolis in Glasgow, Scotland, I realize my mistake. This place is huge. Acres and acres of nothing but tombs. We should have picked a specific monument to meet by, instead of just the property in general. It could take all night to find Joseph.

An unknown fear creeps into my stomach as the rays of morning sunlight start to rise over the memorials in the distance, creating shadows on the glossy grass. The tombstones in this place are no joke. I look up at a rather large one and instantly feel like a doll standing beside a gigantic house. The stone statue, with its ornate details and engraved words, is at least thirty-five feet tall. These are no ordinary headstones like I'm accustomed to in the States. Poetry strikes my heart, thinking about how this culture makes tribute to their dead in such an incredibly expressive way.

My curious thoughts are interrupted by a small wind. It's slight, like when something gradually displaces cold air. It's followed by a rustling of fabric. Not for one second do I delude myself into believing it's Joseph. I know it's *him*, recognize his presence like it's engrained in my soul. Swiftly I turn on my heels and hide my shock as I stand face to face with Chase. An icy, almost debilitating shiver shoots down my spine.

Chapter Nine

He's a foot away. I'm paralyzed. The sun shines behind him, casting a light on his frame but leaving his face in darkness. My eyes focus on the small particles of sunlight around me and his features become clear. Just as I remember from the Grotte, he's unbelievably beautiful. So perfect it hurts. Makes me want to fall to my knees and worship the unfathomable man who stands before me. He eyes me with sensual desire. Instantly I pulse with the same desire. I know this is wrong, but I don't care. Nothing matters but what comes next. And the idea that something's coming next sends me into a torrent of unrelenting anticipation.

Blue morning sky contrasts against his soft, white skin and slick, black hair. The green grass behind him frames his muscular build making it more pronounced. Although I know I should run, I only stare into his electric blue eyes as they pull me in, like he's reeling me in on a taut fishing line. Chase has a godly grace. It's not something to think much about until you're under its control. And like falling into a rabbit hole, I'm engulfed in his spell. I awake to a place where I live in a universe of *him*. And it feels like enough to sustain me always.

Chase's closeness to me is alarming, but I don't make the slightest move as I watch his eyes bore into mine. Only an inch away, his presence wraps around me like tendrils and yanks at my reason until it relinquishes its stubbornness. "I wouldn't hesitate to maim and kill every last person on this earth," he says, his words gripping my skin like an astringent. "But never, would I *ever* harm you." His lips whisper against my ear. I freeze, more solid than before. "You know that, right? I'm not here to hurt you…just the opposite." His mouth, cold as marble, slides down my cheek. I feel his icy breath the entire way. He looks into my eyes and then grazes his lips against mine, but I remain concrete. I don't pull away or give in. He eases back a few inches. "I don't know why you are resisting," he says, articulating every word.

I know why I'm resisting, although it's a poor job. It's harder this time than in the Grotte, like I've lost a survival instinct. In the distant corner of my brain, I remember Chase has an emotional modifier he's using to make me want him, love him. And in the forefront of my heart I'm steps away from not giving a damn. I'm a leap away from declaring my unyielding desire for him. Professing my love.

No! I don't love him. This is wrong. A manipulation of my emotions. Back away. Run!

I move my hand. It works just fine as I squeeze my fingers together. *Now move.* But I don't. I remain frozen, like a stupid block of ice.

"It's not a trick. It's called desire," he whispers inches from my lips. "That's why you're still here." He glides his firm, pink lips up and down my chin. I don't just allow it. I relish it. "Desire trumps reason and logic," he says, as he smoothly sinks down to my neck and his cool breath wisps against my flesh. "You should follow it. Follow your desire. Forget your logic."

His nose and mouth skim up my neck, over the curvature of my chin, until he captures me beneath his stare. His blue eyes electrify me from the inside out. Suddenly I'm hit by an extremely sensual and dangerous thought: *I'm his slave.* And there's nothing I want more than that role. Willingly, I'll put on the shackles and do whatever he beckons…with a smile.

Commanding me with his movements, his insistent demeanor, his power, he sinks down and kisses me. My lips remain unmoving, like before. Again his lips brush mine, persistent. Enticing. Each time his mouth encourages against mine, I lose the connection to the presence fumbling with my shackles. And in a breath she's dead to me and I'm a brand new person moving my lips against his, reciprocating. Chase backs me up two steps until I'm flush up against a monument. The stone is warm compared to his hands. His teeth scrape my lips, unleashing a primal urge. An animalistic desire releases within me. I kiss him harder with each passing second, an overwhelming passion intoxicates me.

Chase eases back, his long black eyelashes parting to reveal a satisfied gaze. His fingers direct my chin to the side and obediently I keep it there awaiting his next move. A finger slides down my neck stopping just under my collar bone. His mouth follows the same path, stopping, hovering at the base of my throat. "How does this feel?" he whispers.

Someone speaks using my mouth, my voice. "Amazing."

In one swift movement he angles my chin forward again, bringing his face even with mine. "Just imagine how much better it would feel in our physical bodies," he says with a wicked grin. My chest heaves in anticipation of his next move. Gracefully he dips down, kissing me again. Voracious fingers bury into his dark suit. Finding the lapels of his jacket I use them to draw him in closer— although he'll never be close enough to satisfy my desire. Greedily my hands sweep underneath his suit jacket, grazing his silk shirt, detailing his muscles. I need to feel more of him, to know his body more intimately than I know my own. Become a part of Chase. Give him everything I have even if it kills me. It will be worth it.

A distant part of me finds it hard to believe that I'm making out with Chase, the psychopath, the murderer. However, I don't care. The only thing I care about is getting to the other end of this seemingly unending desire. One of his hands tugs my hips forward. The other tangles in my hair, ensuring I stay pinned into him, making me his willing prisoner. I've never been this close to anyone. But it still isn't enough for me.

He breaks away and abruptly pushes me back. Instantly I lunge, doing everything I can to get back to him, wanting him and not feeling satisfied. Holding both my arms, keeping me at arm's length, he smiles. "Well, hello, Joseph," he says, still fixed on my hungry gaze.

Chase turns, keeping me caged behind his back.

"Get away from her," Joseph says with a protective snarl.

"She's perfectly fine," Chase sings casually. "I dare say she's never felt so good."

"Leave," Joseph says. I can't see his face. A weird part of me, buried deep, doesn't want to. Senses he finds what I've done distasteful. And strangely…I think he's right.

"Well, you really know how to spoil a perfectly good time." Chase pivots, putting his mouth next to mine again. Without meaning to my lips quiver in desire for his. "I won't hurt him. Not as long as you reciprocate my affections as you have so obediently just done, *mon amour*." He kisses me once, softly. So perfectly, it gracefully unravels my essence like a spell. "*Au revoir*," he whispers and disappears.

Slowly my vision refines until I'm focused on Joseph fifteen feet away. Unable to look directly at him I stare at the ground. "I'll see you tomorrow, all right," I say, before retreating to my cold and lonely bed.

Chapter Ten

Once my consciousness is back in the safety of the Institute, the haze slowly falls away, allowing my rational thoughts to surface again. Like waking from a bad dream, my eyes search the darkness for predators as my blood hammers through my veins. But it wasn't a dream. Simultaneously I shift from shivering with disgust for what I've just done and panting, wanting more.

This is the emotional modifier's doing. On the positive side, its effects feel weakened now that Chase isn't in close proximity. On the negative side, it's been perfected and I'm almost certain next time I won't be able to resist him for even a second.

Over and over I replay the events in the Necropolis. *I'm his slave.* Even now the words don't entirely sound wrong in my head. Rationally speaking I know that being attracted to Chase is utterly ridiculous. Makes zero sense. Emotionally speaking, I'm more in love with him than I ever thought my heart had the capacity for.

My logical side forces me to practice the strategy George taught me. I focus on my heart, thinking of my emotions for Chase, recording them with great detail. Then I do the same, thinking about Joseph. Before, the differences were obvious, like comparing artificial light and sunlight. If I can trust my heart, I swear it's just broken from disappointment. My love for Chase is an unwavering beam of sunshine, brighter than all the bulbs in all the world and inextinguishable.

The only saving grace is that my brain knows this is wrong, but that's of little hope. There are those more resilient and fortified with greater motivations who have failed in the face of logic, been scorned by their heart's desires. Great warriors have died for their passions, sacrificed their own well-being for lust and pleasure. How do I stand a chance of battling this? At resisting Chase?

If I could go for a long run right now I would. For a second I consider it, not caring if I rip back open the bullet wound Amber gave me. But Mae spent so much energy healing me, after everything she's been through—losing Pearl—I can't take her efforts for granted. *Just a few more days*, she promises, and I'll be able to work out. Hitting a punching bag right now would definitely take some of the crazy out of my being. Instead I settle for Tao Te Ching. I'm not hoping for enlightenment, as much as answers. Ancient Chinese wisdom feels like the perfect place to look at the moment. If this doesn't work I'll try some pop psychology.

Maybe what happened in last night's dream travel wasn't real. Maybe I fell asleep before dreaming. Maybe Chase only visited me in my dreams, like before. Because it's impossible that even if he has improved the emotional modifier he could entice me to act so seductively, thrusting myself into him—all but tearing his clothes off. Yes, that makes more sense. It's the answer I've been looking for. Chase might make me love him, but he can't make me act on those emotions, right? That's still up to me.

Patrick's familiar knock startles me. The sun hasn't even risen over the ocean that separates the Institute and the real world. I get up from my safe place surrounded by bed sheets and march to the door on autopilot. I should just ignore the knock, pretend I don't hear it. Sometimes my nature, ruled by customs, irks me. The door slides back revealing a droopy-eyed Patrick. "Only you would get a meeting request at this hour."

Oh shit. It wasn't a dream.

I gulp, taking the note from Patrick. "Thanks," I say, unable to even feign our usual banter right now. He trots away sluggishly, no doubt off to return to his dream travels.

I unfold the note, my hands already shaking.

Roya,

Report to Room 222 immediately.

Trey

Well, I knew he was known for brevity, but you'd think his own daughter could earn a formal closing. Apparently, it's too early for such formalities.

I consider curling up in my bed and ignoring the request. But I know whatever I have to face is better done using courage. I'm not going to hide like I'm humiliated of what's forsaken me without my ability to control it. I won't be shamed. Not this time.

43

Trey hovers just beside the entrance when the door to room 222 slides into the recess. "Thank you for joining us so quickly, Roya," he says, stepping back, revealing Aiden and Ren sitting slouched at the table.

Oh shit.

I'm going to need more than just courage to get through this. Aiden's hair is matted to his head in what I believe is actually bedhead and not his usual crazy 'do. Ren's wearing a crumpled button-up shirt and an indignant expression.

Trey takes a seat beside the two officials, gesturing that I should take the one opposite of them. "I'm sorry to call on you so early, but I also figured you *weren't* sleeping," Trey says, spreading his hands on the table.

Ren suppresses a grin that begs to be slapped. Aiden's face is slack, devoid of emotion. All three of them have red, puffy eyes and look dangerously close to needing coffee.

"I've called this early meeting because Joseph has just informed me that a Chase situation is desperately in need of our concern," Trey says, reporting facts like they aren't the sordid, gross details of my personal life.

A moment of aching hush follows his words. I want to curl into the tiniest of balls and become a simple organism—one without the major systems. Something that relies on so little, which isn't affected by emotions, specifically humiliation.

"Roya." Trey says my name with a new harshness. "Did you just see Chase while dream traveling tonight?"

As if Chase was in front of me right now, I freeze.

"Roya?" he says again, this time his voice softer, pleading.

All I feel is Aiden's eyes, quiet and speculative on me. He's in Head Scientist mode. But I know he can't wall off his heart in the name of his career. What's about to come out is going to color everything.

"Ummmm…" I say, like contemplating a food choice. "Hmmmm…" I continue, as casually as I can muster.

"Roya," Trey repeats, now cautiously. "We're here at this early hour because I fear you've had an encounter which warrants our immediate attention. It's important that we stay in front of Chase at all times, otherwise your safety will be compromised. With that

44

being said, will you please answer my question? Did you have an interaction with Chase tonight?"

There's no getting out of this. Either this is going to be the most humiliating moment of my entire life or I'm going to take control now. What falls out of my mouth sounds more like a response from an injured horse. "Well, yeah," I say, stretching out the last word into multiple syllables.

"Will you please describe in detail what happened during this dream travel?" Trey says, his turquoise eyes heavy with stress.

"Nothing," I say, my voice sounding dead.

"Oh, come on missy," Ren sings in a hoarse voice. "We've heard rumor you snogged Chase tonight."

I refuse to be made a fool. Trey thinks he can parade me in front of his Head Officials for my own good. He's not protecting me right now; he's downright torturing me. I'd rather die a thousand times from one of Allouette's knives than give into this stupid interrogation.

"Is this true, Roya?" Trey asks.

"Guess what, Trey." I say his name like it's something repulsive. "Who I make out with isn't your business. It's not the business of anyone in this room."

Aiden stiffens. Ren snorts with suppressed laughter. Trey leans forward, the knuckles of his clenched fist white. "If it involves you, it's my business," he says.

"Since when?" I seethe.

"Since always."

"Fine." I point at Ren and Aiden. "I don't see why they need to be here."

"They're here to help," Trey says flatly.

"I don't need help," I say. What I need is a freaking lobotomy of the heart. What am I supposed to do? Ren and Aiden can help me, but in this circumstance I can't bring myself to ask for it or accept it.

"Roya, you're in danger. The closer you let Chase in to you, the harder it will be for us to help you," Trey says, his voice no longer harsh or riddled with anger. Fear coats his words now. "You can't see it because you've been infected," he says, like I'm diseased. "Chase is using you. You have to let us stop it."

45

"Chase wants me," I say, resting my hands on the table, leaning back, feigning nonchalance. I'm not sure who's within me speaking right now, the embedded part or the resentful child Trey abandoned. "He's not afraid to show it either."

"Don't make this about us," Trey says, sweeping his hands through his silver hair.

Lucky for me, I have multiple angles I get to play here. "Who says I am?" I say, careful to keep my eyes off Aiden. "And if Chase wanted to hurt me, he would have. So far all he's done is the exact opposite."

"He's deceiving you. He can't be trusted," Trey says, his voice climbing.

"By that rule," I say, my tone even, "neither can you. Or anyone else in this room."

For the first time Aiden's eyes meet mine, a quiet protest in them. In that one look I know he's begging me to back down, not drop these subtle hints about us. To make everything easier right now by being compliant.

"Aiden informs us that you've had dreams recently which were invaded by Chase. Is that right?" Trey says.

Whatever Aiden was begging for with his penetrating gaze has just been lost. My eyes, still locked on his, narrow. "That's correct," I answer like a robot.

"Roya, you really should have confided this in me," Trey says, sounding exasperated.

"Really? Because there are about a dozen things I can say the same of you, *Dad*." I spew the last word with an angry inflection.

"This is not about us. It's about your safety." Trey turns to Ren. "What do you make of Chase invading her dreams? Is there something we can do to stop him?"

Ren shrugs indifferently. "Honestly, I think she might be screwed, especially with that kind of attitude," he says, scrunching up his nose. "If you're not careful, Little Miss Hothead, you're going to find yourself literally screwed."

"Ren," Trey says in a reprimanding tone.

"Oh, all right." He waves his hand dismissively at Trey. Why the hell does my father even employ this redheaded jerk? What the hell kind of leverage does he have over him? "Obviously Chase is using the emotional modifier, coupled with dream invasion. A two-pronged approach that will be treacherously difficult to combat."

"Thanks for the optimism," I say.

"Isn't there something we can do to stop him?" Trey says, his eyes fixed on Ren. "Something else besides Aiden creating a patch for Roya's protective charm to guard against the modifier?"

"Tell you what, I'll give it a go and see if I can find a strategy that might work," Ren says.

"Thank you." Trey turns his attention back on me. "Right now I need you to tell us exactly what Chase said and did tonight so we know how much progress he's made with the emotional modifier, which I know is to blame for everything that's occurred between you and him."

I exaggerate a long yawn. "Glad to know you don't believe I'd be willing to fall for a murderer. What a blessed relief."

"Enough with the antics," Trey says, obviously annoyed. "Tell us what happened."

I have him exactly where I want him. And Aiden and Ren too, judging by their faces. "Well, Trey, I'm not going to give you a play-by-play. Some things have to remain private," I say, flashing a look at Aiden. "Anyway, Chase said he wouldn't hesitate to maim and kill the entire world, but that he'd never harm me." I lean back in my chair, flick a rogue piece of hair off my shoulder. "Isn't that funny? Because it sounds like I'm not the one who should be worried for my safety, but the rest of you should probably think about protecting yourselves."

"This isn't a game. This is serious," Trey says, looking uncomfortable as he readjusts himself in his chair.

This is my cue to stretch out my arms and stare around casually. I've learned this technique from Ren and I can tell he's appreciating it as he stares at me with a brooding look. I wink and slouch in my chair before turning to Trey. "Well, that's pretty much all that happened. What do you think?"

"I think you've left out a great deal of detail," Trey says.

I rock my head back and forth, shrug.

Taking a steadying breath, Trey revolves in Aiden's direction. "Since Roya isn't going to be forthcoming with information, based on the report we received from Joseph, how close do you think Chase is to perfecting the modifier?"

"I think he's fairly close," Aiden says, eyes fixed on the blank notepad in front of him. "But I'll need more info first. Roya, I need you to answer a few questions and only you can," he says, looking up at me, his voice so unlike the one I'm used to. "When you were around Chase, were you able to resist him?"

"At first," I chirp.

"But then what happened?" Aiden asks.

"Do you mean at which point did my logic give way and I found myself inexplicably making out with him? Is that what you mean?"

Aiden presses his lips together. "I only meant, at what point did your logic recede," he says, a firmness in his voice.

"Oh, well, it was about thirty seconds after he forced himself onto me," I say, staring at my fingernails like the current conversation isn't worth my full attention.

Aiden removes his glasses and wipes them off on his shirt. He may think this hides his disgust, but he's wrong. I can more easily see the flames burning in his eyes with his glasses off. "Now that you're not with Chase," he says, "how do you specifically feel about him?"

Staring directly at Aiden, I taper my eyes but remain silent. A full ten seconds tick by.

"Do you feel like you love him?" the Head Scientist asks.

I tilt my head slightly, eyes still locked on Aiden's.

"Roya, answer the question," Trey commands.

"Why don't you go ahead and deduce the answer from my silence," I say, cracking my knuckles.

"For God's sake, Roya, this isn't a game. You could get hurt," Trey says, a punishing tone in his voice.

"We've already established that Chase doesn't want to hurt me," I say, feigning innocence.

"What he wants from you isn't going to hurt you in the beginning," Trey says through clenched teeth. "But believe me when I say it will kill you emotionally in the end."

"What?! You know why he's after me?" I ask, my attention suddenly ripped from the act I've been playing. "You told me you'd inform me once you knew."

Trey thrusts his fingers through his silver hair and doesn't make eye contact with me. "Currently, I don't think you need that information."

White-hot anger engulfs me. At my back I sense a breeze stirring. "Trey!" I hear myself boom. "Why is it I'm only on a need-to-know basis with you? How can you keep so much from me?"

Trey's already shaking his head before I finish speaking. "Knowledge isn't always power. You should know that by now. Everything you know changes you. Not only that, but it can hold you hostage. Look at you now. You're already consumed by emotions since you found out I was your father. This isn't a productive use of your energy. I fear that any more information will just overwhelm you and right now we need you focused."

"So let me get this straight," I say in a measured voice. "Chase orchestrated this huge mess. He had Aiden abducted so he could get to the plans for the modifier. He's responsible for Pearl's death and now he's stalking me by night. And you're not going to tell me why? That's ridiculous!" My attention shoots to Aiden and Ren. "Let me guess, you both know, don't you?"

Ren nods curtly, a pleased grin on his face. Beside him Aiden shakes his head, giving me a pointed stare.

"Well, it's not like you'd tell me if you did," I say, staring straight into Aiden's cold, blue eyes. "Not if Trey forbid you, right?" I fix my anger on Trey again. "Isn't it nice to know you have such loyal lemmings?"

"Roya," Trey cautions. "This is not productive."

"*This* is all your fault," I say, ignoring his attempts to control my behavior.

"It's not."

"Oh really? Well, if you hadn't ordered your employees to build an emotional modifier, Chase wouldn't have the technology. Maybe consider that the next time you sanction some evil device, huh?"

He takes a long breath, nostrils flaring. I've never seen him so angry, not even when he exploded at Joseph for reviving Zhuang. This rage is worse because it's quiet, boiling inside. I'm well acquainted with that type of fuming. It burns you from the inside out. "If you're dream traveling," Trey says, taking each word one at a time, "and Chase shows up, you must leave. If you're sleeping and

49

he invades your dream I order you to wake up. Is that clear?" Trey says, his tone deliberate.

"Is that order coming from you as my father or as the Head of the Institute?"

"It shouldn't matter."

"Well, I don't have to listen to either person," I say, feeling like a selfish child, but I can't help it. My heart is kerosene, my mind a match. I'm seconds away from igniting.

"Damn it, Roya, this isn't a game! Don't you get that?"

"What I don't get is why you won't tell me the reason Chase is after me. Tell me what he wants. I deserve to know."

Surrender darkens my father's face. He places his forehead in his hand. Takes a long breath. When his eyes meet mine I'm struck by the familiarity. His eyes are the exact same color as Joseph's. As mine. A chill runs down my back. The pang which precedes tears rolls through my chest. In that fleeting moment we share a pain, one which serves to obliterate my rebellion. I don't want to hurt Trey, not like I'm doing. All I want is the one thing he owes me: the truth.

He shakes his head, seeming to recharge his motivation. "You have to believe me when I say I'm trying to protect you. Knowing everything will make your life worse, just the same way that you're tortured now that you know I'm your father. Save yourself this heartache...please," Trey pleads, a cruel self-loathing in his voice.

"Look, Trey," I begin. "Keeping the truth from me is the only thing that's ever broken my heart. You may think you're protecting me, but you're not. I'm not a child. Give me a chance to decide what I can handle."

With a deliberate shake of his head, he averts his eyes. "No, my decision is final."

And the match is lit. The fire ignites. Fast burning. "You know what? That's fine," I say in a quick rush. Jerking to a standing position, I lean across the table, hovering there until he meets my gaze. "Don't tell me. Delude yourself into thinking you're protecting me. Meanwhile I'm going to find Chase and ask him directly."

His eyes widen with sudden horror. I don't catch anymore of his expression of disbelief because I pivot and stride to the exit.

"Roya! Roya! No! Get back here now!" Trey yells at my retreating back, desperation in every word. My threat isn't empty either. I have every intention of finding Chase.

Chapter Eleven

The sun has risen in the real world, where Middlings worry about love or whether their dreams will ever come true. How similar and devastatingly different we are as races. The Tao offers only riddles to my problems so I abandon it for the *Collected Works of Carl Jung*. After a night of drama and little rest, his words should confound my troubled mind. In reality, every sentence flows into the next creating a beautiful volley of questions and answers, insights and interpretations. The continuity of his words feels like it's begging me to keep reading, like hidden somewhere within the passages I'll find the clues I'm looking for. The one great truth which quells the fires within me.

The second knock that morning sounds at my door. I don't jump this time. Actually, I've been expecting him. I ready my angry expression, take a breath, and say, "Come in," through clenched teeth.

The door "shushes" as it slides back.

"Do you always just let anyone stroll into your room?" George says, coming around the corner.

I sit up in my bed with sudden surprise. "Oh, it's you. I was expecting Joseph," I say, letting my head fall back on the headboard, a tiny bit of relief oozing out of me with a sigh.

"Are you mad at him? Is that why your emotions are so strong?" George says, standing at the foot of my bed, regarding me with a sensitive look.

"Is that why you came by?" I ask, tossing the iPad to the side.

"Yes," he says a bit sheepishly. "I hope you don't mind."

"I have crucified you too many times for being sensitive to my emotions, haven't I? You apologize almost every time you worry about my well-being," I say. "Most people would be grateful to have someone who cares like you do."

"Our situation is different from most people's," George says, his eyes heavy like he hasn't slept most of the night either. "I don't blame you for sometimes trying to have some emotional privacy."

"Well, I think it's only fair if I return the favor and ask after you. You look exhausted. Is everything all right?"

George yawns, his eyes closing for a second like he's about to pass out right here. "Yes, I'm fine. I want to know about you. Is it Joseph who has you so upset? I've felt a hurricane of emotion from you the last hour."

"I'll tell you all about it, but you have to do something for me first," I say, moving over to the other side of the bed.

"Anything," he says, swaying a little.

"Come lie down here," I say, patting the bed. "You look like you're going to fall over." George's eyes slide to the bed and back to me. "Oh, get over here before I drag you onto this bed," I threaten.

A sly smile curls his mouth up slightly, but still he's too tired for it to light up the rest of his face. Sluggishly he takes the spot next to me. I hand him an extra pillow. He grabs it, propping himself up.

"Now tell me first why you look like a zombie," I say. "Have you been off resurrecting ancient villains, because if so—"

A tired chuckle falls out of George's mouth. He closes his eyes and for a second I think he's fallen asleep.

"George?"

"No villains," he says, opening his brown eyes and turning his face to me. "I dream traveled last night to watch da Vinci paint the *Mona Lisa*."

"Oh. Is that all that has you looking so tired?"

"Yes," he says, an edge to his voice. "How did you spend that entire night following Bruce Lee around? I'm exhausted and couldn't manage competing right now, like you did after the fact."

"Well, dream traveling in the past is taxing and the further back you go the more draining it can become. The *Mona Lisa* was painted in the sixteenth century too. There's a reason we can't go back and see the birth of Christ, you know…it could kill us. What were you thinking going back that far?"

"I was thinking I wanted to see one of the world's greatest histories being made," he says, a meaningful look in his eyes.

"And…how was it?"

"Anticlimactic and not worth all the effort," he says, his voice scratchy. "Watching a painter create is like watching Hemingway write: it's all introspective until it's complete. Even when the *Mona Lisa* was done there wasn't any glamorous payoff. I see the painting as genius, but back then the momentum was slow to build. I realize how so many great artists and writers go crazy. They must always expect something exhilarating when they complete their work only to be stared at with long glances and indecision as the masses make their judgments. It must slowly kill them inside to know they are constantly under the scrutiny of the world."

As usual, when George makes a thoughtful insight, I find my mind suddenly charged. A new inspiration takes residence in my heart. "How did da Vinci feel afterwards?"

"You know I can't expose other people's emotions," he says, tucking his hands under his head, suppressing a smile.

"Unless we're training to face a madman, right?"

"Exactly," he says, humor in his voice.

I don't throw in his face that he recently told me when Aiden was jealous. This rule has never applied to the Head Scientist, not when it's worked in George's favor. "Fine, don't tell me," I say, pushing him slightly with my fingertips. "But you're going to have to let it all spill if we find out daVinci is an evil villain we have to take out."

Another smile. "He wasn't evil, but he was a Dream Traveler."

"Figures," I say. "All the greats are."

"All right, your turn," George says. "I actually would have just returned from my dream travels and gone to sleep, but when I got back I was assaulted by your feelings. You've had some pretty exhilarating emotions, but never before have I felt *that* much from you."

"More than when I found out that the Head Asshole of this place was my father?"

"Yeah, more than then."

"Seriously, you look like you're about to faint with exhaustion. Why don't I tell you later?" I say.

"Roya," he reprimands in that way he does that I half enjoy.

"Why is it that people keep using my name to scold me?"

"If you don't want to tell me—"

I wave him off. "There's no one else I do want to tell," I say, sliding down so our heads are a bit more even. I tell George what happened, omitting the fact that I made out with Chase. I more or less make it sound like he cornered me and then Joseph swooped in to the rescue. I explain that Trey is once again keeping secrets regarding my personal life.

"I told him I was going to find Chase and ask him directly. I'm fairly certain I've been grounded for my outburst." I laugh.

"You're not being serious, are you? You can't go seeking Chase."

"I actually am. Chase won't hurt me," I say and immediately regret it.

George graces me with a single punishing glare before returning to staring at the ceiling. "Honestly, Roya, sometimes you're too impulsive. Chase is dangerous."

"I know. It's just that I need the truth. I don't know how else to find out and the whole thing is driving me crazy."

"I sense that," George says in a restrained tone. He lays his arm over his eyes like the dim lighting of my room is hurting him. "At least you're feeling better than you were when I first woke up."

I do feel better, partly because of Jung and also because of George. Critical thinkers put me at ease.

Time passes with only the sound of George's gentle breathing. Silence with George is usually comforting with a cathartic quality. Finally he says, "I'm not sleeping, if you still want to talk."

I coerce a piece of hair from my ponytail and twirl it around my finger. "Can you feel the emotions I have for Chase, right now?"

George removes his forearm from across his eyes. "Yes."

"Do you still sense them as not real, as imposter emotions?"

A sour remorse briefly blankets his face. "No, they're becoming more real. You're asking because you can't feel the difference anymore, between your love for him and real love." It's not a question and his definitive tone empties me of hope. "He appears to have perfected the modifier. I'm sorry, Roya," George adds.

"I am too," I say with a melodramatic groan. "In my brain I don't want to feel this way...but I'm becoming possessed by something so strong I can't battle it."

"Don't worry, Aiden is going to fix your bracelet and then this will all go away."

"And until then?"

He peeks one eye open, closing it with a half-smile before he says anything. "Until then, you can lean on me."

"Thanks, George," I say, bending over, kissing his forehead. "Now you get some rest, you look awfully tired."

He tries to get up, but I tug his arm back to the bed. "Stay," I say, a question in my voice.

"Here?"

"Yes, here. How am I supposed to lean on you if you're not present," I say.

"What about you? Are you going to sleep?"

"No, I'm not sleep material, and dream travel is out of the question right now, until my protective charm is updated." I pick back up my iPad. "Thanks for everything, George."

"Thank *you*," he says with a smile, then within three breaths he's asleep.

Jung's words, again a steady streaming of comfort-producing philosophy, lull me further into an introspective state. With George sleeping peacefully beside me and Jung's verses trailing across my vision, I feel for a moment that in all this mess there's a delicate balance I need to achieve. George once spoke to me about synchronization. The idea strangely hones my eyes on a particular sentence, one that makes me gulp. Knocks on my chest.

"Your vision will become clear only when you can look into your own heart. Who looks outside, dreams; who looks inside, awakes."

Something I suspected from the beginning solidifies until I know it so completely to be a truth that I would stake my life on it. Jung's words are a clue and they've unearthed the confidence I need to believe. The secret Trey is keeping can be revealed. I don't need to ask Chase. I don't need to threaten Trey anymore. All I need to do to discover the truth is to go within.

Chapter Twelve

Our fingers interlock, and the rest of our bodies don't touch for almost an hour. I don't sleep, just watch George, quiet and still as he slumbers. The door slides back suddenly, causing me to spring upright. Cautiously, I lean until I catch Joseph's stern face stride around the corner, a white paper container in his hands.

"Way to knock, Joseph!" I snap in disbelief.

"Figured it was a waste of time," he says, tossing the container at me, then eyes George with a contemptuous look. My outburst roused him, and he's stretching into a sitting position. "What's wrong with your bed, Anders? Is your room flooded or something? Heard this place was prone to nasty leaks."

"Shut up," I say, tossing the container on the bedside table. "George is here because I invited him in. The same can't be said for you."

Guiltless, Joseph shrugs. "Just wondering why a boy is sleeping in your bed. If Pops finds out…well, I won't tell him. He's already had a big day in regards to you."

"I better give you two some space to talk," George says, rubbing his eyes as he stands. His shirt is twisted around his torso and I just catch a glimpse of what lies beneath before he tugs it down with a graceful smile.

"Thanks for everything, George. Get some more rest. I'll see you later," I say, tucking a piece of hair behind my ear.

He affirms with a wave.

The clock says it's after lunch, and although I haven't eaten, I'm not the least bit hungry. Still I open the container of food Joseph brought.

"Chicken?!" I yell, shoving the container away like it's a box of eyeballs. "Are you insane?"

"Well, Stark, I thought now that you've been bitten by the vampire you were into meat." He chuckles, too amused for his own good.

"Very funny."

"Had to make sure you were still the same person after last night. Thought you might be a possessed demon freak by now," he says, plopping down on my bed and almost causing the grotesque salad to spill on my bed covers.

I thrust the container at him. "I've been embedded. Would you give me a freaking break?!" I say, my face suddenly hot. "You think I like what happened last night?! I thought you were supposed to help me in situations like this, not make them worse!"

"That's what I was trying to do," he says, tossing the container on the table. "I was trying to get you the help you won't ask for. That's why I went to Trey. He's contacted you, right?"

I turn and face Joseph directly. Pinning both my hands on the bed, I stare into his eyes—murder written on my face. His left eye twitches, but he doesn't budge while I stare him down. "Oh yeah, he contacted me all right. We had a little meeting around four this morning. *Your* father asked me to explain in detail what happened between Chase and me…in front of Ren and Aiden. Thanks for the help, Joseph. Next time leave me the hell alone."

Joseph's eyes go wide. Color drains from his face. "Stark, I am so sorry," Joseph says, covering his face with his hands. "Our father is thicker than you, apparently. What an idiotic thing to make someone do."

"He seemed to think it was some strategy session or something," I explain.

"That's a real jerk move," Joseph exclaims when I tell him that Trey refuses to reveal why Chase is after me. "I thought he said the Institute was forever in your debt. I say you cash in on that now, and make him pay interest."

"I threatened to go and ask Chase directly." I laugh morbidly.

"Stark!" Joseph reprimands.

"Oh, don't worry. I'm not going to do it. I've got a better idea now," I say, purposely being elusive.

"Well, can I help?" Joseph asks, leaning forward.

"Nope, I think I'm at my limit with *your* help."

"Well, since you already hate me, there's no harm in saying that watchin' you make out with Ted Bundy was just 'bout the weirdest thing I've ever seen," Joseph says with a shiver.

"Well, I hope it makes you feel exponentially uncomfortable to know that I was minutes away from wearing way less clothing."

"Your hopes have been achieved."

"How would you like to be forced to love a crazy person? To not control how you act around them?" I say, a new bitterness in my voice.

"I'm sorry. I was making this about me…as I'm prone to. But this is almost too much for you to have to handle," he says, softening.

"It's about time someone wonders how I'm dealing with this all."

"No one worries about your emotional well-being as much as they should, but that's your own fault." I stare at Joseph, waiting for him to continue. "You're just too tough. It changes people's expectations. They treat you differently and that's probably how it should be anyway."

"Whatever," I say.

"So, news reporting?" Joseph changes the subject. "You wanna go and take some money outta Pop's Institutional pockets?"

I smile at his casual tone. He can switch gears faster than anyone I know. Although I seriously want to punch him for going to Trey, I still find him the easiest person to forgive. Who else could revive my archenemies and still have my unwavering trust but Joseph? Hating him would be like hating myself.

Before I have a chance to answer someone knocks. I angle my head at the door, giving Joseph a look.

"I'll get it," he says with an exaggerated sigh. A minute later he deposits a note in my hand. I look at it blankly, certain that whatever is inside I don't want to read.

"All right, Stark, let's see it. Can't be all that bad," Joseph commiserates.

"Your scale and mine of what's bad are drastically different," I say, unfolding the note. Trey's handwriting is flowery. More so than most men's.

Dear Roya,

I'm sorry I disappoint you so often. I know you must feel deserted by me. You have every right to be angry at my choices. It took me too long to tell you this: sending you and Joseph away tore my soul in two. I'm not good at showing it, but I do care about you two. All of this is to protect you both. Please don't be foolish. Please don't seek out Chase. He wants to use you as a weapon against the Institute.

Sincerely,
Trey

"Weapon?" Joseph says, reading over my shoulder. "How?"

I fold up the message, feeling strangely sentimental, and shrug. "It doesn't make much sense, but welcome to the world of the Lucidites. Nothing makes sense in this place."

"What do you think he means by that whole soul bit?" Joseph asks, watching his feet as he kicks them back and forth over the side of the bed.

"Hard to tell," I say. "The thing about Trey is that he has the capacity to care, but he also has an agenda."

"I guess I should reserve judgment," Joseph says after a moment of deliberation.

"That's mature of you."

♦

A half an hour later another note comes. Another meeting request. I love Patrick, but he's only brought bad news all day. Maybe the guy should take the rest of the month off.

Ren's office is surprisingly well lit compared to what I envisioned. In my imagination he worked in a dungeon, tortured enemies pinned to the walls in rusty chains, an interrogation light swinging in the corner, every now and then illuminating teeth and bits of hair sprayed out on the dirt floor.

I am surprised when I walk into a tidy office with multiple floor lamps. A large British flag ripples across the entire back wall. A row of shelves, full of jacket-worn books, flanks the side wall. There's no blood or pliers or anything else that can link Ren to the torture of innocent people. My eyes continue to search.

Ren spins around in his swivel chair and faces me with a keen grin. "Well, thank you for gracing me with your presence. I expected that you wouldn't be here until after all the Pokémon cartoons were over. Pull up a chair, won't you, luv." He motions to a folding chair lying against the wall.

"Wow," I say, unfolding the cold metal chair. "Looks like you went all out."

"Can't have guests getting too comfortable. Then they'd want to stay and that would just about kill me," he says.

"Would it? Well, I've got nowhere to be any time soon, so let's put that to the test."

He raises an eyebrow, looking almost entertained by my quip. "Oh, clever girl, you wouldn't be so quick to make jokes if you knew why you were here."

"I'm one hundred percent certain it has absolutely everything to do with making my life hell, so without further ado, please get on with it."

"You're taking all the fun out of this," he says, crossing his arms and feigning disappointment. "Can't you grimace a bit? Be a tad more repulsed by me? That would make this move along a little better."

"Keep doing what you're doing and I'm certain I'll vomit."

"That would be lovely," Ren says with a toothy grin. Maybe it's the lighting in his office, but for the first time I notice gray hair flecking between strands of red. "We're here so I can help you combat your horny attraction to Chase. Specifically, I've been cursed with the opportunity to teach you about dream invasion. Oh, woe is me. Good thing I have such a sunny disposition."

Dream invasion. It's how the Lucidites originally contacted me. It's how Aiden informed me he was still alive while being held captive in the Grotte. And, it's how Chase regularly enters my dreams, forcing himself onto me.

"Do you know how lucky you are to have private lessons with me?" Ren says, breaking into my reverie.

"This is luck?" I say without emotion. "Remind me to throw away my rabbit's foot."

"Dream invasion," Ren begins, ignoring me, "can be avoided but only if you control every aspect of your sleeping dreams by limiting what can be introduced. It's actually quite a fun way to dream. A caveat is that your subconscious still can introduce things into the dream that aren't limited. So don't be surprised if you're eating a scone that turns into a squirrel and then the Queen of England sits down and tells you that you just ate her pet. You can control the location, the details, and pretty much everything else.

61

But there will be surprises. If you're doing your job, as I'll teach how to do, then Chase will be forbidden from entering. He won't know you're dreaming or even that it's a possibility that he could visit. He'll simply be banned without evidence as to why."

"Trey told you to teach this to me, didn't he? What if I decide I don't want to stop Chase? What if I decide that I want Chase to visit my dreams so I can ask him why he wants me in the first place?"

"Well, you can do whatever you like. Certainly you do that already, don't you?" He sneers. "Thing is, Chase is about as likely to tell you why he's after you as I am to indulge you on that fact. We both have simply nothing to gain by revealing this information. So go ahead, allow him into your dreams. You've got nothing to lose…well, except your virginity or whatever other innocence you're pretending to have at this point in your adolescence."

"Fine, tell me what I need to know to keep creeps out of my dreams," I say, slouching down in the chair.

For over an hour Ren divulges every last thing he thinks will help me guard my dreams against invasions. I don't take notes and pretend I'm barely listening, but still I absorb every word he says.

Finally, he leans back in his chair, eyeing his gold ring like it's a new piece of jewelry. "You know, Trey isn't the monster you want him to be."

"Coming from you that means nothing."

"Oh, I get it, you like to pretend my opinion is worthless."

"In regards to my personal life, it is," I say. "You love to give me your unsolicited opinion. But I think we're close enough that I can tell you I don't give a damn what you think."

He smirks. "You know, that was quite the performance you gave this morning in Room 222. Think you might have even ruffled some feathers, if it makes you feel better."

"Glad you enjoyed my raw, unfiltered emotions."

"You got a recorder?"

"A what?" I ask.

"A voice recorder."

"No, why?"

"Too bad, you could record what I'm about to say next. It's the only direct compliment you may ever hear from me."

"Well, I've got a memory like an elephant, so fire away."

"You're just like your father."

"Is that my compliment?"

"Indeed it is," he says, propping his red leather shoes up on his desk.

"As I said before, keep your opinions to yourself. You obviously have a skewed sense of judgment."

"You're a real heartbreaker, aren't you? Why don't you use that to tear Chase's heart out?"

I lean forward, daring to put my face inches from Ren's. "I have every intention of doing just that."

He doesn't budge, but does allow a pleased grin to unfurl. "Good girl. I knew my efforts wouldn't be completely wasted on you. Now get out of here before your presence zaps me of the will to live."

Chapter Thirteen

I awake from dreams unspoiled by lunatic murderers. The high degree of lucid dreaming it takes to stop dream invasion leaves me in a state of euphoria. Then I remember who I have a meeting with first thing this morning, and all bliss turns into a storm-tossed sea of bad emotions.

If my education at the Institute has taught me anything, it's that people can act in a host of different manners which are all contrary to their sincere states. Pretense is an integral part of the fabric which holds these stainless steel walls together. I've hated it from the beginning. Hated the lies and secrets and all the acts. But right now I'm going to immerse myself in this culture of pretenders. I'm going to forget that I'm a person with real emotions. I'm going to pretend there isn't a long list of feelings I want to express. For one hour I'm going to be someone else.

"I'm here," I announce from the entrance. "As requested."

Aiden's back is to me. He moves his chin slightly, his peripheral vision capturing my presence. "Come in," he nods, voice clipped.

Shoulders back, chest high I stride until I'm on the other side of the table where he's working. He's stacking binders and moving them to the bottom shelf. I drum my fingers on the table top casually as if I'm waiting in line at the post office.

"Is this a good time?" I say. *Drum drum drum.* "I can come back." *Drum drum drum.*

Finally he flicks his eyes up, not to me, but to my wrist. "Give me your bracelet," he says not in his usual tone, or even the one he uses when in Head Scientist mode. This is a new one. He's mad. So mad he won't look at me.

I pause, study him. "Do you have a patch? One that will block Chase?"

He bristles at the mention of his name. His nostrils flare. "No, I just need to take some diagnostics," he says, extending his hand. "Bracelet. I need it."

"Does no one in this place use manners?"

He finally brings his eyes to mine. Hurt, laced with pain, engulfs me. I hadn't expected it to be so poignant. It almost breaks my fake exterior. Almost.

"Please," I say. "That's the word I was looking for, but whatever." Pressing the pin, I release the silver and copper cuff off my wrist. "Here," I say, immediately feeling naked without my charm. Putting it on the table, I push it in his direction.

Aiden regards me for a moment, not looking at the bracelet sitting between us. What he's thinking is all too apparent in his gaze. And what he's feeling is as clear as the glasses on his face.

"Ummm…is this going to take long?" I say, nudging the bracelet farther in his direction.

He shakes his head, a deliberate anger flares across his face. What I'm doing right now is like the trial of long knives, pressing a blade between my forearm and bicep. It's agonizingly painful. I don't know how Lucidites keep this act up for so long. It will surely kill me.

He plucks up my protective charm and immediately drops it like it's burning hot. A new worry stretches across his face. "What?" I say. "Is something wrong with my charm?"

He shakes his head roughly. "It's nothing." Slowly, as if afraid of it, he picks it up again from the table, this time holding it with a lighter grip.

"Why did you drop it?" I ask, my forehead creasing with worried concern. "Why are you holding it like that?"

"Just having a psychometric moment," he says, placing it on another workstation table, his back to me as he examines my charm.

"Is that the thing where you sense energy on objects?"

"Yes," he says, then nothing else.

"And…" I prompt.

"And, nothing." His tone is spiked with frustration.

"No," I counter. "You sensed something from my bracelet. What was it?"

"Nothing."

"Oh, that's a big fat lie."

Aiden sighs, pretending to work.

"Tell. Me," I say in two giant, angry words.

He swings around, irritation blanketing his face. "It's nothing to concern yourself with."

"It's *my* bracelet. I think I should be concerned."

He peels his eyes away from me, staring at nothing.

"Tell me," I say again.

Pinching the bridge of his nose he shakes his head. "Roya, it's just your energy—it startled me."

"Oh," I say in quiet surprise. "Is that a bad thing?"

"No, it's not bad and it's also not something I want to discuss further."

Aiden's never spoken to me like this. Treated me with such heartbreaking indifference. In my mind I see myself racing up to him, untying his arms from his chest and urging him to just love me. Fantasies are stupid.

"Are you done with my charm? I don't want to be without it long enough to give Zhuang a chance to embed my thoughts. A heart controlled by Chase and a mind controlled by Zhuang will have me on the America's Most Wanted list in no time."

"You're safe from Zhuang while in my lab. It's protected with a VDR shield, same as the rooming corridors," he says, not the least bit amused. "And yes, I'm done." Aiden hands me my bracelet, careful not to touch me.

"When will you have the patch ready?"

"I don't know," he says, leaning against his workstation, crossing his feet. "But hopefully it will be soon, then you'll be free to feel how you want."

"Is that supposed to be a joke?" I spew and immediately scold myself for it.

"No, it's a factual statement," Aiden says, staring at his Converse shoes. "I don't go around making insinuations."

"Any other *factual* statements you care to share with me?" My act is slipping, along with my resolve to keep my distance. I take two steps in his direction. He flicks his eyes up at me, a warning in them.

"No," he says, and I can't tell if it's an answer to my question or my sudden closeness.

"Well, maybe you'll share an opinion with me."

He draws in a tired breath, sweeping his eyes to the right.

"Don't I deserve to know why Chase is after me?"

"What I think in this situation is irrelevant."

I've failed to be a pretentious Lucidite. And I don't care anymore. My mask is on the floor in pieces. "How about how you feel? As a friend, don't you feel like I deserve the truth?"

"Roya, anything I say in answer to that will be wrong in one vein or another."

"Thanks, *friend*. Glad to know you have my back."

"Err," he says in a frustrated growl. "Since you've guilted me so well I'll say this much. What you're getting based on what you deserve isn't enough. And I can't invent anything on Earth that can change that. For that I'm sorry. As your *friend,* I wish I could help you."

I believe him and it breaks my heart—my real one. It feels good to know even in pain my heart still works.

I hadn't realized I was still holding my protective charm, not wearing it. The latch makes a gentle chirp when it catches. Unable to resist, I look up at Aiden, his eyes pinned on mine. There are a thousand words we're leaving unsaid. A thousand things I want him to say and also worry I can't stand to hear. I must be a glutton for punishment because all I want is to feel him, knowing it will haunt me later—tear the pieces of me that exist in two.

"I think we're done here," he says, pushing up from the table, now close enough I can reach out and touch him. "I'll let you know if I need any other measurements."

My eyes close with the sudden weight in my heart. I open them and he's already moved across his lab. When I'm almost to the exit I turn around. He's staring at me, was watching me leave. "I think for the first time I feel like life is unfair," I say. "I've always thought there were reasons that justified everything, but right now I'm not sure what I believe."

He nods, agreement written on his face. "There's something I wish I could tell you right now to make things better. To ease the pain created by all this confusion."

"Go ahead," I almost beg.

He gives a remorseful smile. Swallows. "You asked me not to do that anymore. I respect you enough to honor that request. Even if it tortures me."

Pressing my lips into a firm line I nod, disappointed. "Right."

"Mind shutting the door behind you?" he says, putting his back to me.

"Sure," I say, hitting the button once in the hallway. The stainless steel door, which hardly ever closes Aiden's lab off from the rest of the Institute, slides shut. If not saying how I feel makes me a Lucidite then I don't want to be one. Feelings were meant to be expressed. My fingers brush the cold steel door in front of me. "I love you," I declare, wishing I had the courage to say it one minute earlier. Wishing I had the nerve to erase boundaries and obstacles and everything else we've self-imposed on ourselves and our happiness. But people like Aiden and me don't live happily ever after. Our pride would never allow it.

Chapter Fourteen

Joseph has already eaten half a slice of pizza by the time I sidle up next to him in the main hall. Squeezing his shoulders I say, "Hey, you're going to be my dream travel buddy tonight since I obviously need supervision."

He laughs. "What if I don't want to be the one stopping you from making out with Chase?"

"Too bad, you owe me big," I say, tossing a plate of field greens and lentils on the table. It looks as appetizing right now as pig's head. "You'll remember that I was supposed to break your nose and I spared you." At our birthday party I told Joseph that if what he was secretly working on wasn't brilliant then I was going to punch him in the face.

"That's cold, even for you, Stark," he half laughs, tossing the rest of the pizza back onto the plate.

"Yeah, well, I hear I take after dear old Dad," I say. "Thinking of calling him DOD for short. Thoughts?"

"I'm not really ready for jokes on either of those subjects just yet," Joseph says, looking resentful.

I know he's feeling sentimental on the whole Trey situation. Actually I have a sneaking suspicion that he's going to great lengths to consider the possibility of building an actual relationship with the guy. The whole idea makes my stomach turn.

"Well, actually, tonight Trent and I were planning on—"

"Going to Iceland," I interrupt. "Yeah, my Joseph-radar is finally working so watch out." I see and sense the cringe that follows my words. Joseph has much to hide and I'm just a thought away from unearthing some secrets. The worried concern on his face makes me certain he knows it too. "I'm tagging along. Is that all right?"

"The more the merrier," Joseph sings without enthusiasm. "Hey George," Joseph calls over to him. "You wanna go to Iceland with us tonight?"

"Sure," he says without a moment of deliberation.

"It's getting merrier," Joseph says like he's playing a game. "Hey, Samara?" She stops, beside our table. I suspect she was trying

69

to sneak by, intent on sitting somewhere else. I also sense she isn't really over her breakup with Joseph or to terms with killing Pearl, but at least she's brushing her hair and wearing something besides yoga pants.

"Yes?" She halts, looking at him with surprised anticipation.

"Wanna go to Iceland tonight?"

Her face breaks into a relieved smile, her lighthouse eyes flashing with a new energy. "Yes," she says, taking the seat next to me.

"We're all going," Joseph says, circling his arm around the table.

"Sure," Samara says again, disappointment edging into her voice.

"What are we doing?" George asks, buttering a roll.

"Snipe hunting," Joseph says. "Be sure to bring a bat and bag. It will be the time of your life."

♦

I dream travel to the dewy meadow. Sadly I'm early. This is my curse. I'm always overly punctual, to a fault. Half expecting Chase to be standing behind me I fling around, scanning the area. All I see is a brilliant green field dotted every so often with small mounds of rocks. A smell of salt and dirt wafts through the air. I didn't bring a bag and bat as Joseph requested because I'm not going to be made a fool.

Seconds later I sense someone behind me. I turn, feeling reactionary. My defenses lower as soon as I face a meek-looking Samara. "Hey there."

"Hey," I manage back at her.

"You forgot your gear," she says, holding up a burlap sack and a small bat.

"Oh well, I guess I'll be the referee," I say.

"There's no need for referees in snipe hunting," Joseph says at my shoulder.

"Well, I guess I'll just sit out." I stick my tongue out at him. His blond hair is brighter in the Icelandic sunlight.

A slapping sound behind me arrests my attention. I turn to find Trent smacking his bat into his outstretched hand. "Let's get this party started already!" A dreadlock falls into his face as he holds up both his arms victoriously. "I'm ready to beat all you fools."

"Nice spirit, T," Joseph hoots, looking around. "We're just waiting on Captain Emotions and we can get started."

George materializes beside me, bringing with him a soft smile. "I prefer Mr. Emotions," he says, glancing down at me.

"Noted," Joseph says, scrutinizing George with an irritated look. "Here's the game. Y'all will be catching snipes, which are notorious for inhabitin' this area. They respond to sound and vibrations. Additionally they live in the ground. Here's what you gonna do: take your bat and beat it on the ground. I suggest doing it rapidly as that usually gets a better result. You'll wanna keep your eyes low to the ground and peeled on the earth because if you've been successful a small, cuddly little creature will come tearin' out of the ground looking for shelter. These are snipes. They won't hurt you one bit. Once you spy them, though, you'll wanna make haste and catch and put 'em in your bag. The person who catches the most snipes will win tonight's games. How does that sound for fun?!"

"Man, I'm going to school you peeps!" Trent shouts, pointing his bat at Samara and George, who look less than enthusiastic.

"I think I'll let you," George says, adjusting the mail bag lying across his chest. "I'll watch the first round."

"There will be no watchin', Anders," Joseph says, heat in his tone. "Stark is the only one allowed to watch and that's only because she's lousy at following directions."

"And besides, if you aren't playing, I'm not either," Samara says, pushing the burlap sack further into the back pocket of her jeans. "Trent is scaring me. I don't want to be alone with him out there."

"It's called zest," Trent says. "It's a key ingredient in my irresistible charm."

"Why exactly do we want to catch these innocent creatures?" Samara asks.

"They're *not* innocent," Joseph says, suddenly offended. "They've overpopulated this area and are killing the natural vegetation. You mess with that and it affects the temperatures which in turn affects the icebergs, et cetera, et cetera. What you're doin' is saving Iceland. And we're not going to hurt them. I have a buddy in

71

Georgia that runs a snipe ranch. He's taking them in…if you all ever get your asses out there and catch them, that is."

"All right," Samara says, timidly. "I'll do it if George does."

George glances at me and then to Joseph. "Sure," he says with a shrug.

"Good! This is a prime snipe hour, so let's not waste it," Joseph says. "The first round will be one hour long and starts now!"

The three of them scatter across the rock-filled meadow. Trent wastes no time, sliding down onto his knees and wildly beating the bat against the soft earth. It looks like he's trying to kill a million fire ants. He stops every thirty hits and hunches down lower, checking for snipes.

Samara bangs the ground softly with her bat only every other second and looks around, bewildered. Only once she catches Joseph gazing at her does she put a bit more effort into the game. George ran so far down the meadow that it's hard to tell exactly what he's doing. His movements are rhythmic so I guess he's following Joseph's instructions, but definitely not with the same gusto as Trent.

"You're evil," I say, allowing the smile I'd been suppressing to unfold.

"Oh, Stark, you have no idea." Joseph gives a fake evil laugh as he puts his arm around my shoulder. "Did you get the inside scoop on snipe hunting by spying on my thoughts?" he asks.

"Well, and my fake brother took me one time," I say, bitterly remembering the wasted summer night.

"I think I would have liked Shiloh."

"Yeah, too bad Zhuang had to murder him. You two could have exchanged stories of ways you like to antagonize me."

"I really hope if Zhuang kills me, that you don't speak about my death so casually," he says, squeezing me into him.

The thought of something happening to Joseph sends aches orbiting around my chest. My emotions for my fake family aren't undeserving. It's hard to truly love people who were embedded to accept me, but never truly did. I wonder if the emotional modifier had been invented then if they would have loved me. Maybe it wouldn't have worked on them, because the original modifier didn't work well enough. Maybe we're *that* different. But I love Chase and I'd like to think that I'm nothing like him.

I push away these worried thoughts. "So how long are you going to let them go on like this?" I ask Joseph, who's resting his arm on my shoulder like I'm a piece of furniture.

He shakes his head. "I started the game, but they're the ones who have to end it." He turns me toward the water in the distance and points. "Our job now is to bathe in that geothermal spa. I have no doubt they'll come and find us when the game is over."

The light turquoise water is mysteriously beautiful. Steam billows off its surface giving it a magical quality.

"What's that?" I ask in awe.

"*That* is Iceland's Blue Lagoon. It supposedly offers its bathers some nice healing properties. I say we check it out firsthand. But don't make any unnecessary splashes. We don't wanna freak out those Middlings over there," he says, gesturing at the figures bathing in the distance.

"When *do* we get to freak out Middlings?" I say, summoning my bathing suit underneath my clothes.

"Probably when we inherit the Institute and make our own laws."

A laugh bursts out of my mouth. "Oh, is that what you think is going to happen? I don't think Trey is leaving us his legacy." I pull off my shirt and jeans, leaving them in a pile on a nearby rock.

"One can dream, right?" Joseph says, a twinkle in his eye. "I've always wanted to be the president of the country. Being a leader over an entire society actually sounds much more appealin' now."

"You are ambitious," I say, toeing the water. It's hot.

"And you're too cautious," Joseph says, entering the water with a small dive. He swims under the surface for a few seconds and then pops up some thirty feet away. "Get in already!"

I hesitate briefly before walking into the Blue Lagoon. The water is smooth against my skin. After a few careful strokes I turn over and float on my back, looking up at the brilliant blue sky, enjoying the feel of warm water in my ears. The steam rises in columns all around me. Remembering what Joseph said about the water having healing properties I sink down until it almost covers my eyes. The water here may heal physical ailments, but I'm doubtful it fixes emotional problems.

"Roya," he whispers, his voice caressing my name, making it sound like something he needs, enticing me with the promise of something indulgent. I flip upright. The steam is denser here, so thick I hardly see my hands wading beside me. I turn again and again, not knowing which way to swim to return me to Joseph. Not knowing if I'll swim right into Chase's arms. Not knowing which one I prefer. I picture this is how it feels to be lost in an avalanche of snow.

"Roya," he says again. I stiffen.

I don't love him. The words are strong in my mind, trumping the messages from my heart. Without hesitation I bound in the opposite direction, my heart suddenly hammering in my chest. Four strokes bring me out of the thickest steam. Joseph is on the bank.

Like I'm competing in the Olympics, I race for the shore, feeling a weight start to tear into my chest. The hold my mind had on my heart wanes. Only slightly but it's enough to make me hesitate. To consider turning back, swimming into Chase's arms which I know with such certainty are waiting to hold me. I'm roughly twenty-five feet from Joseph. Although I'm still cutting through the water each movement is slower than the last, not filled with as much urgency.

"Joseph," I yelp, like I'm drowning. It's my last rational idea to avoid my heart's wrong desires. He swivels his head around, confused concern written on his face. The moment his eyes connect with mine the spell is weakened. Looking at Joseph reminds me of who I am in my heart. Realization dawns on Joseph's face. The concern that blankets his features next constricts my throat. He dives back into the water, making hurried strokes until he reaches me.

"Where?" he says, pushing me in front of him, paddling behind me.

"Over there," I motion with my head.

When we reach the banks, he looks me over, like I might be hurt. "You should have known better than to go off by yourself," he reprimands.

"I didn't realize I had," I say, an apology in my tone. Making him worry is the last thing I want right now. He has too much to deal with already.

Joseph gives me a measured glare, then lets out a relieved sigh. "Stay on the bank, away from the steam, would you?"

"Yeah," I say, distracted by the three figures racing over the hill, George is in the lead. There's a look of horror in his eyes. It's expressed perfectly by the words that spill out in gasps as he sprints to me. "Where is he?!"

"He's gone." I rush forward and have to stop myself just before I throw my shaking arms around him. "It's all right. He disappeared as soon as Joseph showed up."

George bends over, breathing deeply.

"Damn it, Roya," Trent says, sounding irritated and winded. "You can't join us if I you're going to bring your stupid stalker with you. Not that he interrupted anything of real importance," he says, angling angry eyes at Joseph.

A mischievous smile springs to Joseph's mouth. Trent smacks his bat into his hand. "That's a rotten game, mate."

"Oh, you didn't catch any snipes? Too bad. Maybe it's the wrong season for snipe hunting," Joseph says, laughter in his voice.

"I suspect there's never a good season to catch made-up creatures," George says, standing up straight, trying to sound menacing although it isn't effective.

"Now, now, George, just because you're a poor hunter doesn't mean you have to call snipes made up." Joseph splashes water at the three of them.

"Hey," I say, "I thought you said no splashing."

"The Middlings left," Joseph says, sending a wave of water in my direction.

Scanning the lagoon, I realize he's right.

"You're so cruel, Joseph," Samara says. She sounds on the verge of tears as she throws her bat and bag onto the ground. "I can't believe you brought us all out here just to play this stupid trick on us. You're the worst."

Joseph has been moving forward in the water as she speaks. "Oh, that's not the only reason I brought you out here." He bolts forward, picks her up, and throws her over his shoulder.

"No! No!" Samara screams. Laughs. It's the first genuine one I've heard from her since we've returned from the Grotte. Joseph leaps back out into the water. "Don't! Please don't!" she pleads.

A treacherous smile flashes across his face. "Begging only encourages me," he says, dropping her into the water. She bobs for a second, looking furious and on the verge of laughter all at the same time. Joseph's already striding back up toward George and Trent. "Who's next?"

George laughs, pulling off his shoes and throwing them at Joseph. Trent dives at Joseph, and the two explode the water around them with a giant spray. The three take turns flinging water and insults at Joseph for the next hour. As usual, Joseph smiles, taking it all in like he's being lavished with compliments. For Joseph attention always does the trick. It's what he wants at the end of the day. And although I've been restricted to the shore, I still enjoy watching my friends take turns tackling my brother, so much so my sides ache from laughter.

Although Samara has laughed and smiled over the last hour, none of it has appeared easy, like each positive emotion is one she robbed from someone else. Too many times I catch her staring at Joseph, only to realize he's engulfed in antics that don't involve her. The disappointment in not having his attention isn't something she's hiding well. And Joseph doesn't appear to have any hint that her attention is hinged on his every move. Finally she floats away, leaving the three guys wading in the lagoon water. Soon after, George breaks off, headed in my direction.

It's precisely at that moment that I know something extremely important and personal about Joseph. It springs up the moment he's alone with Trent. The realization stems from his thoughts, but is validated by my observations. Not only does it feel wrong to have access to someone like this, to know his darkest secrets, but it's made worse that this one is shrouded in shame. Not only do I now know something deeply personal about Joseph, but I also know I can't confront him about it. He isn't ready.

George wades out of the water, distracting me from the most recent epiphany. The brilliant blue water drips off his face and body. He's built perfectly like a statue—like something an artist would want to make—trimmed waist, broad shoulders, sculpted chest. The knife wound from Allouette is pink with fresh new skin. My eyes linger up his torso until I catch the gratified look in his eyes. I blush furiously.

"I'm going to keep my distance," George says, taking a seat a few feet away. "I sense that a certain someone wouldn't want me too close to you."

"Oh, Joseph doesn't care," I say.

"I think he does," George says, chewing on his bottom lip. "But he's not who I'm referring to. Although Chase is gone, I sense he'd return if the situation warranted."

"Which means you and I shouldn't dream travel together," I say, knowing the implications laden in the statement.

"Right," he says with a subtle smile.

My mind travels to Chase and his preoccupation with me. The question keeps my mind constantly searching. It's the question that precedes every meditation and awakes me from every dream. Still I'm no closer to knowing the truth. And my confusion is steadily morphing into anger which is spiraling into hopelessness.

"Hey, it's all right," George says softly. "You want to get out of here?"

"Yes, but I think I need to be alone. I'm going back to the Institute," I say, my mood having plummeted from thinking about Chase.

He nods, staring off into the blue. "I understand."

"You always do." I go to pat his arm but stop myself. "Thanks," I finally say. "Would you tell everyone I left?"

"Of course," he says just before I recede back into my own bed.

Chapter Fifteen

After returning from Iceland I conjure up a place to begin my lucid dreaming. This is part of how Ren taught me to ground my thoughts inside a dream. If I begin in a place of my choosing rather than falling into a dream, then I'm more likely to keep my awareness. Slowing my breath, I repeat the phrase that delivers me to a dreamland where I will have control:

I'm about to dream. Stay aware. Stay awake inside the dream.

Again and again I repeat this until I'm standing on a cliff staring out at a gray sea. The winds sweep furiously at it. Although I'm dreaming, I'm still highly aware of everything. The thoughts in my head are active, possessing the power to shift everything around me. *Chase is not allowed here,* I say in my head, locking the door to my dream.

As Ren instructed I can limit specifics, make conscious choices, escape and even invent elements in the dream. Still, my subconscious is free to drop in its own unprocessed thoughts and emotions. This is the part that's made lucid dreaming the most fun. To actively witness the strangeness of my subconscious is like exploring a carnival funhouse. Each room plays on reality and is also spiked with something so askew it entertains and also baffles.

I gaze down, feeling a constriction around my torso. Champagne-colored silk corsets my body. At my waist the fabric billows out, curving into a bell shape and draping all the way to the grass under my feet. A wedding dress.

"It's an antique," a girl with a French accent says, pinning up curls on the top of my head. She leans around my shoulder. "It vaz his mozer's," she says, a proud look in her opaque eyes.

This must be what Ren was talking about. *Hello, subconscious. Thanks for dropping into my dream.*

The girl hands me a mirror. The handle is gold and ornately decorated with flowers and vines. Spots from age fleck the surface. "You are a most striking bride," the girl says, sounding pleased. Before I have a chance to bring the mirror up to my face I'm interrupted.

"You can't do this!" Aiden yells behind me. "You can't marry Chase!"

I turn to see him stride through an isle of chairs, hydrangeas lining the ceremonial space.

"She can and she vill," the girl says, stepping in front of me, blocking Aiden. My mouth feels sewn shut.

"Roya, you don't love him," Aiden petitions, fists clenched by his side. "I will die before I allow you to do this."

"Then you vill die," the girl says, snapping her fingers. Two men materialize on either side of Aiden. They are towers of muscle, dwarfing him between them. Horror rips across Aiden's face, but his attempts to fight their holds are futile. One seizes his arms, the other places two meaty hands on either side of his head. The next movement is swift, followed by a sickening crack. Aiden falls to the flower-covered earth as loosely as a bundle of rope.

"No!" I scream. My eyes snap open in my darkened bedroom. Hands jerk to my chest, which feels as if it's been shattered. Bolting upright in bed I'm immediately restricted by the sheets tightly swaddling my body. Hot breath hitches in my throat as the image of Aiden's dead body burns into my vision.

◆

"Can I have a private word with you?" I say to Shuman, interrupting a meeting she's having with a dark-haired girl.

Her eyes glance at the clock on the wall, a surprise in them. Joseph and I had planned to news report after breakfast. I skipped the meal and came straight to the Panther room.

"We will continue this later," Shuman says to the girl, who nods at her, then regards me with thoughtful interest before leaving the conference room.

"Something is troubling you," Shuman says. It's not a question.

"Yes. Ren explained to me how to stop Chase from entering my dreams, but I just had one and I'm not sure it's working."

"Did Chase actually invade this dream?"

"No, but it was about him. And it was violent, reeking of things he would have done," I say, loosening the lump in my throat before continuing. "And there were Voyageurs I don't know in the dream."

"I think the answer to this is evident in why you sought *my* advice, rather than Ren's. Your instinct told you I would be of most help, is that right?"

"Well, yes," I almost stutter. Although I'm worried the dream means I'm failing to block Chase, I also sense it needs to be interpreted, which is a specialty of Shuman's.

"Chase did not invade your dream. It sounds as though no one did. What you experienced was partly your subconscious playing out its own fears and also I suspect something else of great importance." She cracks her knuckles before continuing. "Tell me, what did these Voyageurs look like?"

"One was a girl, maybe my age. She had reddish, curly hair. Then there were these two brute-looking men. They appeared so similar that I could have sworn they were twins. Maybe they invaded my dream," I reason with a sigh.

"No, that is not what happened. For one, dreams cannot be invaded by multiple people. The way it works when someone enters your dream is they have tangled their subconscious with yours. This is impossible to achieve with more than two subconsciouses. Secondly, the people you have just described to me are Voyageurs who were once under Chase's command. They are now dead."

"What?! How would my subconscious know about them?"

"Your subconscious is connected to the universal source."

"What does that mean?"

"Dreaming delivers you to a plain of existence where you plug into the source. As a clairvoyant you plug into the source when awake, but your connection to it is heightened when news reporting, meditating, and dreaming. All information, past, present, and future, is stored in this universal source. It is impossible for me to know why these figures were sent to you in your dream. Your subconscious retrieved them from the source for a reason. The reason is most likely connected to the assorted details in the dream, which I would strongly encourage you to interrupt. Your brother might be of great assistance with this, since he has a knack for the art of dream interpretation."

"Can you tell me anything else about these Voyageurs that will help us interpret the meaning of the dream?"

"Actually, I can. I will tell you that when Chase tired of them they were murdered. Much the same way he does when he no longer has use for someone."

I sit quietly, listening to the clock tick.

"Can I offer you an insight?" Shuman asks.

"Yes," I say, desperate for anything that can untangle this web.

"Now that you know your subconscious delivers information about real events of the past while lucid dreaming, it will affect the weight you put upon it. It is possible that this dream has been a setup, to prepare you with the confidence you need to accept information yet to come."

Shuman, too many times, has spoken like this. Like she's aware of future events regarding my life and only gives me enough clues so that I'll continue down the path she sees. I used to resent her for this, but now I understand that this vision of hers is probably a burden. Moreover, I sense she's trying to help in her weird and mystic way.

"Be careful not to limit anything but Chase while lucid dreaming," she continues. "Also do not try to control too many aspects of your dreams. If you do, you will miss messages being sent to you. Be a quiet observer."

"Okay," I say, spotting Joseph lurking by our familiar station, giving me a puzzled look. "Thanks for your help."

"Is everything all right?" Joseph asks when I take the chair next to him.

"Yeah, it's just whoever runs this universe is sending me weird messages. So everything is pretty much status quo."

"All right, we'll discuss the mysterious meaning behind *that* statement after we news report. Have fun and get good stuff, little sis," Joseph says, lying down in his own recliner.

"You too, big Joe." I smile, clapping the headphones into place and closing my eyes.

Darkness seeps across my mind's eye, replacing the glow of the purplish light overhead—a sign I'm about to receive a news report. I've entered the void, the place where all my news reports are delivered. A sound similar to thunder echoes around the blackness. A light, like sun reflecting off a mirror, pierces my vision, blinding me momentarily. The ground in the premonition rocks with

81

a minor earthquake. Fabric arises into my vision, flowing like a flag in the wind. White and black.

The camera lens retracts until I spy two legs marching across iridescent blue carpet in slow motion. Each confident step is a trespassing, dripping with an ominous threat. One that rockets across my chest, assuring that what comes next doesn't just endanger me, but everyone I know.

Everything speeds up into real time. The vision blacks out, like I've lost the signal. Then it flashes with a new intensity. It's almost too bright to focus upon, like I'm staring into the sun, trying to make out its shape. Still I stay focused until the foreboding presence is as crisp as a blade of grass. Right then I know something which empties all hope from my being: soon Zhuang will invade the Institute.

Chapter Sixteen

Panic spears me at the sight of Zhuang. Somehow he's more majestic than the last time I saw him. Starched black and white robes sharply whip around his body as he strides, closing the space that exists between him and a door. A yellow fingernail—filed into a sharp point—presses the button. I glimpse the placard above it:

Head Official
Trey Underwood

The door hasn't even fully slid back when Zhuang slithers into the office. A guttural sound of frustration explodes from the ancient madman. Instantly he's back in the hallway, standing stock-still. He sniffs the air. Narrows menacing eyes. Charges forward.

Determination marks his snakelike golden eyes, which look rimmed with coal. He reaches behind his head, his sleeve falling down to reveal long, sinewy muscles. With a jerk he rips the sword out from behind his back. The one he used to kill Whitney with. Stab Joseph with. Was a moment away from ending me with.

A roar like that of a territorial lion erupts from Zhuang's mouth. To my horror an individual runs out of an office, a look of concern on the white coat's face. Instantly the man's expression falls slack. He stumbles, dropping on his rear end and crab walks backward in sudden panic. Zhuang raises a hand up, up, up into the air. Simultaneously the scientist levitates horizontally until his nose is touching the cold stainless steel ceiling. His head rips back and forth, tortured by the uncertainty of what comes next. A cold chuckle falls out of Zhuang's paper-thin lips. At lightning speed, he zigzags his bony hand through the air. The hovering body follows suit slamming back and forth between the Institute walls like a ping-pong ball. Each collision is harder than the last, accompanied by the sounds of cracking and screams. Finally, the body crumples to the blue carpet, blood smearing the places where it waylaid the steel walls.

A swarm of white coats empties out into the hallway. Individually their eyes dart to the man's body, then to Zhuang, standing squarely in the middle of the corridor, some ten feet away. Most run. One dives back into his office. A woman slumps against the wall, most likely dream traveling.

Zhuang gives an irritated expression as he steps over the dead body, continuing on his path. "Run or hide but you will all still die." His voice comes out in a low growl.

♦

A choking scream rips me out of the premonition. "They have to get away! They have to!" I yell. Shooting upright, I cause my headphones to be yanked off my head and clatter to the floor. Sweat drenches my shirt, making it cling to my chest. Joseph flings his headphones off and is at my side at once.

"What is it?" he says, gripping my arm. "Are you all right?"

"Third level! They have to get away!" I say through hyperventilated breaths.

"Stark." Joseph searches my eyes, which wildly dart around my head. "Is someone in danger?"

"We all are." A shiver shoots down my spine, worsened by the sweat against my back. "Come on." I tug Joseph's hand as I sprint out of my chair and down the darkened hallway.

How long do we have? What if we have only minutes? What if all the white coats are already in danger? The adrenaline has a hold of me right now, but as soon as it abates I'm going to be riddled with anxiety.

I scan the conference room and don't find Shuman. Still sprinting, I check each of the training areas with haste. Left with no other options I slam my hand against the button for the door at the end of the long corridor. It slides back and gold light streams through the dark hallway, causing my eyes to squint. Shuman jerks to a standing position behind the table in the center of the room. A map sits in front of her.

"Excuse me, Roya," she says, confounded and enraged by my interruption. "These are private quarters."

"I'll remember that next time." I stride across the room in three steps. "For now I have a report that needs your immediate attention."

84

I take a tentative glance at Joseph beside me. His expression makes me certain that he half suspects what I'm about to divulge.

"Well, go on." Shuman's voice is calm but anxious.

"Zhuang," I say, trying to steady my breath.

Joseph straightens. Shuman blinks with disbelief.

"You have seen a report that involves Zhuang?" she asks, her words uncharacteristically fast.

I nod. "In the future, maybe in a few minutes or several weeks, Zhuang is going to break into the Institute." My words taste like cement in my mouth. I want to spit them out, but instead I swallow the harsh bits of rock.

Shuman's chin, which is held high, slowly lowers until it is an inch from her chest. Her eyes shift from side to side. Mouth pinched. "Go on."

"Zhuang was looking for Trey," I say, feeling Joseph jerk beside me but unwilling to look at him. "That's where the vision started. At Trey's office."

"He did not find him?" Shuman asks.

"He did not."

"What did you see of Zhuang's actions?"

I shudder, too easily remembering the man's broken body. "Murder. A scientist. Third level. And he was after more," I say in chopped sentences.

"He's coming to destroy the Institute," Joseph undertones as if talking to himself.

"I suspect he is coming for much more than that," Shuman says, drawing in a long breath. "He is coming to steal power. Trey's for sure. And yours," she says, eyes pinning on me.

"But he's still gonna kill us all," Joseph says.

"I only saw him kill *one* person." My attempt at reassurance is lousy. This is the news Joseph has been bracing himself for, but not exactly in this way. He knew Zhuang would return, but none of us could have guessed he would enter the Institute. I actually didn't even think it was possible.

"I will need a description of this person Zhuang killed." Shuman appears to be calculating. "Your report might have just prevented the deaths of many scientists."

"But the rest of us are doomed," Joseph says in a ghostly whisper.

85

Although we're usually pretty disagreeable, I lock my eyes on my brother and nod. He's right. Soon we're headed for a catastrophe.

Chapter Seventeen

Joseph and I agree not to discuss Zhuang over lunch. I feel the regret and shame swelling in him like rising dough. With each passing minute the pressure grows and soon I think it will cocoon both of us. I nudge him under the table, a gesture he's done to me a dozen times when I'm wearing a melancholy face. He nods in understanding and plasters a giant, fake smile across his mouth. "Better?" he whispers through clenched teeth.

"Now people are going to stare at you for totally different reasons. Tone it down a bit," I say in a hush, careful not to let anyone else at the table pick up on our conversation.

"How's it that you're so calm? Zhuang is coming after you."

"It's called a poker face. I inherited it from Trey."

"Yeah, you must have. It's brilliant."

"I'm even better at pretending doom isn't about to fall down on me. Watch this," I murmur, pushing my asparagus and white bean salad away. "Hey, George." I turn my attention to him sitting on the other side of me, not quite as close as Joseph.

He finishes the line he's reading in his book and looks up at me. "Hey."

"Sorry to interrupt," I say.

He flicks his eyes across my face, studying me. A knowing smile forms on his mouth. "No you're not."

"Oh, all right, I'm not," I say, grabbing a bean from my plate and tossing it at him. "Just trying to be polite."

He ducks out of the trajectory of the bean. "You don't have to use pretenses with me."

"What are you reading?" I say, gesturing to the book his hand is still pinned between so he doesn't lose his place.

"*Love in the Time of Cholera,*" he says, tucking his bookmark between the pages and showing me the cover.

"Is it good?"

"It is."

"Well, maybe I'll start it. I like the idea of us reading the same book at the same time."

"Me too," he says with understated satisfaction.

"It would give us more to talk about."

"Yes, more."

"Maybe we should start a book club," Joseph says, breaking the lovely tension that was building. "But we can only read stuff that's ancient, written with flowery language, and about characters that live miserable lives of lost love and sacrifice. I for one cannot wait to curl up, eat a scone, and bore myself to death reading that drivel."

I turn and give Joseph a wink that only he can see. Of course he's fantastic at pretending. It's his thing. "Those sentences you just constructed are the most intelligent things I've ever heard you say. I don't think your hillbilly accent flared up once during your monologue. I already see that this book club idea is going to be good for you."

"Oh, it will do somethin' for me, that's for sure," he says, over-embellishing his southern drawl.

Turning back to George, I say, "Some people just can't be helped. Anyway, I was wondering if you'd help me practice emotional shielding this afternoon. Ren thinks it might help me against Chase."

"He's probably right." George nods. "And absolutely I will. I'm meeting with Aiden after lunch, but how about as soon as I'm done?"

"Sure," I say slowly.

Aiden and George are still working on the emotional modifier together? I'm not sure why this surprises me, but it does. It's not that I worry like I used to that they're perfecting a device that manipulates people's emotions without them knowing it. What bothers me is that the two of them are working together and I still feel strangely tethered between them, even though Aiden and I are history. But we still have just that: history. I wonder if they talk about me during these meetings.

"I think the emotional modifier is close to complete," George says, interrupting my thoughts. "Then Aiden can begin working on the patch for your protective charm. We think that it will prevent Chase from embedding you."

"I hope so," I say.

"Aiden's been working on it nonstop, churning out different models that get closer and closer to working seamlessly."

Although I'm glad they're trying to help, it still feels strange to know their work is centered on me. For a person who is used to a whole lot less attention, I'm kind of on overload. And the two guys who've owned pieces of my heart, teaming up to protect me from a love affair from a third guy, is the most peculiar arrangement I can imagine. I feign a smile. "Well, thanks for working on the project, although I know you have mixed feelings on the whole device."

"My feelings aren't mixed," George says, voice low. "It's wrong to manipulate emotions, even if against a dangerous person. There are other ways to protect ourselves. I wish I would have known that before I started the work. Then you wouldn't be in the situation you are."

I'm shaking my head before he's even done speaking. "Don't. You can't berate yourself for hindsight. You're working to save me now and for that I'm grateful."

"I need everyone's attention." Trey's voice echoes from the front of the room. "At one-thirty this afternoon everyone is required to attend a meeting in the auditorium. That is all. Thank you." Trey walks across the stage with practiced grace. His confidence looks unmarked by the weight of what I know he's dealing with. And although I wish I didn't care, I still take in his every movement, studying him for the similarities that I undeniably share with him.

My eyes flick to Joseph. He's already looking at me, obvious apprehension covering his features. Usually I'd just imagine how a person like him felt in his position. However, now I know how awful Joseph feels. Guilt and dread swim around, threatening to tear him into pieces from the inside out. The only other person who feels this as keenly as me is George. I can't be certain that he knows the details of what's coming next, but from the expression on his face I believe he's aware of the torment that's slowly scraping away at Joseph's insides.

◆

Half an hour later I dutifully head to the auditorium. I'm rounding the corner into the large room when I collide with Aiden, who's scribbling on a notepad as he hurries in from the opposite direction.

"Hey," Aiden says, almost knocking me over. "Sorry." Something skirts across his face before he recovers his stone expression. Angst maybe?

"Hey," I say as casually as I can muster. We pause in the doorway, letting people jostle past us into the auditorium. I could stand here forever enjoying the torment in my heart and the opportunity to watch him bury his own. I must love abuse.

"Nice work," he finally says after an awkward moment of silence.

"Huh?"

"Your report."

"Oh."

"Your father is really proud of you."

"Hmmm…funny I learn this from you and not him." I roll my shoulders, a sudden tension gripping my back.

"He's been very busy."

A hand grabs my arm from behind with a gentle yank. "Hey, sis," Joseph says, biting on the words. "Saved you a seat."

I turn to see him not staring at me but giving Aiden a threatening look.

"Thanks." I turn and let Joseph guide me, not saying another word to Aiden. However, as I walk down the main aisle I feel him behind me, his presence crowding, hoarding every available place in my head.

"Right here." Joseph stops, encouraging me into the row second from the front. "Right next to my squire," he says, indicating a seat beside George. Aiden takes the seat in front of me in the front row—just between Ren and Shuman.

"I suppose you're deluding yourself into thinking you're a knight, then?" I jab Joseph in the ribs as he takes the seat on the other side of me.

"Suppose whatever you like," he says, fending off my mild attack.

I turn to George, ready to commiserate over my brother's immaturity. He halts me with an appraising gaze, worry growing in his eyes.

"Bad news, huh?" George states after searching me. During lunch I had up a shield, which I've taken down now since he and everyone else is about to find out about Zhuang.

"The worst," I reply.

"Anders," Joseph says, leaning across me. "I find it creepy that you ransack Stark's emotions every chance you get."

"I only read emotions Roya gives access to," George says evenly, unflustered by Joseph's obvious aggression. "She knows how to shield me."

"It's true," I say, angling Joseph back into his seat with my shoulder. "And I don't mind."

George rewards me with a gentle smile which reaches his brown eyes, making them glow. "Reading your emotions is like watching a sunrise," he says, all his attention on me. "You want to do it every chance you get."

Aiden sits forward suddenly, resting his elbows on his knees, head hanging low. There's no convincing myself that he hasn't heard this exchange.

"It's strange to think that the last time I was in this room was when I first entered the Institute," I say, breaking away from George's eyes, pretending to take in the details of the auditorium. "You know, when I came here it was because *someone*"—I jab a finger in Shuman's direction—"told me I was the one to challenge Zhuang. They forgot to mention that I would compete for that role."

"I still remember seeing your face and wet hair when Ren shoved you into the room in front of all of us." George's voice carries a hint of nostalgia.

"Yeah, you were the epitome of a deer in the headlights." Joseph laughs.

"I should have realized right then that this place was going to be a confusing mess of games and lies," I say, keeping my voice low so hopefully just George and Joseph can hear me. "Instead I decided to willingly compete for an honor I didn't want while Trey hid the real details of my life."

"Hey, Stark," Joseph says, looking around the room watching the various people take seats.

"What?"

"Your bitterness is showing. You might want to tuck it in a bit."

"I'll try," I say, not meaning it. "Hey, maybe in our next life, we'll be born to some boring Middlings?"

"Good idea. If you were the daughter of an insurance salesman you wouldn't have to fight some ancient madman and worry about being impregnated by a hot French guy." Joseph cranes his neck around, seeming to be looking for someone.

"Well, I might, but the details would look a little different," I say with a morbid laugh.

"Do you really have to put it *that* way," George says, pressing two fingers against his temple.

"The hot French guy part or the impregnate part?" Joseph says, spinning back around, sliding low in his chair.

George shudders. "The idea that Chase would ever touch you makes—"

"Would you buffoons mind shutting your traps," Ren says, spinning around. "Every word out of your mouths kills a dozen of my brain cells. Although I have more to spare than most, I'd still like to hold onto all I can."

"It's a free Institute. We can do what we like," Joseph says, sticking his tongue out at Ren.

He responds to the gesture with a derisive glare. "Well, I guess I'm free to inform George here that Chase touching Roya isn't just an idea. It's a reality that has come to pass, which will probably repeat itself over and over and over…"

Aiden's hand claps Ren on the shoulder, steering him back around. "Lay off them, would you?"

Ren shrugs Aiden's hand off and faces forward again, muttering something under his breath.

"What does Ren mean?" George whispers in my ear, almost scolds.

I'm just about to lie when I catch Samara moving into the aisle, about to take the seat next to Joseph. Before she can Trent hops over from behind and plucks himself down, stealing her seat. Arrogance beams off Trent's face as he dusts off his shoulder nonchalantly.

"What was that about?" Samara says, scrunching up her forehead, taking the seat next to Trent.

"Just trying to be a gentleman," he says, stretching out his long legs. "Didn't want you to sit behind Shuman where you wouldn't be able to see properly."

"Wow, I'm blown away by your chivalry," Samara says with a bitter edge.

"I do try," Trent says, sliding his chin around and exchanging a look with Joseph. The two stay locked on each other and although I can't see Joseph's expression, I can feel his emotion.

There's a new tension between Trent and Joseph now. The twitch of a smile on Trent's face makes me certain he enjoys it. But it fills the open places in Joseph with discomfort. I want to pull my mind from his, but my instinct tells me not to. I can't help him unless I know everything he's dealing with. And what I learned in Iceland about Joseph is now confirmed by a tiny spark of emotion he just felt for Trent and quickly admonished himself for. Soon I'll help him confront this, but right now we have more urgent matters.

"Thank you all for joining me on such short notice." Trey's voice carries across the auditorium on a loudspeaker. He's wearing his usual white button-up shirt, sleeves folded up to the elbow, medallion winking out at the base of his neck. Although I fight the urge, I find myself studying him again. "I recognize that your time is valuable," Trey says, clearing his throat. "I'll cut to the reason I asked you here. For a short time now we have known that Zhuang was alive and growing stronger. Although our efforts to defeat him on June thirteenth were effective in weakening him, they didn't destroy him entirely. He has now risen back to power. This morning a news reporter learned that Zhuang *will* enter the Institute."

Sudden gasps fill the large space. An eruption of shuffling and muttering follows. Trey holds up his hand; the room silences immediately. "Although authenticating this report isn't possible, I have every reason to believe these events will come to pass. This news reporter has never given a false report," he says, eyes careful not to meet mine. "While our security has always been strong enough to deter attacks from Zhuang we are now in danger. He has most likely been able to tap into and determine the specific details that keep us shielded and therefore find a way to forge his way in here." Beside me I feel Joseph tense. I press my shoulder into his slightly, offering the most subtle bit of comfort I can think of. It was from Joseph that Zhuang learned how to break into the Institute. Sucked it out of him, along with his energy and power.

Silence fills every crevice of the room, mounting the tension brewing in my chest. No one stirs now. All remain focused on Trey, hinged on his next words. "It's unknown when Zhuang will enter the Institute. Certain security measures will be put into place to alert

93

you, the residents of the Institute, as soon as we know that Zhuang has entered the premises. We do know that he will enter on the third level; therefore, this level will be shut down immediately. All who are officed there will be relocated to new spaces." Trey drags his hand through his silver hair, looking out at the crowd, which has been absorbed in his every word. "When you hear the siren overhead, signaling that Zhuang has entered the Institute, or if you have any other indication, then it's imperative that you all dream travel to a GAD-C location. No one, and I repeat no one, but the Head Officials will be staying to battle Zhuang."

Only the Head Officials? They aren't enough. They're all going to be killed. My eyes study the back of Aiden's head. Suddenly I feel snapped in two and every emotion I've masked all morning seeks to spill out of me. Aiden doesn't stand a chance. Zhuang will kill him. And although it's not my place to care, I want to stop it. I want to stop Zhuang from killing anyone. A battle I didn't know I wanted to be a part of has instantly become a personal crusade.

"This is all of the information that I have at the current time," Trey says. I pull my eyes away from their focal point to find my father staring at me intently. There's a message in his eyes, a warning. "I know this creates a new level of stress around the Institute," he continues, sweeping his gaze around the auditorium. "Please stay alert at all times, report anything suspicious, and be willing to escape this place with no notice. I'm sorry that the Institute, which has been a safe haven to us for so long, will face danger. Please know that the Head Officials will be working diligently to restore the sanctity of this place as well as to protect Lucidites everywhere from Zhuang. Thank you." Trey walks off the stage and disappears behind a door.

We all stay seated, staring ahead blankly, like we're waiting for another show to perform on the stage where Trey exited.

"Zhuang sucks," Samara finally says as people move around us toward the exit.

"You have no idea," Joseph says, with a perverse laugh.

"Wonder who gave the report?" Trent says, puckering his lips like he's sifting through possibilities.

Shuman stands and twists around. "The identity of the persons who make news reports is anonymous. Only the Head Officials are privy to that information." She stalks away.

Trent rolls his eyes, not looking the least bit deterred. "I wonder if it was that old hippie lady who does the strange stuff with crystals," Trent says. "Hey, Doc!"

Aiden, who's been scribbling on a notepad, swivels his chin in Trent's direction, looking unusually contemptuous. "Are you talking to me?"

"Well, I know you're listening and yeah."

"What can I do for you, Mr. Reynolds?"

"Who made the report?" Trent asks, eyes eager with curiosity.

"I'm not at liberty to say," Aiden says, standing up. "Only that person has permission to disclose their identity." His eyes flick to mine, then down to my hand lying less than an inch from George's on the armrest. He tips his head at the group and hurries away.

"It was you, wasn't it?" Trent asks Joseph, giving him a look of unabashed pride.

Joseph shakes his head and inclines it at me.

"Roya?" Trent asks.

I pinch Joseph's forearm. "That wasn't your business to tell."

"It's T," Joseph says, rubbing his arm like it might bruise. "He deserves to know."

"Ah, man, Roya!" Trent says, jaw dropping. "If you knew why didn't you tell us? We're your team."

"I just found out myself," I say. "Once I turned the information over to Shuman I didn't feel it was my place to tell anyone else. How was I supposed to know what I saw was real, anyway?"

"Because you're freaking Roya Stark," Trent says like that reason carries real weight.

"Well, let's hope that Zhuang doesn't decide to visit us right now," Joseph says through a long yawn. "'Cause I need some rest."

Trent shakes his head and laughs. "Funny how you act like the axis of this planet, while we're trying to figure out how to save it."

A vicious chuckle comes from Samara. "Yeah, exactly."

Joseph looks at the group with an overexaggerated expression of hurt. "Oh, I didn't realize you all were playing superheroes again. If so, I would have rethought my sleep schedule."

I know Joseph is running to the end of his witty act. Soon the real emotions of what he's feeling will boil to the surface, but I can't let that happen. "Come on," I say, tugging him up from his seat. "I'll tuck you in and read you a bedtime story."

95

Chapter Eighteen

"So why this place?" Steve asks as he and Bob join me on the slippery rock. I can hardly hear him over the crashing water of Sutherland Falls. Steve summons a parka and Bob quickly does the same. In unison they flip the hoods up over their heads, flinching from the cold spray. Although I back up so the roar of the plummeting water doesn't interfere with our conversation too much, I actually enjoy the chilly mist as it sprays my face and arms. I don't answer right away, just allow myself to be mesmerized by the water as it descends the last part of the multitier fall before entering Doubtful Sound.

"Well," I finally say, "I chose this place because it's the second largest waterfall in the world."

"Second?" Steve asks curiously.

"Well, the first isn't supposed to have the 'wow' factor that this one has," I reply, looking up at over nineteen hundred feet of waterfall. It's hypnotic, making me feel out of control and uninhibited. Much the same effect Chase has on me. I cringe at the uncanny similarities. Leave it to me to be stalked by a man who's akin to a waterfall. Couldn't have been the quiet-pond type, could it?

"You sure have a knack for choosing strange destinations, don't you?" Bob notes, putting his soft arm around my shoulder and squeezing me in, but, I suspect, also using me to stabilize his balance.

"Well, I want our reunions to be memorable." I shiver out a smile, watching the white water plunge into the sound. The endless cascading quickens my pulse like the steady flow of adrenaline during a battle.

"No worries of that." Steve laughs, drawing his long frame up straighter and looking around cautiously.

"Don't worry," I say, patting his arm. "I don't sense Chase is here right now."

"You sense him when he's around?" He raises a concerned eyebrow.

"The modifier he's using is more powerful when he's present, drawing me to him," I say, my mind suddenly boggled by the strangeness of the words coming out of my mouth.

"Well, if you get any urges, let us know and we're going to retreat from our dream travels," Steve says, sounding almost as harsh as Trey.

"Yes sir," I say, giving Bob a sneaky smile. He returns it with a wink.

"How is it when you're at the Institute? Does whatever Chase is trying to do to you work there?" Steve asks.

It sounds as though when Trey informed Bob and Steve of the Chase situation he didn't include that he was trying to make me fall in love with him. For that I'm grateful, but not surprised. Most everyone is used to getting only relevant details when being briefed by Trey. "Chase's programming isn't as strong there, and some of the time I can resist it," I say, holding my hands out to greet the mist. It falls like dew on my fingertips.

"Then why do you dream travel?" Steve scratches his head, confused. "Why not just dream freely until this whole thing is fixed?"

I give a defeated shrug. "Wouldn't matter. There are other horrors waiting for me when I dream," I say, trying not to sound pitiful. "Everything with Chase has lent to rather awful dreams. I get that my subconscious is trying to work through it all, but it can be exhausting. And now with the newest threat…"

"We know Zhuang has returned," Bob says, consoling me.

"And that he will enter the Institute," Steve adds.

Right. The information would have been published on the Lucidites' newsfeed after the Institute was informed. "Without sounding melodramatic, it feels like everything is crashing down right now."

"Hence the reason you've brought us here," Steve says after a long minute.

"Probably."

"I'm sorry, Roya," Bob says, the corners of his mouth pinching together. "If we thought you'd be safe from Chase you could live with us and avoid the threat of Zhuang."

A strange silence fills my head, drowning out the waterfall as I realize there's no safe place for me in the world. Except here and now. Right now I'm safe, but that won't last long.

"Did you know Joseph was the one responsible for bringing Zhuang back?" I ask, toeing the moist dirt and moss under my feet.

"What!?" Bob grips my arm in unexpected astonishment. "No, we were told that Zhuang was restored by the collection of hallucinators he had control over."

That settles it. Trey's covered this up for Joseph. That's at least a sliver of sunshine in this dark day.

I nod. "I'm afraid so. He was tricked by Zhuang to think that he was reviving our estranged father. Sadly Joseph transferred a whole host of powers and information to Zhuang when he regenerated him. I suspect this is how Zhuang is now able to enter the Institute. He knows how it's protected. Unfortunately, he probably knows everything that Joseph has ever known, which is too much for me to think about right now."

"That's really heartbreaking. How's Joseph doing now?" Bob asks.

"About like you'd expect: a lot of self-loathing, a fair bit of depression, and bouts of anxiety since he can't disclose any of it."

"At least he has you," Bob says.

"Yes, I'm grateful we have each other."

"When Zhuang shows up," Steve begins, looking earnest, "then the both of you need to dream travel to the GAD-C in Oklahoma. We will pick you up there. Once we're all together we can decide on the next step given the immediate situation."

I nod, without saying a word. No one knows, not even Joseph yet, that I have no intention of leaving the Institute. It isn't pride that's urging me to stick around when that dismal day comes. Maybe a part of it's revenge, to kill Zhuang for what he did to Joseph and also Whitney, but there's also a deeper reason. When I was elected as his challenger I didn't want to believe our fates were somehow tied together, but now I know it without a doubt. Even if I escaped the Institute he'd still find me, or me him. We are as certain to meet as this waterfall is to crash into the sound below it. There's just no way the two won't find each other. I'm the one who gave the news report about Zhuang's return. It was my brother he used to revive himself. It's my father he's coming to steal power from. When the

98

sirens alert me that Zhuang has entered the Institute I'm going to finish the fight we started.

♦

"Hit me again," I say.

George's deep brown eyes, which right now remind me of fertile spring soil, stare intently. He nods and instantaneously I sense him press against my emotional shield, attempting to break through it and into my heart. The stress causes his jugular vein to rise to the surface of his skin and pulse with an incessant force as he concentrates. My eyes follow the vein down his neck and drift along his broad shoulders, taking in the contours of his chest. The momentary distraction is all it takes, and George surges through my shield and straight into my emotional center.

"Why thank you, Roya," George says, voice low and husky, obviously sensing my attraction.

I flush, cracking the tiniest of smiles. "All right, that was a lousy attempt." I rake my eyes over the blue carpet, trying to regain my composure. "I can do this. Just give me a minute to concentrate."

"Take your time," he says.

Backing up a few paces I shake my head, hoping my distractions will fall out of my ears, making this whole process easier. I spent the entire morning meditating upon my heart—something Shuman suggested. Although it does make me feel lighter, I'm unnerved by what I learned. The fears regarding intimacy and abandonment were of no surprise. Once those known emotions had been unearthed, however, I peeled back the layers until I was face-to-face with a blunt message.

Like warm sunshine, I feel George's eyes on me. And know he feels this confusing emotion I'm allowing myself to review. In my meditation, I learned my heart felt secured by the fact that no matter what, George is always trying to fulfill my needs and desires. That wasn't the startling part of the meditation though. The astounding message was almost like a direct order from my heart: *Let go and love him.*

I awoke from the meditation like it had been a nightmare where I'd been running from a three-armed monster. For half an hour I tried to rationalize to myself that the message was false and just some stupid rambling from my subconscious. However, my subconscious doesn't ramble quite like that and the word "love" is hardly ever used, especially in that context. There are times I know deep down when a message is authentic, and begrudgingly I have to admit this is one of those. But it's weird to consider striking up a relationship under my current situation. I'm more afraid of the steps it will take to follow this direction. Also I'm worried of what everyone will think. I'm worried about how final this decision feels, like cement around my knees.

"May I offer some advice?" George slides his hands into his pockets, chin down.

"Go for it."

"Motivation is key. You want to keep Chase out, right?"

"Of course," I say.

"Well, I don't get the impression you're motivated to keep me out." George angles his eyes up a bit and catches mine.

He bites his lip and I'm instantly enamored by this moment. I like the look in his eyes, the draw I feel to him, the way his teeth look as they bite into the soft, pink flesh of his lips. His hands push into his jean pockets, like he's restraining himself. I even like the emotions deep inside me that are afraid to fully embrace the moment.

Pulling his hands out of his pockets and straightening, George says, "Why don't you pretend I'm Chase. Maybe you'll be motivated to keep me out."

His advice does make sense. I'd been playing with this new attraction to him since we started practicing today and haven't really committed to the idea of keeping him out of my heart. Actually a part of me believed that if he felt what I felt the next steps would be easier because he'd initiate something. That's what I like most about George anyway; he reads me and gives me what I want when I want it.

"All right," I nod. "You're the despicable Chase."

In my head I picture Chase: his captivating blue eyes, slick black hair, features so perfectly balanced I want to lose myself in them—but I don't. I make myself remember who he is. I separate the facts in my mind from the deceptions Chase has done to my heart. The meditation this morning makes this easier.

With a steadying breath I beckon George with my hand to commence. Although I'm looking in his direction, this time I make sure not to make eye contact. Instead I stare just over his shoulder, my thoughts consumed with all the awful things Chase has done. In many ways, he's worse than Zhuang. Although his abilities are comparable, his motives are unknown. At least with Zhuang we know he wants power. Chase's mystery makes him scarier.

Knowing my thoughts are firmly centered on Chase, I scan my shield to ensure it's reinforced in all areas. Not only do I feel zero attraction to Chase right now, but I want him destroyed. I'm empowered by this hate. Enlivened with a determination. The anger and heat from my thoughts tear through my body like a torrent, carrying momentum. The self-righteous urge to take the power back from this deceitful man churns in me as my shield pulses with intensity.

"I can't get through." George breaks into my focus and for a second I'm surprised that he's standing in front of me. Forgot he was here.

In a wave, my present reality surfs over me. Like a beam dispersing, I let my shield release and with it the space between George and me grows softer. A smile yanks at the corners of my lips as I let the thoughts of Chase retreat.

"I did it!" I say, feeling triumphant.

"You did. Nice improvement," George says.

"Thanks."

"So that advice helped?"

"For sure." I finger a lock of hair, twirling it with sudden nervousness.

"I was right, wasn't I? You didn't want to keep me out?" George takes a step toward me.

I glide the hair over my fingers repeatedly, enjoying the softness. "Well, I don't want to be an open book for you to leaf through, if that's what you're thinking. What did you get earlier?" I ask, knowing what I'd given him access to.

"Enough." Satisfaction mingled with heedless desire surfaces on his face.

I'm enjoying tiptoeing around the obvious truth. "Enough? What does that mean?"

I'm not sure where the space has gone but now George is right up against me. He leans down, brushing my hair away from my face, off my neck. "Enough to bargain with you."

"Bargain?"

He nods, the smile on his face not faltering. "I know what you want, and I'm more than willing to give it to you. I will commit my whole heart to you. God knows it already belongs to you anyway. I will give you all of me. Do anything you ask. Protect you how I can. And doing all that for you will provide me with more satisfaction than anything in this world. In that way I'm greedy to give you my heart."

My fingers, which always long for the softness of hair, thread into his. "That sounds like a bargain for me actually."

"Here's where the negotiations come in," he says, looking suddenly serious. "I also selfishly ask that you commit to us one hundred percent. Because if there's an obstacle blocking your heart, we're doomed to even try to be together."

"But Chase? I can't help what he's doing to me."

"I don't mean Chase. You know who I'm referring to."

Mirroring him, I bite my lip, a desired pain erupting from the action. *Kisses seal deals, right?* Isn't that what I told Aiden? The guy I can never have. The coward? The obstacle George is alluding to now.

Pressing my hands only slightly against his neck, I urge George down, a smile upon my lips. "How can I not want this?" It sounds like a statement out loud and like a question in my head.

"How can you not," he agrees.

"You are the sweetest, George. My sweet George," I say and can't believe the words have come from my mouth.

Drawing in a soft breath, I kiss him. In between each time our lips meet I feel his satisfaction. It's as if I'm the one who has the power to read emotions as I sense the currents of gratification ripple through him. I'm swept away as his emotions and lips and breath and my own fulfillment fuse into elegant perfection.

The smile on his face presses against my mouth before he eases back so that I can see it. His fingers lace into mine and twirl my hand up until it rests against his chest—the exact same one he caught me admiring earlier. It's solid, begging for me to lean on it.

George scans my eyes and kisses me tenderly again.

102

Chapter Nineteen

Joseph waits for me by our now-permanent news reporting stations. He takes one look at me and rolls his eyes. "Oh man, Stark! Y'all made it official?" He sighs with frustrated disapproval.

I scowl at him, pinning my hands to my hips. "How do I keep you out of my head?"

"Only thing that worked for me was being under Zhuang's influence but I wouldn't suggest that technique," he says, scrunching up his nose.

"Well, why is it that we're so connected now? More than in the beginning?"

"I think it's because we want to be."

"I would also like some privacy," I say.

"More than you want the connection between us?" Persuasion in his voice.

Actually no. This link between us nourishes me. Provides me with a unique strength. The more it builds, the more powerful I feel. My news reports are of greater significance and delivered a dozen at a time. The reflexes that were spiked since the moment we met are even faster now. And every other skill of mine has been honed.

"No, the connection is more important than privacy," I finally say. "You're the only person I don't need secrecy from anyway. I trust you implicitly."

"I agree. You're more than my sister," he says, and his words carry weight and meaning and also a great deal of power. We're a source to each other.

I return his words with a smile, one he mirrors before his face lines with disappointment.

"All right now. So back to the first topic. George? Really?"

"What's the deal? Why don't you like him?"

"Psssh," he scoffs. "Him. Livingston. Chase. I despise them all 'cause I fear they'll break your heart and then I'm gonna rip theirs out through their throats."

"Damn, you're twisted," I say, but smile still.

"Yeah, but in good ways." Joseph takes a seat in his recliner, still facing me. "Truth is, I know I can't protect you forever," he

103

says with defeat. "I've been tryin' to be more accepting of the idea of you with someone, but it's tough. I keep tellin' myself that I should be happy if you find love. I mean, I see the way Anders looks at you. And you truly do deserve to be with someone who lights up when you come around."

"He lights up?"

"Like a freakin' lightning bug. Actually, most of the time, the guy has the personality of a cardboard box. But when you're around, he opens up and becomes almost tolerable. You're definitely good for him, but I'm not sure I agree with the reverse. That's probably the thing; I don't foresee a person in the world good enough for you. As T said before, 'you're freakin' Roya Stark.'"

"That's not fair."

"No it's not, and who wants to live on a pedestal all alone. I sure as hell don't want that for you. But you did climb up there on your own," he says, giving me a clever grin.

"I did no such thing." I hop up onto my own chair, swinging my legs back and forth. "Speaking of Trent…"

Joseph raises an eyebrow at me, giving me a cautious glare. "How long have you known?"

"Since Iceland."

"Right…Well…"

"How long have *you* known?" I ask.

"All my life. Or as long as I can remember anyway. There wasn't another option for me."

"And Samara and all the other girls?"

"Just an attempt to pretend. To fake it, hoping maybe I'd change."

"Because?"

He pushes out a breath. "Because I was raised in a place that didn't tolerate such things and even if that's not where I am now, it's still engrained in me. And now there's Trey and his reputation and all those surroundin' implications."

"Do you really think he'd care? And who gives a damn if he does? For the life of me I can't figure out why most of the people in this place are afraid to live their life the way they want because of the opinion of some silver-haired hippie."

"He's more than that. You may not want to admit it but our father influences the lives of thousands of Dream Travelers and millions of Middlings. His power is far reaching. He isn't just our father and he isn't just the leader of the Lucidites. He's one of the most powerful Dream Travelers on Earth." Joseph pauses, suddenly exasperated. "What if it *does* disappoint him?" he hisses, tossing himself back slightly. "I've already revived our greatest nemesis. I just don't need anythin' else to color me in his eyes right now."

"But Joseph, this isn't something you've done. This is about who you are." I move to sit beside him. Grab his hand and squeeze. "No matter how powerful a person is, if they don't love you for who you are, it makes them the stupidest person on Earth."

His mossy green eyes quiet a bit. "Although you're right, this just isn't somethin' I want to deal with right now. I've got enough to worry about."

"And Trent? How does he feel about it?"

"Similar to how you feel about Aiden's cowardly behavior."

"But he still loves you, doesn't he?"

"You know better than anyone that even if someone disappoints you it doesn't diminish the way you feel about them."

"And how about how you feel?"

"I feel like an unlovable wreck."

"You are neither of those things."

He leans his head on my shoulder, an endearing gesture he been doing more and more lately. "And you deserve to be happy. I'm going to try and be that for you."

"Thanks," I say, pressing my head into his. "You deserve to be happy too."

"Well, hopefully there's time for that later."

"Oh, Joseph…" I say with a sigh.

He picks up his head and waves me off. "Why don't we table this discussion for another time? I'm sure there are a few hundred people who need to be saved, but that will only happen if we settle our happy asses down and news report."

"Well, when you put it that way…" I say, stretching to a standing position and crawling into my own chair.

"See you in a few," he says with a wink.

♦

"You paged us," I say to Trey when he answers the door to room 402—his new makeshift office.

"I did," he says, welcoming Joseph and me into the small room.

I slide the note he sent to the Panther room into my back pocket.

"Thank you for coming so promptly," Trey says, taking a seat behind a metal desk.

The plain white walls and empty bookcases are the wrong backdrop. I'm accustomed to seeing him in his rich and intriguing office with the oversized furniture and random artifacts. "Please take a seat," he says, gesturing to two dark leather armchairs. In the bare-bones office they stick out like china on a picnic table. "How are you both doing?" Trey looks at me, then Joseph.

Is he kidding me? Is this social hour?

I stare at him blankly. I'm entirely willing to continue this action until he becomes too uncomfortable to sit here any longer.

"Pretty good," Joseph finally chimes. "I like news reporting. Think I've got a long-term future with it."

Reflexively I roll my eyes. *What the hell is Joseph doing?*

"That's good news," Trey says, encouraging. "I'm not surprised though. Shuman is especially happy that you two have agreed to report together. The information you're reporting is a huge benefit to the Institute as well as the world at large."

He crosses his hands on the sleek metal surface of the desk and looks at me. "How about you, Roya?"

I realize my shoulders are pinned by my ears. Taking a slight breath I release them. "Yeah, I'm fine."

Disappointment edges Trey's eyes. He regards me for a few seconds. Lines form around his mouth as he presses his lips together, assessing me. "Your news reports have drastically improved since you began. And, of course, the report regarding Zhuang is probably the most important one ever forecast." His eyes remain on me as a long second passes.

Of course. This isn't a personal meeting. This is Trey. This is business. "Thank you," I say in a dull monotone voice.

"That's actually why I've asked you both here," Trey says, worrying down the fabric on the sleeve of his shirt. "When Zhuang descends into the Institute, you must flee right away. If my inclination is correct you two will be second and third on his list.

106

Roya, you'll remember from your report who Zhuang comes after first."

I remain still, providing no response.

"You two will be the next on Zhuang's list because you're a threat," Trey says, like he's advising employees rather than his offspring. "Zhuang is seeking power, and both of you are rich sources of that. He's already communicated his interests in consuming your consciousness, Roya. And Joseph, I'm sure he holds similar ill will toward you. One of you almost killed him and the other restored him. You're both a valuable asset and a threat to him in different ways, and that's all he needs to target you."

It's weird to hear things boiled down in this way. It's even weirder to be in this office, staring at this man who's supposedly our father. None of it feels real, but when I push myself back to the days of toiling around the woods with my cats that time doesn't completely feel real either. Is none of my life real? Are all my perceptions skewed and never to be made clear?

"When Zhuang enters the Institute," Trey says, beckoning me away from my thoughts, "you both have to dream travel to a GAD-C. You can't hesitate or try and stop what's coming."

"Yeah, of course," Joseph says, like this is a no-brainer.

Trey nods his approval at Joseph and turns to evaluate me. Again I remain silent.

"Roya, I suspect you're going to try to stop Zhuang," Trey says, sweeping his hands though his silver hair. "It isn't your job this time to fight."

"Why would you suspect that?" I say, narrowing my eyes at him.

Trey shakes his head with obvious frustration. He desires compliance and instead I'm asking questions. "Because I can sense things and they're always correct."

"Hmmm…" I say, spiking my tone with skepticism.

"One of my gifts is knowingness," Trey says. "Your gift is ruled by Anahata. Mine is governed by the sixth chakra, Ajna. Informally you know this as intuition."

"Everyone has intuition, how can that be a gift?"

"The reliability and frequency of my intuitive notions is what makes it a gift, much the same way as your clairvoyance."

"So yours is never wrong?" I say, doubt oozing in my tone.

107

"Exactly."

"How do you know what's intuition and what's just some hunch or idea or worry?" I ask, not understanding how something so flimsy as intuition can be classified as a gift.

"How do you know the visions you see are of the future?" he counters.

"Because it comes through me, instead of from me," I say automatically.

He nods, a knowing in his eyes.

"What are your other gifts?"

"I control water. Produce it in a dreamscape and govern bodies of water in the physical realm."

"What?" I say, disbelief streaking the word.

Trey holds up his hand. "Currently I can't grace this conversation with the time and attention it deserves. I will, though, in the future."

Why does he always have to do that? Dangle something of great importance and relevance in front of me and then postpone the conversation. How many times has he promised we'll discuss something more in depth later and that moment never comes?

"My main concern is your safety when Zhuang enters the Institute," Trey says, looking at me, then Joseph. "You both must leave the Institute as soon as you hear the sirens. Is that clear?"

Joseph nods.

I have zero intention of leaving as Trey is dictating. But arguing with him will get me nowhere. Really his determination to control every aspect of my life just incites my bitterness. And more than anything I want Trey to feel the undeniable heartbreak he's done to us.

"So you're sending us away again?" I say, threading my arms together and leaning back in the chair. "It's like a game, isn't it?"

"Do you honestly believe I wanted to send you away? Separate you?" Trey says, a tiredness in his words.

"You've offered us no other explanation. I get separating us in the Middling world, but we would have been safe here from Zhuang. So, if you sent us away, I have to assume the reason is—"

"It isn't because I didn't want you," he cuts me off, jaw tensed. "That's the furthest thing from the truth."

"Well, you're the only one who knows the truth, as usual," I say, careful to keep a tone of indifference.

"The truth is when your mother died, any hope of you both living a normal life died too."

The mention of our mother assaults me, briefly knocking the mask off my face.

"She planned to raise you two together in the Middling world," Trey says, taking in the surface of the desk under his hands, like that's where his crafted speech resides. "What she didn't know then, and I didn't learn until after you were born, was that you couldn't be together in an unprotected environment. Your energy fields are too strong when together. I wanted to raise you here, but the technology that protects us in the Institute was unreliable then. We didn't have the VDR shield, or energy buffers, or protective charms. We were constantly a target for Zhuang and other enemies. I couldn't ensure you'd be safe here. Sadly, even if your mother had survived we would have had to make tough choices regarding your upbringing. But we would have shared that burden. In the end, *I* alone made the only choice that I knew would keep you safe and also be in line with your mother's wishes. She wanted you to know grass and sunsets and wind. The only way that was going to happen was if I split you up." Trey flashes his eyes on me and only me. "It's simply false to think I sent you away because I didn't want you."

I refuse to break under the pressure of Trey's eyes focused on mine. How dare he speak of our mother so casually? Act as if the idea of her and the choices that shaped our lives should easily be digestible. If he thinks his little speech is going to soften me, then he underestimates my resilience.

"In the time that's allowed to us," he continues slowly, "I hope I'm able to prove how much I really do love the two of you."

"Don't you dare use that word!" I jerk upright, all pretenses of apathy abandoned. "Things are complicated enough without you defaulting to manipulation."

Trey turns his head suddenly, as if I just slapped him. He stares at the wall. Swallows. Mouth twitches. Nostrils flare. From his profile I spy a restraint in him I've never seen before.

Slowly he fixes his eyes on me, a sunken grief floating to the surface. "Saying words I've never had the privilege to express freely to my children isn't manipulation. It's a right I was stripped of when

I made the choice to protect you. Hate me for all the reasons you have, but don't for one second think I'm a monster who doesn't love you."

Chapter Twenty

I believe when a heart breaks a substance spills out like cement and pours through the bloodstream, hardening everything. In time, I know my heart will mend and the rock inside will crack and crumble away. But for now I'm as solid as a column. And alone I stand.

Unconcerned for Trey's forbiddance, I dream travel alone to the forest outside the house where I grew up. The path through the trees overgrew a few years ago, but still I can make my way through this place blindfolded. The ground cover and thick vines don't deter me from stalking deeper into the woods until I come to the small clearing. I could have dream traveled to this spot, but I wanted to take the trek. Wanted it to remind me of who I used to be. To relish the memory of living a simple life, uncomplicated by conspiracies and danger. I'd hoped that along the journey I would wake in my old bed and find that although my parents still despised my existence, they were in fact my true blood. That my life wasn't a lie and my fate wasn't haunted by death.

The old log is exactly where I remember it—nestled in a patch of sand and dirt, encircled by a column of trees. It's a relief to find the refuge I spent so many hours in as a child untouched by the last few months. I wish I could say the same about me, but my short time at the Institute has left branding marks on my insides. I sink down onto the fallen oak tree and feel the weight of my confusing emotions settle on the log along with me. The last time I was in this clearing I'd been such a different person. None of this dream travel or Lucidite business was even a blip on my radar. Now, I'm fully engulfed in this life and it's drowning me. The Roya from a few months ago would never have believed all this.

The stagnant air swishes gently. I should have known better than to think I'd get a moment to myself. I don't escape by dream traveling because my forlorn heart wants to play with fire and prove it's strong enough to stomp it out. I stay unmoving, waiting for him to approach. First I take stock of my heart's messages. Then I lock it under the logic of my mind, which knows not to trust any emotions. With a practiced effort, I push my emotional shield out, ensuring whatever fleeting wrong or right feelings I have remain private. I chant in my head the words which have become my mantra: *I don't love Chase.*

The twigs don't even crunch under Chase's feet as he advances. I look up and see him for exactly who he is: A ridiculously gorgeous murderer.

I don't need a patch for my charm. I don't need anything from the Institute. I can do this alone.

A chain drapes off the middle button of Chase's vest and disappears behind his open suit jacket, probably into a side pocket and connected to an elegant watch. He's even more impeccably dressed than usual. As casually as a man waiting for a train, he kickstands himself up against the tree closest to me. Unafraid, I meet his enchanting eyes, holding his all-pervading gaze which threatens to swallow me whole. Dancing with the devil tonight actually sounds like a good idea.

"What a gift," he says, his voice like warm silk to my arctic-scorched soul. "I've got you all to myself."

A reply stays locked in my mouth. Instead I indulge myself by taking in every exquisite detail about him. Murderer or not, he's still the most striking specimen to ever live. He shouldn't be here. He should be in a museum so all the world can relish his beauty and experience the raw intensity that radiates from him. Suddenly I wish I was up against him, because at least from that vantage point I couldn't see just how flawless he is.

"What are you doing here?" The offense I was trying to inject in my tone comes out sounding more like curiosity.

A ghost of a smile flicks across his face. Motionless eyes watch me for a few seconds. "The reasons I'm here are many. And the result of our visit shall hopefully be successful."

Unwrapping my arms from around my legs I stand up. To know I can move is encouraging. I'm not frozen by his allure like usual. Deliberately I take steps until only a couple of feet separate us. "Why do you stalk me?"

Pushing off the tree, Chase stands upright, face amused. "They have not told you?" He clicks his tongue three times. "How come you trust people who are unwilling to be honest with you?"

"Told me what?" I say, again the words mine, the ability to move and think still within my control. But my heart is manic with a flurry of competing emotions.

"I need you to know who I am before I tell you why I'm here."

"I know who you are," I say. "You're a deranged murderer." Instantly my heart races, frantic that I've offended him. I clap a hand down on it. Steady my thoughts.

Chase, unflustered by my name calling, slides his palms back and forth across each other. "And you know this because the Lucidites have deemed it so, is that right? The same people who hide important information from you?" He pouts his lips, shakes his head. "Roya, you're so much smarter than that. Don't let your judgment be clouded."

"I don't trust anyone. How's that for judgment?"

"That's a good place to start," Chase says, his long black eyelashes falling down slowly as a pleased smile forms on his face. "Now, the Lucidites have told you who I am, but I'm willing to show you."

"What does that mean?"

"You're intrigued, are you not?"

I draw in a long breath, my heart racing, beating itself against the bars of its cage.

"Close your eyes," Chase demands, a lovely harshness in his voice.

"Absolutely not."

Chase huffs, looking aggravated for the first time. "Have I ever hurt you? No, I haven't. And I don't intend to. I haven't even touched you since we met tonight, have I? I simply want to show you some things."

My mind, which is completely lucid, considers the idea. If Trey knew I was here right now, he'd be livid. My heart flushes with rebellion and it's the first time since Chase arrived that I think I've experienced an authentic emotion. I unlock the cage and let my heart free as I close my eyes.

"Good girl," Chase purrs. "Now watch."

Light explodes across my vision, not blinding me, but warming my mind. I see no images, but instead feel a host of memories pour into me. Instantly I'm aware of Chase's thoughts and emotions, as if they're my own. Then I receive a volume of information about him, detailing past hurts and successes, dozens of his likes and dislikes, and intimately acquainting me with the image he holds of himself. Gasping from the sudden rush of experiences I snap my

113

eyes open. In less than a minute I learned more about Chase than I would after a dozen dates. And what I know is startling. He doesn't see any of his acts of violence as senseless, but rather retribution for crimes committed against him…by Trey.

"You see, *mon amour*, I'm willing to give you all of me," Chase says, taking a step closer. "This is not a game. I show you who I am. The Lucidites tell you who they are. Who do you really believe?"

"I don't… I don't… know," I stutter, my mind a mess of images and unfathomable thoughts.

"What do you feel?"

"I feel confused," I say.

"Take my hand and we will figure it out together." His long-fingered hand extends, palm open.

It's both a rod pulled from hot coals and a rope thrown over the cliff I hang from. I shake my head roughly.

He tightens his eyes, furious disappointment in them. "The *reason* we keep meeting," he says, biting on each of the words, "is because you belong to me."

Maybe it's being capsized by so much of him, but I suddenly don't have such a tight grip on my heart's urges. Can feel my attraction to him. Pulsing. Racing. My heart begs to embrace the undying love we share and still I feel half in control. It's a joy ride where each curve threatens with near-death and each straightaway soothes the adrenaline rush. "I belong to you…" I say, like I'm testing out words, learning a new language.

"Yes, that's right," Chases coerces gently. "Are you still confused?"

I nod, because I am. I'm split in two, half wanting to run into his arms and also away.

"Take my hand," he commands, all softness gone.

I remain frozen. Not running. Not accepting the outstretched hand.

"Don't you want me?"

"Yes," I say, without meaning to. Believe it with half my being.

A sliver of a smile carves his lips. I convulse softly under the weight of his brilliant gaze.

"Do you want to spend an eternity with me?"

"Yes," someone says and the voice sounds uncannily like mine.

"Good, touch me."

I want to. More than anything I want to. But clamped down firmly upon my being are chains from my mind, controlling my body even though they fail to control my words.

"This time I won't tempt you, although I know that will work. This time I want you to make the first move. Do it. Touch me."

The word "no" is trapped inside me. And the need to flee is as well. The temptation to press my mouth against his increases rapidly and the longer I hold out the more my blood boils. I reach my hand up to his face but pause when it's almost there, yanking it away. Chase doesn't look deterred, but rather entertained.

"I see we still have a disconnect here," he says. "My guess is that your own conservative nature is blocking you from what you really want. This might be fortunate for the Roya who operates you right now, but soon you will evolve and be the person *I* control. Isn't that what you really want anyway? To do what pleases me?"

Again words fall out of my mouth unsanctioned from my brain. "Yes, Chase."

Beside us something flickers but I don't turn to look at it, afraid to take my eyes off Chase. Afraid he'll disappear.

"Roya," Shuman's deep voice calls at my back. "It is time to go." There's a vicious caution in her words.

Chase makes a half turn. Still slightly tethered to his thoughts, I know he plans to hurt her. Can kill her all too easily right now if he chooses. Is more powerful than she and I and all the energy that created the forest around us. Disconnecting from the shadows of his thoughts I turn to find a standoff. Shuman has risked everything by showing up here.

Risked. Risked. Risked.

Why would there be a risk where Chase is concerned? One that would bring Shuman here? To bring me back to the Institute? I know the answer and I don't. Can't quite locate it inside my mushy brain.

"You really shouldn't have interrupted, rattlesnake handler," Chase says in a voice he's never used when speaking to me. Threats coat each word, like a curse to the recipient. His fingers flex. I know enough from witnessing his memories to recognize he's building the minuscule energy it will take to send Shuman into a deadly hypnotic state. One she won't be able to resist. One that will end her.

Dashing forward I cut Chase off. Spin around until I'm facing him. His eyes stay focused on Shuman. My hand sprays out against

115

Chase's chest, pressing into it gently, encouraging him to retreat. The feel of his body under my fingertips rips through me with unbridled desire. Chase's gaze lowers until he's focused upon my hand, on him. A victorious smile laces his lips. Now that we're connected through touch rationality is slipping out of me. It's like a hurricane, sending debris in all directions, shattering every window inside me. With the last bit of logic I have left I say, "Please don't hurt her."

In a blur, Chase pins my wrist in his hand and yanks, whirling me around until my back is flush up against his chest. He secures my head in place by pinning his face up against mine. Pinching my wrist he imprisons the hand I used to touch him, pushing me so firmly into him that my chest hardly has a space to breathe. By my side he restrains my other hand, jerking it back, fastening it to his leg. I stare out at Shuman, without seeing her.

Cool breath dances across my cheek. "I see now you only need to be properly motivated. I'll keep that in mind," Chase says, his jaw moving in firm movements against mine as he speaks. "Next time there will be no resisting me. I can promise you that. Because *vous êtes né à m'aim-er*. You were born to love me." Like a flame being snuffed out, he disappears, leaving only hungry emotions behind. I clutch the night air that used to be him and stare into Shuman's impassive eyes.

Chapter Twenty-One

"How did you know I was here?" I say, straightening up, brushing the cold off me.

"I am clairvoyant," Shuman says, searching the forest around us, although I can guarantee her that Chase isn't anywhere around. I'd feel him if he was.

"Right. So you knew I was with Chase?" I ask, embarrassment spreading up my neck

"I knew you were soon going to be in trouble," she says, settling her eyes on me. "I realize you thought you were strong enough to resist him." Her tone is soft as she speaks, but not quite sensitive. "And you are, but you need to recognize that he is stronger."

"I was able to resist him, though," I defend, watching branches sway behind her in the wind.

"Yes?"

"Yes, I had the emotions from my heart locked down and was solely operating based on my thoughts."

"Then what happened?"

"Somehow he was able to connect to me. Show me things about him. It wasn't like he was in my thoughts, but rather sharing his with me," I say.

"One-way thought transference," Shuman states.

"Oh, well, it's totally creepy," I say. A shiver runs down my spine as his memories rush back to me.

"And this information you learned confused you, is that right?"

"He said that what I knew about him was wrong. That what I know about the Institute is false. And he showed me details that made me…"

"Sympathetic to him?"

"Yes…I mean no…." I sigh with defeat. "It made everything confusing and the moment my thoughts were jumbled I didn't have a way to stay grounded."

"Do you think that he censored what he shared with you?"

"Of course he did," I say, the idea suddenly dawning on me. I want to slap myself in the face. *How stupid am I?* His memories had instantly endeared me to him, created a foundation that otherwise would have taken months, if not years, to create. And I fell for it, slowly slid into a pit where I identified with him until I was unable to fully control myself. "But he did share dark things with me too," I say, trying to rationalize my faulty judgment. "For instance, I was still connected to some of his thoughts when you arrived. I knew he planned to..."

"Kill me," Shuman states, a little too calmly.

"Yes," I breathe. "Why did you show up knowing that was a possibility? Chase is dangerous, and as his grip on me tightens he's more likely to kill anyone who comes between us." Those words are true and yet I can't believe they're my observation. Half the time I don't know where the information inside me comes from anymore.

"I did take a risk showing up here in the forest. But it was one I knew was necessary," Shuman says, her words all tidy and matter-of-fact. "You have heard me speak of the fabric of our reality before. Well, my gift, along with reason sometimes informs me that intervention either in the past or the present will bring about certain events. I interfered because it secured a more peaceful future for all."

As usual, Shuman's statement is bold and makes zero sense. The thing is, as long as she keeps intervening in my life, I can't prove that she's in fact wrong. She's like the fairy godmother I never wanted. And with her there's no gown and fancy shoes, but she'll surely send me to a ball in something that'll explode into a vegetable if I don't mind the time. I swallow down the untimely laugh. "Do you know why Chase thinks I belong to him?"

"I do not," she says in an airy whisper, still searching the shadows for predators.

"I need answers though."

"I cannot offer those. All I can tell you is that if Chase succeeds in recruiting you then a delicate balance will be lost."

"And what will that cause?"

"It will destroy the Institute."

No pressure then, right. I've never asked for any of this and still it feels like so much relies on me and what I do. How can that be? How can I be so pivotal when it's not something I desire?

"Are you going to tell Trey about this?" I ask, again taking a seat on the old log.

"Are you going to attempt to dream travel before your protective charm has a patch?"

"No," I say.

"Well, then I see no reason to concern him with this. He has enough troubles."

"Yeah, I'm sure it's a bit consuming for him to know he'll be hunted down by the Lord of Nightmares soon."

Shuman never likes my jokes. Now is no exception. "I believe the future concerns Trey, but not his own. I believe he's mostly concerned with yours and Joseph's."

"Why is it that since everyone's found out I'm Trey's offspring all conversations are different? Why can't I just be the girl who almost drowned coming to the Institute? Why does everything have to now be about my relation to that man?"

"If you renounced your life here as a Lucidite, would it mean you were never one of us? Would it erase your time at the Institute?"

"Of course not," I say, picking at the bark on the tree, upsetting a dozen ants.

"The same is true for your blood. If you disown your father, it does not change the fact that he made choices on your behalf. You are forever tied to those decisions because they molded you. It would be a great benefit to accept the choices as well as the blood that runs through you. Right now you are divided by pain. But your father is not your enemy. He is the roots to our society, which is in more danger than ever before."

"Does that make me an acorn on this Lucidite tree?"

Shuman leans forward, narrows her almond-shaped eyes. "If you wish. But know this, 'no tree has branches so foolish as to fight amongst themselves.'"

"Thanks for the advice," I say dully. "I'm actually not real consumed with Trey and the Institute right now. I've got Chase to worry about. I don't know why he's after me. And it feels important. You more than anyone can appreciate that gut feeling."

"I do. And I think you should heed its warning."

"Well, what do I do about it?"

"Wait," Shuman says, crossing her arms tightly so they make a squeaking noise against her leather vest.

"What?"

119

"*Wait,* and an answer will be provided to you," she says with finality.

Chapter Twenty-Two

Wait? Waiting seemed like the last thing I should do with Zhuang's impending invasion, Chase lurking in the corner of all of my dream travels, and my long-lost father making ridiculous efforts to repair a defunct relationship. However, wait is exactly what I did. Slowly the hours dissolved into long days and then rather quickly they accumulated into a week. The threat of Zhuang was always in the air. It was the edge at the back of everyone's throat, the reason so many words came out terse. It was the tension that rippled through the main hall, causing cautionary glances over shoulders every time a resident who could be Zhuang entered for a meal. I was proud that no one had fled the Institute. They might have all been victims of fear, but they were willing ones.

Every day Zhuang didn't thunder through the hallways and blast us all to smithereens heightened the stress. One might think I'd be relieved that I was given another day to live, but as each one passed the doom mounted higher and higher. The fear of Day Z, as we were calling it, was three hundred times worse because it hung overhead with the ever-growing weight of my stress.

The enjoyable moments that I allowed myself to have, when I wasn't looking over my shoulder and listening for the sirens, were riddled with odd feelings. It sometimes felt strange to laugh, like that was the cue for Zhuang to end us all. Nothing at this point was pleasurable. Fruit tasted like mushy sweetness. Hot showers were just warm water splashing against the surface of my body. George's lips were just lips that I used to comfort me, but still too often left me feeling empty.

Things between George and me were easy and for that I was grateful. He was always there when I needed company and when I wanted to be left alone, he was absent. I never had to explain myself to him, and that was the best gift that he gave me. Most evenings we spent lying in my room or discussing literature or philosophy. The conversations were often deep, but rarely stimulating. I mostly had them because they passed the time and I liked the way he'd look at me when he didn't think I was paying attention.

Having George's affection felt good. I'd never been in a relationship, and for that matter I'd hardly had many friendships. The closer we became, the more I wanted what he gave me; however, there was a catch. This little catch made my heart ache every time George said something so ridiculously sweet and looked at me for reciprocation. What made all this worse is my heart told me to enter into this relationship and oddly my heart wasn't totally in it. I now could see how good it felt to be loved and adored by someone—committed to that love. It was a brand new satisfaction. One I couldn't believe I'd waited so long to experience. But the awful catch was that most of the time I didn't want it from George.

My whole being was poisoned by the emotional modifier. When I was with George I wished I felt the same draw I had to Chase. So badly did I want to be in love with George like that. The meditations and shielding helped, but still when everything was quiet and I wasn't concentrating I felt Chase penetrating into my heart and forcing me to love him. Half the time his efforts worked and I'd ache because I couldn't have him and also because I knew wanting him was wrong. I hadn't dream traveled since the last time I saw him. Patiently I waited, like Shuman had directed, hoping that soon a way would be provided that helped me combat Chase's powers. Each night I spent allowing confusing dreams of Chase to rip across my subconscious. Usually, I awoke multiple times throughout the night screaming with my bed covers twisted absurdly around my sweat-drenched body.

The days had actually become mundane. I'd eat, run, shower, eat, news report, eat, and hang out with George. My runs were still the highlight to every day, but without music they lost the same pleasure they had before. I'd put the iPod in a box, within a box, within a box in my closet and refused to listen to any music. Aiden, who had given me the iPod, was a part of a different life, one I was trying to forget I ever had. Music would certainly remind me of that old life and a whole host of emotions that I'd shoved down to the recesses of my soul.

Every time I ran, it burned my side where the gunshot wound was almost healed. Still, the clarity I received while running was worth it. I didn't get a runner's high from the experience as much as a runner's release. I was freed from worries and uncertainties and all the guilt I kept layering on my heart. When I ran, all my thoughts were sucked into a vacuum and for that one hour I was unrestricted by them. To meditate on nothingness was pure bliss.

The saddest moment of every day was when I rounded out the last mile. Mae had asked me to keep it to under five miles. As soon as my legs slowed, my thoughts filtered back in, until they swarmed inside my head like angry wasps. And what always followed my run was half the reason I needed the one hour of meditation.

For five days straight Trey had pretended to be crossing my path when I left the workout facility. I knew I could alter my routine and avoid him a time or two, until he figured out my new schedule, but I wasn't willing to do that. Maybe falsely, I equate my strength with my predictable routine. I'm not just a creature of habit. It's embedded in my DNA and changing it would be like forcing a lion to eat green beans for the rest of its life. It's just not going to happen.

"How was it?" Trey says as he approaches me after this morning's run.

I tug the towel with both hands on either side of my neck. "Not long enough."

"It surprised me that you take such a joy in running," he says as I try to pass him in the hallway.

I want to say "oh really," and stroll by nonchalantly. But my curiosity gets the better of me. "Why's that?"

"Because you disliked it so much as a child."

Rapid blinks seek to zip the surprise out of my eyes. "Is that something you 'know,'" I say, using air quotes over the word, "because of your gift?"

"I know it because I've watched you from the dreamscape." A fond smile angles his lips up slightly. "You went to some pretty impressive lengths to get out of track-and-field day."

Zhuang punched me in the gut during our battle. That feeling shoots through me and I reflexively want to double over but remain standing. To know Trey watched from the other realm fills me with a strange confusion, like I've been immersed in breathable liquid. "Did you visit when I had class trips too?" My voice is dripping with sarcasm.

"I watched you every single day. Didn't miss one."

My mouth puckers; my eyes follow suit. Fierce tears rake up my throat. "Stop," I say, my voice constricted.

"Roya." He says my name like it's a plea.

123

Stepping backward, I shake my head at him and I don't know why. It must be to stop what's about to burst out of me. "I have to go," I say and twist around almost tripping over my shoes. Quick steps take me halfway down the hallway. And then an image flashes in front me, flickering a few times before solidifying. I halt like I've been pressed between two walls. Standing in front of me is Trey. I flip around to the hallway where I left him. It's empty. Pulse racing, I swivel back around, mind boggling. "How did you do that?"

No pride marks his features, only fatigued determination. "I can teleport. Short distances," he says, breathless. Several wrinkles spray out around his eyes as he clenches them shut and steadies himself with one hand on the wall. "It's energy consuming though."

"What? That's a gift? How's that possible?"

After composing himself Trey looks up at me. "Most anything's possible. We're just energy and thought. Between the two we can manipulate any reality."

"Well, thanks for the performance," I say, looking past him at the path I want to take but can't will myself toward. Am I being unfairly cruel to him? I can't decide. And since I feel hollow it's hard for my conscience to accurately inform me.

"I'm not going to stop trying, Roya," he says, drawing in a long breath. "Like I said before, you were better off never knowing I was your father because it's too much to process in retrospect. But I think I never wanted to admit that I always knew you'd find out." A pained smile flashes on his face. A sound like a laugh falls out of his mouth. "Actually I believe you finding out strangely saves me in the future, but we're not there right now."

"Why are you speaking so cryptically?"

He presses his forehead into his hand. The buzzing of the lights overhead is excruciatingly loud, drowning out our silence. Looking up, he casts his eyes on mine. "It's going to take you time to process everything and I will offer you what I can. But it's clear to me now more than ever that even if it hurts, you need to know I care."

"I'm not sure what I need," I say, resentment welling up inside me.

Trey chews the inside of his bottom lip. A resignation forced into his intense eyes. He wants me to say more. I know that with as much certainty as I know the sneakers on my feet are mine. "Okay," he says, a strain in his voice. "I'll see you tomorrow." And there's a promise in his words.

"Okay," I agree and sidestep around him, moving not as quickly as before.

Chapter Twenty-Three

I sit in my room staring at the blank wall, waiting for the long hours to pass. I imagine that somewhere in the world it's raining and that's where I want to be right now. In a house. With windows. That look out on a yard. Rain spatters against the glass, forming designs that are quickly covered with new droplets, like a constantly evolving canvas.

There's a road outside the house and it takes me to a store, a museum, a park. It takes me away. Is it poetic that I can go anywhere in my dreams and still I feel trapped? Poetry is for the romantics. I'm the cursed.

A knock sounds at the door, awakening me from my modest fantasy. It's Patrick. I know his knock. One long one, followed by three quick. Aiden had used that knock once to trick me into answering my door. He won't be trying to trick me anymore. For all I know Aiden's forgotten I exist. I've hardly seen him since the meeting in the auditorium.

"Well, hey there, sassy," Patrick says when the door slides back.

"Hey to you," I say.

"You want me to carry this inside for you?" he says, gesturing to the large box he's balancing on one hitched knee.

"Sure." I move aside to allow Patrick into my room.

"I'll just leave it here on the bed for you, sweetheart," Patrick says, strain in his voice from carrying the heavy package.

"Thanks." Curiosity mounts inside me.

The box makes my bed springs squeal from its weight. "Tell whoever sent this to you that they're buying me a massage," Patrick says with a wink.

"I'll write them a letter straight away, but you have to deliver it."

"Clever girl. You're ensuring the Institute gets its money out of me, aren't you?" Patrick chuckles.

I flush red, wondering if that's a jab at me because of Trey being my father. I'm going to have to outgrow my paranoia at some point.

The clear packing tape comes off the top of the box in one long strand. As I suspected, there's a crisp white envelope lying on top of a piece of tissue paper. All Bob and Steve's packages are wrapped this way. I rip open the envelope to find a lacy white and blue card inside.

Dear Roya,

Bad dreams will deprive you of so much important energy. This should help you combat those nightmares. This Egyptian god has long been known for his power to protect dreamers from nightmares. Furthermore, Bes might be able to offer information and power to you while you sleep. Put him to the left of your bed for best results. Sweet dreams.

Love,
Bob & Steve

I fold the card and put it to the side. The tissue paper is crisp, brand new. Not something recycled from another event. Underneath I find an object that strikes me as familiar, but takes several seconds to locate in my memory. The last time I saw this it was behind a glass case in Bob and Steve's library. Now it sits in this box in my room staring back at me. I'm nervous to put my oil-ridden fingertips against the stone, afraid in time they will mark it. Damage it. Still I trace the carving. Too curious to know how it feels.

As I anticipated, the tablet of Bes is rough and hard, like how I'd expect it'd feel to swipe my hand against the Sphinx. The raised portions of Bes are mostly bulbous, protruding outward with great detail of his features. Most Egyptian gods are portrayed in profile, but not Bes. His Buddha belly, flat nose, and outstretched tongue are best captured from a frontal view. It's hard to believe that a barely dressed dwarflike man is known for warding off nightmares, but I'll try anything at this point.

♦

As I drift off to sleep that night I'm careful to remain lucid, creating a landscape that grounds me inside my dreams. After the first nightmare of Aiden being murdered I abandoned the location of the ocean and came up with this one. Thankfully none of the dreams have been quite that bad.

The location is always the same, night after night. A giant green hill, unmarked, save for a large oak tree. I stand beside the giant tree, looking out at a night sky and the stars of my imagination. All my dreams begin this way, until my subconscious paints it with colors and people and usually fears. Still, as long as I remain lucid, I can watch everything from an objective place, make alterations if necessary, and pull myself out of a dream that's too terrifying. Detail by detail the scenery around me shifts and people come in and out. Ideas are processed. Conversations from the day repeated. And so my dreams pass tonight, one after another. Nothing frightening. And as a quiet observer, I sit in the background, enjoying the simplicity of it all.

When the scenery shifts to one that's both familiar and strangely new, my attention is piqued. I'm in a room inside the Institute, but it's different. The walls are paneled in shiny stainless steel, which clearly reflects everything in the room. It confuses my senses and isn't as appealing as the brushed stainless steel that the Institute is presently known for. The carpet under my feet is black, not iridescent blue. It's like the Institute has been remodeled.

A figure appears, one I know, but only from the picture in the main lobby. I watch everything, careful to absorb the details, knowing I'm observing a reality that has come to pass. Other people enter into the vision. Conversations are had. Everything moves almost too quickly for me to process, but it's only because emotionally I feel tied to it all.

"Please, Monsieur Underwood, I beg of you, do not tell him." Those are the last words I hear before I bolt upright in my bed.

◆

Even though I want to charge into Joseph's room, I stop and softly rap against the door, being quiet enough not to wake anyone.

Shuman's words come back to me in a rush: *Now that you know your subconscious delivers information about real events of the past while lucid dreaming, it will affect the weight you put upon it.*

128

Wrapped in a sheet and bleary-eyed, Joseph answers the door. "What?" he growls.

"It's almost morning," I say, pushing him aside and marching into his room. "Quit acting so tired. I've got something important to tell you."

"I'm not actin'," Joseph says through a yawn, sending the door shut behind me. "What's so important that you have to barge into my dreams so early? Don't you have the rest of the day to harass me?"

"Oh, I'm sorry, I didn't realize you already knew all about our mother's history. Since you do, I'll just be leaving." I start for the door, expecting the hand on my arm.

"Hold up there, li'l partner," he says, pinching my wrist with a tired smile. "Go on now."

"I've just had the most peculiar dream." I rub my head, refreshing the images in my mind. "In it I saw Flynn and Trey, and they were much younger. Trey was hiding a woman."

Joseph rotates his hand through the air, beckoning me to hurry up and get to the point.

"The woman was Eloise—our mother."

No emotion or shock or anything registers on Joseph's face.

"She begged Flynn not to report her relationship with Trey to her father," I say, careful to report the dream in the order in which I experienced it. "The three of them argued and Eloise said that if her father found out he would punish her severely."

"So?" Joseph gives me a petulant expression. "I don't see the significance of these events. Why are you wakin' me up to bore me with this crap?"

I close my eyes; secure the words exactly as I heard them in the dream. "Flynn refused to keep the secret. He said, 'I have to tell your father about this, I never keep anything from Pierre.'"

"What!?" Joseph says, dropping the sheet. Thankfully he's wearing pajama bottoms. "As in the guy who was the leader of the Voyageurs?"

"Yep," I say.

"Our mother's father was Pierre!?"

"Exactly," I say, encouraging with a nod.

"This means…"

"She wasn't a Middling," I say, completing Joseph's thought.

Chapter Twenty-Four

"I sure hope you're right about this, Stark," Joseph says over his shoulder with tired eyes as I sidle up next to him.

"Oh, don't even start."

"Are you gonna knock?"

"No, you are," I say, crossing my arms in front of my chest.

"One of these days, I'm gonna have a dream with ultra-important significance, then I'm gonna order you around. How does that sound?"

"It sounds like you're wasting time. Knock already," I say.

Joseph knocks, although a rabbit could have made more noise than him. Still Trey answers the door, a look of surprise on his always-tired face.

"Well, I didn't expect anyone this early, especially you two," he says, a smile reaching up to his eyes.

"We just had a few questions for you," Joseph says, a meek smile on his face.

"If you want to teleport to the nearest exit, now would be a good time," I say dully.

Joseph elbows me in the ribs. "What your very rude daughter is trying to say is this will hopefully only take a minute."

"That's not at all what I was trying to say," I scold Joseph, who's looking too sheepish. "Please save the world endless confusion and don't become an interpreter."

Unflustered, Trey welcomes us into his office. It's as drab as the last time we were here. "You both may have as much time as you like," he says, walking behind us and sitting at his desk.

"I just had a dream. I witnessed certain events from the past," I say, looking directly at Trey. His expression grows hard as I speak. "I need to know if the information I learned is true."

"What is it?"

"Pierre, one of the cofounders of the Institute, is our grandfather, isn't he?"

Trey rests both elbows on the desk, rakes his fingertips over his eyebrows multiple times. "You have quite the knack for picking up on information, don't you?" he says with a frustrated laugh, although I don't think he feels it's the least bit funny.

"So it's true?" I say.

He delivers his answer to the far corner, like it asked the question. "Yes." Trey should be talking, explaining himself, but he isn't. He keeps his eyes pinned on the corner, like some imaginary force is there advising him on how to proceed.

"How could you not tell us this?" I finally say, breaking the silence. My tone is quiet, but sharp. "You made us break into *this* man's headquarters. The Grotte. We could have been face-to-face with our grandfather, killed him, and not have even known," I say, drawing out the last word as the implications sink in fully. "I want you to tell us everything and I want you to tell us now."

"Roya," Trey says, voice steady, "I've cautioned you before about the truth. It won't set you free. It will weaken and disarm you. Don't ask for something that will only weigh you down."

"I'll be the judge of that," I say, matching his tone, but through clenched teeth. "Why don't you let me decide for once?"

"Because you're not in that position." He looks off, pigments of his skin flushing red in places.

"I've almost died for this place...twice, and you can't be straight with me?" I lean across the desk, daring to separate us by inches. "Your deceptions make me ashamed to be a Lucidite."

His turquoise eyes flash with coarse surprise. "You don't mean that."

"You leave me no other way to feel," I say.

"Then that's how you feel. You don't need to know any more than you do, even if it makes you hate the Institute."

I stand up, almost toppling the chair behind me. "And therefore I have no legitimate reason to stay in this hellhole." His face drops into one of sudden horror, but I don't study it long. Joseph tries to grab for me, but I swish past before he has a chance. The button for the door is inches away from my outstretched hand.

"Stop, Roya!" Trey commands.

I freeze. Glance at him over my shoulder. He's leaning over his desk, hands pinned on it. "Pierre is your grandfather," he says. "It was my relationship with your mother, Eloise, that broke up Flynn and Pierre."

131

I turn and dissect him. Angry eyes like blades cut him open. "You said our mother was a Middling."

"He lied," Joseph says, not glancing at me, but rather staring at the floor in a daze.

Trey nods. "I did lie, but I'll tell you the truth now, if you stay at the Institute."

"I want the whole truth." I take three steps back in his direction, leaving a good three feet between us. "None of this 'that's as much as you get to know' bullshit. I'll stay if you answer everything." I stare at him with a hard expression and hope this translates to confidence. "And I do mean everything," I finally add, noticing his right eye twitch.

"Sit down, Roya," Trey says, as he takes the seat again at his desk.

I remain frozen, uncompliant.

"Yes, all right." He nods and looks down at the blank contents of his desk. "I'll tell you everything, but I want you to live at the Institute for two more years."

"What?! That's too long."

"You've been gone too long. That's the least amount of time I'll settle for."

"NO! A year. That's as long as I'll stay."

"Then you won't get the truth from me."

This is a wrench and we both know it. As I stare at him, trying to gauge his determination, I realize we're playing a game. He holds half the chips and he's willing to make me go all in to get what I really want. I don't blink for a good minute while I match Trey's expression and try to determine my next move. Finally, I take the seat again next to Joseph, this time sitting all the way back, crossing my legs casually. "That's fine, because Zhuang plans on killing us all anyway."

"You won't be here to kill, remember," Trey says, offering me an equally casual smile. "We'll take care of him and you and Joseph can return to the Institute."

I nod, willing to wager this bet. "Okay, you've got yourself a deal." I turn and flash a smirk at Joseph, but he's not looking the least bit amused by my negotiation skills.

Behind me the ventilation system clicks on, followed by a steady flow of cold air on my neck. "Your mother," Trey begins in a clinical tone, "as you've learned, was Pierre's daughter. My father, Flynn, and Pierre founded this place in the 1970s after the US government abandoned it. Flynn had already secured the appropriate technology at that time in order to keep the government from coming back and taking ownership of the property."

"The modifier," I say.

"Yes," Trey confirms, intertwining his fingers. "Flynn was in favor of technology, which was the first rift between the two founders. They also didn't have the same vision for the Lucidites, but they had complementary powers and a lifelong friendship. Flynn thought the Institute should have three missions: research, reconnaissance, and protection. Pierre thought the Institute should have only one mission: power. The two were able to balance their interests for the good part of almost two decades." Trey draws his fingers apart and pulls one hand up to his protective charm. He fingers his medallion through his thumb and forefinger. "I'm not sure what you saw in your dream, Roya, but here's what happened. Elle had been living here for quite some time. She was raised at the Institute, which was one of the main reasons she didn't want this for you two. I spent most of my developmental years at a Tibetan temple, raised by Buddhist monks. When I entered young adulthood, Flynn asked me to come to the Institute and consider taking on some of the work he'd pioneered. This is when I came to know your mother. We fell for each other instantly."

From beside me Joseph shuffles his feet. Trey's attention is briefly caught by the nervousness before he continues. "Although we asked Flynn to keep this a secret, he refused. He thought if he approached Pierre about it that he would be reasonable and accepting. Elle warned my father this wouldn't be the case, but Flynn thought he knew Pierre better than his own daughter. He was wrong." There's a quiet regret in Trey's eyes. "When Pierre found out about our relationship he became enraged. He went to Elle and forbade her to see me, but she was already pregnant with you two. She told Pierre and he did everything he could to terminate her pregnancy."

Trey tightens his mouth, hesitates. A sorrowful shudder rips through him. "Somehow she was able to get away from Pierre. When she showed up at my door that night I had no idea how she'd survived his attack. I was certain that Pierre had succeeded in killing our baby, since at the time we didn't know she was carrying twins. Elle wouldn't allow Mae to heal her broken ribs, her concussion, or the bruises around her throat where Pierre had almost succeeded in strangling his daughter. She made Mae center all of her powers into saving her child. That's when we learned there were two of you. It was a surprise, one we couldn't enjoy at the time like we wanted to," he says with a smile suffocated by pain. "Your hearts were barely beating on the monitor but we knew for certain we heard two. Throughout that night I listened as Mae worked and with each hour your heartbeats grew stronger.

"I'd never seen my father more sickened with hostility," Trey continues after taking a short, replenishing breath. "My own mother died giving birth to me and I know that night brought back emotions he hadn't visited in decades. The next morning all his loyalty to Pierre had vanished. He never apologized to Elle for betraying her secret to her father but what he did was more meaningful. Before Elle and I left the Institute the next morning Flynn spoke his last promise to her, for he never saw her again after that. He promised that he would do everything in his power to protect you two. As you know, Flynn died trying to find and kill Zhuang, because he knew that he couldn't allow you, Roya, to do it. He was a man of his promises."

A volcano of emotions erupts inside of Joseph. It almost makes me double over. Guilt like lava pours through him, but to his credit his face remains stone, only marked by stress that could be excused to the torrent of information we've just received. I want to reach out and take his hand, but I keep mine folded in my lap. Flynn, our grandfather, spent the last bit of life keeping his promise to our mother. And Joseph killed him. The poetic injustice sears my soul. I can't imagine being Joseph right now, having to deal with unforgivable actions.

"After watching the brutality Pierre showed his own daughter, Flynn made a decision to wage a war against him," Trey says, like reading a story out of a book. "This is exactly what happened when Pierre realized that Elle had gone missing. Flynn was one step ahead though. He lured Pierre in physical form to the desert. My father confronted him about all of his concerns: Pierre's unhealthy craving for power, his abuse to his daughter, and his resistance to advancements. He told Pierre things needed to change and asked him to come up with his terms for negotiations and they would both meet in one hour in the Institute to discuss them. Flynn disappeared, knowing Pierre would take his time to form his demands." Trey pauses for a second to breathe. He's been speaking nonstop for more than a minute.

"Once Flynn returned to the Institute he activated the security that we now have in place here. As you both know, you cannot dream travel directly to the Institute. The only way you can gain access now is if you're fully submerged in water in physical form. This was an idea that Flynn had from the beginning, but never shared with Pierre. He executed this plan while Pierre was in the desert and when his partner tried to return to the Institute he was unable. Flynn had hidden Pierre's daughter and taken the Institute from him. He had declared war and that's why to this day we regard the Voyageurs as enemies."

Trey's taciturn tone is betrayed once again by his eyes. Hate and pain surface time and time again with each sentence. These are words he has not strung together in quite some time. His usual cool manner isn't just threatened by this topic, it's torn in half, exhibiting the person Trey doesn't want anyone to see. He isn't a whole individual. I see that now. Hasn't been one for quite some time. My study of him is cut short by a distracting fidget from Joseph. He's been all jitters and scratching and shuffling since he sat down. Now he's pushing forward in his chair, drumming his fingertips on his knee.

"So why?" Joseph asks. "What was Pierre's big deal with you and our mother havin' a relationship? I don't get it."

Trey pushes back from his desk and pins his hands on his knees. He lifts his chin. I watch as a tense knot in his throat bobs up and down as he tries time and again to swallow. What he'd just divulged hadn't been the difficult part. He'd hoped all along this would be enough to satisfy us, but Joseph had to ask his question and now Trey was facing what he didn't want to answer.

"Elle was forbidden to be with me or anyone else because…she had already been promised to someone else." Trey says the last part in a rush. He isn't looking at either of us as he speaks, but rather his own hands. "Pierre had made an arranged marriage for her. In exchange for a union with Elle, every Lucidite would willingly give their powers over to Pierre. Taking power from someone diminishes

135

it, but if someone freely gives it over its purity is maintained." Trey's hands slip through his silver hair. The reflex reminds me of how I often absentmindedly twirl my hair through my fingers when I'm nervous or lost in thought.

"Your mother was promised to Chase. In exchange, Chase would control any Lucidite Pierre chose and have them relinquish their consciousness and all the power it held to him. Very much like Zhuang, Pierre wanted to take the powers of others to strengthen his own. When Flynn learned of this in the desert, he knew that this war wasn't just necessary, but inevitable. I don't think my father ever forgave himself for not seeing Pierre for who he truly was. Thankfully Pierre never fulfilled his end of the bargain and it appears he's even slipped from power with the Voyageurs."

Trey steeples his hands and rests his forehead against them. I shiver from a sudden chill, as though the air from the ventilation system is breathing down my core. When Trey lowers his hands, he regards me with a burning concern. "But Chase is back and has found a way to collect on what he was promised. This, Roya, is why Chase wants you."

None of this adds up. I'm not good at math, and this is like a complex equation. "I'm not my mother. Why wouldn't Chase just find some other Dream Traveler to seduce?"

"He's after your blood," Trey says. "There are only a few pureblood Dream Traveler families still in existence. These bloodlines will always produce a Dream Traveler. Not only that, but the offspring of these families are incredibly strong and skillful."

"What you're saying..." Joseph says slowly as he pieces it together, "is that our mother was from one of these ancient lineages? She was a pureblood? And so is Chase? That's the reason that he wanted to marry slash breed with her?"

"That's part of what I'm saying." Trey pushes his hands automatically through his hair.

"The other part is that Chase wants Stark because she has the same blood, right?" Joseph almost sounds matter-of-fact, like we're discussing the best growing season for tulips instead of my love life.

"Not the same blood," Trey corrects.

"Right," Joseph says, nodding. "Well, her blood would be less potent, but still enough to interest Chase, huh?"

136

"It's more than enough." Trey looks down uncomfortably. And I realize I'm twisting a strand of my own hair so tightly it's about break. "Your mother was a direct descendant of one of the most ancient lineages of Dream Travelers. I come from another."

Trey flips his head up, gauging our reaction to another bomb he's dropped. The silence fills a place in me that was about to overflow and is now flooding. I begin making graphs and charts in my brain trying to piece all this together, but the more I try to understand it the more the confounding aspects of it cloud my brain.

"You two are both Dream Travelers with pure blood. This is quite rare." Pride marks Trey's words, which stuns me even more. I'm being hunted for this blood. How can I be prideful about this?

A loud, dramatic sigh sprays out of Joseph's mouth, making me jump. "Damn! Stark is in a lot of trouble, isn't she?"

"Yes, this is why it's imperative that we protect her. Chase only wants offspring with founder blood." Trey turns and looks at me. "And after he has what he wants he will have no use for you. Actually, I fear he will physically punish you for your mother's betrayal. Maybe imprison you or get into your head. And still the cruelest thing he will do is take your children from you. There's nothing worse."

The ventilation system switches off. Then a soft silence fills the space. Trey's expression relaxes. I guess now that the truth is out he's finally unburdened.

"I can't believe," I begin slowly as if I'm choking on the words, "that you've known all of this for so long and kept it from us. How could you pretend to be confused as to Chase's motives when I told you how he treated me in the Grotte? You knew, didn't you?"

He nods, his eyes reeking with guilt and the weight of too much stress.

"A few days ago I let Chase seek me out in a dream travel. I was all alone," I say, my words cold and almost practiced.

Trey stiffens.

I keep my eyes locked on his. "I wouldn't have done that if you'd shared this history with me. I'll guard myself now that I know this information. Now that I know what Chase wants, I'll die before he gets it." I stand, arms by my side, back straight. "Funny, huh? How you thought all this information would make me weaker and all it actually makes me want to do is protect myself more. Imagine if you would have shared it with me earlier. Imagine all the hell we could have avoided…"

Chapter Twenty-Five

"Let's not talk about this anymore. I want to relieve my mind of it for a little while," I say, twirling my fingers through George's hair. We've been discussing the secrets Trey revealed for a solid hour.

He turns to me from his sitting position on the floor. "I understand."

I scooch back on the bed and cross my legs. "You always do, don't you, my sweet George?" I say, staring fondly down at him.

"That's my favorite nickname ever," he says, lying back on the carpet, cradling his head in his hands.

I smile. "You know what I'm going to do?" I say, tracing an invisible pattern on my bed covers with my finger. "I'm going to flee the Institute. Go work on a goat farm. I'll change my identity and tell the nice family I work for that Chase and Trey are stalkers, and to shoot them if they set foot on the property."

"That sounds like an especially flawed plan," George says with a sideways smile. "And you promised to stay here for two years."

"Trey lied. I think I should return the favor."

George gives me a handsomely stern look. Jaw set. Eyes piercing. That perfect pinch to his mouth. Lately I've been making statements just to encourage him to look at me that way. Guess I like getting in trouble. Fortunately I'm good at it.

"All right, I wouldn't really break my word even if Trey is a skinny little liar."

"I know you wouldn't. Still, if we're pretending, what would your life on this goat farm look like?"

I beam as the ideas spring to mind. "Well, as long as I'm pretending, I'd own the farm. It would be off the grid and surrounded by blankets of lavender fields. From the goat's milk I'd make artisan cheeses that I sold at the farmer's markets. Also I'd send a bundle of it to Misty, aka Goat Girl."

"That's extremely thoughtful of you. Would you have a garden?"

"No!" I say with mock offense. "My job is the goats. *You're* in charge of the garden."

He strokes his stubbled chin, a slow grin sliding over his face. "Of course. I'm remiss to not realize you'd put me in charge of the fruits and flowers."

"Indeed you are," I say, suppressing a laugh. "From the garden you make jams and other goods."

"And sell these and the organic produce at the market, right?"

"Yes, we have side-by-side stalls. And we're known as 'that mysterious couple' who never talks to the locals except to explain our exemplary production processes. As soon as market closes we ride back to our cottage, which is a good distance from society."

George props himself up on his elbows, a dimple-producing grin on his face. "And I read you *Madame Bovary* or *Leaves of Grass* by candlelight."

"But not too late into the night," I scold.

"Of course not," he agrees. "We have to get up early to milk the goats."

"Exactly," I say, drawing the word out. "You know, if I keep up news reporting, in two years I'll have enough money to buy this farm."

"I'd be all too happy to be your farmhand to earn my keep."

Shuffling back to the edge of the bed I kick my legs over the side. "You will be no farmhand."

"No?"

"No. There's other ways you can earn your keep," I say, a bashful smile making my ears burn.

"Oh?" he says, sitting up all the way. "Like offering you my endless love. Is that what you had in mind?"

The mention of *that* word strips the smile off my face. *Love.* I'm not sure why—it just makes everything suddenly real, and not a safe fantasy.

I expected that my sudden seriousness would make George retreat, but he stands, a heated look in his eyes. "Come here," he says, extending his hand to me. I take it and he easily pulls me up from the bed and to him. "Farm or no farm. Whether we're in the Institute or traveling the world, you have my unwavering affection. Roya, I love you."

I freeze. I know how I feel about George but I can't voice it. Everything I say sounds too small in comparison to his unyielding love. "George, I...I'm bad at this."

"That's not true, you just don't know how."

"Remember in *Love in the Time of Cholera* when Fermina says love is a natural talent?"

He nods, his expression growing worried.

"She says, 'You are either born knowing how, or you never know.'"

"Even poetic words can be wrong," George says, sliding both his hands up my arms. "Love isn't inborn, it's learned. You never learned how to love unconditionally because your parents never loved you that way. I don't understand how though. How could anyone spend a minute in your presence and not fall crazy in love with you?" He half smiles. "Well, from my observation, most people do. You have the adoration of everyone in *this* place."

"No." I shake my head, pinning my eyes on the middle of his chest.

George guides my eyes back to his by tipping my chin with his forefinger. "You believe love is a curse because it will never last and always dissolve the moment you stake faith in it."

"Maybe I've closed off my heart for too long because I don't understand unconditional love and don't feel I'll ever have the capacity to love like that, and then what's the point?"

He gives me a reassuring smile. "The point is to open yourself up to the possibility. Remember when Florentino told Fermina, 'Think of love as a state of grace; not the means to anything but the alpha and omega, an end in itself'?"

I nod, liking that George memorizes his favorite quotes from books too.

"The beauty of love is you don't have to think about it, it just happens," George says, sounding much more mature than he should be at the age of seventeen. "Love isn't governed by logic or understanding. You don't enter into it like an agreement. It crashes down on you. You wake up one morning and realize the reason you can't take your eyes off someone is because you're in love with them. Over the long hours you've spent together, you've fallen for them. If my time loving you has taught me anything, it's that love grows with every returned smile, every second of communal silence and every word exchanged. Unconditional love is built and when it's finished nothing destroys it."

141

I press my lips together. Who knew George would be the one to teach me how love works. When I threw the frequency adjuster at him I thought he was my downfall. But his purpose in my life is more about growth than anything else. "I want to believe in a capacity like you speak."

"That's the first step," he says, cupping my chin with his firm hand.

"What's the second?" I say, a nervous laugh in my throat.

"After that, the steps are kind of interchangeable," he whispers against my lips.

"Oh, well, that's confusing."

"Stop overthinking this." He leans down and kisses the corner of my mouth. His thumb swipes along the curve of my jaw and he trails kisses behind it.

"Is this one of the steps to unconditional love?" I say, my voice aching in my chest.

"Yes," he breathes against my throat.

George brings his eyes up to meet mine. I'm suddenly captured beneath his glare, which isn't cloaked in its usual firmness. My fingers find the loops on his jeans and with a small tug I encourage him closer. He takes my face in both his hands and kisses me once upon my mouth. And again his lips grace mine. On the third kiss I open my mouth to his, tasting his warmth.

On top of his shirt, I walk my fingertips up from his waistband, along his stomach, and slide my hands around his back. I pull him into me, inciting a more passionate kiss. Too curious, I slip my hands under his shirt. He pauses, a heated expression hooding his eyes. Hastily, he throws his arms over his head, binding up the fabric of his shirt and pulling it off forward. Greedily, I take him in, running my eyes over the angles on his chest.

Suddenly my hands are weighted down by my side. I want to touch him, and I also don't. I don't know how to start. Everything feels too real as we stand a foot apart watching each other. George reaches down, seizes my hand and presses it into his chest. His skin has a lovely warmth under my fingertips. I glide my hand up, taking in the contours that make up George, studying them. His muscles flex under my fingers. I glide my hands along his body until they're around his neck. I'm not surprised when my eyes look up to his face to find him biting his bottom lip. I untuck it from his teeth with my finger and cup his chin, drawing him into my eager lips. His face leans forward into mine and the kiss that follows I expect, but the ferocity behind it I don't. His lips smash into mine hard, his breath hot. Unleashed by my hands and my wants, George releases the aggressions that he's harbored for too long. I don't back away from it. Instead I push my body more firmly against his. He knots his hands into my hair, his lips moving against mine with a firm intensity.

Without a second thought I tug my shirt off too and pull George down on the bed on top of me before he has a chance to give me a proper glance. My hands eagerly explore the parts of him—the curves of his chest, the slope of his waist.

Each of my hungry emotions encourages him, making him wilder moment by moment. His large hands tangle in my hair. I wrap my legs around him pressing our bodies more firmly together, enjoying our skin touching. He groans. A sound that releases a thousand stallions from my gut. All racing to him.

"Sorry to interrupt, Stark, but your immediate attention is needed."

Horrified, I whip my head to the side. Joseph is squatted down giving me a devilish grin.

"Joseph, are you out of your mind?!" Blood thunders in my head, roller coasting my thoughts into a million places. George tries to sit up, but I pull him down on me to cover up my toplessness. "Have you decided you're too good to knock?"

"I did knock, but I don't think either of you could hear it over...well, you know. Seriously, Stark. Important news. Get your shirt on, we need to talk."

"Turn around," I command.

As he does, I give George an indignant expression which he returns, his face flushed. He hastily finds my shirt and tosses it at me before tugging his own over his tousled hair.

"Oh, and..." Joseph says, tottering back and forth, back still to us, "nice abs, Anders. Do you work out?"

"Shut up, Joseph," I say, pulling my shirt over my head.

Breathless, George leans down and whispers in my ear. "I'll be in my room." He grabs my hand and gently squeezes it. Stepping up on my tiptoes I give him a peck on the cheek.

"Okay," I mouth, taking a few steps back. When George is gone I spin around and face Joseph. "What in the hell is your problem!?" I say loud enough George can most certainly hear me from the hallway.

Joseph pivots, a mischievous grin on his face, eyes dancing with joy. "I know how we're going to defeat Zhuang. We're going to use the greatest weapon on earth. One that *you* happen to have direct access to," he says, firing his hand at me like it's a gun.

My face falls into dumbfounded embarrassment.

"Chase," he says finally, triumph revolving on every one of his features like a strobe light.

Chapter Twenty-Six

"I just had a dream of the future. It was exactly like how you described the one of Flynn, Trey, and Eloise. It was real."

"A premonition, but while you were sleeping?"

"Yes, but it wasn't in the distant future. It's going to happen soon."

"It's eight o'clock. Why were you sleeping?"

Joseph slides his hand along the side of his head. This nervous gesture is in essence the same as Trey's but doesn't disrupt Joseph's spiky hair on top of his head. Funny how we're all just a conglomeration of our nervous habits. I see them like road maps in each conversation telling me more about the people than their words.

"Did you forget that you woke me up at the crack of dawn this morning? *And* sleeping is a great way to avoid people."

"Like Trent?" I ask, knowing from dipping into his thoughts that I'm one hundred percent right.

"Do you want to know how we're gonna demolish Zhuang or not?" Joseph says with an exasperated sigh.

"But we're supposed to leave the Institute as soon as he arrives," I say, although I never had any intention of doing that.

"And in my vision, we stay."

"But do we survive?"

Joseph whistles through his teeth. "Who knows."

♦

"That's all you saw?" Disappointment riddles my voice.

"I think it's enough for us to figure out what we need to do," Joseph says, voice jittery with nerves.

"You mean what I have to do." I tremble at the thought.

"Well, my part isn't all that easy either. You have to admit that if we can pull it off it will be brilliant."

"I'm willing to consider this strategy for one and only one reason," I say, working my fingers through the knots George made in my hair. "I fear Trey will fail and Zhuang will still be our problem."

"I see your faith in Pops hasn't recovered since you figured out he's a compulsive liar."

"I guess that's where you get it from, huh?"

Joseph ignores me. "You on board?"

"Sure, I don't have anything else to lose…well, except my virginity," I say with a chuckle.

"From what I just saw, you were desperately close to losing it tonight." He jerks back, but not before my punch connects with his arm.

"Why don't you finally learn some kung fu so that you survive long enough on Day Z for our plan to be executed. I don't want to be responsible for protecting your ass."

"Yeah, yeah. I'll do my best to hold my own. Lord knows you'll have your work cut out for you."

◆

"Why Vegas?" I ask, watching the Bellagio fountain, waiting for the show to start.

"Just thought you could use some superficial flashy nightlife," Bob says, leaning over the edge of the railing, peering down. "I know you prefer dream travels that are more nature based, so we can go somewhere else if you'd like."

Violin music starts and with it the cascading water perfectly mimics every beat of the compelling notes. The combination of the two entrances me immediately. A woman's elegant voice begins singing in Italian.

"What's this song?" I ask, feeling the music convulse in my heart oddly.

"'*Time to Say Goodbye*,'" Steve says, staring at the incredible display of spiraling water shooting in uniform rhythms along the large pool of the Bellagio fountain.

"Besides from the obvious, based on the title, what's she singing about?"

"She just said, 'Into me you've poured the light, the light that you found by the side of the road.'"

"That's gorgeous," I say, accosted by a sudden rush of emotions. The intensity of the water and lights speed up and with it my heart.

"Wait until Andrea Bocelli starts singing," Steve says, and almost as if cued, a man's voice fills the air. It's as smooth as the pool of water was before the fountain started.

"Tell me what he's saying," I urge, a desperate need to know.

"'When you're far away I dream of the horizon and words fail me. And of course I know that you're with me, with me,'" Steve says, his eyes closed, a peaceful look on his face.

For a good minute I'm captivated by the music, the water, and the lights. I don't know how to waltz but as I listen to this music I feel the need to move, to sway like one might if they were waltzing. The night's air wraps around me with its warmth and strength, leaving me fully content. I want to look up and take in one of my companions' expressions but I'm too overwhelmed. I'm accustomed to being stunned lately, but not like this.

The man's voice is full of confidence. It assures me that his love for her will overcome anything. I don't understand Italian, but I feel enough of the emotions to know their message of love. For the first time in my life I understand something.

I draw in a long deep breath and stare at the night's sky. I hold the breath and wait, but I'm not sure what for, it just doesn't seem right to breathe freely right now. The drums pound once and then both voices join in unison and harmonize with such soul. Water shoots to new heights. How could it be possible that in the most commercial of places I'm having a truly spiritual moment? The tears slip down my cheeks, unleashed by a tender ache I didn't even know lived within me.

Bob half encircles me with his arm, squeezing me into him. It makes me feel slightly less dramatic to notice his eyes wet with moisture.

"Shall we walk?" Steve asks.

I nod, knowing my voice will crack if I say something aloud.

Luckily for me Steve starts talking right away. "The reason we love Vegas is pure and simple. It's where we met." Steve laughs, exchanging a fond look with Bob. "It was a total accident."

"That's usually how the best things in life happen," Bob chimes in as he strides beside me.

147

"I was walking down a busy part of the strip, just like here," Steve says. People mill about everywhere and although we move to avoid them, many times they pass through us like ghosts. "The experience was very much like this. I wasn't paying much attention to the people who I passed through, too busy taking in the sights. Bob was doing the same." The memory seems to surface in Steve's vision. "We crashed into each other, sending both of us to the ground." Steve laughs again, shaking his head. "Can you believe it? Out of all the places we could have been walking. It just means we were on paths that were destined to collide."

"It took a minute for it to register what had actually occurred," Bob says, reaching out and offering his hand to Steve. He wrings it sweetly. "I'd dream traveled my entire life and had never accidentally run into another Dream Traveler. There's just not many of us and this Earth is so vast."

My head easily moves back and forth between the two men on either side of me as they take turns telling the story. "After we'd recovered from our fall, we chatted, sharing our backgrounds, dream travels, interests." Steve winks at Bob. "I liked him immediately."

"That's the best story of how two people met that I've ever heard." I beam.

"We like it." Steve slows and turns, facing the turquoise water at the Venetian Resort. A gondola sails through the waters. A couple sits in it cuddling as a man in a black and white striped shirt pushes the boat. I lean on the railing, looking down into the water as it churns from the movements of the sleek boats.

Even though it's late, crowds of people shuffle down the sidewalk behind us and over the bridge in front of us. Stopping, laughing, taking selfies. The traffic on the streets buzzes loudly. I find myself strangely enjoying the energy that this city exudes.

"So, tell us, what's new with you?" Bob watches the couple in the boat until they move off from our sight.

Pulling in a long breath of air, I sigh. "Where do I begin?" I eye the large column to the right of us and decide to take a seat at its base. Bob and Steve squat down next to me on either side.

"Uh-oh." Steve gives Bob a worried look. "This must be big if we've got to sit for it."

"It is," I confirm. I watch the gondola passengers take their rides through the Grand Canal. They all appear so happy and carefree. Suddenly I have the urge to jump into one of those boats and let all my worries float away. Shaking off the thought I fill Bob and Steve in on the newest bit of lies. After my long and sordid explanation, they both do a poor job of hiding their grave expressions.

"It's so hard to believe Trey would keep all this from you." Steve has a look of seriousness that grips his eyes, making the wrinkles around them suddenly pronounced.

"It's getting less difficult to believe this kind of stuff though," Bob says. "I mean, I respect him as the Head of the Institute, but it's hard to look at him the same way anymore."

"However, it isn't fair for us to judge." Steve gives Bob a chastising expression.

"You're right," Bob says with an edge of reluctance.

"Well, although I reserve the right to change my mind, I'm doing a fair bit of judging," I say.

"I think you're allowed," Steve says, patting my arm. "I just don't think Bob and I should. It's not productive."

"That situation with Chase is incredibly unnerving though." Bob shivers, like he's suddenly cold.

Bolting upright, I twist around, feeling his presence like a hot match on my skin. A figure lurking on the other side of the column shifts but not before I spy a few trademark features. And if I had any doubts, he, like us, doesn't cast a shadow.

"He isn't a bad man," I say, cringing inside with sudden rampant fear.

"Roya, of course he—"

I cut Steve off. "No, what you know about him is a picture painted by the Lucidites." With a great intensity I point with my eyes, my expression trying to reveal everything I can't say out loud. *Chase is here. Over there*, my eyes seek to say. "I think of all people you'd want me to be with someone who would protect me the way I know he will." My voice comes out shaky. Scanning the area, I look for weapons. Ways to protect Bob and Steve if I need to. Inside me I feel the trace of a connection to Chase. He's angry, and it's such an unbelievably gorgeous anger—like flames dancing in a bonfire.

Astonishment and understanding dawn on both men's faces almost simultaneously. Bob cautiously turns his head to peer behind him, but I know Chase is well hidden on the far side of the pillar. Steve rebounds upright like a plank, almost stumbling to his feet. "You're right," he says, taking my arm a bit tighter than usual. "If he makes you happy, that's all that matters."

"He does." I force a smile into my voice. "I truly love him."

Bob joins me on my other side. "How about we walk?" His voice a high-pitched rush.

I hold my breath, nod.

Chapter Twenty-Seven

Worrying down my thumbnail I take the once familiar trek. The hallway outside Aiden's lab is quiet, devoid of its usual overflow of music. Strategically, I chose to wear the pink visor Bob and Steve just sent, along with new running gear. Although I told them I could buy my own clothes with the hordes of money I'm making news reporting, they scoffed at the idea. Since I'm planning on running after this meeting, it doesn't look strange if I hide every rogue emotion behind the protection the visor provides. Head down, thumbnail firmly pressed between my teeth, I round the corner into Aiden's lab and run straight into him. A half a dozen books fly out of his arms and land haphazardly on the ground. The corner of one pokes me in the chest during the collision, but the embarrassment smarts way worse.

"I'm so sorry," Aiden says, catching only one book. "You all right?"

I rub my forearm, which also took a good portion of the impact. "Yeah. You?"

He kneels over in a rush, scrambling to pick up the books splayed out on the floor. "I was just headed down the hallway to drop these off for Ren."

"Oh, well, you sent me a note saying the patch is ready. I can wait here until you return."

Handing me a book, Aiden smiles, his eyes briefly lighting up behind his black-rimmed glasses. Then, almost like remembering a grim detail the smile fades, whisked away and replaced by a more guarded one. "Or you can help me with the delivery?"

"Ha-hah," I pretend to laugh. "Nice try, but I've managed to avoid Ren for a while now and I feel better for it."

"Come on now. Obviously I can't manage all these books on my own." Aiden lays another heavy book on the one he's handed me and walks off at once.

I roll my eyes, hurrying to catch up with him.

"Have you considered getting a rolling cart?" I ask, pinning the books to my chest. "Since you obviously don't like to make multiple trips and always carry more than you can handle?"

"I'll put it on my Christmas list." He points with his head, indicating a door. "Mind knocking?"

Just above the button is a label: Scape's Escapes. "Is this?"

Aiden nods. "Yep, it's where the Strategy department meets."

"Ren's secret lair," I say in a ghostly whisper. "No doubt riddled with bones and teeth."

"And here I thought you'd never been in there," Aiden says, matching my tone.

I rap against the door. Like he'd been waiting for us, it slides back almost immediately. Ren stands glaring at us in his usual dark green suit. "Oh, you lot are obviously lost. The playground is on the third level."

Aiden steps forward, handing the books to Ren. "Here are the books you requested, sir," Aiden bows slightly. He turns and relieves me of my books, placing them on top of the stack. "If there's anything else I can do to help you, please just let me know."

"If there's anything else I can do to help," Ren mocks in a high-pitched voice, nose crinkled. "How about you sod off, that'd help." He elbows the button, sending the door shut at once.

"I think what he meant to say is 'thank you,'" I say, smothering a laugh. "Does anyone have any idea why that guy is so crabby?" I ask as we retrace our way back to Aiden's lab.

"No, but honestly I find his rough nature a bit endearing."

"Oh, you would," I say, trying to sound wry, but it's bordering on amusement.

"So, it's kind of nice to know I'm not the only person you're avoiding lately," Aiden says, directing me over to a certain workstation. I pretend to be interested in the current arrangement of his lab, which is always changing.

"I'm not avoiding you. Just been busy." I chew on the inside of my cheek. "Besides I don't have much reason to stop by."

"Well, you're here now." Aiden extends his hand and eyes me nervously.

I almost reach out and take it, confused and elated by his gesture.

"May I have your bracelet?"

"Oh, yes, of course," I say in an embarrassed rush.

"This will only take a few minutes. Can you hang out?"

"Sure."

Aiden opens a microwave-like box that sits on a nearby counter. Placing my bracelet inside, he hits a dozen or so buttons before shutting the door and placing a reinforcement lock on it.

"Are you nuking my charm?" I ask, trying to peer around him.

"Kind of," Aiden says, a laugh almost in his voice. Not facing me, he drums his hands on the countertop, watching a dial on the front of the machine.

"Where's the music?" I ask, hopping up on a stool. The action strangely brings back a rush of memories—all connected to Aiden.

"Just felt like having some quiet time for a change." He turns around staring straight at me, making my skin prickle with unease.

Yeah, me too.

"So, I hear you're royalty," Aiden says, daring to take the seat next to me.

I pick at my running shorts like there's a problem with the fabric. There's not. They're brand new. "Wow," I say in a dull voice. "Gossip travels fast around here."

"Yeah, you're the center of a lot of talk these days."

"Lovely…" From under my visor I spy on Aiden, who looks to be as interested in the floor as I am in my running shorts. The sharp angles of his face appear to make him even more smartly handsome than the last time I studied him. Clenching my eyes shut I rebuke myself for the sudden thought. "So who told you Chase wants me to breed him an army of pureblooded Dream Travelers?"

"Trent," Aiden chirps. "He loves a good scandal."

I should have guessed Joseph would have told him. Neither one of them can keep their mouths shut about much. "I'll be grateful when everyone gets their own lives. Then maybe they'll quit being so fascinated by mine."

"You might have to wait a while for that," Aiden says, eyes still pinned downward. "Even I have to admit that when you get over the morbid parts of this whole Chase thing, it's highly interesting."

"So you really learned about this from Trent? You didn't already know?" I ask, risking a direct glance at him.

He shakes his head. "I told you I didn't, remember?"

"Right," I say, the agonizing memory of that meeting with Trey, Ren, and Aiden washing over me. "But Ren knew. I wonder how though. When Trey dropped the bomb that he was Joseph's and my father he said Ren was the only person who knew. It doesn't appear that they're really close so why would Ren know all these family secrets?"

"Probably because he's been here for a really long time. Well, he's been here for as long as I can remember anyway."

Aiden kicks his long legs back and forth, catching the rails of the stool every now and then.

"Isn't it weird to think that if Trey hadn't sent me off, I would have grown up here with you?" I ask, the question like a paradox in my head.

Aiden doesn't look at me. I actually get the impression that he's distracted by thoughts in his own head. "So, you and George, huh?" he finally says, his voice flat.

How can a single question feel like a hot poker on my skin? "Yeah," I finally say, pushing the ache out of my throat. "He was willing to take a risk on me."

"Do you enjoy dropping little insinuations like that into conversations?" Aiden says, swiveling his gaze up, fastening it on me. Emotions, like telepathic links, spring back and forth between us.

I glare into his dark blue eyes, smoldering with regret.

"George doesn't have anything to risk," Aiden says.

"Sure he does. Trey can't like that we're together. He goes to great lengths to take away things that make me happy," I say, not meaning any of it, but knowing it will feel like shards of glass on his skin.

"So are you happy?"

"Are you asking as a friend?"

"As your friend, all I want is for you to be happy. I wish it could be with me." He throws up his hands as if in surrender. "I know I'm not supposed to say things like that anymore, but the way I figure it is things are coming down to a deadly wire and that's how I feel. Sue me."

"Oh, are we putting it all out there after all these weeks? I didn't get the memo," I say. "In that case—"

Beep. Beep. Beep.

The microwave-looking-thingy cuts me off before I have a chance to say something I'll no doubt regret. Without a second glance, Aiden slides off his stool, his shoulders tensed as he opens up the contraption. He reaches into the darkened box with a pair of tongs and removes my bracelet, which is glowing with dangerous heat. Steadily he places it on a mat on the counter. Pauses. With his back still to me he says, "It will take a little while to cool down. I'm sorry but you're going to have to wait here."

I'm not sorry. Sickeningly, I'm enjoying this. After weeks of tension building every time I think about Aiden and his cowardly behavior, it's nice to have a fight. Let it blow up a little.

Exhaling loudly, he turns, leaning against the counter, pinning his hands on either side of him. "Here's a caution," Aiden says, and I tense automatically. "If this works, which I suspect it will, I advise you to not let Chase know it. Firstly, it will piss him off and I think that should be avoided. Secondly, we have the edge on him right now. If he knows you've found a way to stop him he'll find another strategy and something tells me the next one will be more serious. If you do find yourself face-to-face with him then give him the reaction you think he wants long enough to keep him appeased. Trey's working on a plan to rid you of Chase, but his first focus is on Day Z."

"So you're telling me to pretend to be in love with Chase if he comes around?" I say, completely blindsided by the instructions.

"Yes, pretend just like you do with George."

I actually smile. He's being cruel and clever. A new side of Aiden that's strangely fun. "How do you know I'm pretending?" I say, threading my arms together.

"It's more of a hope."

"Seems like a really unworthy drain on your attention."

His eyes flick up to the ceiling, a familiar frustration returning to his face. Aiden and I are spectacularly good at arguing. I'm pretty certain there's no merit in that. "I would test the patch to see if it works by using the emotional modifier I built on you, but…" he says, tottering his head side to side, like he's still considering the idea, "I suspect you wouldn't want that."

"How extremely astute of you. You suspect correctly. I've had enough emotional programming, thank you very much."

Beside him my bracelet still glows hot on the counter. I think he gave me false expectations when he said this would only take a few minutes. "If," I begin, drawing out the word, "you did test my patch with your emotional modifier, what sort of programming would you do to me? For testing purposes, of course."

155

"Hmmm..." he says, thinking the question over with sincere deliberation. "Maybe I'd make you obsessed with something ridiculous like cheese puffs or ancient Celtic folklore."

"Why not both?"

He strokes his chin. "I like the way you think."

"Well, I *think* you could do better. Find a more entertaining way to manipulate my emotions."

"Is that right?" Aiden gives me a heated glance. "Maybe I'll use it to make you stop being mad at me."

"Oh, I didn't know it could work miracles," I say, unable to suppress a sliver of a smile.

"Well, you being in love with Chase is a marvel."

"No, it's downright ludicrous."

"You know, the line between love and hate is excruciatingly thin," he says.

"Whoever said I hated you?"

"I inferred that much."

"Well, stop with the inferences. The truth is—"

"You love me and I broke your heart," Aiden says, his voice full of heat.

Talk about having words which were never going to come out of my mouth ripped from my chest. I gape at him. "What?" I revolt, like he's just said the stupidest thing in the world.

"The walls here aren't soundproof."

"What does that have to do with anything? I'm not yelling," I say.

"When you left my lab last time, I heard what you said after you shut my door."

That memory rises from the deepest layers of my skin. I remember standing on the other side of his lab door, touching it, speaking those three tortured words. Embarrassment quickly morphs into aggravation at my own idiocy.

"Roya." Aiden closes his eyes for a half beat. When they open, the look in them is a forbidden one between us. One I should look away from immediately. "I love you too," he says, like it's a curse.

"Aiden—"

"If we could be together...Would you still want to?" he asks, and the question unleashes an angry dragon inside me.

"Are you intentionally trying to torture me?"

156

"No, I'm sorry," he says, massaging his temples like he suddenly has a headache. "After my parents died I went back and watched them die over and over again." Aiden doesn't look at me during this intimate admission until the last word. Then I see something in him uncovered for the first time. Sorrow. "I'm telling you this because something sick in me has to experience loss over and over until I exhaust the pain."

"Us not being together is nothing like losing your parents."

"No it's not," he admits. "But still, I have that same unhealthy urge to keep cutting myself with the loss. I know we can't be together. Still, I only feel whole when I torture myself with the unattainable possibility."

In the midst of all of these strange topics, there's one question that begs the loudest. "How did your parents die?"

"Two of Chase's minions killed them. Twins."

"Meat heads," I say, remembering the guys from my dream.

"Yeah," he says, looking off, a sad smile on his face. "You're really plugged in, aren't you?"

"Lucid dreaming makes for a good channel." I'm not sure why I cross the distance, but I do until we're only separated by two feet.

"The Voyageurs wanted to know how to dream travel into the Institute," Aiden says.

"Your parents wouldn't tell them?"

"No. They knew that that piece of information would endanger everyone."

"Why didn't they just dream travel away? Escape?"

"My father was a Middling. Yeah, I'm a mutt." Aiden laughs, like this is a funny moment. "Definitely no royal blood in me. My father was one of the US government employees who first worked here. Later, he was the only Middling who stayed. He'd fallen in love with Mom and Flynn let him stay, but it meant it was difficult to leave which is why I was raised here. They had taken a rare vacation away, leaving me with Mae. That's when the Voyageurs took them. Tortured them....Killed them."

Reflexively, I take his hand in mine. He grips it back.

"And your mother stayed with your father? She didn't dream travel away?"

"No," he says at once, like the idea was preposterous. "I don't think she could bear to live without him. No two people were more

157

connected than my parents. Their love is what made this science department what it is today."

"So that's why you love your work so much," I state, the idea crashing down on me like blocks, followed by a rainstorm of guilt.

He nods, a beautiful pain in his eyes.

"I'm sorry I ever asked you to sacrifice this all for me," I say, sweeping my arm around, gesturing at his lab.

He clutches my fingers with a new intensity. Pulls my hand closer to him. "You're the only reason I've ever considered losing anything."

"But you have to stop torturing yourself. I'm not worth it." I squeeze his hand once and let go.

"I'm afraid I can't make that promise," Aiden says, plucking my bracelet from the counter. He grabs my hand, clamping my bracelet on my wrist. His thumb presses into my palm before he lets go. "My parents taught me about two things: science and love. Neither will I forget so easily."

Chapter Twenty-Eight

The button is under my finger when Joseph's angry voice gives me pause. "I can't give you what you want, don't you see that!? You're just wasting your time!"

A cold chuckle. "Asking you to be who you are is a waste of time, huh?" Trent says. "Get back to me in a few years and let me know how *that* worked out for you."

Joseph and I are scheduled to meet in this classroom to train privately, since we don't want anyone to know we're planning on fighting Zhuang. What's Trent doing here?

"It's so easy for you to pass judgment on me, isn't it? You've done what I can't do, but I remember when you were just as insecure about people knowin' you're gay."

I know it's wrong to eavesdrop. Pressing my ear more firmly to the door I bury my conscience under my own curiosity.

"Yeah, it was last month. I'm not acting all high and mighty. All I'm asking is for you to do the same thing. I'm telling you that it makes you feel better. You drop the act and along with it the weight of all the pressure."

"Right, and how 'bout all those people who whisper when you enter the main hall?"

"They're whispering because they're girls who can't have me anymore, men who are glad I'm no longer competition, or guys who are interested. That's why they're whispering."

"You're ridiculous," Joseph laughs, sounding half amused and half irritated.

"But you know I'm not interested in anyone else, don't you?"

"I can't give you what you want," Joseph enunciates each word.

"But you want to, don't you?" There's a small plea in Trent's voice.

"What I want and what I have to do are incongruent. Sometimes you don't get to be who you are."

His words make my heart feel stale, like a piece of bread left out, easily crumbled into bits.

"Don't you see that everyone's going to accept you no matter what? People here don't care about that kind of thing, and everybody's already totally endeared to you."

"Maybe they used to be, but I spoiled my reputation."

"Nobody knows about that."

"No, they just know I disappeared and when I returned I looked as wasted away as a drug addict. I hear the rumors. My mystery is the only thing preservin' my ego at this point."

"Damn it, Joe! Why does everything always have to be about you!?"

"Because this is about me and all the stupid things I do. We wouldn't be having this fight if I kept my mouth shut," Joseph says, regret billowing from his words.

"You think I didn't know that you loved me before you said it!?"

"I think I gave you the wrong impression when I did. I made you think we have a future."

"And why don't we?"

"Because I can't risk anyone finding out."

I jump from a sudden loud crash against the wall. "To hell with everyone else already!"

"Damn…gettin' in an argument with a telekinetic is dangerous," Joseph says, sounding strangely impressed.

"I wasn't aiming at you."

"Well, you're gonna have to pick that chair up."

Something scrapes along the wall. The noise is followed by a soft thud. "There," Trent says dully.

"While you're at it, you mind sendin' my drink over here? I don't feel like gettin' up."

"Can you just be serious for one minute?"

"Ha!" Joseph says without enthusiasm. "That coming from you is hilarious."

"Look, Joe, if you can't do what I've asked then stay away from me. That's my level-headed request and I'm not budging on it."

Joseph laughs like Trent just told a joke. "So you really think we should go public about our relationship?" Another laugh.

"Yes."

"T, I'm a shadow to my sister and a disgrace to my father. Why would you want that?"

"Because...you're the only person who's ever owned my attention. Accosted it unfairly. And here I stand asking you to love me back. It's all I want."

"I told you this was a waste of time. I can't give you what you want."

Silence. Hurried footsteps. I take three quick steps back and drop to the floor, pretending to tie my shoe. "Oh hey, Trent," I say when he enters the hallway.

A fake smile layers over the anguish I saw initially. "Well, hey there, Roya. Tell me, when you and Joe were in the womb, did he hoard most of the space? That's what I'd expect from a selfish jerk."

"You know, he probably did, but my memories as a fetus are kind of fuzzy."

He pats me on the shoulder as he passes. "Few have the wit to keep up with me. In another life, Roya, I'll make you mine."

"Well, then I'm going to start believing in reincarnation right now," I sing, walking into the classroom and shutting the door behind me.

"How much you hear?" Joseph says, not looking up. Arms crossed, leaning against the far wall.

"Hear what?" I know it's absurd to try and lie to Joseph, but what the hell.

"You've never been late a day in your life. It's five after."

"Well, I didn't much think that barging in was a good idea— like you did to George and me the other day."

"I wish you would have interrupted. That would have saved me."

"Saved you from what? Yourself?"

"Oh, so you think I'm being heartless too?"

"I think you're a chicken, and you're going to only hurt yourself and the people you love if you keep down this path," I say.

"You make it sound all tragic. That stuff you read makes you as brooding as a hen clucking after laying an egg."

"And you're so stubborn you can teach a pit bull a thing or two." I close the distance between us, yanking one of Joseph's arms down so they're no longer tied across his chest. "You don't stand in my shadow. It's because of you that I can do anything of great significance. Actually, it's because of you that I survived the Grotte and didn't become Chase's concubine."

"Well, while all that's true, it's not the perception of the people around this place."

"For the life me I can't figure out why you give a damn what others think."

"And sometimes I look at you with your ratty little ponytail and apathetic attitude and wonder how you don't give *more* of a damn."

"People either like you or they don't. And honestly, what other people think about me really isn't my concern."

"You know, it's probably your unlikability that makes everyone adore you so much. People love a challenge. Maybe I should try it and see if it works," Joseph says.

"Just try being yourself. That would, no doubt, win over every person in a ten-mile radius."

"Only ten?"

"And you're not a disgrace to Trey."

"Roya, how about you resurrect the man who's gonna kill our father and get back to me on that opinion."

I want to hug Joseph. Tell him that no matter what he does he can't lose my love, but a dull pain in my chest waylays my attention. To feel someone else's pain so acutely has a unique discomfort.

"Are we gonna train or would you like to spend the rest of the day berating me?" Joseph says.

"I'm not meaning to berate you."

"Nah, you're trying to help. I get it," Joseph says, defeated. "Well, we'd better get started or we'll be late for dinner with Trey."

"What?!"

"Oh, yeah, I meant to tell you, he invited us to dinner tonight," he says casually, like giving me the weather forecast.

"Where? The main hall? Chuck E. Cheese?"

"Nope."

"Well, is he finally taking us to McDonald's for an overdue Happy Meal?"

"Nope." Joseph smiles for the first time since I entered the room.

"I give up."

"He's hosting us in his private quarters," Joseph says proudly.

"Oh, gag."

"Come on, Roya. That's rude."

162

"Do I have to be there? Can't you make up some excuse for me like I'm hormonal and not fit for company?"

"That's not a made-up excuse," Joseph laughs and ducks from the hand targeted at his head. "It won't be so bad, so just try and have a positive perspective."

"Fine, however, if you're too beat up from sparring to attend dinner then I don't have to go either."

"Don't you worry 'bout that. I'll go even with a broken limb."

"Why?" I ask, befuddled.

"Because I like spendin' time with him," Joseph says in a rush.

"Oh God, you've been spending time together? What do you two do? Play catch? Collect stamps? Snipe hunt?"

"We talk," he says. "He's actually an easy person to talk to. He listens."

"I listen," I say, instantly offended.

"Yeah, but you're different. You're in my head. Sometimes it's nice to have a more objective listener."

"Well, now I really don't understand how you'd think Trey sees you as a disgrace. If he did, he wouldn't make the effort to spend time with you."

"Yeah, I hope you're right," Joseph says with a sigh.

Chapter Twenty-Nine

"Maybe we should have brought something." Joseph says, staring at Trey's door like it's made of crystal.

"What, like apple cider?" I ask.

"I dunno." He raps at the door three times.

"I brought attitude. Will that do?"

Joseph narrows his eyes. "Try and behave yourself."

"I'll do no such thing. If you don't like it then I'll be leaving." Seizing my golden opportunity I whip around and trot back down the Head Official's rooming hallway, which was left open for us.

"Not so fast," Joseph sings, jerking me by the wrist.

"Everything all right?" Trey asks from the open door.

Joseph's face flushes red. "Yeah, Roya was just gonna run back and get the apple cider she forgot."

"Although a thoughtful gesture, it's not necessary," Trey says to me, a cynical surprise on his face.

"Then I won't worry about fetching the hash brownies Joseph made either," I say, striding past my brother and into Trey's quarters.

"What?!" Joseph startles behind me. "I made no such thing."

"Well, he was going to, but he used up all the ingredients," I say, swiveling my head over my shoulder in time to catch the look of humiliation on Joseph's face.

Trey shakes his head, amusement hemming his turquoise eyes. "I know when she lies too, don't worry," he says, giving Joseph a consoling pat on the back.

What's that supposed to mean? Have I lied to Trey? Probably.

I turn back around, busying myself, studying Trey's living quarters, which are as expansive as a penthouse apartment. The hallway spills out into an oval-shaped living area complete with an oversized dark brown leather sofa, a six-candlestick chandelier wrapped in rope, curved bookshelves that line every single wall, and two doorways on either side of the room. Vintage books and colorful objects fill the shelves. My feet bring me to the nearest bookcase, my fingertips about to clutch an ancient copy of *The Merchant of Venice*.

"How about you follow me in here?" Trey says behind me.

Sliding my finger down the spine of the book, I turn, disappointed. "Sure."

He strolls through one of the doorways and into a dining area, dimly lit by a few wall sconces. A large glass tabletop sits on a stunted column. Draped across it is a chain like one that might be used on a Navy ship. Each link is as large as my head. The far wall is adorned with a single tapestry. Woven into the shell-colored linen is a neat symmetrical pattern in a rich shade of bark brown.

"It's an endless knot," Trey says, spying what drew in my attention. He appears to be interested in watching my reactions to the various accoutrements embellishing his living space. "In Tibetan Buddhism it symbolizes eternal love since it has no beginning and no end."

"You said before you were raised by Tibetan monks," I say, remembering the disclosure when he gave me the statue of Achi Chokyi Drolma. It was on the morning of the day he informed us he was our father. Our birthday. "Why was that?"

"My mother, your grandmother, died in childbirth. Flynn had help raising me for a few years but then he became busy trying to establish the Institute. I think for him it made sense for me to live away."

"So there's a pattern in the family of sending children to be raised by other people?" I say with a morbid laugh.

"Roya." I hate when he says my name in that reprimanding tone. "Flynn's priority was always the Institute. I didn't resent him for that, it was just a fact. And my priority has always been you and Joseph."

"You have a funny way of showing it," I say, shaking one of those ship in a bottle things I found on a nearby shelf.

Trey plucks it from my hands with an irritated look. "What is it that you want from me?"

"I don't know," I say, slumping into a giant chair that's so high-backed it looks fit for a giraffe to sit in. "I'm obviously not getting it."

"Clearly you're unhappy with me," Trey says.

"Flynn must have cared and made you a priority if he was willing to terminate his partnership with Pierre in order to protect you and Eloise," I say.

"I was always a priority, but Flynn was a born leader and knew the sacrifices it took to secure peace. He also knew the children Elle and I bore would go on to do great things because he was a clairvoyant, as has been everyone in our family."

"Oh." *Just another pawn in this great arms race among the Dream Travelers.* "You said before that you visited us every day…"

"Every day," Trey confirms.

"Well, I'm curious about two things," I say. "How did you choose our fake families and when they proved to be a poor match why did you leave us there?"

A long sigh falls from Trey's mouth. "Right. In hindsight I made mistakes. At the time I thought that both homes were good choices, but with time the reasons I picked them disappeared. Joseph, the mother in your family died, changing the entire dynamic of the home. Roya, you were simply unaccepted because unlike Joseph you're not as good at pretending you're a Middling." Trey's forehead creases as he stares at nothing. "The problem was that by the time these problems inside the households surfaced, you'd already been there for too long. Removing you would have created all sorts of confusion. You were both seven at the time that your family life became neglectful. I don't think it was coincidence either."

Trey takes a seat in an identical chair beside mine. Joseph's doing a ridiculous job of trying to act natural as he props his elbow on a high sideboard. He's eyeing an antique globe and I sense he badly wants to rotate it on its axis, but is too nervous to touch it. Trey watches him for a few seconds before turning back to me. "Have you ever wondered about your name, Roya? It's unique."

"It means dream," I say tediously. I looked up the significance years ago, since neither of my fake parents had any clue.

"Yes, I gave it to you. Elle named you, Joseph," Trey says, indicating my brother. "She was raised Christian and loved the teachings from the Bible although later she abandoned her religion."

"Why?" he asks, curiosity dripping in his tone.

"She believed, much the same way I do, that stories are for the inspiration, but true faith comes from within. The stories from the Bible or any other religion are meant to guide and teach. The Bible or Koran or Bhagavad Gita are not faith. They're stories of faith. Elle didn't need Christianity just the same way I didn't need

Buddhism anymore. They were foundations, but we had risen to new levels of awareness." Trey focuses on me, his head inclined slightly. "I think I told you before, Roya, one religion isn't enough for me. I need multiple philosophies to navigate."

Strange doesn't even begin to explain how peculiar it feels to be sitting in Trey's dining room and discussing religion like it's something we do every Sunday evening. It's no doubt going to take years for my present reality to not feel surreal. This silver-haired man who has the demeanor of an army general and the attitude of a laissez-faire monk is supposed be our father. The idea continues to hit the wall of my brain like a ball of silly putty.

"Are you guys hungry?" Trey asked.

Joseph looks to me, like I'm supposed to answer.

"Sure," I say with a shrug.

"All right, well, I'll fetch dinner and be right back," Trey says, exiting through another doorway on the far side of the room.

Now that I'm free to peruse, I allow my eyes to wander around the room, studying every detail. Burlap fabric ripples in sections across the walls, but it doesn't entirely hide the stainless steel behind it, indicative to the Institute. It peeks out in places where the burlap must make room for a metal filament sconce or a piece of artwork.

On the main wall is a large iron wheel that looks like a gear that would drive a gigantic machine. I want to run my fingers across this piece, but I don't really feel like leaving the comfort of the oversized chair. The whole room is rustic and masculine, but feels warm and sensitive with its multiple curves. It's understated, yet complex and intellectually intriguing.

Carrying two large round platters, Trey walks into the room and sets them on the table.

"I hope you two like Indian food," he says, encouraging us to take a seat at the table. "That's what I've ordered. It's my favorite."

It's my favorite too, but I'm not divulging that.

"I don't think I've ever had it," Joseph says frankly.

"Well, this will be fun," Trey says, handing us both large plates.

The food is done thali style. Rice, chutney, dal vegetables, yogurt, and a few entrees are served in small metal bowls. Along with them are layers of naan smothered in oil and garlic.

My mouth salivates at once. Rich curry spices waft up from the bowls, enticing me with their distinct aromas. I wait until Trey hands me a bowl of vegetable korma before moving an inch.

"Go ahead," he encourages. With that we begin the procession of passing around the various bowls and spooning the contents onto our plates.

"So tell me," Trey says, feigning a casual tone, "how have things been going?"

I have absolutely no idea how to answer that question. I do what's expected of me and defer to Joseph. Predictably, he grins and starts in on a long explanation about how at home he's feeling at the Institute.

Trey nods and listens thoughtfully. I eat. Joseph makes sure that the conversation throughout dinner is never quiet or uncomfortable and I'm grateful for that, because I'm both.

When I've had my fill of curried vegetables and saag aloo I push back from the thick glass table and take a long drink of lemon water.

"I want to thank both of you for joining me tonight." Trey looks at me only briefly before turning his attention on Joseph, who is no doubt much more receptive to Trey's attempts at eye contact. "I know things aren't easy between us and I don't have any illusions about our future relationships. I just want to do what feels right, and giving us an opportunity to spend time together makes sense."

I pretend to be fascinated by the dirty fork lying on my plate.

"Thanks for having us over," Joseph says in a cheerful voice, one I instantly despise. "I'm grateful for the opportunity to be here."

"Joseph, you're just like Elle," Trey says, a strange fondness in his usual rigid tone. He wads up his napkin and lays it on his plate. "The things you say are just like the things she'd say. Your mother was outgoing like you. She could entertain a room with her charm and humble sweetness."

A grin like I've never seen spreads across Joseph's face, lighting up every corner of it. "I'm glad to hear that I got it from her," Joseph beams. "For the longest time I thought I'd inherited it from my prized pig, Betsy."

I roll my eyes. "You never had a prized pig."

"Thanks very much for calling me out, Stark" Joseph says, still wearing the silly smile. "If I did have one, that's what she'd be named. And I did think that I got my personality from our pigs because they were cool and fun."

"I know something you got from the pigs," I say, pushing my plate away.

"Roya, I'm sorry to tell you this, but…" Trey stares at me for a moment under the dim flickering of the sconce lights. "You're actually exactly like me."

Abrupt laughter erupts from Joseph. To my disbelief Trey joins him. I've never heard him laugh and it makes him almost appear human. He covers his mouth, but I still spy the humor in Trey's eyes.

"It's kind of scary," he says. "You and I are almost identical in our mood and demeanor. I swear I know half the time how you'll react and I almost always agree with your response."

I don't dare respond, just continue to look at him like he's trying to sell me a constellation in a distant galaxy. After a few seconds he pushes up from the table. "That's exactly the reaction I expected from you."

Joseph laughs again, the stupid grin looking to be a permanent fixture on his face.

"I have something for both of you," Trey says, a new lightness in his voice. He heads back toward the main living room. "If you would, please follow me."

As soon as I set foot back in this room I'm glad. It makes me feel warm and I desperately want hours alone in here to comb through all the contents. Trey marches off to the opposite wall. This gives me the opportunity to inspect the items on a nearby shelf. Immediately my attention is pulled in by a pair of pink ballet slippers. Something odd runs over my skin, a reaction I've had a few times when encountering objects around the Institute.

"Those," I say, pointing at them, "they were in my closet in the fifth task for the competition to become Zhuang's challenger. The one where I had to choose the object of most importance."

Trey gives a look of surprise. "Were they? Well, that's interesting."

"This isn't the only time I've encountered an object from the closet." I say, remembering the bizarre rush of familiarity I felt the first time I saw the frequency adjuster. "Why is that?"

Trey snatches two objects before spinning back around. "Those objects in your closet were projections from your future. This is some of Aiden's newest technology, and we only allowed him to use it for that task. It's something he'd been working on for a while and wanted to test out, and that seemed like the perfect time. When you came through the GAD-C he captured a sample of your DNA. I'm not well versed in the specifics, but he used this to get a reading of over fifty objects that would come into your possession in the future. Honestly, I find the technology to be a little mind-boggling, and have serious concerns about its usefulness." He eyes the slippers, his expression serious, yet pleasant. "It sounds like one day you'll inherit these slippers."

"Damn," Joseph says with a whistle. "Aiden is wicked smart."

"There's no debating that," Trey says, an edge of irritation in his voice.

Joseph flashes me a curious expression. He caught it too. "Ew, has the golden scientist gotten in trouble?"

Trey shakes his head, dismissing Joseph's curious question. I bury everything related to Aiden six feet deep.

"Here." Trey holds out his hand to me. "This belonged to Elle and I want you to have it."

I hesitate before reaching out and letting him drop a cold, oval object into my palm. It's a polished, green egg-like stone and I instantly like the way it easily fits in my hand.

"What is it?" I ask.

"Jade," he replies, taking a seat on the chesterfield-style sofa. "This is a good time to give you a bit of family history."

Joseph takes a seat on the opposite side of the sofa. I remain standing.

"Your mother's family were known for their telepathic powers. Not only that, but like many Dream Travelers from the Founders' lineage, your mother had multiple abilities. One of those was she could control the forces of the Earth."

Trey pauses, gauging my reaction. Feeling too unnerved by the strangeness of his eyes, I take a seat in an armchair just to have a reason to move my body.

"You'll remember," he continues, "that you were able to control the wind in the Grotte?"

I nod.

"I had no trouble believing that during your debriefing," Trey says. "It's part of your lineage. Your mother could make the earth buckle underneath someone if she chose. However, being raised by Pierre, she often feared her powers and that she would use them for corrupt reasons. Jade often represents balance and peace, and for this reason Elle kept this stone close to her."

Trey turns and faces Joseph. "Elle could control the earth. I control water, and Roya the wind. I believe that when properly motivated you could control fire. It makes sense, but I have no way to affirm this notion."

Joseph swallows hard and I feel the tension and excitement in him.

Trey extends his other hand, which has been firmly clenched around an object. Joseph holds out his hand, just as I had done but with less reluctance. Softly Trey drops a seemingly heavy and shiny object into his palm. "This belonged to your grandfather." Trey sounds suddenly tired, or is it emotional? It's hard to tell in the faint lighting of the chandelier overhead. "This was his protective charm and I want you to have it."

Suddenly I feel Joseph's agonizing guilt. It's a sharp blade on his skin. Fire touching ice. Light on an unexposed photograph. Trey has no idea that his words are further destroying Joseph in ways that can't be repaired. Joseph doesn't close his fingers around the silver pocket watch, but rather keeps them splayed out, ensuring the object touches the least amount of his skin.

"No one was more practical than Flynn," Trey says. "Sometimes I wonder if Elle would still be with us if she'd been more practical. You see, your mother reacted with emotions to everything and it was what I loved about her, but probably what got her killed in the end. I'm giving this to you, Joseph, because you're so much like your mother and I hope that you steal a little of your grandfather's practicality and therefore avoid the same mistakes as Elle." He studies Joseph, who has recently vaulted away his expression under a mask of stone. "Why don't you take it for now and you can always give it back if you decide."

My voice slowly finds energy and rises out of my lungs. "How and why did our mother die?"

"That," Trey says, holding up one finger, "is a good question and one I expected to hear from you tonight, Roya." He stands, peering down at me. I instinctively know the conversation is over. "I'm not going to give you the answer to this question tonight. I actually want you to receive the information from the person who was there and witnessed it firsthand. Ren will expect you in his office first thing in the morning."

Chapter Thirty

"Ren?" I say as we exit Trey's quarters.

"Yeah, that's going to keep me up most the night with questions." Joseph's brow is wrinkled with confusion.

Stricken by a memory I slap Joseph across the shoulder.

"Ouch!" he says, grabbing his arm. "Why'd you do that?"

"I just remembered something."

"Next time, just tell me. No hitting."

"Be quiet," I say, holding my hand up to silence him. "When I was first practicing with George, we were trying to determine if the sensor would allow him to read emotions remotely. Anyway, I accidentally encountered Ren and…"

"Don't stop there," Joseph urges.

I scratch my head, trying to remember the exact memory. "George sensed that Ren had guilt and shame, but that he didn't feel he deserved to bear this wound." I close my eyes, searching for the phrase, the one that struck me so oddly at the time.

"What! Keep going!" Joseph says, gripping both my arms. "What else did George read?"

I snap my eyes open, the memory echoing inside me suddenly. "Ren was tired of blaming himself for what went wrong. He was sorry she was dead. And it made him suffer."

"And you think that's about our mother?"

I shake my head with doubt. "Maybe. If it was any normal person, I'd say yes without a hesitation, but who knows how many people Ren's watched die."

"Man, that's morbid, Stark."

"Welcome to the life of a Lucidite," I sing, turning to continue down the hallway just as Aiden rounds the corner, most likely headed for his own room.

"Hey," he says, a surprised smile flashing on his face.

"Hey." I freeze, studying him for entirely too long. The only thing that makes me feel better is he's doing the same thing, his eyes roaming over my face trying to uncover something.

"What are you doing in my neck of the woods?" he asks, not taking his intense eyes off me. I silently wish he never would and then chastise myself for the thought.

"Visiting dear ol' Dad," I say, pointing over my shoulder at Trey's door.

"Oh, I see." Aiden fidgets with his keycard.

"Well, we'd stay and chat but I don't want to," Joseph says, tugging me down the short hallway.

Without saying goodbye I allow myself to be led away. "So, Stark," Joseph says, draping his arm across my shoulder, "do you need a chaperone for dream travel tonight? I'm free."

"No, after everything we just learned, I'm old-fashioned dreaming tonight—and by that I mean intense lucid dreaming to keep a certain psychopath out of my head." I swivel my head just before we leave the hallway to find Aiden still standing there staring at me.

I give him a half smile.

"You're being really tough on him," Joseph criticizes as we stride back to our rooms.

"No I'm not, Aiden know—"

"Not Aiden, you thick brick," Joseph says with a laugh. "I was referring to Trey."

"Oh, what do you expect? Do you really think we're all going to Disney World on vacation and everything is just going to be easy peasy from this point forward? That's unrealistic, Joseph."

"If you want people to change or to prove themselves, you have to give them a chance."

"Who said I want anything out of this?" I look at him coldly.

"Roya, everyone wants love. Don't act like you're some special exception."

"Trey said it himself," I reason. "I'm like him. He gets I'm standoffish. That's just the way things are going to be between us. Get used to it."

"You should also give yourself a chance to change."

"Is that what you're trying to do? Are you trying to change who you are?" I say, the implications cruel, but also true.

"No, I stopped tryin' to do that," Joseph says, a sad smile flicking to his lips. "I'm just tryin' to come to terms with who I am."

"Well, I can't argue with you there."

"So does George know?" Joseph says out of the blue.

"Know what?"

He leans down and whispers in my ear. "That you still harbor feelings for—"

"Shut up," I say, putting distance between us. "And no, he doesn't."

"Be careful. Hearts will break and you'll be the one convicted of the crime. I know from experience that the sentence is excruciatingly long and undignified for such a thing."

"Would you mind keeping your love advice to yourself?"

"Just one last piece of advice," he says, offering me his pinky. "Promise."

I slap his hand away with a sigh.

"Pops appears kinda peeved at Livingston right now. I pretend not to like the Head Scientist, but he's actually pretty top notch in my book. So do him a favor and don't get him in any more trouble."

"What? How would I...I'm with George."

"Right, right, right," Joseph says, throwing his hands up in surrender. "I'm obviously misreading the situation. Forget everything I said."

♦

I start my lucid dream the same way I've been doing almost every night: on the glossy, green hill. The oak tree is taller than a two-story house. Stars wink at me in the inky purple sky. I stand staring out at nothing, waiting for my subconscious to paint images into my dream, transport me to a new location, and bring in its messages.

Six feet away Aiden appears, wearing the clothes I just saw him in. Everything about him is as perfect as I always remember it.

He looks around, taking in the hill, its tree, my stars. "Nice location, but it's missing something."

I step forward and then have the idea to encircle him, pinning a playful smile on my face. "Oh really, what would that be?"

He snaps his fingers and music plays from invisible speakers. I recognize the band immediately from my iPod. Finger Eleven. Its beat has assorted effects on me. He turns as I stalk the perimeter encircling him, an unsteady smile on his face.

"Although I love being your prey," he says when I complete the first circle around him, "I was hoping that you'd dance with me."

I click my tongue at him. "This is my dream, and that sounds like something *you'd* want to do."

He lowers his head, seduction written in his eyes. "Get over here," he commands, a firm smile gracing his lips.

Bes appears to be working because this definitely isn't a nightmare. I step forward and take the hand extended to me. Aiden spins me around, yanks me to him. "Dance with me," he says, moving to the beat.

"I'm not sure I know how," I say. "Show me."

He nods, not taking his enticing eyes off me. Gingerly his hands park on either side of my hips, moving them in time with his, our bodies not quite touching.

"Good," he whispers in my ear. One of his hands slides to my back, the other takes my hand raising it above my head just as the song ramps up. My shoulders have now found a movement that complements that of my hips. I bite my lip, moving my head side to side, eyes pinned on him. He releases my hand and I instantly wrap both arms around his neck, pulling him down as we move. He's so close our noses touch, our eyes locked together.

"This is definitely no nightmare," I whisper, almost against his mouth.

"You said that out loud," he says.

"It's a dream, it doesn't matter."

A knowing smile quivers on his long lips. "Then I beseech you to say whatever you want," he says, threading his fingers into one of my hands and spinning me around again, pulling me back to him.

Unable to resist any longer I tug him by the shirt down to my mouth. A familiarity I've missed surges through me. His hand knots in the fabric of my shirt at my back. Still moving to the beat he kisses me, his teeth raking against my lip in a deliciously hurt-good way. His lips taste exactly as I remember, salty and sweet, electrifying everything inside me. Transporting me. Nothing feels like Aiden. Nothing ever could. And my imagination knows him so well. Even in dreams.

His kisses speed up, a more fervent desire building inside him moment by moment. And BAM! Something strikes me, like a bolt of lightning. It doesn't hurt, but the realization that accompanies it sends me scrambling out of his arms, breaking an embrace I've wanted for so long.

"I don't…I don't know this song," I stutter, every part of me trembling as I piece this altogether. "And you…" I say, pointing at him with my eyes. Aiden stares at me with a knowing sideways smile. When he kissed me, touched me, it felt exactly the same way it did when Chase invaded my dream. "You're really in my dream aren't you?" I accuse, heat in my words.

"Yes, and you're in mine." He steps in close, his breath against my skin again. "You want this," he says, with pleased surprise.

I step back, the effort followed by a ping in my chest. "Aiden, this isn't right. You shouldn't have invaded my dream."

"I couldn't help myself. God knows I've had to resist you too many times lately."

"This is wrong though. You know the deal." My fingertips touch my lips, like I can still feel his kiss on them. "You kissed me. You know—"

"I didn't break our deal," he says, a clever look in his eyes that threatens every ounce of my inhibitions. "And you kissed me back, quite a lot actually."

"Aiden, stop!"

"Fine, if you truly don't want me here then Ren taught you how to make me go away. Do it, but I'm not going anywhere."

My face finds my hands. "I can't keep doing this." I raise my head, my voice too loud in the quiet night's air of my dream, the song having ended a minute ago.

"Doing what?" he says, acting innocent. "You're not doing anything. Dreams aren't real, just brilliant manifestations of our imaginations and currently we're just sharing one of those."

"But this feels real. And we're choosing what we say, and…what we do."

"Yes, but if you cut me I'll awake with no marks. It's not real in the physical sense or like when we dream travel. Only our imaginations."

"Still, this will only make things harder."

"It couldn't be any harder," he says in a calloused voice. "Roya, if you want to leave then do it. And if you don't then stay."

All I have to do is have a single thought, strengthened by a solid intention, and Aiden will disappear. Be locked out of my subconscious. I can wake myself up if I want. Change the scenery. The possibilities of how to force him away from me are endless. And yet I don't do anything, just stare at Aiden knowing the longer I stay willingly the more guilt I'll have later. And at the same time, the idea of leaving feels wrong deep in my soul.

"This isn't real, Roya. It's all a shared imagination. A dream we're both having together," he says, like he senses my conflicting tensions.

I dream all the time, and my dreams never change my waking life. They may stick in my being, haunt me with crisp images and make me question the true nature of my subconscious—but they don't change anything in my reality.

The same song from before interrupts the silence. Its unrelenting beat is congruent to my reckless desire. Aiden snatches my hand, hazarding a smile. "What's it going to be? One more dance?"

I tug my hand back to me, drawing him in with it. He glides forward until he's against me, his expression echoing my emotions.

♦

In a shared dream Aiden and I danced and laughed for hours. We cuddled in the grass, him pinning imagined flowers in my hair. We talked, easily coasting from one topic to the next. Each one made me more amazed by his humble brilliance. And he listened to me the way he always does, with amused awe. Often words didn't come out quickly enough before I was struck by another inspiring idea that steered my thoughts and the conversation in a different direction. Never before had I been gifted with so much uninterrupted time with him and it confirmed something that I'd been denying. As soon as it popped into my brain, exploding my bubble, I rolled over on my stomach, propping myself up on my elbows.

"I kept thinking that we didn't really have enough in common. That our series of brief encounters meant everything I felt was just an infatuation," I said, picking grass out of the earth and tearing it into tinier pieces. He rolled over on his stomach, the same as me, our shoulders touching.

"And now what?" he asked with anticipation, waiting to feast on my answer.

"Now I know why I always came away from every encounter with you longing for more," I say. "My instinct draws me to you, not because we're compatible, but because we're..."

"Entangled," he said, pulling the leaf of grass from my fingers, bringing my attention straight to him.

The smile I gave him was wobbly, all wrong for the moment. "Yeah."

"Why do you sound so heartbroken?"

"You know why," I said, interlacing my fingers in his.

"I can wake up right now. I can go to your room, slip into your bed, and kiss you in the flesh, cementing the deal. And since I'm a man of my word, in the morning I'll go to your father to tell him that I'm inescapably in love with his daughter."

At the thought I stir away from him, sitting up suddenly. "No, Aiden, you can't do that. You can never risk your parents' legacy for me."

"What if it's what I want? What if it's what they would have wanted for me?"

"Look, I think you've always been right. Trey isn't going to have a favorable reaction to us being together. And lately he's weirdly protective of me and I don't know how to force another way."

"But Roya—"

"I got the impression tonight that he's not thoroughly happy with you," I said, hating that I had to bring this up to prove my point.

Aiden made a sound of frustration. "Trey thinks I dabble in too many projects. He doesn't always see my vision and we butt heads about what technology would best suit the needs of the Institute."

I nodded, his admission erasing all hope in my being. "And all he'd need is a little motivation to choose a Head Scientist more compatible with his mission for the Institute." A stale silence hung between us. Inside my head the opposing parts of this debate battled, neither gaining an advantage, but the raw reality was still clear. "I don't know enough about Trey and I definitely can't trust him to do what I want. He's got his own idea of how things should be done, which is why he's made so many bizarre choices in my life. I can't let you risk everything you've worked for, for us."

"This is important though. It's torturing me that we can't be together. It's not the decision I want to make anymore."

"Well, I think you'd be more tortured if you lost your position."

"You're wrong. As Dream Travelers we're guaranteed a hundred years of good health. I know without a single doubt I will spend every one of those loving you. And my curse is that I'll increasingly love you more with each year that passes. That's more torturous than losing my job," he said with a brutal honesty in his eyes that made my soul ache.

I have died a hundred times waiting for Aiden, only to watch him turn away from our love. And I have been reborn a hundred and one times by a single look from him. And here I stand at this altar asking to transplant my heart, so I don't die another death.

"I won't let you go to Trey. There's too much at stake."

"Roya, you can't stop me. And I'm tired—"

"Look, Aiden, there's no future for us in the waking world. I'm with George, okay?"

He clenched his eyes shut. "And that's what you want?"

"That's how it is. And it's not changing," I said, breaking both our hearts by stringing the words together that would block him, protect him.

"In the morning nothing will have changed for me."

"This isn't real, Aiden," I said, standing, backing away from him. "It's just the imaginations of two people. I can cut you right now, remember? And you'll awake without a mark."

"After tonight I'll awake with a mark, I promise you that."

Chapter Thirty-One

"Why does Aiden keep looking at you?" George asks, stirring cereal which went soggy a while ago. "His shield is up, but something in his expression is failing to hide a heightened interest in you today."

Luckily I'm shielding partial emotions, only feeding George what I want him to know. "I have no idea," I say, not daring to look in Aiden's direction.

I awoke last night and spent the rest of the time finishing *Love in the Time of Cholera*, thinking it would take my mind off what I'd just done. It didn't.

"But Aiden knows we're together, right?"

"I have no idea what he knows," I say, looking at George, tucking my chin close to my shoulder and feigning disinterest in the conversation.

"Well, there's one way to solve this," George says, leaning into me, pausing an inch from my lips. "And this should stop the staring as well," George says, cupping my chin and softly kissing me three times. I return the affection, not knowing how else to react. Easing back, George's eyes glow with satisfaction. "I believe that worked," he whispers, his breath catching on my lips.

I dare to flick my gaze up to see Aiden storming out of the main hall, his strides reeking with urgency. I can only imagine how devastating it is for him to witness that act of affection after the things we said last night. But this is what's best for him. And that's what I want.

George gives me a cautious look. "Do you still want *this,* Roya?" He motions between the two of us. "Because right now, I get the impression your heart is still divided."

"But what do you feel from me?" I ask, not answering the question.

"I feel you want us to be together."

"And don't you trust my emotions?"

"Explicitly."

"Good," I say, leaning my head on his shoulder. I wish *I* could trust my emotions. Again it's weird to seek comfort from George because Aiden and I have hurt each other.

George grips my hand under the table and kisses the top of my head. "I love you, Roya."

I squeeze his hand a little tighter, pulling my head back up.

"Hey, I'm curious, did you know that Joseph is..." I say, knowing I don't need to finish the sentence.

First disappointment falls on George's face, followed by resignation. "Oh yeah, that."

That's not what he was hoping was going to come out of my mouth next. But he's patient and for that I feel I should be even more endeared to him.

"Yes, I knew," he says, pulling both our hands up so they're resting on the table together.

"Since when?"

"Since I met him."

"Oh," I say in quiet surprise. "You're a vault."

He gives a solemn nod.

"Does he love Trent?"

George looks at me sideways, giving me that familiar stern look.

"It's okay," I say. "I know you can't tell—"

"The only person Joseph truly allows himself to love is you," he interrupts. "You're safe and not going to break his heart. Although his worst fear is outliving you."

George has done something rare just now. He's revealed someone else's emotions. "Thanks for the disclosure, George."

"You're the only person I've ever wanted to share everything I feel with. Unburden myself to. But by doing that I'd only put unnecessary stress on you."

"Always the selfless one, aren't you, my sweet George," I say, rising from the table. "I've got to actually go and find Joseph now. We have a meeting with Ren."

I lean down and give him a peck. I'm not sure why, but once he kissed me publicly a few minutes ago, it put an expectation into place between us. And besides, the more people who see, the more who talk, the further away I'll push Aiden.

182

I'm almost to the elevators when he calls my name at my back.

"Roya," Trey says, in that reprimanding tone that's quickly becoming overused.

I whip around, fixing a puzzled look on Trey. "What can I do for you?" I say, pretending I didn't hear the sharp edge in his voice.

To my shock, he grabs me by the forearm and pulls me around the corner, to the less trafficked hallway leading away from the main hall. "George's display in the main hall just now wasn't appreciated."

I suspected Trey got wind of our plan to battle Zhuang. I even expected he was going to privately chastise me for some of the impolite remarks I made last night. I totally didn't anticipate *this*. "Oh, you've got to be kidding me," I say, pulling my arm out of his grasp. Embarrassment should accompany this conversation, but since I've already had to disclose the details regarding making out with Chase to Trey, this is actually not as big a deal. "Don't you have bigger things to worry about, like not getting murdered?"

"Actually this *is* important for many reasons. And it brings up something related I've wanted to address with you. I worry that with everything going on, having a serious relationship isn't a good idea."

"When is a good time? Can you put it in my calendar?"

"Roya, your mother and I made our life more complicated than it had to be by going too fast."

"Are you saying you regret being with her?"

"No! Not at all, but she had you when she was eighteen. If we could have just waited..."

"I can't believe we're having this conversation. George and I are not the same as your relationship. Times are different."

"Are they? Chase is after you the same as he was with Elle. What do you think he will do if he finds out you're in a relationship with someone else?"

I roll my eyes. "He's not going to find out. George and I don't dream travel together."

"And not only is Chase a concern, but I've been worried about you wearing the adjuster for a while. Maybe the Institute isn't the right place for George."

183

"I thought you felt he was good for me," I say, remembering what Aiden had bitterly disclosed.

"Who told you that?" he says, narrowing his eyes.

"Doesn't matter," I dismiss him at once, the way he always does to me.

"Well, I did think he was good for you as a friend, but I'm not sure if I approve of the current relationship."

"You can't kick him out of here!"

"And I won't. Not right now. But I also want my concerns to be known to you. And if it comes down to your safety and preservation, then he will have to leave." Trey says this so evenly, like we're discussing paint swatches.

"Is this really about George?"

"No, it's about you." He levels his turquoise eyes at me, a mini-standoff in the works. Finally, he throws up both of his hands, shaking his head at me. "You're too young for a relationship. You have too many things you should be focused on right now."

"You're such a hypocrite."

"I'm trying to help you learn from my mistakes."

"Well, I might have to stay here because of a bargain I made with you, but I don't have to do anything you say. I'm not dumping George because you think it's a good idea."

I can't believe what I told Aiden is correct. Trey doesn't want me to be with anyone. Aiden was right all along. And I almost let him risk everything he'd worked for. His parents worked for. And he would have lost it...because of me. I'm some sort of asset to Trey, and he's protecting it. The idea infuriates me and also seriously piques my interest. Why is Trey trying to keep my attention clear? What's his agenda?

"Do you not want me in a relationship so I'll provide a dozen news reports for the Institute each day?"

"No," he says, like it's a ridiculous notion.

"Why you do care?"

"Because you have a future to fulfill and you're only going to do it if you're free to make choices based on..."

"On what?" I almost yell, but find the tact to keep my voice in check. "Is this another ploy to hide information? What do you know, Trey?"

"Roya, this conversation is over."

"It's not over!" I say, stomping two feet in his direction.

"I'm going to ask you to keep it polite between you and George in front of the Institute, as well as behind closed doors," Trey says in a steady, almost unrecognizable tone.

"Oh, so I should move out of his room?"

He cuts his eyes at me. "I know you're not living in his room."

"Because you have spies on me, right?"

"This conversation is over," Trey says, shaking his head at me, more disappointment than anger in his eyes.

Chapter Thirty-Two

The moment Joseph answers his door he rolls his eyes at me. "You could save yourself a lot of trouble and just stop arguing with him."

"And what fun would that be?"

"What was it about this time?"

"George," I say, tugging him out the door and down the hallway.

"Oh, so Pops doesn't want you dating George, huh?" Joseph says with a clever grin.

"More like anyone at all. I'm supposed to remain 'focused.'" I use air quotes for the last word.

"So you really think it's a good idea if I come out to him right now and make my relationship with T public?" Joseph whispers.

"Yeah, I do. Just don't make out with him in the main hall. It's not printed in the Institute Code of Conduct, but it's apparently a no-no."

"Oh, no! You didn't?" He breaks into hysterical laughter.

"No, I didn't. It was just a few innocent kisses."

Joseph narrows his eyes at me, reading something deep within. "Sure," he says, his tone full of disbelief.

"I'm still having trouble understanding why my personal life is everyone's damn business all the time," I say.

"Enough about boring you," Joseph says. "I wanna talk about why Ren was there when our mother died."

"That's why we're going to his dungeon to meet with him right now," I say, my thoughts still absorbed in the Trey mess.

"I know, Stark," he says petulantly. "It's called speculation. Curious people do it."

"Well, here's something to speculate, Mr. Curiosity. Isn't it creepy to have a meeting set up with the dark leprechaun so we can learn the sordid history of our mother's death?"

"It is, but not in comparison to everythin' else in our present reality," Joseph says as we disembark from the elevator.

He's right. Having a prearranged meeting to learn how our mother died is really not the creepiest thing going on in our lives right now. Lately, I'm on edge and hardly present because I half expect to hear a siren signaling Zhuang is on the third level about to start a killing spree. If that isn't enough to make it ridiculously difficult to keep my breakfast down, then there's also the Chase reality. I think the idea that he wants to impregnate me with little Voyageurs who'll certainly grow up to do evil things is worse than Zhuang's imminent attack. Yeah, in retrospect meeting with Ren to find out how our mother died sounds almost normal.

Ren's office door is open. He's expecting us. My shoulders tense and a dull ache runs down the middle of my spine. I don't want to do this. Joseph gives me commiserating look. "Me either," he says in response to the hesitations in my head. "Don't worry, this will be over soon."

"Have you so soon forgotten how lengthy Ren's lectures can be?"

"I'm trying to create my reality."

I force a weak smile and let him take the lead.

Ren's sitting at his desk, tapping a pen on his bent knee and looking more repugnant than usual. I sense he would rather be doing anything else than this. Two metal folding chairs sit opposite of him. With a dramatic wave he motions to them like he's presenting us with side-by-side thrones.

"Go on now. Take a seat so we can get this show on the road."

Ren drums the pen a few more times before looking up and catching my gaze. His emerald eyes are bloodshot, which amplifies the color of his red hair. He's obviously not a morning person from the way his face is more drawn than usual. Setting down the pen he exchanges it for a mug, taking a few sips. "So, Trey has requested I fill you kiddos in on a bit of history. You'll have to excuse the brevity I'm going to give this lecture. You see, I'm not a history teacher and I absolutely disagree with the idea that you two will benefit from learning anything about what I know. However, I've been overruled on the subject." He drums his fingers against the side of the coffee mug. A nervous habit. One of the first he's ever exhibited. Maybe I should be enjoying this.

Ren flashes me a look of contempt. I like to think that he reserves that one especially for me.

"It looks like you've softened Trey up after all. Bravo," he says with zero enthusiasm.

Taking in a long breath, he stares at the floor. "Oh, all right, here we go. After Eloise became pregnant with you two, Trey moved her to Stockholm, Sweden." Ren's speaking at lightning speed. "Here's some random, yet related information. Once a pregnancy has progressed so far, and the fetus has its own consciousness, then a mummy-to-be cannot dream travel safely. That extra consciousness could get tied up in the layers. Therefore your parents made the decision to live outside the Institute until you two hatched. The place they chose was well known to be safe and had the proper medical facilities in place, which was the biggest part of the equation for Trey. All went fine for the first few months, well, as far as anyone knew. However, Eloise was being haunted by a foreboding feeling that someone would come and try to kill her and her children. She was right."

Ren pauses, but he doesn't make eye contact. Instead he keeps his eyes low, like the light of the room is too much to bear.

"Allouette had been charged by Chase to find Eloise and kill her and her children. Your mother was always a bit passionate and driven by emotion, however she was a trillion times more charged when she was pregnant. She awoke one night and decided that the only way she could escape this nightmare was to face it. Apparently she left a note for Trey and popped off to the docks where she planned to charter a ship to France. She believed, because that's what she'd been told to believe, that the safest way for her to travel at that point in her pregnancy was by boat. It had all been a setup. Everything to get her to that boat had been a part of the plan. While your mother looked over her shoulder during the first and second trimesters, fearing her own death, Allouette knew that the only danger was toward the end, which is how long it took that dirty witch to put her plan into the works."

Ren coughs and takes a sudden gulp of coffee, probably to erase how uncomfortable he's obviously feeling right now.

"As you've already learned, Allouette is especially dark. She's also especially crafty. She had constructed the perfect plan for how to give Chase exactly what he wanted. It didn't involve long brutal months of hunting down a pregnant woman and slaying her in a dark alley. Instead she used her resources and bored into this young woman's brain to implant the message that there was no safe place on Earth. That no matter what, she and her children would never

188

ever be safe. Allouette made it her mission for a long nine months to find every possible way to make Eloise believe that the only means of survival was to board a ship and sail back to her father, who would find compassion in his heart to end this war and protect his daughter and grandchildren. Eloise believed these dreams and thoughts that laced through her mind and knew that no one would ever support what she was preparing to do as each month of pregnancy ticked by. This was also a part of the planted message Allouette used because she knew if Trey got wind of this he'd reason with Eloise and stop the plan immediately. Obviously your mother never shared her concerns with Trey. She held these fears close to her until the day she awoke early and chartered that boat.

"Now Eloise was on this chartered boat and it was not sailing to France, as she had expected, but just to a set place where it would briefly pause before disposing of some *cargo*."

Ren's eyebrows twitch, another nervous tick I've never seen on him. "Not only did Eloise not know that the ship she was currently sailing on was not actually chartered by her, but she also didn't know that the person she'd been running from was onboard. While Allouette hung back, waiting for the ship to get to its halfway point, a few unexpected things happened. The first is that Eloise went into sudden early labor. The second is that Allouette's companion, who was now facing a laboring and completely defenseless woman, had a change of heart.

"You see, someone has to be properly motivated to want to kill a pregnant woman and her unborn babies, because not only is it raunchy, but it's also something only evil people can do. Allouette was motivated though. You see, she is on the long list of women who have fallen for Chase's charm and good looks. She was, and still is, in love with him. She was motivated to kill your mother and you without the slightest hesitation."

Ren pauses for a second and rubs his teeth together a few times. There's tick number three.

"Let me rephrase that. Allouette *did* kill your mother. She guided the knife that slit her throat just after a ship's mate was wiping off a disgusting newborn baby boy a few feet away. And with Eloise's last dying breath she forced out a repugnant little girl." Ren shudders like an invisible source has shaken him.

He sits up straight and does something quite unexpected. Ren looks at both of us. Something flashes on his face. Another new look, one strangely bordering on sympathy.

"I wish I could say I was the ship's mate. I wish I could tell you I was the captain or even the guy who swung in from an adjacent ship and saved the day. The truth is, I was Allouette's companion."

A rock sits in my throat. Blocking air. Head swimming with lightheadedness borne from disbelief.

"I was the one who Allouette seduced and asked to bore into your mother's brain," Ren says, like recalling a past life. "For all those months I was the one who put hypnotic images in her head and made her believe she was unsafe. Your mother knew how to shield Chase, but she was unaccustomed to me and I was successful at getting through and laying the trap. However, as I watched her die and realized the depths of filth I'd gotten myself into, I had a change of heart that I never expected. Right there in a cabin with a dead woman, the second mate holding two screaming infants, and the person I thought I loved, I became someone very different. It's only because Allouette never expected this possibility that I was able to take her over so easily right before she was about to turn and kill you two. Using mind control, I forced her to go to the bow of the ship and throw herself overboard. After realizing in those last horrible ten minutes that my companion was the grossest murderer I'd ever known and also in love with another man, I had no trouble sending her to a cold and wet death. The ship steered its way back to Stockholm and once it arrived I took you both to Trey, who I was well aware of and knew where he'd been located for quite some time."

Ren pauses again. I rustle my hands back and forth on my legs, earning me a contemptuous look from him. "I'm not proud of being a part of Allouette's plan. However, if it wasn't me, it would have been someone else and that someone might have let you die."

Joseph clears his throat. "I think we owe you a strange bit of gratitude."

"Oh, golly gee, shucks…don't flatter yourself. I didn't do it for you." Ren gives us a cold expression. "I did it because I didn't agree with killing people, but I didn't know that until I was witnessing it. I also didn't like being used. If I had it to do over, I'd have had the ship circle around and run over Allouette, but unfortunately I took my mind control off her long enough for her to recover and dream travel to safety. Damn bitch."

Chapter Thirty-Three

Not one word came out of my mouth during our meeting with Ren. Strangely, his long monologue filled in all the gaps. It left me with only one question, but not one Ren could answer. Only one person can answer this question, and there's no way I'm ever going to confront him with it. I turn to Joseph, stopping his progress down the hallway. He's almost sprinting, like he needs to get as far away from Ren's office as possible before a bomb goes off.

"Stop," I say, clutching his arm.

He looks at me, not quite seeing me. Blinks rapidly. "You wanna say it, so just go ahead. It's all right to have a little sympathy for the guy. Maybe more now than ever."

I do *want* to voice the question rolling around in my head, like a bowling ball in a clothes dryer. "To find out that the woman you loved, the mother of your children, died like that," I say, my throat quickly turning to cement. "To be handed your two children and told…what was that moment like? How devastating would that be?" I speculate, trying to remove myself from the equation, but it's impossible. I was one those babies, handed to my father with the news that my mother was murdered during childbirth.

"Trey doesn't seem like such a monster anymore, huh?" Joseph says.

"No, he seems like a man given a heart-wrenching fate. I suspect his scars run deep."

"I know they do."

"Maybe he resents us though, for living, when Eloise died? Maybe that's why he sent us away?" I say.

"I think you don't want to believe that he loves you as much he does because you'd have to start caring too."

"I don't know," I say in a sincere state of confusion. "I think this information will help me to understand him better. Maybe even forgive him…one day."

Joseph's eyes are sharp, rimmed with a new hostility, but it's not aimed at me. "Who could do something like that? What kind of person murders babies?"

192

"I can't even begin to understand the evil…" Every inch of my skin feels like its crawling with sharp-legged beetles.

"Will it make what you have to do with Chase harder? Now that you know he's responsible?"

A humorless grin spreads slowly on my mouth. "Oh no, now my motivation is firmly in place. More so than ever I'm certain I can pull off the plan. And make him suffer a painful death."

"Damn, that look in your eye right now kinda scares me…in a good way." Joseph pats me on the back as we resume the walk to the elevator. "Good luck tonight. I feel sorry for the man you're meeting."

"I don't."

♦

The marble steps of the Parthenon feel both solid and fragile under me. I sit. Wait. I don't know how he does it, but he will find me. I'm like an antelope prancing in front of a hungry lion, but this circle of life is about to be revised.

Two and a half minutes. That's how long I have to wait. Behind me his rubber-soled shoes barely make noise as he crosses through the inner chambers of the Parthenon—the *cella*. Its walls, no longer standing, make this possible. I pretend I'm enjoying the morning light as it kisses the tops of the buildings of Athens. But I'm not taking in the view or the magnificent structures around me. I'm rehearsing. Reinforcing my shields. And slightly worrying what will happen if my protective charm fails. Aiden knows what he's doing though. With this I can trust him.

I rarely pray and when I do my agnostic heart doesn't quite know who I'm praying to. But right now I know exactly who I need to direct this prayer to: my inner goddess. *Please help me to deceive this man. Unleash inside me what I need to convince him that, to me, he's irresistible.*

Standing, I straighten, like my senses have just been lured by something deliciously human. I slide my chin around until my eyes seize him strolling around a column. I know how an intense desire feels. At the sight of him my chest convulses forward once, but only an inch. My lips part, like breath has just escaped my lungs. And my eyes scream "I want you." The way my body reacted to Chase before

193

I had the patch to my protective charm is engrained in my memory. And right now I'm triggering that memory, making my body live in the past.

Chase's eyes are like two round-cut aquamarine diamonds, a well in their middle. A bottomless well, as empty as his soul. Still, it's impossible to not appreciate such beauty. He's like Niagara Falls, breathtaking and deadly.

To my inner goddess's pleasure he's wearing a tuxedo shirt, the neck opened, no bow tie. The best part of his ensemble is the taut suspenders. My job is getting easier by the minute. When he's only a foot away I slip two fingers under the paisley silk suspender at his waist. Watching my fingers as they slide up, I wait until they're just at his chest and then I tug him forward.

"I didn't even have to ask this time," he says, his cold breath greeting my face like I've just opened a refrigerator.

"Ask?" I say with a shiver.

"For you to touch me." His eyes are like that of a proud cat's, all self-serving.

"I've been slow to warm," I say, slipping my fingers out from under his suspenders and running them down until I find the place where they attach to his suit pants. Again my fingers tuck inside the fabric and tug. "But I can't resist you any longer."

In a rush he grips my other arm, his fingernails pinching into my skin. "Although I'm pleased to hear this, I must ask that you not play games with me, Roya."

My breath hitches. "I...I...I..."

Pressing his fingers harder into my arm, he crowds his face up against mine. "You might think the streets of Las Vegas were loud enough to conceal your conversations," he says through beautifully white clenched teeth. "They weren't."

"Chase." A subservient plea in my voice.

"Yes?" he says in a hiss, his canines flashing at me.

"You're hurting me." I let my voice quiver, and swivel my gaze to my arm. The skin has turned blotchy in places due to the constriction caused by his fingers.

Loosening his grip on me he skims his hand until it meets my wrist. Like a handcuff he cinches around it, but not as tight as before. "Imagine how upset I was to hear your recount of your revelation to

194

those men in Las Vegas. It almost sounded as though you were unhappy to know why I wanted you."

"I'd never want you to be upset," I say, realizing my fingers are still inside the waistband of his pants. I pull them away and step back as far as he'll allow me, his grip still on my wrist. Staring down at the crumbling marble under my feet, I practice a look of shame. "I'm sorry if I hurt you. It's only that the circumstances involving us are so complicated and have been a lot to digest." Bringing my submissive eyes up to his I say, "But I've decided that no matter your reason for wanting me, I'm grateful." He searches the features of my face, with an expression that isn't quite anger.

He tucks his chin, swallows hard, and turns his gaze to the distant corner of Athens. "Who are they?"

"They're like my parents," I say.

With a lift of his chin he flicks his eyes back to mine. "Will they come between us?"

"How could anyone come between us? Will your parents be a problem to our union? Please tell me there's no one who has that power," I say, my voice dripping with fake desperation.

"Oh no, it's our marriage that will finally put me back in my father's graces. Bearing children with pure blood will not only reinstate me into the Blain family, but it will put me in the highest position."

"It appears that our relationship will mend many fences and for that I'm glad."

A wicked smile quirks his lips up, a clever gleam in his eyes. "Oh yes. It will mend castle walls and once I'm back inside the Blain estate...I'm going to kill every last one of them. Then you, my queen, will have a proper place to birth my children, since the Grotte is no place for them."

In a palace of blood. How romantic...

"How do you always know where I am?" I ask.

"Roya." He shakes his head and clicks his tongue. To my relief he's softened a bit in appearance and with his grip. "You haven't been paying attention, have you?"

"Not enough, apparently," I say in a meek voice.

He releases me and gracefully steps closer. "I'm targeted on your energy. I know it like I know the contours of most people's minds. Even when you're awake, I know where you are. I wish I could say that I knew what you felt and thought, but you're too good at shielding. Soon a day will come where you will never use a shield against me, but for now I'll allow it. I do enjoy the game of love and it isn't as much fun if I have too many advantages."

He's sick. Corrupt and sick. I lace a smile across my lips, plant my hand softly on his chest, and feign a shudder as though his heartbeat under my fingertips is erotic. The only thing turning me on right now is the idea of ripping his heart out.

With unhurried, deliberate steps he begins snaking his way around me. "Did you know that the word *Parthenon* refers to a virgin's apartment? Funny place for us to meet tonight." He's completed the tight circle around me. "So, Roya, now you know why I want you. Why don't we cut to the chase?" His smile is inches from my mouth. I run my eyes over the features of his intricately beautiful face.

Cupping the side of my head, he pulls me in to him. Sickness rises in my stomach, but I make a silent plea just as his mouth covers mine. Under all the breath and movement I find a way to forge the lust and the allure. The animalistic desire I once felt for him is gone, replaced by repulsion as deep as the pits in hell. I know the moves to this dance, though, even if I'm forced to do them with the devil. When his mouth grazes mine I push into him, thinking maybe I'll make his lips hurt and he'll mistake that as passion. He bites me. I let him pull away first and then I lunge for him, pretending to still be hungry. His pink mouth twitches with a smile. I thank my inner goddess.

"Well, it's settled." He flattens his shirt, like I've wrinkled it. "You'll be my wife."

I pull him toward me, enjoying this little game he's unaware I'm playing. With a shaky hand I find the place where his shirt opens to his chest, three buttons down, and slide my fingers up until I feel the blood beating in the vein along his neck. I push up on my tiptoes until my lips meet my fingertips and kiss him softly. His purr masks the revulsive shudder I let slip out. He tastes like juice concentrate, making my mouth feel like it's now coated in syrup. His skin is as hard as what I suspect the statue of Zeus on the east pediment feels like. If it wasn't for the beating under his skin, then I'd question whether he was human.

"Yes, but we have eternity to be together," I whisper against his skin. "I don't want to rush this."

My scalp suddenly screams. His fingers yank my head back, almost ripping out a chunk of hair. "I've waited a long time for this. Don't you forget that." He releases my hair and stares at me behind sinister eyes.

"As grateful as I am for this opportunity, as much as I want you," I say, "I need to know you want me, and not just my blood. Now that I know the truth it's more confusing than ever." I pause for effect and then look at him like he's the answer to all my problems. "Make me believe you want me. Prove you love *me*."

His black eyebrows furrow in confusion. This gorgeous and powerful man is suddenly lost. "How?"

I thread my fingers through his smooth hair, rubbing them against his scalp. "That's the thing about love. It's a mystery. You'll figure it out and when you do, I'll be yours…forever."

I pull my bottom lip into my mouth, my top teeth press down against it. He yanks me to him and growls. His excitement is palpable; it almost courses through my body. Chase loves games and that's what love is to him. A game. He probably thinks I'm smiling due to the ecstasy of the moment. He leans down, his mouth going wide. I almost don't hide the horror in my eyes before his teeth pierce my neck and rack against my skin. Pain sears from the bite, like a hand held too close to a flame. However, if this is a battle scar, I'll endure it. His breath presses against my skin sharply, eliciting a response that even my revulsion can't overcome. Goose bumps rise to the surface. His eyes meet mine and I smile back at him with feigned unabashed adoration. He kisses me once upon the lips and steps away. A distance I've been looking forward to.

"Until next time, *mon amour*," he says, lowering his chin.

Chapter Thirty-Four

"Are those teeth marks on your neck!?" George says too loud when I sit down with a bowl of salty grits. After last night if I never have anything sweet again I'll be fine.

"George," I reprimand in a hush. "Be quiet." Keeping my eyes low I scan the main hall. Thankfully it doesn't appear Trey is present, but half a dozen people are twisted around in their seats, curious looks on their faces. One of them I stare at too long. Aiden's. He's wearing a look that matches George's horrified expression.

"He did that, didn't he?" George grips my hand and points his gaze at Aiden. The three of us are locked in a staring contest now. Thankfully, most everyone else has turned back to their breakfast.

Aiden must have read George's lips or sensed the allegation because he shakes his head with a deliberate force. Unable to stomach the look of gross disbelief on Aiden's face I slip down in my chair, using my hands as a visor over my forehead. "No," I say so only George can hear. "It wasn't him."

"Chase did this to you?!" Again his voice is too loud, drawing uninvited attention from neighboring tables. The only thing I'm grateful for is the onlookers are mostly a group of research scientists visiting from our sister society in the Pacific Northwest, the Reverians. Hopefully they don't know who Chase is. More importantly, hopefully they don't know who I am. Ungratefully, through the crack in my fingers I spy that Aiden is still staring, his mouth now gaping open.

"George, it isn't like you think."

He slips my hair back, taking in the pair of long, red streaks running from just under my earlobe to the middle of my neck. "And what should I think?" he says, his voice flat with hostility.

I rearrange my hair so that it covers the marks. "Look," I say, finally daring to glance at him, "I have everything under control."

"It doesn't appear that way," George snaps. "Did he hurt you anywhere else?"

I remain silent, pinning my eyes on the table. Although I found it impossible to cover up the bite marks completely, I was able to wear a long-sleeved shirt that covered the bruises where Chase had gripped me too tightly.

"Damn it, Roya," George says in an angry hush. "What are you getting yourself mixed up in?"

"I just needed to see if my protective charm worked against him, that's all," I lie.

"And?"

Planting my elbows on the table I cradle my forehead in my hands. "It works."

"But it looks as though things got out of your control," George says, still sounding on the verge of exploding.

"No, I need Chase to think he's in control. I need him to…" I stop, realizing that I can't divulge any more to George, especially with other people likely to eavesdrop.

"Roya, what are you not telling me?"

"Don't worry about it, George," I say, flipping my head up and meeting his eyes, which look like they're about to bulge out of his head. "I'm not going to dream travel while Chase is still after me, okay?"

"You're hiding something though." He slides his eyes in Aiden's direction. To my horror, Aiden is still locked on us, not even remotely trying to hide his interest in what's going on at my table. "I get the feeling," George continues, refocusing on me, "that you're hiding a lot." He pushes up from the table and stares down at me contemptuously. "I need some time to think about this."

His ominous words hang in the air as he charges out of the main hall. I crumble onto the table, not caring an ounce what everyone's spying eyes see. Not even Aiden's. The idea that I've hurt George takes over my being. Wraps around my mind and constricts.

♦

"That's more than rough, Stark," Joseph says after hearing my recount of what happened during breakfast. "You can't catch an emotional break lately, can you?"

I shake my head.

"Well, maybe you should consider staying in your room for a while. I'm not sure if Mercury is in retrograde, but there's definitely something affecting your interactions lately," Joseph says, taking a seat in his news reporting chair. "Not that you ever have an easy time of it, but you seem to be extra provoking lately."

"Thanks for the concern, but I can handle it. And besides, we need to get some strategizing underway. Zhuang isn't going to kill himself, if you know what I mean."

Joseph's laugh sounds especially loud in the serene space of the Panther room. "Yeah, that's true."

"Tomorrow morning let's meet in the same classroom as last time," I say. "Since we don't know when this whole thing is going down we need to go ahead and work through the entire strategy. If you could hone this fire business, that would be extra handy."

"Oh sure, I'll just get right on that." Joseph rolls his eyes. "I can't so much as start a campfire by rubbing two sticks together, so I'm not sure if we should hold our breath that I'll make a spark out of thin air."

"But have you really tried?"

"With the persistence of a hummingbird after nectar."

"Well, these kinds of things take practice," I try and console.

"Oh, yeah, really? How much you practice before you made a mini cyclone in the Grotte?" Bitterness wells up in Joseph's tone.

"Actually, that's a fantastic point. I was super emotionally charged then. Maybe we can get you really riled up and see if that helps."

"Yeah, maybe," Joseph says, dispirited.

"I'll practice harnessing the wind and see if I can figure out a strategy. How does that sound?"

"Sounds like we're a bunch of stupid kids pretending we're super heroes," he says in an uncharacteristically melancholy voice.

"Everything is about perspective." Bob and Steve said that to me once. It's helpful advice that grounds me sometimes.

"And currently I'm having a hard time wrapping my mind around this ridiculous idea that through the forces of my mind I'll control an element like fire." He throws his hands up in the air. "This whole idea is absurd!"

I caution Joseph to be quiet with a single look. "George Bernard Shaw wrote that all great truths start out as blasphemies."

"Thanks, Shuman, I appreciate the adage."

200

"Fine," I say, lying down in my chair, "you're allowed to be cynical this one and only time. But I want you to get it out of your system and show up with a better attitude tomorrow morning."

"Sure thing." Joseph salutes me. "So while I'm being allowed to act like you, I mean pessimistic, I'd like to say that I'm doubtful about how this whole plan can realistically be executed. There's tons of security in place that specifically protects us from being able to do this kind of stuff. How's it all gonna magically go away so that these events unfold?"

"We know Zhuang enters the Institute," I say, holding up one finger. "So right there tells you that something in the security system doesn't work on Day Z. Secondly," I count off another finger, "you saw the vision so it can happen. We just have to figure out how." I tick off a third finger. "And lastly, maybe in the end it will take a bit of magic to save the day. After everything I've witnessed, that wouldn't be so unbelievable."

♦

Each hour that passes that I don't see George makes the open wound deepen. How would I feel if the roles had been reversed? If he showed up with teeth marks from another woman? I'd be hurt and that's exactly what I did so dismissively to him. He's my sweet George. And sometimes I wish I knew how to punish myself for my apathetic attitude. The look in his eyes this morning scratched my heart and throughout the day it's become infected.

"Come in," he says, a few seconds after I knock.

Pressing the button, I will myself forward. Willing myself to make apologies. Willing myself to take off my pride if it repairs the mistakes my stupidity caused.

George sits on the ground, a few books splayed out around him. One in his hand, clasped shut. He's wearing the brown T-shirt that has a chest pocket. I always pretend to stick something in there and only the last time did he call me out, saying I was just looking for an excuse to touch his chest. Looking up at me, he lays the book to the side. His expression reminds me of a dust storm for some reason, brutal and also blindingly unreadable.

"Do you want to see me or should I go?" I say, threading my fingers together in front of me.

201

"Don't go," he says, and although it's what I want to hear, the way he says it is all wrong. Kneeling down next to him, I wait until he looks at me. Deep in his brown eyes there's a pain, but preceding that is still his love, so unwavering it hurts. "I'm sorry, George. I know the way I reacted earlier was insensitive. It was—"

"It's all right, Roya," he interrupts. "I trust you if you say you have things under control with Chase. I just worry."

"George, Joseph and I have a plan."

"I get that," he says, picking at the fabric of the blue carpet. "But he hurt you and do you know what I'd do if anything—"

"Nothing is going to happen," I say, knowing I can't make that promise. So to make up for my words I move forward, crawl into his lap, and wrap his arms around my torso. "I don't want to make you worry. I..."

"You what?"

I love you. Why can't I say it? I feel it with all my being, but the words are somehow stuck inside me.

I lace my fingers into his, turn sideways, and put my ear to his chest. "I'm an idiot, undeserving of you."

He uncurls his fingers from mine, taking back his hand and moving in such a way that I have to sit up. "Roya," he says, his tone bordering on frustration.

I turn and look at him. For some reason I just want to kiss him, make his lips erase all the pains in my heart, all my doubts and fears.

"Roya," he begins again. "I don't...there's..." He sighs, at a loss for words.

Swiveling around so I'm fully facing him, I perch on my toes right in front of his curled up legs. "George, whatever you're about to say just stop."

"I can't. I need to say something and I don't want to."

"Then don't," I say, taking his face in both my hands. "Just kiss me, please."

He doesn't respond, but a bit of tension resigns inside him. I lean in, feeling a new tenderness between us. It's magnified when I brush my lips against his and feel only half his normal intensity. Hands grip my shoulders, urging me back. I can only guess my face is a portrait of bewilderment when George scoots away so we aren't touching.

After sitting back and hugging my legs to my chest I chance a look at him. A wise and scorned look reflects off his face. "If you love me then why can't you say it?" he says, his voice not sounding the least bit tragic, which is how his words make me feel.

"I don't know," I say. "I'm just not ready."

"Roya, this morning in the main hall your shield came down briefly."

Bemused I stare at him, search him.

He clears his throat and looks off before returning his focus on me. "Aiden's came down too, more so than ever before."

"George, this isn't about—"

"I really don't think your heart is in this." He motions between the two of us.

"How can you say that? And isn't this the wrong time to make that judgment, with everything going on?"

With a tight mouth he stares off. "I told you before that at some point this was going to have to be solely about us and not *him*. I fear that will never be the case. I haven't wanted to admit it, but your feelings for Aiden never dissipated. Even though you know you can't be together, you still love him. And sadly I know that it's pure, it's not emotion arising just because you can't have what you want. I think he will always own your heart, whereas you've only given me a lease on it."

"Everything you've just said is absurd. We're friends, that's all," I say in a voice that sounds so convincing even I believe it.

"Roya, think about who you're trying to fool right now." His eyes fix on me with a new seriousness.

"You're being incredibly stupid," I say, my words vexed.

"No, I'm being honest."

"You think you know me so well." I push up to a standing position. "Have you considered you're misreading emotions?"

George stands up beside me, a new determination in his eyes. "I'm not wrong, although I've been trying to convince myself otherwise."

"Please don't do this," I say too weakly. "Not right now. I need you."

"And I'm here." His eyes soften as he speaks. "But I'm not willing to keep pretending with you anymore. I won't be the guy you're almost in love with," he says, his words devouring my heart.

"We both know this relationship isn't reciprocal. I'm in love with you, Roya. Can you honestly return that emotion for me?"

"I want to," I say, and he reflexively backs away, shaking his head with a knowing he's denied.

"That's not enough." George clenches his jaw. "Especially since I know you're capable of more."

Usually I'm prepared for danger, but I'm not prepared for this. And this situation feels dangerous, because it has the potential to scar me. "What do you want me to say?" I respond, standing up straighter, looking at him boldly. He created this confrontation for one and only one reason. I know there's no running away from where it's going.

"You don't have to say anything. I just don't think we should be together anymore."

I'm suddenly aware of my hands and how they hang loosely by my legs. I transfer weight back and forth between my feet, unable to figure out how to stand properly. With great effort I will my shoulders to relax. There's nothing I can say to change his mind right now. The only option I have left is to allow my emotions to surge through the room freely. Taking down my shield, I stand back and let every emotion I've held regarding George free to gallop between us. I imagine my emotions as tiny sparks of pink and blue lights spiraling through the room, little iridescent pigments for George to pick up and read. They tell the story I can't through my lips. They tell him that this hurts, that I need him, that I don't want to lose him. My emotions tell him that I want to love him like he deserves. And the last flickering emotion, a spark of sapphire coated with gold, describes how not loving him like he deserves is my tragedy, not his.

His hands clasp mine, making my eyes go wide. I suck in my breath, hold it. Inside him I see the all-familiar mirror of my emotions. Regret. Betrayal. Confusion cloaking something so close to love…but far enough away, I can't describe it. And then like a soft wind on a spring night, it all disappears and before me stands George. No emotions, just a wall of stone.

"Please, George, give me another chance. I can really try, I can—"

"It wouldn't matter," he whispers in a voice I don't recognize as his. He's already changing…into not-my-George.

"Please, don't do this," I say, through the threatening tears. Swallowing pushes them down, but not for long. "I need you."

Firm hands grip my shoulders. "You don't need me. Never did." Desperately I want to touch the scowl on his lips, kiss him until it disappears, but he holds me away from him.

"Please...don't," I argue again.

He sucks in a breath, stares off at a distant corner. "I kept wanting to believe I was your Florentina," George says, referring to the main love interest in *Love in the Time of Cholera*. "I wanted to believe our love was the one that would last. But I am Juvenal and if I remain in this relationship then we will live, but only half a life. If you were to be mine, over time your love would grow complacent and although there would still be love, it wouldn't be enough."

"You're wrong," I say with only half conviction in my voice.

"You don't love me like you love Aiden."

How can words feel the same way as a head-on collision? "But George, I do."

"Then say you love me."

I wring my hands. Fidget. Remain silent, unable to voice anything new.

"Like I said, you don't love me like you like love him," he says, nodding, confirmation written on his always serious face. In not saying anything, I've said everything. "But I'm happy for you," he says, in a distant voice. "I'm still bitter, but also happy. Because no matter what Aiden does you'll always love him." His heartbroken smile etches into my mind, a haunting in the works. "Congratulations, your heart's allowed you to love someone unconditionally."

"I want it to be you." My words are as broken as me.

"But that's not how love works. We don't choose who we fall in love with and we can't make someone love us the way we want."

"George, we can make this work, just give me—"

He shakes his head. "No, because I want all of you and I think that will never happen. Not for me."

"But there's no future for Aiden and me," I say, searching his eyes.

"Well, then I hope you find someone who lets you love them with half your heart."

"That's cruel. Why would you say that?"

"You want to know what's cruel?! What's cruel is I know exactly how the two of you feel about each other!" His deep voice bounces off the stainless steel wall, and all his anger soaks into me. Chest rising up and down from the sudden rush of emotions, he takes a few steadying breaths. "You love me," he says in a calmer tone, "but I know you're capable of more. How can I settle for less when you look at him and your heart blazes?"

Cringing with denial, I shake my head.

"It's all right. I don't blame you for it. We aren't responsible for who our heart chooses." A shaky, heart-rending smile graces his mouth. "I wish at times my heart chose someone else."

Closing my eyes, I pretend to be transported to a giant warehouse where I can scream and hear my voice echo back to me. When I open my eyes I glare at the carpet under his feet. There's no begging left in me. There's no changing his mind.

George places two fingers under my chin, tipping it up so I'm forced to look at him. "Roya, the irony of our relationship is you think I taught you about love, but the reverse is really true. I never thought I could fall in love with someone before you. Those were emotions and experiences other people had. But you changed that for me. Half my heart will always belong to you. How can it not? Before you, I thought I was doomed to the shadows of other people's emotions. You brought light to my feelings. Made them the central part of my universe for the first time. You're the girl who made me hear my own heart beat for the first time." He leans down, brushes his fingers across my cheek, and kisses me once upon the lips. "Forever and ever I will love you, and that's as it should be."

Chapter Thirty-Five

As usual, my twin brother is late for practice. I scan through the list on my iPod trying to find a song that inspires angst rather than grief. Last night after I left George's room I pulled the iPod out of the boxes where I'd imprisoned it. There's no point in hiding from emotions anymore. Also, they've always served me in battle. Facing Zhuang this time is going to take a new level of emotion. Good thing I have an overflowing storage.

"Did I not get the memo?" Aiden pokes his head through the door, taking in the empty classroom.

I jump, startled by his sudden presence.

"Are you teaching a seminar?" he says.

Words from my conversation with George last night spring into my head, making my face flush red. I busy myself wrapping up the ear buds, making a great effort not to look at him. "No, I'm just waiting for Joseph."

"Because…?"

"Uhhh…because…we're practicing a theatrical performance for once Day Z is over."

"Oh," he says, nodding like this makes perfectly ridiculous sense. "Well, that was quite the scene in the main hall yesterday. Bravo," he says with a sarcastic clap.

"Thanks," I say dully, the ache still living in my being. "We were rehearsing for the play."

"Oh, so everything between you and George is all right?"

"If by 'all right,' you mean he dumped me, then sure." There's a stain in the shape of a deformed duck on the carpet. I trace it with my eyes.

"George dumped you?" Aiden asks, walking further into the room, standing on my duck. "Why? Is he insane?"

"You were right about Trey," I say, bringing my eyes up until they find Aiden's. His expression is as hard as granite right now. I remind myself I haven't just hurt George with my apathetic nature, I've hurt two guys. I'm the bomb and the shrapnel. I'm the explosion and the debris that maims.

"Oh?"

"Yes, Trey doesn't want me with anyone. He threatened to deport George out of Institute."

"Is that why he broke it off?"

"No," I say, voice clipped.

"Is it because you're playing a dangerous game with a psychopath?" His eyes dart to my neck, narrow.

"No," I say. A sudden desperation I should have used initially with George unleashes. "And my meeting with Chase was nothing. I was only trying—"

Aiden holds up his hand. "Shhh…" He steps forward, almost grips my arm. "I've seen you operate enough to know you're calculated. If you're playing with Chase then I suspect…" He stops, scratches his chin, smirks. "Well, I'm no scientist…oh wait, yes I am."

"You suspect I have a good reason?" I ask in disbelief that this conversation could be so easy.

"I do," he says at once. "I mean the idea is still hard to stomach, but who am I to judge?"

"Right," I say, taking a seat on the desk in the middle of the platform. Aiden moves forward, leaving only three feet between us.

"So George broke it off, huh?"

"Yes," I say with conviction. "And it's probably best that he did. Trey wants me focused. And he's probably right."

Aiden gives a slow nod. "Ms. Stark, I do believe you just said your father's name without your usual bit of revulsion."

"Did I? Well, I guess learning my family history has softened me up a little."

He raises a curious eyebrow.

"You don't want to know," I say, with a trivializing wave. "It's sick and demented."

"I do want to know because it involves you, but I'll wait for you to tell me another time," he says, anticipation in his voice.

Silence. It hangs between us, enticing me to say things that I shouldn't, that I can't. *Where in the hell is Joseph?*

"So why did George break things off?" Aiden dares to ask. Sometimes I want to slap him for being so bold.

I clench my eyes shut and push the words out past the ache in my throat. "You know why." When I snap my eyes open Aiden is slow to cover up his satisfied expression.

He points to the iPod sitting next to me. "Do you want me to load that song on your iPod?"

"What song?"

"The one we danced to. Twice," he adds a second later.

Any doubt I had about our night spent together in my dream on the hill is gone now. Every word we said was from us. And I truly walked away. Rejected him. As I will have to do over and over if necessary.

I've been silent for too long. Aiden gives me a sideways look. "Is that a yes? Do you want the song?"

I shake my head roughly. "No," I say in hush.

He nods, disappointment flaking off his features. "For the first time in my life I'm sorry to be right about something."

"Trey?" I ask.

He nods.

The look in Trey's eyes when he confronted me about George surfaces in my mind. It was a more serious look than normal. An unrestrained protectiveness. *"You're too young for a relationship,"* I remember him saying. *"You have too many things you should be focused on right now."* Anger flares up in my head like a match being struck.

"Yeah well," I finally break the second patch of silence, "I guess I was naïve to think that the dictator of the Lucidites wouldn't want to dictate my life too."

Aiden leans against a nearby wall, giving me a look of sympathy. "What are your plans for when Zhuang arrives?"

"Trey told everyone to dream travel and generate."

"That doesn't answer my question." A corner of Aiden's lip twitches with a slight smile.

I pull at a piece of hair and twirl it through my fingers. "Something tells me to face what's coming."

"Then you'll do it," he says, kicking off the wall.

"You're not going to tell me not to?"

The grin on his face slowly undoes me. Unlaces my heart. "We both know that's not even an argument worth constructing. Are there other people who have the ridiculous notion they can argue with you and change your mind?"

"There are many."

"Time wasters," he says, shaking his head with a smirk.

209

"But you argue with me sometimes."

"For the plain and simple fact that I like to," he says, breeching the distance we've held between us.

I swallow down his words, his ploy at my heart. Dismissing it instantly. He doesn't quite get yet that I'm his downfall. "What will you do? On Day Z?"

"I'll hold down the fort. Much of the security has to be manually controlled," he says matter-of-factly.

"From your lab?" I ask.

He nods.

"Will you be safe there?"

"Probably." His eyes dart to my neck, which I now realize is exposed since I've been playing with my hair. "So would your game with Chase have anything to do with Day Z?"

"You should have become a detective, not a scientist," I say, covering back up the marks on my neck.

"I'm sure you have a good plan, I'm just hoping it—"

"I'm here," Joseph sings, strolling around the corner into the room. He sizes up both of us and scowls. "Well, well, well. It appears I'm interrupting something. Good."

"Hello, Mr. Jordan," Aiden says, bowing his head formally at Joseph.

"Hey Livingston, I think I saw one of your white coats milling around in the hallway, looking lost," Joseph says, taking a seat on the desk next to me. "Why don't you go fetch him?"

"You must be mistaken, I mentally know where they all are all the time. There's not one on this level right now," Aiden says, winking at me.

Joseph turns to me. "You know what I was just thinking about?" he says, a mischievous gleam in his eyes. "Remember the time I walked in your room and you and George were top—"

"Joseph," I say in a rush, my eyes going wide.

"Well, I think I've missed my cue." Aiden's mouth twitches, eyes narrowed. "I'll be taking my leave."

"Is it your mission to make my life hell?" I ask, shutting the door to the classroom after Aiden exits.

He gives an angry sigh. "I already warned you that you're only bringing trouble for that guy."

"I'm well aware of that and doing my best to push him away."

"Well, you need to work on your strategy because he didn't look too deterred," he says.

I cover my face with my hands. "I know. It isn't something easy to do."

"Especially when you're in love with him," Joseph says, hopping down from the desk.

"Oh shut up, would you?"

"Not a chance. You know, sometimes even when two people love each other the universe still conspires against them, forces them apart."

"I don't like the evil universe you speak of."

He shrugs. "Actually the universe is kind and wants what's best for us. It just wants to push us to become a better version of ourselves. The only way we'll do that is if we're forced to fight for what it's keeping from us."

"And how does that relate to you and Trent?"

"*That's* an exception."

"Whatever," I say with a laugh. "So you're late," I scold.

"And you're always early, so I figure we balance each other out."

"You're bad at math."

"I apologize for my tardiness. I was busy."

From a quick dip into his thoughts I answer the question I'm about to ask. It's actually pretty awesome being in someone's head at times, albeit creepy. "So I guess Trent couldn't hold himself to his ultimatum."

"I'm irresistible. You would know that if you weren't my sister."

◆

Unfortunately, Joseph's prediction had been correct: He's absolutely incapable of controlling fire. Not only can he not create a spark in the darkest of rooms when I do everything to try and put him in the darkest of moods, but he also can't control fire when it's already present. I brought along a candle and matches thinking that maybe we were mistaken to think that Joseph should be responsible for creating the fire in the first place—after all, I don't have to create wind, but rather just control what exists. It didn't matter, because after an hour of staring at a flame off and on Joseph hadn't as much as made it flicker except with his exasperated breath.

"I think we'd better come up with a different strategy," I finally say, pushing my hands on either side of my head like a vise.

Joseph punches the air angrily and paces back and forth.

"Don't worry," I say. "We'll figure out a backup plan, if you can't do this."

"Like what?!"

"Look," I say quietly, hoping to encourage him to do the same, "in your vision you just saw me, right?"

He narrows his eyes, shakes his head abruptly. "And who's going to protect you when the time comes, because according to my vision you're going to need backup."

"I really don't know, but if this doesn't work then why should you—"

"No, I'm going to be there too."

"You and I both know this is sounding more and more like a suicide mission."

"Clearly."

"Why should we both die?" I fold my arms across my chest.

"Nope, I'm not even entertaining this discussion. We're workin' together this time."

"But you don't need to be there," I reason.

"I do if you're going to survive," Joseph says, flashing an angry look. "You'll remember I brought this man back from the depths of nothingness. It's my fault that soon he'll stroll through this place and destroy it and every person he comes across. I really appreciate that once again you're willin' to die for me and everyone else, but stop 'cause I'm sick of it. This time I'm there and if one of us has to throw our neck in front of Zhuang's sword, it's going to be me."

Furiously my stomach turns in a series of knots. I've only known the guy who stands before me for a few months and I also know him better than I've ever known anyone my entire life. He isn't just my brother, he's a part of me. It aches to think that there's a reality where he dies and I live. Now I know how he felt when I faced Zhuang.

"I'm not going to let you get killed by Zhuang just because you brought him back," I argue. "We're going to have to come up with a better plan or otherwise we're abandoning this whole thing and running like cowards when he shows up."

"Fine."

"Maybe we need some special weapon," I say. "Something that doesn't rely on our mental focus. Something that will work even if we fail."

"And I think I know exactly what would work," Joseph says, scratching his head, his eyes lighting up. He nods. "Yes, leave it to me. I'll make the arrangements. It's the very least I can do, since you were assigned to seduce a psychopath."

"Yeah, in our next life you get that assignment."

"Deal," he says definitively.

"All right, well let's break for the day. After the last twenty-four hours I don't think I can dream freely tonight," I say. "I said I wouldn't dream travel, but I really need to get away. Will you join me?"

"Where?"

"How about Machu Picchu?"

"Pssh, that's the best idea ever."

Chapter Thirty-Six

Thin air shivers against my skin. Under my feet the grass of the Central Plaza is slick with morning dew. Surprisingly even at this early hour we don't have the ancient wonder of Machu Picchu to ourselves. Middlings with HD cameras and smartphones stroll through the grounds, setting up to capture the sunrise, which is already kissing the eastern-facing top of Huayna Picchu—a pyramid-shaped peak.

"If I was the entrepreneur type," Joseph says beside me, "I'd build a Starbucks right here and make a killin'."

"I think you'd be haunted by Incan gods for the rest of your life," I say, taking a seat on the edge of the nearest terrace.

"Well, doesn't matter anyway. I'm not that sort. I'm the sort to inherit the family business and try not to steer a society of loyal Dream Travelers into the pits of hell," Joseph says, walking across the field to inspect a couple of grazing wild alpacas.

"That's quite the lofty goal. I think I'd rather run an alpaca farm. I hear their wool is pretty desirable."

"Oh yeah?" Joseph turns, giving me a sideways smile. "And where did you hear this from?"

"Fine, you caught me. I read it."

Over half of Huayna Picchu is now bathed in morning sunlight, and the terrace where I'm kicking my feet back and forth is growing lighter by the second. Joseph has trekked a path to the opposite terrace, and I almost can't make out the outline of his shoulders since that area is still not graced by the first rays of sunlight.

A breeze carrying the songs of rousing birds and ancient traditions wisps across my skin. Places like this awaken sacred parts of my soul. Remind me I'm connected to more than just Joseph. We're all connected through consciousness and a history of dreams and ideas. Of course, it's hard to understand those connections to the degree I feel them with Joseph. His consciousness is almost as familiar as my own. When it presses up against mine, it feels as natural as the sunlight that now caresses my skin. Opening my eyes I can now see Joseph inspecting the far wall, made of rectangular stones.

214

Two levels up from him a Middling strolls back and forth on the grass, no camera in hand. She looks to be swaying as she walks, like a ghost haunting a hallway. When she reaches the first wall she turns, continuing her march. And across the field I hear her voice, singing a strange melody. Joseph hears it too. He stops, raising his chin to inspect her. She must be thirty feet higher up on her terrace, but it's hard to tell from my distant vantage point.

The girl's voice travels softly through the ancient space and greets my ears. Her tone is high, almost piercing. And as the sun rises higher over the mountain ridge her voice climbs with it until her words ring clear in my head.

"I'll pluck the feathers off your head. Off your head! Little lark! Little lark!" she sings, now doing something that's more classified as a dance, twirling and sashaying like a young child. She hums, still dancing. Joseph turns to me, gesturing with his thumb over his shoulder at the girl and rolling his eyes. I shake my head, bewildered as well. "I'll pluck the feathers off your eyes. Off your eyes! Off your beak! Off your head! Little lark! Little lark!" the girl sings, now even louder than before. I revolve my gaze around at the tourists now starting to roam through the plaza. They don't appear to give the girl much attention. Zero actually.

Crouching down low, the girl springs off the grassy plaza, landing on the level below with perfect grace. Her sheet of black hair covers her face. In my mind I feel Joseph's heart startle as my eyes watch him peer up at the girl one level above him. He takes three steps back. She flips her head up to reveal a heart-shaped face and large, dark eyes.

"*Je te plumerai le dos,*" Allouette sings with a giggle. Mind racing, heart suddenly hammering, I leap off the wall and sprint for Joseph.

"*Et le dos! Et la queue! Et les pattes!*" she continues to sing, crouching down again, a toothy grin plastering her chalk-white skin. Joseph slips stepping back on the glossy grass, shuffling backward on his hands and feet until he gains balance. I'm too far away from him. Allouette leaps again, soaring through the air at a distance that's humanly impossible. Knowing exactly where she intends to land, I push harder. Joseph rolls seconds before she comes crashing down, swiveling her head in his direction.

215

"*Et les ailes! Et le cou! Et les yeux!*" she continues, stalking toward him.

Rebounding off the ground, Joseph stands, taking a fighting stance.

"*Et le bec! Et la tête! Alouette! A-a-a-ah! Alouette!*" she finishes with a cackle, pulling twin blades from her waist.

"Are your fists going to beat my knives?" she says and backs up, spinning so she's facing me as well. "Or your little sticks?" She indicates the escrima sticks I've just summoned. "I don't zink so."

Joseph's eyes flash on me, a mix of worry and hostility. "What are you doin' here?"

"Finishing a job I started a very long time ago."

"You murdered our mother," I say, taking the place right next to Joseph.

"*Oui.*" Allouette giggles shrilly.

"You're disgusting," Joseph says with a shiver.

"You know, killing a laboring woman is really too easy. Takes zee fun out of it. She waz all panting, not fighting. Bleeding, already tortured by Joseph ripping her open. I got tired of the whole zing and slit her throat."

Revulsion churns in my stomach.

"I waz just about to twist his little baby neck," she says, pointing the tip of one of her knives in his direction, "when ze most horrific surprise happened out of your dead mozer. You," she says, swiveling the knife at me. "A girl. And I knew Chase vould want you. Again, he'd be distracted by the idea of pure blood. Men are stupid animals, but undeniably irresistible. I should have been able to stop this madness a long time ago by killing you, but Ren ruined it all. He knocked me out before I had a chance and stole you away. I've spent my whole life trying to find you. Killed many a Lucidite trying to gain information on your whereabouts. And now here you are. You will not become Chase's trophy, your fate is the same as your mozer's."

"I don't think so," Joseph says, stepping forward. "You've gone unpunished for too long and today you'll pay."

She sighs, looking tired. "Oh, am I going to have to kill you first? Oh fine, just line up in zee order you vant to die."

Unexpectedly Joseph disappears. Dread curls through my stomach. *He left me!* He retreated, like a coward. The space between Allouette and me feels more expansive without Joseph.

"He's much wizer than he looks," she says with a high-pitched laugh. "You shouldn't try and run though, because your time is due."

"I have zero intention of retreating." I lunge forward, bringing my sticks up in a block.

The sunlight shimmers around Allouette's petite frame, making her somehow appear less sinister. Behind her something flickers and without warning she tumbles forward, struck from behind. A stone half the size of her head barrels to the ground beside her. Joseph stands in the morning sunlight, a triumphant smile on his face. "Remember that one?" he says, standing over her heaving body. She's crouched on all fours, hair shading her face. "T did that one to you the last time with a book. The rock probably hurt a lot worse."

"Joseph," I say in a warning, as she tries to stand up again.

"I got this," he says, giving me a wink. He kicks her once in the stomach, making a guttural sound spill out of her. He gives me another triumphant look as she spits blood onto the pristine grass. "You didn't think I'd left ya, did ya, Stark?"

"Maybe," I say, frozen by the grotesque scene.

Again he pulls his leg back and sends it straight into her gut. This time, though, she's expecting it and grabs his foot and twists it so that he falls down flat on his backside. Looking to be strangely recharged, she whips around, plucking the knife from the ground where she dropped it. Before I can move fast enough she twirls around, holding the knife against his throat. "Let zis be a lesson to you both, zat two on one doesn't give you advantages, especially when facing me. Now say goodbye to your brozer."

Joseph's eyes go wide. He swallows, pushing her blade away slightly from the movement of his throat. My chest is suddenly vibrating with terror. Allouette pricks the tip of the blade to his neck and I spy the tiniest of crimson peek out from underneath it. His eyes wince with shock.

"Go ahead. Say a proper goodbye. And don't vorry, you'll see him very soon,"

"It's me you want dead, not him. Let him go," I say.

"Oh, no. Do you see zee gash he's made in my head? Zat's unforgivable."

"Well, you've got to make a decision, because you can't kill us both and I'm the one you want dead," I say, taking three calculated steps backward. Joseph's brow knits together with confusion and his eyes scream at me. But I don't care, I've made my decision. "You want me, Allouette, come and get me."

And I disappear.

♦

The chance I've taken is monumental. I've risked everything, hoping Allouette knows time is of the essence. Even the seconds it will take to slit Joseph's throat will cost her my ripple. It will dissipate almost immediately. Ren would have taught her to track the same way he taught me. Time is crucial. She knows that.

Birch trees, none bigger than two feet in diameter, most much smaller than that, surround me. Using the time of day to my advantage, I traveled back to dusk. The forest floor makes notes with each of my hurried steps. I'm twenty feet from where I landed when I hear her singing.

"*Frère Joseph, frère Joseph.*"

Sliding behind the closest and largest birch tree, I suck in a breath. Leaning forward, I catch the sight of Allouette grabbing a birch tree in one outstretched hand and swinging to the next, like she's performing in some demonic musical. "*Dormez-vous? Dormez-vous?*"

I have zero idea how I'm going to kill her, but I know without a doubt that I can't allow her to continue to stalk me. The forest ground, padded with twigs and leaves, is unforgiving to the three steps I take to a more solid-shielding birch tree.

Allouette covers the gleeful giggle that falls out of her mouth. "Roya's steps are ringing! Roya's steps are ringing!" she sings, swaying faster in my direction. Only ten feet away from her I crouch down low, knowing I need to move out of the track she's currently on. If I just move quietly enough that I can shift my position to an unknown one, then I'll gain an advantage.

"Ding, daing, dong. Ding, daing, dong," Allouette sings, continuing her pursuit. I shuffle my feet backwards on each of the words, hopefully covering the sounds of my movement. When she whirls around, sensing I've doubled back, I'm already another ten feet away from her. Now I squat down, hiding my figure sideways behind a birch tree, which has plates of bark falling off it, giving it more width than normal.

"Remember vhen you lied about killing Zhuang?" she sings, snaking a path back through the trees. "I have zeen him. He's as real and beautiful as ever. By 'kill him,' did you mean 'make him better'?" She's now moving faster, head whipping back and forth, almost amused as she searches the forest for me like I'm an Easter egg. "If zo, come and do the zame thing to me."

Allouette half skips to the birch tree in front of the one where I was hiding. I think she's spotted me because she instantly slows her progress. She throws her hands in the air and spins around like she's practicing for the role of Maria in *Sound of Music*. A giggle, which sounds almost nervous, chills the air, and then she continues her march. One of her black lace-up boots steps, surfacing on the other side of my tree, and to my relief it's quickly followed by its companion. When she's just about to march past me I spring out of my hiding spot, walloping her lower back with my escrima stick. Instead of falling down, she sprints forward. I take this opportunity to scurry backward, darting through the trees. Now my location is known. Worse than that, she isn't as injured as I'd like her to be from the assault.

I have two options now: turn around and face her or run like hell. I choose the second, crisscrossing my way through the white trees. Sometimes they're too close together for me to negotiate between, causing me to have to retrace to another path. This only makes me worry about the precious space I'm allowing between us. And then a new worry strikes. A knife sticks into a tree, inches from my head. Squatting down lower I weave my way through the forest. I know this stance gives more surface area for a blade to hit and makes me slower, but since Allouette looks to be going for a head injury, I feel this is a calculated risk.

Blades now fly past my body every few seconds, most accompanied by a "zing" sound and a splash of displaced air. Each makes me worried that a misstep will take me into the trajectory of a blade. I'm all instinct, being led through the forest path, not making any conscious decisions of my own. I've always felt safe in

219

the forest, been protected by one force or another. I make an abbreviated prayer that this will remain the case here.

Blindingly hot pain scorches my calf as a knife slices through my flesh. My feet lose their footing and my stomach lurches at the idea that the muscle of my leg is separated unnaturally. Fire races up my leg, all my other muscles paying the price for the injury that I must ignore as I stagger for a cluster of trees, more close knit than the prior patch.

The sunlight now casts horizontally through the leaves and trees, giving everything a weird shimmer. From my hideout in the cluster I'm partially hidden by a bush if I remain low.

"I like zee decoration you've left on the ground here," Allouette says, too close. "Your blood splatters out zo prettily." She giggles, like a girl told an especially good secret. "And there's zo much of it. I like to zee that."

Allouette's obsidian eyes follow the path of the blood and then they light up with evil delight. "Are you going to come out and play or shall I encourage you?"

Behind me is a stupid clearing, no places to hide, only an open field of dirt and patches of grass. In front of me is Allouette surrounded by a few thousand birch trees. Tons of tiny hiding places, none big enough. I don't even chance a look at my leg, but for some reason it feels better than moments prior, not as fragile. Still, the fire around the cut is quickly draining me. Making a split-second decision I dart to the left, sprinting as fast as I can back through the birch trees. If I can just find a place to hide for a moment I can lure her to me.

And then the second blade intrudes on my skin, nicking me like a spear along my forearm. It feels like a paper cut. Still I continue to sprint and weave.

"Come on, little lamb, you've got to be tired now," Allouette sings as more blades whistle by my head, all sticking into immature birch trees or straight into the earth decaying with bits of bark.

I second-guess a passage through a grouping of trees and my punishment comes in the way of another blade ripping across my bicep. This one is deeper than the last, guaranteed to mark my steps with blood. Running won't work anymore. I dart forward, picking up a stick that's about the length and width of the escrimas I dropped while running. Backing up three steps I stride out, so that I'm facing Allouette on profile.

She halts immediately when I come into view. Evening sun casts around her dark frame, outlining her like she's made of coal and ice. "You know, Chase vill not be coming to your rescue tonight. No one vill."

Chase is usually stalking me in every dream travel. I half expected him to be sitting on top of Funerary Rock at Machu Picchu, staring down at Joseph and me. Observing us.

"You see, I have made him indisposed for zee night. I've made him indisposed for several nights, waiting for your energies to pop into zee dream travel realm, and here you are." Her laugh sounds like that of a coo from a demented pigeon. "Your little stick is really cute. But you're zo deluded to think it stands a chance against my knives?"

Sweeping forward, she moves with a practiced grace, her long skirt punctuating every movement, like it's a part of the dance.

Advantages happen in battles when a person can take their opponent by surprise. For this reason I step forward. "Ren said you kiss like a horse gobbling up an apple and have the table manners to match."

She halts, lowers her pointy chin, and gauges me. "Did he?" She shakes her head, like shaking off a memory that attached to her like a spider web she just walked through.

"Is it true that you start to smell like bad eggs if you haven't showered in a while?" I ask, starting to meander my way through the trees, not toward her, but rather making an arc.

She begins her familiar cackle when I cut her off. "That's what Chase said," I say nonchalantly. "But maybe I didn't hear the details right since I was breathless and naked."

A hiss pierces the almost night air. "You'll go to hell for lying, girl."

"They're not my lies," I say, completing a half-circle around her. She twists around, having lost track of my progress through the woods. "These are only the things the men you've left unsatisfied have shared with me." I take two steps toward a smoldering Allouette. A knife with a dark handle is pinned in her hand, her knuckles going white from the fierce hold she has on it.

"When you're dead, I'm going to cut out your heart and make pâté out of it," she says, no sing-song quality to her voice any longer.

"Do you know where we are?" I ask, weaving my way through the trees, allowing her to trail me.

"I do not," she says, pacing her steps with mine. "Vell, I know you'll die here."

"Actually, I thought this was the perfect place for you to die tonight," I say, retracing my steps to the place where we started. Turning, I flash her my murderous eyes. "This is the Voyageurs National Park. A proper resting place, don't you zink," I say in my worst French accent.

She grimaces. "Americans are really obnoxious people. You especially."

"I can't argue with any of that," I say, planting my feet and spinning around to face her.

As I suspected she's racing toward me, the knife high above her head. I crouch down low, send my front leg back, and pivot around completely, throwing the stick into her abdomen sharply as she closes the distance. Without taking a breath I bring my opposite elbow down on her back, sending her body flat to the forest ground. She crumbles and I almost do too, from the effort my sliced muscles have endured. I stumble backwards, deciding how to finish her off. She's panting on the ground, slowly rising up onto all fours. Now that I must face the idea of killing someone it feels all wrong. Would watching my back in fear of attack for the rest of my life be worse? Too fast Allouette has her feet underneath her, perched so low that her behind must be close to grazing the floor.

"You've hesitated to kill me. You're not a killer. And that's the reason you're going to die," she says, a look of cold satisfaction on her face.

I lay the palm of my hand out flat, comb my fingers forward twice. "Bring it on."

"Consider it done," she says, her eyes hovering above my head.

I chance a glance in that direction and to my horror a glint of silver catches my eyes. A knife with a dark handle dances through the air above my head. It teeters to the left and to the right, not giving me a proper idea of which way I should retreat to avoid it. Then, like a missile zeroing in on a target, its point pivots downward and cascades toward the earth.

I step backward and to the left. Invasive pain, worse than a bullet wound, surges through my body. Hot. Breathing fire. Tarnishing everything around it. When the blade sinks down into the place between my shoulder blade and shoulder I question the judgment I made to escape it. *But it could have been my head,* I reason to myself. Still, the blade makes no place for me to move as it takes residence in my body. I stagger, reaching for it and then stopping, afraid to bring my hands around the knife that's now connected to my flesh. Allouette looks too amused, coolly watching as she leans against a nearby tree.

"Vould you like some help vith that?" she says, in a voice so sweet you'd think I should offer her a compliment in return. "Here you are," she sings. The blade, tearing muscles and ligaments, rips back out of my flesh and rises into the air. I stare up at it, a point coated in blood staring down at me with menacing grace. A single drip of blood falls off its tip and lands on my cheek, like the first droplets of a summer rain storm. In a rush I take three steps back, my shoulder making mention of each step like a trumpet blaring in my head. "You're afraid I'm going to stab you again?" she asks, like we're deciding which restaurant to patronize tonight. "Oh, no vorries. No more knives. Your death is a personal one and one I want to enjoy…vith my own hands."

I clatter backwards, finding a dead end at the same cluster of trees I'd hidden behind earlier. How had we traveled back and forth that much across this forest? The dark-handled knife is now hovering beside Allouette's face, like a bodyguard. It soars up in the air and turns downward, rocketing at my face. I suck in a sharp breath and roll in the opposite direction, landing on my backside, arms splayed out behind me on the earth. The blade sticks into the base of the birch tree I was stationed in front of.

"Good girl," Allouette cheers. "You learn so quickly." She takes two steps toward me and I kick back on my hands and feet, but find the same dead end as before—the tight cluster of trees.

The forest is now coated in mostly blacks and blues of the approaching night. For this reason I don't see Allouette's dark frame until it's pressing up against me. She's managed to pin one of my arms under her knees. Then she straddles me, pinning my other arm right where its bleeding from the laceration under her other knee.

"Are you comfy? I do vant you to feel cozy as you move into ze next life."

Her long fingernail comes closer to my face, almost in slow motion. I jerk, trying to free myself from the pin she has me in, but she's impossibly strong. "Now, now," she soothes in a most unsoothing voice. "Ztay still." The finger traces the contours of my forehead, along my nose, around my lips, over my chin, and down my throat. There she joins it with her other hand. "Zay goodbye, you filthy Lucidite, the dark spot of my life, the ruiner of all things." Her hands clamp down on my esophagus. Air is no longer welcomed into my body. Air inside me has no place to go. I'm trapped inside my prison of suffocation. Again I try to move under her pinned stance, but she has me restrained from the elbow up. She picks me up by my throat and rams my head back down on the base of the tree. Stars circle in my vision, but I maintain consciousness—barely. My fingers search the earth, dirt pushing under my nails, twigs grazing my hands and then…the smoothness of the hilt greets the palm of my hand. It's stuck firmly into the base of a tree. And with each passing second I lose my hold on this earth. On this motivation.

Being strangled and rapidly losing oxygen strangely heightens every detail. From this close distance I spy flecks of gold in her almost black eyes. Spidery veins drape her eyelids.

The rosewood handle is smooth. Taking a gigantic breath that brings me no air and empties my lungs of none of the used carbon dioxide inside me, I jerk the handle once. It stays pinned. Again, I try and release the blade, this time working it back and forth. Splinters of wood flake from the tree as I wiggle the knife free. With a force only leant to me because Joseph is somewhere close in the physical realm I lurch my arm out from under her bony knee, swing it up, and send the blade of the knife like a speeding dart into her temple.

♦

My eyes snap open. Joseph sits right up against me in my bed, his face popping with relieved surprise when I awake.

"There you are!" He grabs my hand, peers into my eyes. "Are you all right?"

"I've had better nights," I say, wincing from the pain in my shoulder as I try to sit up. "What about you?" I say, touching his neck which has a small gash and is bleeding more than I like.

"Oh, I'm fine," he says, dismissing my concern. "But I think you're lying. I bandaged up the wounds I could find, but are you hurt anywhere besides your arms and legs?"

I look down to see he's used pieces of a T-shirt to make tourniquets around the lacerations on my arms and the one around my calf. "Thanks," I say. "I have a couple other injuries, but nothing serious. Why don't you use the rest of that shirt to wipe up your neck?"

"What happened?" he asks, pressing the wadded up shirt to his neck.

My head swims in a sea of images and dizziness. I'll tell you, but I only want to go through the story once," I say, standing up and swaying slightly. "Take me to Trey."

Chapter Thirty-Seven

Shouts echo from Trey's office as we approach. I'd press my ear up to the door and listen if I wasn't certain passing out was a mounting possibility.

My knock is weak, and sounds more like a cat pawing. Joseph gives me a nervous look. "You lied. You're not all right," he says, searching my body for the other wounds.

"Not right now!" Trey answers through the closed door, his words on fire.

"Yes, right now!" Joseph says, beating on the door.

A second later it slides back, revealing a red-faced Trey and beside him Aiden looking equally flustered.

"What is it? I'm in the middle of something," Trey says, gritting his teeth. I'm not sure if the blood loss is making me imagine it, but he's almost hostile.

"Whatever it is, this is more important," Joseph says, half dragging me into Trey's office. I'm leaning on him increasingly by the minute.

"Fine," Trey says, throwing his hands through his hair. "Aiden, we will continue this later."

Through my swimming head and blurring vision I spy Aiden burning a hole in the floor with his eyes. "You're dismi—" Trey stops. Reaches out. Grips my shoulder. "Roya, why are you bleeding?" he says, picking up my hand and inspecting Joseph's dried blood. "Are you all right?"

"I'm fine," I say, surprised to hear my words slur. "And that's not *my* blood."

He grips my shoulder harder, not realizing his fingers have just reached into the gash in my back. Pulling his hand away he looks at the fresh blood now covering his fingers.

"Oh, well, *that's* my blood," I say, aware that I sound drunk.

"What? What's happened?"

"I just killed Allouette," I say, and then all my body weight slumps against Joseph and the world goes black.

♦

"Why didn't you take her straight to the infirmary!?" Trey says.

"She wouldn't let me!" Joseph answers.

"Would ya keep it down?" I say too slow. "I'm trying to sleep." The bed underneath me is all too familiar. I'm in the infirmary, the stiff brown covers tucked up to my chest.

"Roya," Joseph says, moving around Trey and grabbing my hand. "How do you feel?"

"Like someone stabbed me in the back," I say.

"Top of your shoulder," Joseph corrects. "When I asked you about your other injuries you left that one out. Oh, and the bloody gash on the back of your head."

"I actually forgot about the last one." I wince from the light in the room, my head an explosion of unrelenting pain. "Not anymore though."

Trey moves to the position beside Joseph, worried frustration coating his face. Aiden eyes me from the corner with a cautious look.

"Roya, what happened?" Trey says, his tone still frantic.

"I told you," I say, gasping for breath between each word. "I killed Allouette."

"I was hoping for details," he says, pinching the bridge of his nose.

"With a knife," I say.

With a heavy sigh he turns to Joseph. "What happened?"

"Hell if I know. She abandoned me."

"I saved your life," I say, pressing up into a sitting position, my shoulder screaming about the effort.

"After I saved yours," he says.

"Fair enough," I say, smiling a little at Joseph.

"Would you two stop?!" Trey says, flaring his nostrils. "Roya. What. Exactly. Happened?"

"Allouette followed us last night. Was planning on murdering us. She was about to slit Joseph's throat." An audible gasp falls out of Trey's mouth. "I knew, well seriously hoped, she'd track me using my ripple, so I disappeared. I'm the one she wanted to kill most. I traveled to the Voyageurs National Forest."

Joseph bursts into a laugh. "Nice!"

"Silence," Trey commands.

"Anyway, we danced around a bit," I say through measured breaths. "She stabbed me. I gave her a few bruises and I stabbed her. That's the story."

"And you're certain she's dead?" Trey gives me a skeptical look.

The memory rushes back to me, bringing with it bile in my mouth. "Yes, usually people don't recover from a knife in their brain."

"Damn, Stark!" Joseph says, gripping my fingers tighter. "You're twisted. Why didn't you go for something less disgusting? Like the chest?"

"I didn't have much of an opportunity to plan my attack since I was being strangled to death," I say, pinning my eyes on the fresh gauze bandages wrapped around the wounds on my arms.

Joseph raises my hand, placing the back of it against his cheek. "I am so, so, so sorry I wasn't there."

"I'm not," I say, repeating the scene in my head of propelling a blade into another human's brain. I don't want anyone to ever see what I did.

"I do understand that you two had to defend yourself," Trey says, glancing between Joseph and me. "But why didn't you escape by dream traveling?"

I look at Joseph, knowing our answer is the same. "Because we wanted to kill her."

"She could have killed you," Trey says too loud, making my head sear suddenly.

"Do we want to talk about what happened or didn't?"

"You take too many risks," Trey says.

"You have no idea," I say, thinking about Chase.

"What does that mean?"

"Nothing." I dismiss the question. "And it's funny you say that since all my enemies are because of you."

"Please know that I realize I'm one hundred percent responsible for all of this. I apologize," he says, his tone weighted with guilt. "Until I give you different instruction I do not want you to dream travel. Is that clear?" His authoritarian tone has a quality of protective fear. It does something strange to my insides. Unable to look directly at him, I nod, staring intently into Joseph's green eyes.

All right, let's give Roya a chance to rest," Trey says, placing a hand on Joseph's shoulder.

Joseph gives me an uncertain look, my hand still in his. "It's all right," I say. "I'll call for you as soon as I wake up."

"Before you have any visitors though," Trey interrupts, "I want a full psych evaluation done on you today."

I nod and watch them leave. "Wait," I say when all three are filing through the exit. "I need to ask Aiden a question about my patch. It will only take a minute."

Trey gives Aiden an unreadable look and nods. "Make it fast and then I want you in my office, Dr. Livingston."

Once the door closes, Aiden hurries to my bed, tentatively peering over his shoulder. He looks like he wants to reach for me but doesn't. "Roya, if you show up in my presence one more time half dead, I'm going to have a heart attack," he says in an angry rush.

"Well, if you survive it, you can recover in the bed next to me."

He allows a small smile.

"I just need to know why Trey looks like he's infuriated at you. I won't be able to rest until I do."

Aiden shakes his head. "You just stabbed someone in the head and you want to know about my drama?"

"Oh, believe me, I'm about to have an emotional breakdown about what I've just been forced to do, but I wasn't going to allow myself to in front of Trey," I say, battling a sheet of tears. "Just tell me what's going on because the extra worry is more than I can take. Is this about...?"

"No." Aiden takes a seat on my bed and holds my hand. I close my eyes, suddenly relieved by his touch and that one word. "It's about me and my work."

Aiden releases a long, furious exhale which makes my eyes spring open. His eyes are burning with anger. "Trey wants us to keep our current security," Aiden begins. "But I'm demanding that he allow me to upgrade it. He refuses. He thinks that the upgrade fails and that's how Zhuang gets into the Institute. But I think the reverse is true. I know about Joseph," he says, his tone milder suddenly. "I think Zhuang knows how to break the security because of the access he had into Joseph's thoughts, the things he would have seen. But

Trey isn't willing to see that. He keeps taking my pleas as attacks at Joseph. He's colored by his protectiveness of you two."

"And you think this is how Zhuang gets into the Institute?"

"Yes." Aiden grips his hair like he wants to pull it out. "And Trey won't listen to me," he says with a growl.

"But Bob and Steve once told me that Trey is usually right on these kinds of things because of his gift. Could he be right?"

"I don't think so because I don't think his intuition is guiding him here, it's his bias toward Joseph. Zhuang will know to submerge in water to enter the Institute. If we just changed that to something he didn't know then we could stop this whole thing."

Aiden's right. Instinctively I know he is. And it burns the blood in my veins to know Trey won't listen to reason. That he's taking it as an attack on Joseph. "Do you want me to say something?"

"No!" he says at once. "He's too mad, he'd kill me if he knew I discussed any of this with anyone...especially you. Just...don't even worry about it."

All I want is to comfort him, wrap my arms around him, ease his pain, and that's the last thing I can do.

"Really, I don't want you to worry about this," he repeats. "You have enough to think about." He gives me the look visitors offer the animals who have been at the pound for too long, those animals that are no doubt lonely and bordering on insanity due to the confines they've been sentenced to.

"You think I'm a monster, don't you?" I say, a searing pain spreading through my chest.

"No," Aiden says, shaking his head furiously. "Not at all. You defended yourself and you purged this world of a disgusting person."

"I've killed someone, marked my soul with their blood. It's not like when Amber died. This time I actually performed the act that ended someone's life."

Aiden shuffles forward on the bed, leans headfirst, and presses his forehead against mine. It's warm and his eyes are so close our eyelashes are almost touching. "Your soul is perfect. And if it's even possible I love you more for what you've done. I love you for—"

"Please stop," I choke out. Tears spill out of my eyes in a torrent, all of them racing to be the first to spill over my chin.

Aiden eases back, unbridled heartache in his eyes.

Pulling my hand from his, I wipe the tears away, but not faster than they are replaced by new ones. "You have to go—or otherwise Trey's going to be even angrier with you. The longer you stay here the—"

"I don't care, Roya," Aiden says, wiping a tear off the side of my chin with his thumb and resting it against my jaw.

I pull back, angling my face so he's no longer touching me. "I do," I say, unable to look at the expression of disappointment I know he's wearing right now. "I care what happens to you."

"Then stop pulling away from me," he says in a half whisper.

"No." I lie back, pressing the side of my face into the pillow and staring as far away from Aiden as I can manage. "Trey could walk back in here at any minute. And he probably will if you don't leave right now."

"And he'd see me comforting the girl I—"

"And he'd have another reason to fire you," I say, revolving my gaze to Aiden's.

"Please stop worrying so much about me."

"Fine, then leave so you stop giving me more to worry about."

Chapter Thirty-Eight

"Only ten sessions?" Samara says in disbelief. "I had double that when I killed Pearl."

"Apparently you're assigned fewer therapy sessions when you kill your arch nemesis versus a friend." Self-consciously I rearrange my pillows, disliking so many eyes focused on me.

"I'll remember that," Samara says dully, her eyes working their way over to Joseph and climbing up to his face. "Joseph, I bet you were terrified when Allouette held the knife against your neck," Samara says, her voice dripping with sympathy.

"Oh, only a little," he says with a sidewas smile.

"Really," I say. "Because you looked like you were about to pee in your pants."

"And she cut you too," Samara says, ignoring me, her fingertips touching the cut on his throat.

Beside Joseph, Trent looks a breath away from reaching out and slapping Samara's hand.

"It didn't hurt," Joseph says coolly, giving Samara a long smile.

"Roya was stabbed in the shoulder, Samara," Trent says, folding his arms. "Do you want to caress that too?"

Samara shoots Trent a dagger stare. "What's your deal, Trent? Can't you be a bit more sensitive about what these two have been through?" Her hand slides down Joseph's arm and she hugs it to her. Samara once told me she had a thing for bad boys; I wish she knew that she had a thing for gay boys. Joseph has done an impeccable job of shielding that information from her.

Trent plops down on my bed, sending me bouncing slightly. Melodramatically he grabs my hand and strokes my arm. "Oh, Roya, Samara has brought to my attention how insensitive I've been. Please forgive me. Can I do anything for you? Paint your nails? Braid your hair? Rub your back?"

"No, no, and hell no," I say, jerking my hand away from his with a smile. Over his shoulder I spy an amused look on George's face. He knows the true nature of the behavior being displayed here and he looks to be enjoying the drama as much as I am. He hasn't said a word since he arrived, has hardly made eye contact until now. We haven't even seen each other since he broke things off. I want him to take Trent's place so I can wrap my arms around him, but it wouldn't be like before. It would be torture for both of us.

Joseph slips his arm from Samara's clutches and comes to lean against my bed, giving Trent a curious look. "Hey, T, you better get off George's girl," Joseph says. He knows we broke things off, but he's a master at deflecting. "He's gonna get angry that you're touching her."

"I think George knows I'm harmless," Trent says, glaring at Joseph.

"It doesn't matter," I say, catching the uncomfortable look in George's eye. "We aren't together anymore."

"I bet that now you're all laid up needing comfort you wish you hadn't dumped him," Trent says.

"She didn't dump him," Joseph says in a gossipy tone.

Trent stands, turns, and gives George a nod. "Yep, that settles something I've suspected for a while. George, you're a first class idiot."

I busy my attention checking on the bandage around my calf, keeping my eyes low. "Well, I love all of you," I say, faking a yawn. "That being said, would you all get the hell out of here? I need to sleep."

"Yes, madam," Trent says, hooking his elbow through Samara's and pulling her away. She gives him a cold look. "Come on, girl, I'll put dreads in your hair. I'm certain it will look dreadful." He laughs at his own joke.

Joseph kisses my forehead. "Sweet dreams, sis."

"Thanks."

Joseph slaps George on the shoulder as he passes him. He hasn't moved, the brooding expression on his face taking up residence inside my chest.

"I've got something to tell you," George says when the infirmary door closes. He's more unshaven than I've seen him, his short beard flecked with tones of gold.

"I'm super tired. Can't this wait?" I say, fidgeting with the sleeves of my periwinkle pajamas.

"I wish it could," he says, taking three steps until he's right beside my bed.

"Okay, well, at least sit down so I don't have to crane my neck looking up at you. It hurts my shoulder."

He tentatively peers at the space beside me where Trent had sat.

"You can pull up a chair if you want," I say, hating this moment. Hating him more than he deserves. And strangely loving everything about how he looks right now.

He sighs and perches on the side of my bed, hands clasped between his legs. "Roya, all I want to do right now is be close to you, but this is just a recipe for disaster," he says, chewing on his thumb. For some reason I've always found his teeth attractive, maybe because I've grown accustomed to watching his pointy canine chew on his bottom lip. "I've been crazy ever since I found out what happened to you. I've had so many doubts."

"George, I can't discuss us right now. My brain is too full. My heart, too heavy."

"This isn't about us, it's about me." He stops and waits until I look directly into his eyes, a silent hopelessness in them. "I'm leaving the Institute."

"What?" I sit up, feeling sideswiped, and seize his forearm. "Is Trey making you do this?"

He shakes his head, confused. "No." He eyes my hand on his arm, but I don't pull it away. "This is my choice. Why would he make me leave?"

"When we were together…" I say, the words catching in my mouth sharply.

"Yes?" he encourages.

"He's just protective of me. Doesn't want me to get distracted."

"Oh." George nods, digesting the idea easier than I would have liked. "Well, no, this is about something I've been thinking about for a while. I'm going to pursue a degree in psychology at Dartmouth. For some reason I think I'll make a good therapist."

"Oh," I say, disappointment crashing around like a bumper car inside my body. "Yeah, you'd make a stellar therapist." I realize my hand is still resting on his warm forearm. I slip it away but he seizes it before I've retreated too far.

"I've had my doubts, but I feel like this is the right thing to do," he says, both of his hands holding mine, stroking my knuckles.

"How could you get into Dartmouth on such short notice? Don't you have to apply and go through certain processes for that kind of thing?"

George releases a smile. "You should know that your father is a well-connected man. He can make things happen."

"Yeah, he made a lot of things *happen* in my life." Resentment saddling in my tone.

"It's not like I'm ever really gone. I'm only a dream travel away."

"I've been forbidden from dream traveling," I say sullenly, pulling my hand free. Sitting all the way up I cross my legs under me, careful with my injured calf. We're closer now.

The idea of the Institute without George in it feels wrong. He may not be mine anymore, but he's still like an important fuse inside me. "Is there something I can do to make you stay?"

He rubs his lips together, an undeniable hope in his eyes.

Tell him you love him, my brain beseeches. *Make him stay*. My lips part. Mouth hangs open until my tongue is parched. "George...I..." I finally force out.

Earnest desire rings from his eyes.

"I don't want you to leave," I say in a rush. "I know we're not together, but I still need you in my life. And that's the most selfish thing I've ever said, but after everything I just don't want to lose you. Your presence brings me such comfort."

"Roya, I know you're experiencing a lot of heightened emotions right now. More than anything in the world I want to be the one to help you through them. But I'm going to be selfish too because if I comfort you, then in the end I'll break my own heart with possibilities that will never be fulfilled."

"So there's no way to change your mind?"

"Is there any way to change your heart?"

"Maybe...with time."

"I'll be here until Tuesday," he says.

Chapter Thirty-Nine

Sleep was not a companion to me during my stint in the infirmary. When my eyes closed Allouette's face swam into my mind. Dozens of times her sharp cackle ripped through my head as I slipped into dreams. And the few times I successfully slept, I killed Allouette over and over again. The therapist, an older man with wiry gray hair and droopy eyelids, urged me not to run from the dreams or make them go away. But I couldn't take the experience of feeling the knife in my hand plunge through her flesh and veins and bone and brain. So I didn't sleep.

My room greets me oddly. It looks exactly the way it always does, with books neatly stacked in various places and the peacock headdress Bob and Steve gave me hanging unceremoniously from the lamp on the desk. The bedcovers have been changed, leaving no reminders of my blood that stained the sheets during the battle with Allouette. Somehow it feels like the room has been washed clean of that night and all its trauma. My eyes find the tablet of Bes leaning against the wall beside my bed.

"I've missed you, old friend," I say to the empty room, eyes on the Egyptian god. "You're what was absent in the infirmary."

Sliding down on my bed, I'm suddenly sucked into the warmth that only a familiar space can provide. Somehow this room has taken on an energy. My energy. And now, feeling the comparison between it and the infirmary I can definitively say this space has a quality of home to it. Sleep, a welcomed friend, so soft and gentle, slips down on my consciousness. There are promises, as I visualize my green hill, that the dreams to come will be as mundane as sweeping a clean floor. My deprived body is instantly drawn in by the presence of sleep, yielding to its healing forces. This experience of sleep is almost melodious, lightly carrying me off like the notes of a breeze through the trees.

Knock...Knock. Knock. Knock.

"No," I groan into my pillow.

Knock...Knock. Knock. Knock.

My calf doesn't appreciate the roll I do to get out of bed. It will have to get over it. Sluggish as a manatee I drag myself to the door and miss the button twice before finally slamming my flat palm against it. "What!?" I growl.

The chipper look on Patrick's face slides into one of disappointment. "Well, excuse me for living. Just thought you'd like your package, Sassy." He pushes a small box into my hands, his mustache twitching slightly.

"I'm sorry, Patrick. I was just trying—"

"Don't sweat it, sweetheart." He tips his hat at me. "You're allowed one or two of those." He turns and whistles as he trots off.

Too tired to enjoy whatever thoughtful gift Bob and Steve have sent, I toss it on the bed and roll back onto my sheets. It takes only seconds for sleep to crash down on me, this time not gently, but more like a tsunami, quick and inescapable.

An hour and half later I'm roused by a sharp corner in my back. I roll over to find I'm lying on the small box. Although I probably could use more sleep, I'm half grateful to be awoken. It's time I made an appearance in the main hall for dinner, since I suspect Joseph will be waiting to see me. And I hope George, since he leaves tomorrow. Groggily, I shake my hand, which is tingling with numbness since I spent most of my nap lying on it.

Feeling forty-six percent better than I did a couple of hours ago I pull the small package Patrick had given me on to my lap. The apple-sized box piques my curiosity due to its tininess. Bob and Steve usually send huge boxes which contain dozens of wonderful gifts. There's only a small rustle when I shake the box next to my head. Pulling back the folds of the box I find a single piece of paper:

Dear Roya,

Since you can't come to us, we decided to come to you. Surprise!

Love,
Bob and Steve

About a minute. That's how long I stare at the piece of paper completely bewildered. Apparently I need more sleep. I read their note again, doubting my comprehension skills. On the third time through something clicks in my fuzzy brain. "Oh!" I squeal, jumping up too fast from my bed. Again my stupid calf complains.

Again I ignore it and sprint for the entrance, sliding to a halt and slapping the button. When my door slides back the best surprise I could have hoped for is waiting for me. The faces of these two men can't be a more welcome sight. Bob and Steve in the flesh. How long has it been? Since before I'd come to the Institute. Too long.

"Oh my God!" I shriek. "I'm so sorry! You've been out here waiting this whole time!" I throw my arms around each of their shoulders, pulling them in for a double hug. "I'm such an idiot. I'm so sorry. I fell asleep."

Steve's chest vibrates with a chuckle. He's smiling from one end of his face to the other when he pulls away, shaking his head. "From the sound of it, you really needed to sleep."

"Don't worry, honey." Bob squeezes my arm gently and then grimaces. He eyes the bandages nervously. "I'm so sorry. Did I hurt you?"

"No, they don't hurt really anymore. Mae's a fantastic healer. She said she kept the bandages on to remind me to take it easy." My voice is overflowing with a giddy excitement. "The one on my calf is being pretty stubborn though, but Mae says that's to be expected when a large muscle is severed so deeply. You want to see it?" I joke.

"Maybe after we've eaten," Bob says through a laugh that makes his face turn red.

"So you're dealing with everything all right?" Steve says, his voice turning the conversation serious suddenly.

The show of a fake smile on my face tells more than my words. I try to make it sincere, but I know it's laced with the trauma I can't escape. "Yeah. Each day I feel better."

"Oh, Roya," Bob says, wrapping arms around me that I've only felt while dream traveling. They're softer in the physical realm, even more welcoming. "No one should have to bear all that you have, but if anyone can, it's you." He pulls back, holding each of my arms, a tender ache in his eyes. "I hope you don't mind, we've taken to calling you 'Ms. Astonishing.'"

And just like that I become a victim to my emotions when a single tear escapes and rolls down my cheek. "I don't mind," I say in a croaky voice.

"We've had the opportunity to meet some of your friends while we waited," Steve says, the sudden tenderness of the moment obviously making him uncomfortable.

"Who'd you chat up?" I say, pushing the tear away, hoping it won't be followed by more.

"George," Steve says. "He's an awfully nice gentleman."

"Yes, he's the nicest."

Bob eyes me. "Things not rosy between you two anymore?"

"Oh, how do you do that?" I say.

"This time I can't take credit for any intuition," Bob says. "Your face just went pale at the mention of his name."

"Well, it's because he broke my heart for breaking his and now he's leaving," I say, trying not to sound overly pathetic. "It's for the best and I get that, but I just don't want to deal with one more thing right now."

The two exchange uncomfortable glances. "I'm sorry. I'm a little melodramatic at the moment," I say with a sigh.

"No apologies necessary. I think we," Bob says, motioning between him and Steve, "just feel a little helpless and that's a difficult place to be when it involves you."

"You didn't by chance meet a smooth-talking guy with blond hair and green eyes while you were waiting?" I ask, steering the conversation in a more positive and less tear-provoking direction.

"We did not," Bob says. "Are you referring to Joseph?"

"I am and I would be honored to introduce you to him." Excitement coasts through me at the idea that I get to introduce my favorite people to each other. I pull them down the hallway, headed to the main hall. "Hey, you had to go through the GAD-C when you entered the Institute, right?"

"Yes," Steve confirms.

"Which white coat was attending?" I ask.

"Hmmm." Bob looks off, thinking. "I think his name was James."

"Oh," I say, a little deflated. "Yeah, James is cool."

The main hall is mostly empty when we arrive. It's still a bit early, but I know that before too long white coats and other Institute staff members will scamper between the various buffet tables filling their plates with roasted meats, steamed vegetables, and one of the potential starch offerings. I point to our usual table and the three of us take some seats.

It's almost surreal to have Bob and Steve here with me and it makes me realize how quickly and slowly the last three months of my life have felt. Truly it has been the longest three months of my life, and that's mostly because never before have I done, learned, or experienced so much in so little time. Now I know that this is the life of a Lucidite. When you have the option of spending your nights traveling the globe and history then it does seem as though a week is a month and a month is a year and I can only imagine how a year will feel like a decade. If I make it past Zhuang's attack, then I have potentially centuries to spend evolving as a Lucidite, as a person.

"There's something I want to tell you about Joseph before you meet him," I whisper, although there are only a few people in the main hall.

Bob and Steve both incline their head in my direction. "You see, he's keeping a secret and I wouldn't usually tell anyone about it, but you guys are different. I actually think maybe you can offer some of your incredible advice on the subject. Joseph is—"

"Coming our way right now," Bob says, pointing over my shoulder.

I turn my head to find my brother walking in with a crowd of about half a dozen other people. A sentimental smile I don't usually grace him with breaks out on my face. Must be having Bob and Steve here that inspired it. He abandons his place in line as soon as he sees me.

"How'd you pick him out?" I turn and ask Bob.

An easy laugh tumbles out of his mouth. "How'd you not realize you two were related from the beginning? He looks just like you, except for the obvious differences."

Joseph presses his hand on my unscathed shoulder.

"Hey, Joseph," I say, looking up at his jubilant face. I sense he already knows who's keeping my company at the moment, but I introduce them anyway.

"Pleased to meet you. I've heard all sorts of wonderful things about you two." Joseph shakes both of their hands.

"The pleasure is all ours," Steve says.

"So first things first," Joseph says, his face turning grave. "Did Roya tell you she's pregnant?"

My fist connects with Joseph's arms before he finishes the sentence. He doubles over laughing, and to my relief Bob and Steve join in.

"Have I mentioned that my brother is a compulsive liar?" I say.

"Not compulsive," Joseph corrects, with his finger held high in the air. "That would suggest that I can't control it. However, I have the ability to control what comes out of my mouth and I just choose to say things that are considered slightly exaggerated."

"Even that statement you've said is oozing with untruths," I say.

"She's acting out a bit because I told her that she wears too much gray. And by too much I mean she should erase it from her wardrobe because no one should ever wear it. I suspect that, like all drab things, my poor sister is married to this color. Poor thing."

"They bought me all those clothes that you're referring to, so watch out."

"Right." Joseph turns and looks at the two men seriously. "I wear a size medium and love the color red and I'm much more entertaining than my sister and also available for adoption."

Bob slaps Steve's arm as they both fall into another fit of laughter. "You two are truly bookends." Bob waves at the two of us. "One amazing pair."

"Astonishing," Steve corrects.

"Right. Mr. and Ms. Astonishing," Bob says, his voice brimming with merriment.

I give Joseph a quick look and avert my eyes. There's something about him that I love so much and sometimes it fills me up and catches me off guard.

"So what brings you two here?" Joseph asks.

"We had a bit of business and also we were overdue to see Roya," Steve explains.

"Are you two staying long?" Joseph asks.

"No," Bob answers. "We have to get back in an hour or two."

"Oh, that's too bad." Joseph has the most incredible ability for making whoever he's speaking to feel like they're the center of his attention. "Well, I'll just do my best to fill you in on Roya's quirky and unorthodox behavior. Maybe between the three of us we can have a positive influence." He leans in close and whispers, "You know she reads Emily Dickinson's poetry compulsively, although

241

I've told her it will only lead to a life as an old maid with three thousand cats."

To my shock the three shake their heads in unison. Steve clicks his tongue. "Yes, Dickinson is good in small amounts, but too much can be lethal."

I slam my palm against my forehead, utterly flabbergasted by this scenario. "Oh my God, you've got to be kidding me."

"And there's my sister's obvious poor manners," Joseph says, shaking his head with disappointment.

"I want to see if I can track down a few other people who I'd like to introduce you to, and aren't quite as offensive as my dear brother," I say, scanning the main hall.

"Your brother is quite delightful," Bob says, his cheeks red from laughing. "But we'd love to meet anyone and everyone you'd like us to."

"That sounds good." I push up from the table. "I'll be right back." I turn to Joseph, giving him a stern smile. "Just keep your opinions to yourself, would you?"

"If you don't mind I think I'll go and get something to eat." Joseph smirks. "I do have other activities to occupy my time rather than obsessing over what a ridiculous mess you are."

The three of them snicker together. I wave them off as I stride down the hallway, bent on finding one person in particular who I want Bob and Steve to meet before they leave the Institute.

I have the elevator to myself for the trip to the fifth level. Excitedly I half skip to the Panther room, hoping to find Samara. Maybe I can even convince her to fetch Trent from Scape's Escapes while I—

I never have a chance to finish the plan in my mind. The flash rockets across my attention, stealing it and laying undeniable claim. The vision buckles my knees under me, and due to the weakness of my calf I lose control and fall to the ground, choking on breath and spit. After less than ten seconds I'm released back to my reality to do the only thing left: run.

My feet don't stop racing until I round into his lab. I could have stopped at the Panther room, warned Shuman. Or Ren's department. But I knew deep in my soul the one place I need to go next is one that will restore my hope.

"Aiden!" I scream, coming around the corner. He's at his main work station and whips his head around to find me, his eyes already crazed with worry.

"What?!" He races for me.

I'm already expecting the tremor that throws him off balance as he closes the distance. It's small, but enough to rattle the cabinets and their contents.

"Zhuang is here," I say, and watch his eyes go wide.

Chapter Forty

Aiden stumbles from the jolt, but recovers quickly. "That's the reason for the shock?"

I nod.

"Did you just see this in a vision?"

"Yes," I say, wanting to reach out for his hand, which is shaking slightly as he pushes his glasses more firmly up on his nose. He bolts off to the nearest computer station. Hurriedly, he strikes the keyboard like it's done something wrong and is deserving of the rough treatment. I turn to leave, not sure why I'm standing there staring at him when I have so much to do.

"Zhuang disabled the elevators when he entered the Institute," Aiden says, to my retreating back.

I spin around, brow knitting together. "What?"

He nods, staring at the screen. Dissecting it. "It's true. I won't be able to get the system that manages them operating for over an hour," Aiden says, like this is the most preposterous idea he's had to digest in a while.

"But I have to—"

Aiden cuts in, still engrossed in the data running across his screen. "He's knocked down our entire security system. Anyone can get into the Institute now." I've never seen someone strike a keyboard so rapidly before. His eyes race over the screen as he does, a furious concentration in them.

"Trey was wrong and you were right," I say, the realization crashing down on me. "About Zhuang getting in here."

"I wish I hadn't been," he says.

I dare to walk up to where he's standing and peer over his shoulder, like I have any idea what the information on the screens means.

"All right, I've shut down our GAD-Cs, so at least no one can enter that way," he says.

"Aiden," I say in a voice that's startles me.

"Yes?" he says, still typing on his keyboard wildly, each stroke of his fingers deliberate and forceful.

"Zhuang makes it to the first level."

He freezes. Turns. Looks at me. "Oh…"

"Isn't there a way we can contain him on the third level before he moves?"

"There's about a hundred ways but who knows which will work."

"Bob and Steve are there. And Joseph. I have to get up there," I say in a rush.

"They'll know to leave. Don't worry about them. Now you've got to get out of here."

"Bullshit!" I refuse. "I'm not leaving."

"Well, you're not getting back up there. You have no choice but to dream travel at this point," Aiden says.

"I'll find another way." I stare around his lab for some sort of clue to how I can get back to the first level.

Without looking away from the screen, and as if he's computing a complex equation at the same time, he says, "You don't have to do whatever you're planning."

"You know I do." I chew on my lip, scanning everything I know about the Institute trying to find an option. "I have to get up there. You have to help me. This is something I need to do."

He spins around, giving me an intense look. I want to avert my eyes from his sapphire ones, but I can't turn away, especially if this is the last time I'll see them. "Here's the deal, Roya. I'll tell you how to get up there because I'll *never* stand in your way if you really want to do something. But I want you to treat me with that same respect."

"Yes, fine. Of course," I say, urging him to continue. "Just tell me how to get up there."

"I know we don't have time for this kind of thing, but there's something I have to say. Please come here." Aiden grabs my hand, wrenching me in close to him. "We may not survive tonight. I can't die with regrets for what I haven't been allowed to say or do." He takes my head in his hands. "If we survive, I'm going to exclaim my relentless love for you to the Institute. And I don't want you to even try and stop me."

"But…" I dare to argue.

He almost laughs. "No arguments. If you want to know how to get to the first level then that's your deal."

Aiden leans down, his lips hovering an inch from mine. He pauses, capturing this moment. Relishing the seconds that precede this kiss. I'm the one who's forbidden our closeness for over a month. Only in a dream did I allow my true desires to be experienced. But even in the dream, it wasn't enough; it only teased me. "Yes, fine, I agree," I say, starving to actually feel him. He lays his lips against mine, resurrecting a soul I'd questioned if I still had. Giving rise to a spirit I'd thought had deserted me. Finally he releases me at the same moment I release him. Breathless, I suck in the gasp spilling out his mouth.

"I really hope we don't die tonight. I don't want to wait another lifetime to love you. But if I must...I'll wait a thousand," he says. And again in his arms I'm reborn, by the kiss we share, the stolen moment we give to ourselves. Reluctantly he pulls away, a small smile on his lips. "I kiss, I tell. That's the rule, right? If we survive this, you can't stop me. Okay?"

"Okay," I agree, pressing my mouth to his one last time.

"All right, I'll keep my word. I'll tell you how to get up there. You're going to keep taking this corridor away from the elevators. When it T's, take a left, a right, and another left. There will be an unmarked door. It's the stairwell for the Institute. It will get you up there."

"Thank you." There's a look in his eyes that gives me pause, keeping me from whipping around and running. I need to race to the first level. I need to escape his arms so we all escape what's coming, but I'm afraid that it won't matter and this is my last moment for happiness. So selfishly I soak in everything about us one last time. And then I make myself back away from him, knowing I need distance to say what I have to. "I need you to know that no matter what happens, that no matter what you hear about what happens up there, that—"

"Roya, what are you going to do?" he says, all his passion churning into worry.

"Aiden, if I don't come back, if I can't, wherever I end up, I need you to know if I ever had a choice, it was always you."

"Roya, what are you going to do?" he says as I back away. Panic in his eyes.

"I'm going to sell my soul to the devil."

"No," he whispers urgently.

"I have to. It's the only way, and it's my choice."

Hopeless grief hoods his eyes. And, heartbreakingly, Aiden is true to his word. He doesn't try to stop me, just shakes his head.

"I love you," I say, backing away. With urgency like I've never known I take in every ounce of him before I force myself to spin around and run.

Chapter Forty-One

Each stride takes me farther from Aiden and deeper into an unknown passageway. After fifty feet, it T's. The size of the Institute has always astounded me but now it tightens my chest. How far will I have to run to get to the stairs? And then there will be the hike up all four stories. I know the climb won't go unnoticed by my injuries, but I have no choice.

The siren assures me my new reality is no illusion. It pierces the air, which is more humid in this area of the Institute. Zhuang is here. A force so evil he'll stop at nothing to obtain what he wants. And still, a parasite like him can never be happy. Those who have replaced their heart with greed and allowed their pride to direct their mind will never be content.

The first time I met Zhuang it was as his challenger, a fate neither of us could escape. Now I know for both of us this is personal. When I challenged him he said he'd waited a long time for me to be born, that absorbing my consciousness was an ingredient he needed to gain powers. How is it I was born into these impossible roles? Zhuang wants my consciousness. Chase my blood. Was I only born to die, like livestock that fat Americans slaughter to feast upon?

Strange that so soon after feeling the life within me grow brighter from Aiden's kiss, it has already dissipated, my heart a numb organ. Its purpose is now only for pumping blood to the rest of my body. And my body's purpose is to take commands from my mind, the commander bent on ending a war which has gone on for too long.

The unmarked door is immediately after the second left. Without hesitating I barrel through it and come to a halt. Suddenly I've been tossed through the rabbit hole where everything I know is turned upside down. A stainless steel staircase stands before me. The cylinder walls are bathed in the shimmering blue carpet. A mahogany banister, as red as the rubies on my necklace that holds the frequency adjuster, follows the path of the stairs. The newel post, a large orb, is covered in a thick layer of dust. My hand grabs it to pull me up the first set of stairs and my fingers catch on an engraving. I pause and displace what feels like decades' worth of dust. I choke out a cough as I read the inscription.

"Take the first step in faith. You don't have to see the whole staircase, just take the first step." –Martin Luther King, Jr.

Guilt scratches at my insides for stopping to read this when time is crucial, but these words feel strangely important. The meaning can be considered literal when found here at the bottom of a spiral staircase, but for the mission that lurks ahead of me there's something important to take away here.

In an effort to make up for my pause, I take the steps two at time. Often I catch my shoes on the nosing of the tread, but I maintain my balance by gliding my hand along the railing. Round and round I go, so fast, so many times my head begins to spin. My senses swimming in a cloud of dizziness is actually a welcome state. I know without too many stresses on my body, my mind will be centered on the battle being waged a few flights up. The battle I'm quickly closing in on, but might be over before I even arrive.

At the fourth-level landing I'm assaulted by a flash so vivid and violent my knees fall forward on the step above me and my hands cradle my head. My elbows slam on the step, the cold stainless steel pinching. I suck in a breath so sharply it constricts my throat. Stiffens my chest. Delivers no real nutrients, just an ever-real message that shock is shooting through my body.

Bolting upright, I push away the tremors vibrating through my muscles. I push forward. If I can just get there in time then maybe I can stop it. I have to stop it. Now I'm racing up the stairs, taking the steps three at a time. My insides burn with vengeance for an act that hasn't even occurred yet. It doesn't matter because now I know more than ever I have to kill Zhuang. After witnessing what I just saw I don't doubt that I'll do whatever it takes to rid this world of that vile man once and for all. This has gone on for much too long and I don't care if I die sending Zhuang to hell. Actually I'm pretty certain I'll die trying, or worse, be imprisoned in an awful fate. But it doesn't matter. Nothing matters more than killing that man. There's no point living in this world if he kills every single person I care about. And there's an entire world outside the Institute which has suffered because this man was allowed to exist. The world deserves to live without this evilness and as a Lucidite it's my responsibility to purge it of him before he burns it down.

Pushing through the exit I barrel down a hallway I recognize. The main hall isn't too far. *Thank God.* And then a hand grips my wrist and yanks me back with such intensity I consider throwing a fist against the force. But I know it's him immediately. I know his presence almost as well as I know my own.

He pulls me into him so tight that I have hardly any room to negotiate a distance. "Joseph," I say, tucked up right next to him. Too close. But after everything I've seen, not close enough. "You're all right?"

He nods, a stern look in his eyes. We're pushed into the corner right beside the display case in the lobby.

"I knew you'd find a way up," he says, pushing me back, looking me over like I might be hurt.

I can't help but to reach out and touch his cheek. After what I saw in the vision, I have to know.

"I'm real," he says, a smile in his voice, but absent from his face. "I made it out."

My brow wrinkles. I can't compute everything I've seen with my present reality.

"You got out of the main hall? How? What are you doing here?" I ask, looking around the lobby to confirm we're all alone.

"Retrieving this," Joseph says, laying a small two-inch sheathed blade in my hand. "I stashed it here," he indicates to the display case.

"Thanks," I say, distracted by the track outlining in my head. I tuck the knife in my waistband and cover it up with the back of my shirt. "Come on, we've got to get back to the main hall." I start off in that direction, mustering the courage to tell Joseph what I've seen and know we need to prevent from occurring.

With a jerk, he tugs my hand, pulling me backwards, causing me to spin around. I scan his serious expression and something in me dislodges and cascades in the pit of my stomach. "It's too late," he says, his tone careful.

"No," I whisper, pulling my wrist free from his grasp. "I've just seen it and we still have time. I have to get to them before—"

"It's too late. What you saw already happened."

There's a prickle in my throat as I scan Joseph's face and then his thoughts and then his emotions. My chest convulses likes the beats of a drum as the harsh reality washes over me.

"No," I whisper again in disbelief.

"I'm sorry. Everyone who was in the main hall is dead. I'm so sorry," he says, his lips barely parting.

"But maybe you're wrong. How do you know? It just happened." The dull ache starts in my back and spasms until it's around my stomach and threatening to cut off my ability to breathe.

"I know because I was there. And it happened before the sirens went off. What you saw wasn't a premonition. I'm sorry." Joseph places his hands on either side of my shoulders and stares straight into my eyes.

The flash which I've refused to replay in my mind suddenly fast-forwards over and over until the pressure in my throat is enough to block my air way. Patrick's limp body lying in the process of regeneration. He never completed it. If the flash I saw came to pass as Joseph says, then the lighting overhead crashed down, frying him, crushing him when he was so close to escaping. And so many others. Inside of less than thirty seconds the vision I saw showed the deaths of dozens.

And the two I replay now in my mind convulse my being. It was easier than it should have been to walk away from my fake parents. To enter this place and know my entire life was a lie has been manageable. Learning my father's true identity has swallowed parts of my being. But to watch Bob and Steve die in my mind is an aching curse, one that scars my soul, rips hope from my heart. They were the ones to first bury any faith inside me. To love me when I thought I was unlovable. Without them…

I sink my head into my hands and feel tears push against the silk barrier. I can't try and contain this. If there's no time to grieve then let Zhuang strike me down, because all I have audience for is the tears erupting out of my being. Joseph's arms pull me into him. His hands stroke my head; rub my back.

In my mind I watch Bob and Steve laughing in the main hall. Zhuang enters, but they don't know it; all their attention is on each other. Inside my mind I scream to them, but they're unaware. They have no idea of the weapons being prepared to attack them. They laugh. Bob pats Steve's arm. And I watch, imprisoned in my vision.

Two twin carving knives, dripping in grease and shreds of meat, spiral through the air. Their trajectory clear. Bob and Steve see the weapons too late. The same as everyone in the room about to be impaled by an innocent object repurposed for destruction. The blades strike each of them like bullets, finding residence in their chests. Steve stands, reaching for the blade and simultaneously pulling away from it. Bob kneels over, disillusioned by the attack and quick change of events. Bloods spurts out of the gashes where the serrated metal intrudes inside their bodies. Collectively they suffer. Gasps for breaths which are limited.

Their faces turn to find each other's gazes and capture a moment of comfort in the other's eyes. It isn't poetic that they died together. It's horrible and only happens in worlds where the wrong people are allowed to live.

My stomach churns with revulsion. Sickness reaches up all the way to my esophagus, and when it's about spill out of me I swallow hard knowing that now I have to hold it together. The pain sinks back down to a place deep inside me with a promise of exploding in the near future.

I push back from Joseph, gripping his hands, letting the tears dry on my cheeks. "How did you escape?" I ask.

"I hid behind a nearby column at the back of the hall. When I realized Zhuang wasn't going to move away from the exit I ducked under a table, dream traveled to the GAD-C on this level, and generated my body."

"You did that before Aiden shut them down?" I say in disbelief.

"What?"

"Aiden shut down the GAD-Cs immediately. I was with him."

"Everything happened incredibly fast, Roya," Joseph says, wearing the grief of a person who's just witnessed multiple tragedies. "There was hardly time…"

"We still have to get back to the main hall, even if everyone's dead, because that means there's still one last person to kill."

"Actually we need to stay put."

"But the fight happens in there."

"No it doesn't," Joseph argues.

"But you said…" I stammer.

"Things have changed."

"Well, if the fight doesn't happen in the main hall, then where?"

My brother points down to where we stand. "Right here. In the lobby."

Chapter Forty-Two

A piercing scream tears our attention away from the current revelation. "Someone help me! Please!" Samara shrieks, her voice sounding to be tattered by fearful tears.

Joseph and I exchange a single glance before bolting down the hallway, to the auditorium where the now incessant screaming originates.

"No! No! No!" she cries and the terror in her voice rips through me, propelling me forward faster. We slow as we approach the auditorium, unsure what danger we'll encounter. I pull ahead and crane my neck around the corner to get a read on the room. Samara stands on the front of the stage. Tears streak down her red face and her chest is vibrating with hyperventilated breaths. Her eyes are pinned on the floor in front of her. The two-hundred-seat auditorium is empty.

"Help me, please?" she says, her voice a frantic whisper, eyes still pinned on the ground. "Please, Roya. Please, Joseph. Help me." Something brown and long slithers on the stage next to her. I blink and the object clicks into focus. Only inches from Samara, curled up, is a king cobra. Its tongue flickers out of its mouth and quite suddenly it raises the front part of its body a foot and a half off the ground. It stands, swaying side-to-side, preparing to strike.

Careful not to startle the serpent, I peel around the corner and inch my way into the room. As I move down the main aisle I feel Joseph just behind me. I have no idea how we're going to rescue Samara from this snake, but I also know I can't leave her here to die like this. When I'm only five feet from the stage I come to a halt gently. The snake swivels around, eyes fastening on me. The sideways look I give Joseph communicates the doubt running rampant through my being. Samara's whimpering draws the snake's attention back to her. A strand of her straw blonde hair falls in her tear-streaked face as she gasps suddenly, backing up two steps.

"Wait," I say, gripping Joseph's forearm. "Samara's hair is white blonde."

"Shit!" he says and the projection of both Samara and the king cobra disappear. I spin around on my toes, readying myself for

Zhuang to fall from the ceiling or throw a weapon at me. Nothing happens. The auditorium is a sea of quiet. Joseph scans the area too and shrugs, confusion binding his eyebrows. A long ten seconds later Ren slinks into the doorway, rubbing his hands together with a conceited knowing expression.

"Hey there, you little prats," he says, standing squarely in the entryway.

"Why'd you do that?" I ask through clenched teeth.

"You're daft to think Trey didn't know you'd try and fight. It's kind of cute actually that you thought you could stay and save the day. But this isn't your fight. Leave this one for the adults, would you?"

"Trey put you up to this?" Joseph sounds unconvinced and slightly hurt.

"Well, he told me to make sure you two didn't get yourself killed. Since you're so foolish it's really quite the task. Anyway, here's the deal. You can dream travel out of here like you were told to do in the first place, or you can play tic-tac-toe until you're blue in the face. One thing is certain, you're not physically leaving this room." Ren flashes his trademark sneer and taps the button outside the door.

Joseph and I race for the door. For as fast as I push myself, I'm still unsuccessful at reaching it before it's sealed shut. A click. We've been locked inside. I rapidly tap the button anyway, trying to reopen the door. It doesn't budge.

"Great." I kick it repeatedly, hoping to break whatever device is locking it.

Joseph checks the other doors and a few seconds later confirms we're in fact imprisoned.

"This is ridiculous!" I say. "I can't believe Trey knew all along!"

"Well, you got to give him a little credit," Joseph says.

I scowl at him. "At this point we might as well get out of here. There's no point in sitting around," I say, sliding down the wall and sitting.

Joseph takes a seat next to me. "Don't write us off just yet." There's a curious look on his face. "Is that GAD-C still in Aiden's lab?"

"Yes, but it's probably shut down too. And anyway, that's on the fifth level."

"Mmm, but it's there, huh? And it has the screen that enables him to see people while they're dream traveling, right? Like the other one?"

"Yes, but Joseph, it won't work and besides, Aiden will be there."

"Exactly," Joseph says, scooching down until he's lying flat. "Stay here. I'll be right back."

My eyes bulge in disbelief. "But what are you doing?"

"What I do best," Joseph says with a wink. "I'm gonna smooth talk our way out of here."

He shuts his eyes, leaving me alone in the large auditorium. Not five seconds later something rocks the long wall to the right of me. It shudders for several seconds after the blow. Every hair stands up on my body as my mind begins spinning with questions. Another blow shakes the wall, this one even louder. A major fight is ensuing just outside this room and I'm forced to sit and listen to blow after blow like I'm in a bomb shelter. Are those bodies being thrown up against the walls? Is it furniture? What exactly is going on out there? I know I can dream travel and see firsthand, but I have to stay put and watch over Joseph's defenseless body.

Strikes now ricochet off the walls adjacent to us every few seconds. Some followed by a howl of pain. Others followed by glass shattering and debris crashing to the floor. Every now and then the loud noises subside for a few seconds, which only makes me jump higher when the delayed bang hurtles against the wall. It's infuriating to sit and do nothing. I'm not a "do nothing" kind of person, but I didn't fully understand that about myself until now. I like the drama. I thought it was a curse that I'd been chosen as Zhuang's challenger, but I secretly have always enjoyed that this was my fate. Stopping evil gives my life a unique purpose, one I never had before I set foot inside the Institute.

I look down and realize that without noticing it I bit my fingernails off. Some are partially bleeding where I've ripped them down past the quick.

"Shit!" I curse as the loudest sound yet explodes, making the door behind me vibrate. The lights in the room flicker.

Joseph doesn't stir like waking from a dream, but rather sits bolt upright, a look of consternation on his face. "Come on," he says, standing up in one clear movement.

"What? What's going on?"

"Aiden has this place monitored through a video feed," Joseph says, taking a measured breath. "Roya, this fight is not goin' well. It's actually as bad as it could be. They're out there losing terribly. All of them are about to die."

The door clicks, like a lock has been released.

"You got Aiden to free us? How?"

"If someone doesn't do somethin' then we're all gonna die. I told Aiden we stood a chance of defeating Zhuang. That we have a plan that might work."

"And that's why he let us free?" I ask, amazed.

"No, he's let us free because I told him his future...if we all survive, that is."

Chapter Forty-Three

The door slides back with a sucking sound. Aiden isn't just allowing this, he's supporting it. Somewhere there are cameras showing our progress as we move toward the lobby. No doubt he's watching on them now. He's stronger than me, because I wouldn't be able to watch him do what I'm about to.

The lighting in the corridor is minimal, but enough to illuminate the destruction ahead. As I prowl forward the signs that mass chaos have transpired increase rapidly. I almost trip over the AC vent lying in my path. Water sprays though cracks in the ceiling, oozes through the seams in the panels of stainless steel walls, and soaks the blue carpet, making it squishy. It's hard to believe ten minutes ago this area was completely intact. Shards of glass crunch under my shoes. The display case is demolished. Now that I'm watching the ground for a clear path I see the glass is flecked with blood. The lump in my throat assures me I'm not numb after watching Bob and Steve die. Whose blood is that? Could Trey be dead?

I take each step, careful not to make a single sound. Ahead someone sways, their back to us. They're cowering over a kneeling figure, which looks only half conscious. I'm so focused on deciphering the scene ahead of us I hardly register the flicker in my peripheral. I edge my eyes to the left and what I see sends me to the far side of the hallway in three silent steps. Joseph slides up next to me, grabs my arm. "What the hell?"

"Rattlesnakes," I mouth.

He flips his head to the side and spies the pile of snakes slipping through the open AC vent, tumbling over each other as they swarm to the center of the lobby, the same as us. Joseph shivers. "Damn," he mouths.

I nod, refocusing on the battle up ahead, twenty feet away. Sparks spray above our heads from severed wires in the canned lighting. A small electrical fire brews in the display case, but thankfully the water squirting from various cracks is keeping it at bay. An ache slips through my chest to see this destruction. The walls feel like they're about to be crushed by the water that lies overhead. This water, which has always protected us, now pushes in, threatening to rip the Institute into pieces. And when it does we're all going to float away, just as we floated in here. My heart aches with a giant tenderness for the Institute which is about to be demolished and washed into the ocean, destroyed forever. It's not a place to me anymore. It has such strong characteristics and emotions filling its halls that it's more like a person. Like a family member. Whether I was willing to admit it before, this place has edged its way into my heart. It's my home. And no one destroys my home. I swallow down vengeance, bottling it for a single fight.

Sliding along the wall, I progress closer to the lobby, not daring to take anything more than shallow breaths. The leather couch is overturned. On top it's littered with broken pieces of the coffee table, objects from the display case, and the large ficus tree that used to reside in the far corner. The foliage-rich tree lies on its side, dirt spilled all over the area underneath it. My eyes travel down to find two legs protruding out from under the couch. The black boots are unmistakably Shuman's. She's lying face down and is pinned from the mid-thigh up. The weight on top of her would be enough to crush a normal person. But Shuman isn't built like a normal person, she's built like a warrior. However, her legs lie unmoving. If I was Trent then I could move all that's burying her. Instead, I just stare at her legs blankly, letting the surrealism of this experience wash over me.

The smell of burning hair, sulfuric and bitter, assaults my nostrils. Sparks rain from exposed wires over Ren's head. He's strapped in a chair by cords frayed at their ends. As if they possess a life of their own they slide around him like snakes. Tiny puffs of smoke linger up every time a burst of sparks shower down on him, making his face contort with pain. Similar to the hair of Medusa, the black-encased wires continuously journey around Ren's torso, squeezing him every so often, turning his face a color that matches his hair.

We're roughly ten feet from the action when I recognize the kneeled figure as Trey. Reflexively I gasp. *No!* Tears I never knew could be connected to him spring to my eyes. My heart races with panic.

On all fours, head sagging, he looks so much closer to death than life right now. Zhuang strides in front of him, his sword swinging by his side.

"You have a choice. I can plunge this sword into you, ending your meaningless life. Or I can suck your consciousness out," Zhuang says, pinching Trey's chin and pulling it up so he's looking at him. Most of his face is covered in blood. A sickening feeling unfurls in my stomach at the sight of my father in such a grotesque state. "Your blood does not need to be spilled. That would be a waste. Make this easy and bring down your shield, releasing your consciousness to me," Zhuang hisses in a low voice, pulling his hand off Trey and wiping the blood on his white silk robes. "I want that life force within you. It will be enormously useful as I besiege the world with my presence. And then I want your daughter's. That's all, and I'll leave your precious Institute."

"You're not getting either," Trey says, spitting blood on the floor. "We'd both die before we gave you that."

And Trey's right. I would. I know giving Zhuang the power I hold in my consciousness would allow him to rise to greater strengths, ones that would undoubtedly mutilate the world.

Zhuang tucks the tip of the sword under Trey's chin, holding his head up at an odd angle. "Let me in. Let me have your power. Give it to me now, and this will all be over." He presses the point of the sword firmer into Trey's neck, my father grimacing from the pressure.

"No. Never," he says, angling his head back away from the blade.

Zhuang flips the sword around, sheathing it with a heavy sigh. "Prepare to say goodbye to your friend." The lobby erupts with Ren's guttural scream. It rips though the air as the cords reach around him and jerk in tighter. Ren's face turns a shade of ultraviolet. He looks close to bursting from the pressure. The end of the cord unravels itself from Ren's body and winds its way around his neck. Ren doesn't appear to care as he struggles to bring oxygen into his lungs after being so tightly constricted. I know Trey wouldn't choose to watch this, but Zhuang grips his hair, forcing his face up. The end of the cord treads once more around Ren's throat. Zhuang laughs. Turning his attention away from Ren he presses a thumb into a laceration in Trey's side. "Last chance to give me what I want," Zhuang says in a gravelly voice.

"No!" Trey says through the pain.

Pulling his bloody hand out of Trey's ribcage, Zhuang stands up straight. "Give me your power before I take it by killing every single person you have serving you!"

"You're going to kill us anyway," Trey says through wheezing breaths.

"So true," Zhuang sneers broadly. "But I wasn't planning on killing *them* in front of you." Faster than a cheetah he spins around, facing us. His silk robes billow around his lean and muscular frame. Somehow Zhuang appears taller than the last time we met and significantly more menacing as he peers at me behind black and golden eyes. I search for a place in them that's human, but all I see are the many demonic compartments which possess him with uncontrollable wickedness.

Trey gasps, blood spewing from his mouth. "Damn it, Roya and Joseph! Get out of here!" He tries to stand but winds up on the ground after a failed attempt to walk, heaving on hands and knees.

I try not to look at my father, hunched over on all fours as he spits blood on the blue fibers of the carpet. He clutches his stomach, which is badly slashed. Ren's breathing in the corner, but looks to be on the verge of passing out. The noose around his neck hangs loosely and I'm grateful to see that the cords have stopped moving momentarily.

Sliding his sword through his hands, Zhuang lets the blood from it trickle onto his fingers and eyes it hungrily. "Little girl, I see you have come to die. This is smart of you. I shall suck out your consciousness and then I'll have no trouble obtaining your father's."

"We've come to kill *you*," I say, feeling the adrenaline in me taking effect.

The laughter from Zhuang's tiny frame fills the destructed room. "You're as disillusioned as your father if you think you and your naïve brother stand a chance. Look at this pathetic man." Zhuang pulls Trey up by his silver hair and speaks next to his drained face. "He's as arrogant as you. He thought he stood a chance against me. Now he will watch you both die as punishment for his foolishness." Zhuang lets the blood-drenched hair slide from his fingertips and Trey's head hangs low again. "And then your father will give me what I want."

Joseph pushes his sleeves up to his elbows. Only anger registers in his eyes when he speaks. "Would you shut up already?

261

Put down that damn sword and fight us like a man, you evil parasite!"

The smirk drops from Zhuang's narrow face. The sword hits the ground with a loud clunk. "As you wish."

Chapter Forty-Four

As if cued each of us sinks down low into a fighting stance. Zhuang's gold eyes dart between me and my brother. I confirm that my shield is up and strong so that he can't penetrate my thoughts. This is even more of a concern for Joseph since he and Zhuang now share a link. According to Trey, Zhuang leeching Joseph's power meant he knew the workings of his brain and therefore how to break his defenses. During our practices we worked to find new strategies to shield Zhuang and I'm hoping that it works. If it doesn't then we'll know soon.

I never thought I'd enter a fight hoping to get myself cornered into a place where I'm about to die. However, that's the only reason for this fight. It's a show. The truth is there's no winning against Zhuang. Not in a fight. He will only be overpowered by someone more powerful than him, and none of the people in this room meet that criterion. I nod at Joseph, one that says, *let this deadly show begin.* My only prayer is that Joseph's assistance doesn't get him killed.

Just as we rehearsed, we take the offensive immediately. Joseph spins around to the other side of Zhuang and I take the front. Zhuang's pockmarked chin twitches. He wasn't expecting this approach, which means we're on the right track. When fighting to lose, it's easier to take risks, knowing when they don't pay off, it won't matter.

The three of us dance around each other. I keep a close eye, waiting to see the flex of Zhuang's muscles or the pivot in his foot telegraphing an oncoming attack. I'm fairly certain he's delaying, trying to get through Joseph's shield and therefore capture the workings of our plan. We can't give him this precious time. I have to do the one thing he isn't expecting: Strike first.

Bobbing side to side, I step forward with my back foot, rotate on my front, and whip my leg around in a spinning hook kick. My flexed heel slams across Zhuang's face. He falls back from the attack, but remains standing, his snakelike eyes rimmed with ferocity. As intended, he's pissed. Momentarily he's distracted wiping a drip of blood from his lip which allows Joseph to unleash a series of punches. Being reckless means we aren't conserving our energy. All attacks are meant to push Zhuang to a breaking point.

I reset and throw another round of kicks. The air around me feels lighter as the force of my kicks repeatedly drills into block after block. My feet hardly remain on the ground together for more than a half a second at any one time. However, Zhuang's having no problem blocking my kicks on one side of him and Joseph on the other. At one point he simply sidesteps back and the kick I'd already launched connects with the side of my brother's face. I falter back, giving Joseph a look of apology. That one look costs me the offensive and suddenly I'm forced to block attacks from Zhuang. His punches are fast. His fists thrust heavily against my forearms and legs. The cuts from Allouette are threatened by each assault. I know soon one is going to buckle back open, oozing blood. Thankfully I'm able to hold my blocks, but I'm quickly becoming dizzy from the speed. One false move and Zhuang will have me on the ground. I don't want to be pummeled to bits; I only want to be placed into a position of threat. And I'm not quite there yet.

Joseph rams his body into Zhuang, pulling him away from me. The man hardly budges, though, and it takes him only inches to regain his footing. I've momentarily been tapped out of this fight and it's weird to lamely watch from the sidelines as Zhuang drills punches into Joseph's side and arms with practiced ease. We aren't fast enough, but we knew that all along. It was never our intention to win this fight. Zhuang is stronger, more powerful, and quicker than ever before. Even with two on one we're no match. This must be why he laughs wickedly every now and then after delivering a series of attacks. Our attempts are amusing him.

Now Joseph's face is bleeding in multiple places. We need to progress to the next phase of the plan. I need to tap back into this fight. Joseph lunges low and sidesteps backward, putting a few feet between him and his challenger. Slowly the dance from earlier resumes. Zhuang is mostly untouched and has hardly wrinkled his robes from this altercation.

Trey looks like he's just escaped a deadly car accident, and is only barely conscious. There's something in his gaze that makes him seem somehow lost, like although he's here right now he may never be the same after this. "Don't," he mouths at me.

Does he know what I'm about to do?

Trey's mouth, red from the blood pouring out of his nose, pinches together. He shakes his head with a deliberate force.

Insanely cold water from a nearby leak sprays my back, making me cringe, and reminding me we have multiple ways we can meet our end tonight. "I have to," I mouth back to him. Each of my words sharp and deliberate.

"No," he mouths, his face haunted by dread.

The beat of my heart rams against my head. My face burns with heat as I refocus my attention on the fight. Everything's moving rapidly. But when Joseph and I exchange looks the next sequence of events slows. He retreats. I take the center spot. I feel his reluctance, but he knows this is the way to the end. This is the way his vision informed us to move. I'm all too aware of Zhuang's oncoming attack, spy the telegraphing of his joints as they lock into place. I can avoid it. Duck. Block. Move. Instead I stand upright. Pretend to be too slow for the kick that strikes across my face sending me to the ground. As soon as my head hits the soggy carpet Zhuang is leaning over me, his face inches from mine. "Just returning the gesture from before." Zhuang's breath smells like rotting fish. He bares yellow teeth and hisses into my face. "Surrender your consciousness to me or die by my sword."

Now things are going to plan. I'm finally in mortal danger. *Hurray.* Taking down all my shields I reach out to him, knowing this is the moment he's been waiting for. Although Zhuang is inching in closer to me I force out the fear. Focus on only one person. Like I'm dialing him on a telephone, I reach through time and space until I imagine that he's received my message. Zhuang's sword flies through the air and without taking his eyes off me it lands in his outstretched hand. Only then does Zhuang step back to allow for the distance he needs to swing. I know if this doesn't work that seconds from now I'll feel that blade.

"Please, I need you. Please come to me. Please, if you love me… save me," I plead.

"Little girl, your father cannot save you. No one can," Zhuang growls.

"I wasn't talking to my father," I say through gritted teeth. "And there's someone who can save me," I say, my eyes flicking over Zhuang's shoulder. "He's just arrived."

"I will not fall for your elementary tricks. Now release your consciousness to me," Zhuang says, holding the sword over his head.

"Step away from her now," Chase's cool voice saunters through the air.

Chapter Forty-Five

Zhuang stiffens. His lipless mouth snarls. Stepping to the side he swivels chin enough to take in the solid form which has just arrived.

Chase glides until he's hovering over me. He's unconcerned for the man standing at his back, holding a sword uncertainly by his side. "Get up," Chase says, extending his hand. My fingers curl around his cold hand and he yanks me from the ground. When I'm on my feet he turns, his sturdy frame sheltering me from Zhuang.

With Chase's back to me, I feel protected as he takes control of the room. His tall build stands against mine, and I sense on the surface of his smooth features is a smile mixed with a strong expression of power. From my vantage point all I can make out is the smoothness of his shiny black hair as it meets the collar of his jacket and even just this is enough to remind me of how attractive this man is to the unsuspecting person. However, I'm not unsuspecting.

"Well, well, well, what do we have here?" Chase's voice is clear, deep. He peers around the room taking in the mayhem, then focuses on Zhuang, who is oddly frozen. "I suppose I should congratulate you on your superb work." Chase's hands rub together.

Zhuang eyes him nervously but doesn't say a word.

"Looks like you've managed to do me a series of favors in one single night," Chase says smugly.

"I do not work for you," Zhuang spits through his pointy teeth.

"Everyone works for me," Chase says coolly.

Zhuang separates his feet and zips his eyes around the room.

"You can go ahead and finish those remaining." Chase waves his hand at the three men lying in various positions behind Zhuang. "But the girl belongs to me."

Zhuang flares his nostrils. "The girl dies tonight."

"Make this easy on everyone. Get over your grudge with her. If you don't and insist on killing her then I'll have no choice but to stop you. I really hope you'll reconsider since I'd hate to end your majestic reign tonight."

Zhuang laughs but not like before. This one reeks of insecurity. "There's no stopping me. Now step aside while I destroy her."

The room is suddenly colder even though the fire behind Trey is building with intensity, sending clouds of smoke into the air. Chase's fists ball up and then relax.

"You and I both know the first statement you just made is inherently false," Chase says calmly. "You can be stopped. And no one will destroy her—until I say."

"I'm not leaving until she dies. She almost ruined me and will pay," Zhuang says, taking a rattling breath.

I half expect Chase to say something but instead his fingertips tense and curl into the palm of his hands. The dim lights flicker. A low buzzing fills the space. Everything in the room changes on such a subtle level. The temperature. The light. The sounds. Although I'm watching from my safety zone behind Chase, I sense the terror building.

Zhuang's long pointed nose twitches and then his face follows suit as if trying to fight something off. Spasms flex all over his face. His eyes bulge from an unseen pressure and dart chaotically all over his attacker's face. He's searching Chase for an option that will tell him how to combat what's happening.

This ancient force prepared to waltz in here after learning all of the Institute's secrets and destroy its unsuspecting residents. He'd expected he could overpower Trey, who would die to protect his palace and its people. Zhuang expected he could fight Ren and Shuman, who are talented but still moral. He knew they'd be unwilling to dip into the dark side to pull from the strength that it would take to fully challenge him. Zhuang had expected everything he'd encountered up until this point. However, he wasn't prepared to face the man who stands before him now. Before him is the one person who's not only powerful enough to bring him down, but now has the motivation to do it. And Chase has no trouble selling his soul in exchange for the power it takes to end Zhuang's long life. He's been doing just that for all of his life, which is exactly what makes him Zhuang's perfect challenger.

Chase isn't moving, but I can tell by the way he's holding his hands in a fixed position that he's using all his energy to channel the strongest power he's ever tried to harness. Zhuang's features stretch under an unseen pressure. His long slit pupils dilate. The surface of his face grows smooth. Suddenly he looks placid, like he's in a trance.

An intense roar booms from Chase. He pulls both hands into the air. Zhuang rises three inches off the ground. I back up until I feel the cold steel on my neck. Another growl erupts from Chase and Zhuang stretches out his own hands searching for something tangible in the sticky air.

Zhuang howls, one so high-pitched, I cover my ears. His bony hands shelter his face, claw at it. Something from inside him or all around him or from far away sucks the very life out. Chase appears to be hardly straining as an unknown force suddenly speeds through the air. However, I know Chase has been drained by the power he's exuded through this feat. My bracelet is undoubtedly doing its job, but still a part of me feels won over by this man. He's drained himself. Staked his life on everything to kill my adversary.

I swallow hard. That feels like true romance.

Shaking my head I withdraw from these thoughts, remembering I can never be fooled by the immediate actions of this man. In the end he's only after one thing and it isn't me. This is the man who had my mother killed. Who forged the way my life unfolded. This is the man who killed Pearl and countless others, including Aiden's parents. I remind myself why I'm here. Why I made the decisions I did. This is about choices and right now I'm choosing not to fight, but rather to let those who like to, face each other. Their selfish hate has overwhelmed them so much that they don't even know who they're fighting anymore.

A sound so awful it makes my stomach turn explodes from Zhuang. It isn't words, but still I interpret the hoarse sound exploding from his mouth as a plea. If Joseph's theory is correct, based on what he'd seen in his flash, then Chase is using his mind control to force Zhuang to send the power that he sucked from dreamers back into the ether. Like moisture in the air, it will be absorbed by some cloud of consciousness, where it will build until one day all this power rains back down onto the Earth and its dreamers.

Zhuang's pointy fingers recede from his face. The red streaks start at his cheekbones and slash down his sunken cheeks. Before my eyes his skin wrinkles like a damaged piece of leather. It goes from being taut against his bony frame to dripping from his features. Sunken eyes stare unblinkingly at Chase and then they land on me.

The wheezing in his chest is the first signal that he's trying to speak and therefore abandoning the power he's been trying to use to fight.

"I should have killed you when I had the chance," he hisses at me and blood leaks from the corner of his mouth.

Zhuang is using his last breaths of other people's lives for hate, which makes everything I've done and will do easier to digest. "Don't delude yourself," I say evenly. "You never could have killed me because I've always been the means to your end."

"I'll haunt your dreams, little girl. I'll be there…every…time…you…sleep," Zhuang says, blood spurting from his mouth with each word.

"Go to hell where you belong," I say behind my barrier of protection.

Zhuang eyes flutter like he's on the verge of passing out. He easily weighs twenty pounds less than he did moments prior, his robes slipping off his scrawny shoulders. His greasy black ponytail is now silver and wiry and drapes from his almost sunken head.

Chase casually drops his hands to his side. Instantly, Zhuang falls dully to the ground at his feet in a heap of silk and disillusions. This is the first time I consider stepping out from behind Chase and watching from his side as my adversary wretches in pain and agony. My eyes flicker momentarily to Chase, who's oozing with pride as the man at his feet heaves in a breath and spurts out blood. "That's it. Go ahead and die," Chase says, his voice a welcome sound after all the noises of pain from Zhuang that filled the lobby.

In a quick motion Chase shoots one hand through the air and rips it back like he's pulling something out of Zhuang. A howl bursts from Zhuang's mouth, sending a volcano of blood into the air. Geysers of thick red liquid shoot up and sink back over his face filling in his wrinkles and drenching his silver hair. Instantly the flesh and bones twitch violently and when I think I can't watch any more he grows smaller and smaller and every part of him dries up into itself. Within seconds Zhuang disappears into a pile of ashes and bones and silk. The sight is vile.

However, there's something that isn't despicable and it's that Zhuang is gone. He's dead and that means a new reign. Dream Travelers and Middlings are now safe. I should be happy. Relieved. Grateful. But I know my fate is not as safe as the people I've bargained to protect.

Chase spins around to face me. I take in the electric blue eyes that have just sucked the evilness out of the world and know they're coming for me next. However, my death will be much, much slower.

Chapter Forty-Six

Irrefutably he's the most attractive person who's ever existed. He such a beautiful composition of a man it makes me want to cry. I'm not sure if this is part of his mind control, but it's one of the most useful of any of the talents I've encountered since learning I was a Dream Traveler. Attractive people hold so much power that they don't deserve. People lavish the beautiful with unearned praise, riches, and fame. If you're gorgeous and know how to use it to your favor then you can part a person's consciousness, deceive a reality, or seduce someone into slavery.

Feeling the poisoned-tipped weapon stashed in my pants I ready myself for what must come next. I need him to come close. I need to prepare myself to fake it again. I need to finish him before he realizes this has all been a trap.

Standing three feet from me Chase pulls his wrist up to his chest. He's weakened, but still a power exudes in every one of his movements. I don't doubt for one moment that he's a force I need to fear and also extinguish. Fluidly he taps his wrist like he wants the time. "Take off your bracelet, Roya," he says through his soft pink lips.

Doom crashes down on me.

The confusion and fear wash over Joseph and Trey's faces. I pretend not to notice them, to have eyes only for Chase. "What?" I say like I misheard.

"Take. It. Off."

Stepping forward two feet, I act as if being close to him is all I've longed for. I make my eyes tell him that I misunderstand and just need him to hold me. Chase steps back several feet, keeping distance between us.

"I've done what you asked," Chase says, gesturing at the pitiful pile of Zhuang's remains. "I've killed a powerful man to protect you. I've proven that I love you. That's what you wanted. That's what you needed in order to become my wife, right?" His electric blue eyes pierce me and although I'm being battered by a shower of cold water overhead I'm on fire with fear.

I swallow hard, and again step forward a few paces hoping he won't notice when I close the space between us. As if we're doing a rehearsed dance Chase steps to the side, keeping himself a safe distance from me.

"Why?" I ask, injecting grief into my voice.

"You must know I'm not your fool. I've played your game, but that doesn't mean for one minute I believed that poor act you tried to pull off at the Parthenon. I know you can shield yourself from me. My wife *will* not be protected from me in this way and you *will* be my wife." He points to my bracelet. "Take it off."

"But, I…I…"

"Take it off or your father dies." Chase's voice is even, full of promises.

I consider challenging the threat, but I catch Joseph's gesture. He's inconspicuously pointing to something. With a tiny flick of my eyes I look in that direction. Every hope I have of escaping Chase withers away with that single glance. Trey's medallion, his protective charm, lies in the corner by the far wall. How had I not noticed that Trey had his charm ripped from him? Now it's easy for Chase to overpower my father, make him do whatever he pleases. He can make him kill himself or anyone left in this room. Trey sits beside Joseph, his face crazed with worry even though he looks close to passing out. This man may not have earned much of my respect in the past, but that doesn't mean I want him to fall victim to Chase's mind control. I don't need to weigh my options because I already know what I have to do. Zhuang is gone. The next danger stands right in front of me. I have to get him far away from everyone I love. I think I knew it would always go this way. Had prepared myself for this inevitability.

The pin to my bracelet pinches my fingertip when I press it, releasing the hinge immediately.

"No! Roya, don't! Please!" Trey's voice is panicked.

"It's all right, Trey," I say, dropping the charm to the ground, abandoning a piece of me in search of redemption. I believe without the charm I'll still be able to hold strong against the beautiful man before me. Not only that, but I think that I'll be able to plunge the poisoned-tipped knife into his chest, ending his life and thereby securing my fate.

I'm wrong.

As soon my bracelet disconnects from my wrist, an unstoppable force wrangles into my mind and heart, reading them and taking control of my body. A satisfied grin, so elegantly perfect and wrong, spreads across Chase's face. "That's it, *mon amour*. I knew you'd see it my way,"

"Yes, your way." My mind startles at the sound of my voice.

"Good girl," he purrs, taking a step closer to me. He eyes me with a deliberate focus. "Oh, yes, I believe this is a match made by the gods. You have a mind that's equal to mine in many respects." His eyes shift over me, but I sense he's not looking at my physical body. "Oh, and a quick read of your emotions tells me you've been extremely disloyal to me, loving another. Tsk tsk tsk. You will be punished for this, but not now." He leans into me, his cold breath biting my skin. "Now it's time to see if the woman to be my wife can comply with my demands. Let's see how well you respond, shall we?"

I want to move. To take the blade in my waistband and plunge it into him, but I don't budge. My muscles don't respond to the orders from my brain. My heart. Both are locked behind bars. Imprisoned.

"Roya," Chase says, his voice filled with amusement, "take off your clothes."

Almost before he finishes his sentence, my hands grip the hem of my shirt, tugging it over my head in one swift movement, and I hand it to Chase. *No!* I scream in my mind. *What are you doing?*

"Stop this," Trey begs, clenching his eyes shut.

"Look at how well she minds. Her brain so beautifully constructed and easy to control." He tosses my shirt into the flames in the display case. It ignites immediately. "You can wait to take off the rest of your clothes when we return home." Snatching my hand, Chase glides a diamond ring I didn't see until now onto my finger. It fits perfectly, like it's made for me. A large pear-shaped diamond sits in the center, a row of small diamonds accenting the band. "You will marry me. Tonight. I cannot wait a moment longer to conceive our children."

Chase eyes the ring, triumph delighting his facial features. "It looks perfect on you. It was my mother's. She'll die when she learns I have it. Literally." He drops my hand and leans into me, grazing his lips against mine. Bile rises in my throat, but my hands don't care. They grab the sides of his face and yank him into me, my mouth kissing him hungrily. I hike my leg up and wrap it around him. It feels grotesquely wrong, which doesn't explain why I turn my head and make eye contact with Trey. A gratified smile unfurls on my face, while Chase trails kisses down my throat. I need to stop this but my hands aren't my own. My lips make satisfied expressions that I don't feel. I'm locked inside my heart unable to do anything, only watch myself operate like a stupid robot.

Chase withdraws from me, a heat in his electric blue eyes. "Oh, and Trey," he says, keeping his gaze on me. I pant, stupidly. "Please don't worry about your daughter. I won't hurt her. Not until the day I kill her, the day after she delivers me my third child. You'll know when that is, because I'll ship you her body."

"No!" Trey yells so loudly it rings in my ears. I want to look at him. To witness the pain in his eyes, but Chase keeps my gaze pinned on his beautiful frame.

"Don't, Roya! This isn't you. Fight this," Joseph begs.

I'm trying, I want to tell him. *Every part of my being is battling Chase. And losing.*

"Hmmm…" Chase says, sounding pleased. "Does it make you feel better to know she's trying to fight me? She's actually quite the fighter, but she's still losing. Oh, what's happening to her is really brutal," he says, almost laughing with glee. "She can't stand this," he says, wiping his finger up and down my arm.

"Stop it!" Trey says, his voice straining.

"I'm afraid that's not going to happen. I have so much more to say on this matter," Chase says, sounding almost rehearsed. "You see, your daughter is going to fulfill my demands, giving me the pureblooded children I ask for. Then she's going to pay for her parents' transgressions. How does that all sound, *mon amour*?" Chase says, looking at me directly, like he's sincerely interested in my answer.

"Lovely," I reply.

"No!" Trey yells, a raw ache in the one word. "Don't do this to her! Just punish me!"

"Don't you see," Chase says with a sickly smile. "This is your punishment. The worst I could envision for you."

"It's okay, Dad," I say in a voice that sounds too childish to be mine. "I deserve this. You deserve this. Chase has made me see that. It's really so just," I say, stroking my fingers up and down his lapels.

"You're going to make a fine wife. I might even miss you after I kill you. But I'll have my children. My power. My vengeance. And that will keep me warm once you're cold in the ground. And just so you know, Trey, until the day your daughter dies she will suffer." His cool breath wisps against my cheeks. With whirlwind speed he yanks the knife out from behind my back. "She will suffer for trying to betray me today. For thinking that was even a possibility. She suffers now, locked in her mind with a sickening aversion to me. You did an extraordinary job making her hate me, and it's worked in my favor because your daughter is so repulsed by me that I know the things I'm going to do to her and make her do to me will torture her consciousness. For example…" He runs his lips over the contours of my jaw. Tremble inside. "She hates every single minute of this. It's completely tearing her apart inside, which is actually turning me on," he says, biting at my jaw.

"How does that feel, Roya?"

Revolting. Horrid. Unbearably awful. "Like heaven," I say, gripping his jacket.

His cold hand grips my shoulder. He squeezes so tight I wince, physically and inside. His fingers press into the wound on my shoulder, opening it back up. "Never wrinkle my suits. Is that clear?" he says, a look of cold contempt in his eyes.

"Yes," the robot in me answers.

He pulls his hand away, blood from my reopened wound on it. Dragging a handkerchief from his pocket he nonchalantly wipes off my blood from his hand. "I guess we have more work to do finessing the controls on her," Chase says, rolling his eyes and looking at Trey like I'm a defective piece of equipment. "This mistake was my fault, but your daughter will pay the price for my mistakes as well as yo——" His voice turns into a hoarse scream. Horror rips through Chase's eyes. He clenches them shut like an unsightly pain is tearing him into pieces. His hands seize my forearms, fingernails pierce my skin. A yell of distress tears out of his mouth. I want to search the space for what's causing this reaction, but he has me frozen, only allowed to stare into his sharp eyes, raked with pain. Fear splits through me, capturing my breath, abducting all peace within my being. My arms scream from the force he's pressing into them.

Chase shoves me away haphazardly, pushing me so hard I trip and land on my backside. Then I see what I tripped over. Urgently I shuffle back, my chest caving in with sharp breaths. I scramble to my feet, my calf screaming from the many altercations, blood dripping down, sprinkling the pit of snakes that tangle my feet. They swarm around my legs and hands. The snakes are all headed in one direction. To Chase. There has to be a hundred of them.

Still stumbling, crushing the rubbery creatures under my feet, I move backwards. The snakes hiss, but don't strike at me. However, attached to various places on Chase's legs are snakes with their fangs stuck sharply through his pants and into his flesh. Violently he strikes at them, deflecting the snakes. He rips them off and throws them across the room. Kicks them away from him. Chase staggers, almost falling to the ground. He recovers just as his attention darts to Trey, who's hunched against the wall, half alive. "And to think I was going to let you live. Now you're dead," he says through winded breaths. Trey's face arranges itself into a sea of pain as he stands, the effort looking like enough to kill him. Slow, arduous steps take him to the knife lying on the ground. My knife with the poison-tipped blade. He reaches for it, every action not his own.

No! I scream in my mind, but the words stay trapped inside me. And then I flex my fingers. Feel the ability to control my body awaken inside my being. It's minuscule, but starting to stir.

The hilt of the knife is against Trey's throat. All my efforts work to move my muscles, to take back what belongs to me. To stop Trey from killing himself.

Fire from the display case shoots through the air like it's riding on an arrow and lands on Chase's back. It snakes up to his shoulder, but it's slow to spread. Shock and anger blare across his eyes. He slaps at the flames. Slams his back up against the wall. And like a lock unbolting an urge inside me unlatches. It stirs with the greatest intensity. A lifesaving one. The wind surges with tiny puffs, encouraging the flames on him to grow. My wind. From across the smoky room, Joseph almost vibrates with redemption. "That's it, Roya!" he screams, a raw need in his voice. "Help me!"

And just like that I almost break through. And then I'm also still Chase's puppet, one that reaches to him, even though he's coated in fire. My body lunges, intent on smothering the flames.

"NO!" Joseph dives at me, pulling me away from Chase. He tugs me backward, and Chase continues to erupt in a blanket of flames and venom. I'm half charging toward him and half urging Joseph's arms around me, protecting me.

And then a cold, delicate metal wraps around my wrist. Shuman's eyes are in my face, pleading for me to stop resisting. Pleading for me to stay still. And all at once I wither until I hear the click and slip back into the person I used to be.

Exhausted and completely skewed by my experience, I slip into another consciousness where I watch everything from a different realm. And still the currents of wind are my constructions. They encourage the flames that burn the dying man. Winds from inside me whisper against Joseph's flames, stoking them until Chase is covered completely in orange and black fire.

Gripping my copper- and silver-encased wrist I feel the balance return to my soul and watch as Chase burns to his death. He clutches his body as the poison robs his organs of the ability to work properly. The fire licks at his gorgeous face. It's difficult to watch him burn and drip until he's just bits of flesh and bone, but after my first battle with Zhuang I have to know my enemy is truly dead. So I watch until every part of him that's alive burns and the only part that makes it bearable is they're all watching beside me.

Chapter Forty-Seven

Aiden barrels down the hallway as we approach the elevators. His eyes fix on me, revolving down to my bare chest covered by only a lacy, white bra. Silent fury leaks out of his eyes. Racing to me, he pulls off his lab coat and slips it over my shivering shoulders. "Here," he says. Then he takes Trey's other arm and hitches it over his shoulder. Between us we carry the mostly-passed-out man, blood oozing from multiple lacerations, his head lulled to the side, resting on my shoulder. Behind me, Joseph has one of Ren's arms draped over his shoulder, helping him down the corridor. Shuman brings up the rear, limping and face already swelling.

"The elevators are working again?" I ask, wheezing as I lug my father.

Aiden nods, looking at me like I'm suddenly a different species.

"Thank God," I say with instant relief. "He needs attention immediately. I hope Mae is in the infirmary."

"She will be," Aiden assures me.

Once we're in the elevator Ren pushes Joseph off him, preferring to hold himself up in the corner. Joseph shrugs and takes my position holding Trey up. I slip into the lab coat, buttoning it up all the way. Only once I'm fully covered does Joseph look directly at me, relief and anguish partner emotions on his face. "Damn, that was the most F'd up thing I've ever seen," he says, shaking his head at me.

"I..." I say, the tears swelling up in my throat. "I tried to fight him...that wasn't m-m-m..." My teeth chatter, making it impossible to talk.

"I know," Joseph says, choking on his own torment.

The elevator is sluggish, inching downward at half its normal speed. And with each level we pass I retreat inside myself, unable to process the events shuffling through my mind in haphazard disarray.

Someone reaches down and grabs my hand. Reflexively I jerk back, disoriented. My eyes come up to find Aiden standing in front of me, a tremulous look in his eyes. "It's okay," he says cautiously, reaching for my hand again. "I was just going to relieve you of this." He slips Chase's ring off my finger. Seeing the ring brings a torrent of punishing memories to the front of my mind. In an effort not to shatter right here I stare forward. Recede into myself.

"Are you all right?" Aiden says, searching my eyes which stare at nothing.

"What do you think, Livingston?" Joseph says, repositioning Trey, whose breaths sound like air coming through a broken fan. "She was just molested both mentally and physically by a psychopath."

"I saw," Aiden says, his eyes scanning me for injuries.

"I…" I say, slowly sinking farther away, unable to construct words or form unfractured thoughts in my head. "I did…"

"You did what you had to do," Aiden says, still trying to locate me in my lost eyes.

"What she did was absolutely the foulest thing ever," Ren says, sucking in a ragged breath, his eyes pinned on the floor. "And also what she did is the only reason we're alive to congregate in this tiny a space. What the hell is wrong with this damn elevator?"

"The generators aren't fully charged," Aiden answers flatly, his worried eyes still watching me.

When the doors open everyone empties out. I remain frozen. Not seeing. Content with sliding up against the walls of the elevator. Sinking into a safe place inside a dark room in my subconscious. Instead, I remain still, watching fuzzy figures lumber away. The smell of burning flesh is stuck in my nose. A violent shiver reaches into my being cutting parts of me. The silver doors are almost closed, trapping me inside the box alone. And still I can't move. Can hardly will oxygen into my lungs. A hand grabs the door pressing it back. His eyes reach out to me, trying to capture my attention and I swim in a sea of blue.

"Come on, Roya," Aiden says, his voice gentle. He tugs the sleeve of the white coat I'm wearing, careful not to touch me, coaxing me out of the elevator. Like a dog on a leash I allow him to lead me a few feet. And then a force crashes down on me so violently that inside and outside I crumble. My emotions and mind feel like they've finally unloaded the strain of holding up a boulder. And the only option is to collapse. Against my every effort my legs sag and I almost fall to the ground. Aiden catches me, scooping me into his arms, cradling me against him. My head slumps beside his shoulder as he carries me down the silver hallway. His heartbeat assures me life still exists in the world. And his words assure that maybe life still exists within me. "It's all right, Roya. Everything's over. You're safe. So safe."

Gentle as a lamb, Aiden lays me down in one of the beds in the infirmary. I'm only aware of some things, like the look of concern in his eyes, and a dull beeping sound in the distance. My thoughts are clouded somehow. I'm stuck in a weird consciousness, like I'm sheathed behind a layer of plastic.

"She almost passed out just now," Aiden informs someone, pushing hair back from my face. I want to look at him but my eyes stay locked on the ceiling. Unable to navigate anywhere else.

"She's in emotional shock," Shuman's voice replies.

"What can we do?" Aiden asks, his fear pushing my insides around.

"Nothing. She has to come out of it on her own," Shuman says and I sense or see her clap a hand on Aiden's shoulder as he kneels down lower to my bed. "For now you must leave her. There is much work to be done to reinforce the Institute."

Aiden agrees with a reluctant nod, eyes hovering over me anxiously. And when he turns and leaves, I lose my motivation to remain conscious. I float away.

◆

When I awake, a part of me stays asleep. I walk through the infirmary. Ignore the calls at my back. Trudge through the hallways. Take the elevator. And disappear.

Even when I show up at meal times or walk through the corridors, I'm gone.

◆

It had been just over a week since the devastation to the Institute happened and nothing felt normal or like it ever had a chance of returning to that. We had no leader, no one delivering mail or goods. Everywhere were broken fixtures and columns, patched walls, and places where the bloodstains refused to come out of the

281

blue carpet. Ren and Shuman were now making regular appearances at meal times, which just made what they were doing feel more contrived. They were trying to boost our confidence and prove there were still reliable people left at the Institute who the Lucidites could believe in if hard times returned.

Rations and morale were running low for everyone as we ate our rice and frozen vegetables. Most people wondered when the submarine would return to the surface of the Earth for fresh foods. I wondered when my father would return from his catatonic state and take back the reins that belonged to him and no one else.

He broke. The unbreakable man broke. During the battle something in Trey fractured and now the light inside him was extinguished like a burnt-out bulb. His injuries had been treated and Mae was certain he'd make a full physical recovery, but she couldn't fix what had cracked inside him.

Trey was released from the infirmary and escorted straight to the mental ward. There the nice therapist with the wiry hair and droopy eyelids observed him, scribbling notes on a clipboard. Nurses in lavender scrubs made sure he was bathed and his needs met. Trey was a fighter. I knew that. But there was now a look in his eyes that said he was tired of fighting. The staff in the mental ward didn't know what to do to wake Trey up, to reinsert the life inside him. And although I was moving around and feeding myself, I was as lifeless as him, so I definitely had no answers.

I visited him every day, sometimes with Joseph, but mostly alone. The conversation was nonexistent, since he wasn't propelling it like he normally did. Mostly I just sat with him, silently reading and watching him in his vegetative state.

And every day Aiden was waiting for me outside the mental ward. He walked me back to my room, not saying a word usually. His presence was a comfort to me, and I wanted to allow more from him, but I was afraid his hands would feel like Chase's on me. I was afraid he would touch me and think of how I kissed Chase with such intensity. I was afraid we were ruined. And there was no going public about a relationship to Trey, since he was hardly alive. In one hour, the events that led to Zhuang and Chase's deaths warped us all. I never expected that by ridding myself of my enemies I'd ruin a place in me. Nothing comes without a price though.

Aiden knew I was lost, just like my father. Just like Joseph was lost. Aiden knew it and for several days he only walked with me, never voicing the obvious. Yesterday, though, when we paused at my door he leaned against the wall, staring at me with sorrowful eyes. "Is there more I can do? To make you feel better?"

"The problem is everything you do makes me feel better," I said, slumping against the opposite wall.

"And why is that a problem?"

"Being happy right now feels like laughing at a funeral."

Aiden nodded, instant understanding in his eyes. "I know firsthand that when you lose people you want to push everything that isn't that grief away. You remember how I told you that I punished myself with my parents' deaths, right?"

I nodded, displaced from my own anguish by a living memory that surfaced in his eyes.

"I can't tell you how to grieve," he continued. "All I can tell you is that when you do smile again it will not mean that you don't still miss them." The lump in his throat bobbed a few times before he managed to swallow it. A tragic smile actually laced across his lips. "I miss them every single day, but it does get easier."

Chapter Forty-Eight

I don't just want Trey to wake up, I need him to. The longer he stays locked away in his head, the longer I feel I'll never find the part I lost after the battle. His recovery reflects so much on my own. And it reflects on Joseph too. During the battle we all cut out a part of ourselves in order to ensure our triumph. And not just the things we'd done, but the deaths we witnessed are scars on our souls. A person isn't built to witness so much tragedy. That's how I know without a doubt that war is wrong. If I'm pardoned from this pain, given a second chance to live, then I'll fight no more. If my clairvoyance returns, then I'll use it to stop every single violent act I can, because I'm utterly fed up with humans killing each other. To hell with the Lucidites' laws, I'll dream travel and intervene each time war is imminent.

But for now, I'm not a person who makes change. I can't even news report, since my pain has shut down my sixth sense. Right now I'm a lost soul, but I keep searching…knowing there has to be a way to be found.

Every day I make out-of-the-way trips to haunt the lobby. No one comes here. Most make out-of-the-way detours to avoid this area. That's how I know it's a safe place to visit my emotions. The display case, which used to dazzle with hundreds of shiny objects, is boarded up now. The walls around it are coated in soot. The smell of fire damage drenches the air. All of the debris from the fight has been cleaned up and removed—everything but the leather couch that Shuman managed to peel herself out from underneath.

While I haunt the lobby I think about how hard it is to believe Patrick will never knock at my door. He will never grin and tip his hat at me. Harder still is that he'll never deliver another package from Bob and Steve. But I don't want their packages; I want the love that accompanied them. I want the support that exuded in every single one of their notes. What I want is Bob and Steve alive. I want the chance that's been stolen from us.

Every day I question my pain over their deaths, belittling it. I tell myself that to love and miss someone I only knew a short time is ridiculous. And still this reasoning doesn't lessen the pain. The thing is, just because we'd only been acquainted for a short time didn't mean we weren't close. Half of my heartache is that they'd died so early into our promising relationship. Forever and ever I'll suffer from what could have been. What would our lives have been like if they'd lived? Where would we have vacationed together? What would our summers have been like? What would we do on Sundays? At least if we'd had a year or two or ten, I'd have something to miss, but all I have is unfathomable aspirations that will never come to pass.

"I've never wanted to rob someone so badly of the pain I feel from them," he says in a careful tone from the other side of the lobby.

I don't look up from my hands, where I've let the tears fall and dry.

Pushing back uncomfortably on the leather couch, I try to settle into a position that feels normal or comfortable or at least passable for human. Finally, I bring my eyes up to meet his. George wears a gray hoodie and looks somehow cozy as he stands a cautious distance away.

There's a question in his eyes and I nod to him, instinctively knowing what he wants. He moves across the space, squatting beside the couch looking at my hands and then my eyes. I may have let him close, but I can't be touched right now. And I know that's the second question in his eyes. It hurts to look at him, but that's true for everything I do lately. Truly, human contact just makes everything more difficult and that's why I've shunned it off.

"Roya," he says, loosening a breath. "I don't have to leave the Institute. I could stay."

I blink in surprise. "Why would you want to stay here?" I say, motioning around the lobby.

"Because I'm a Lucidite, and this place needs people who want to rebuild."

"That's honorable. I should have expected that from you," I say, wishing I had something to do with my hands. "But this place is also a prison of emotions right now. More than anything, I don't want you suffering from all of the sorrow you must be feeling from everyone."

"The only grief I'm feeling that's unbearable is yours. And that's only because I love you so much." He must sense that his words obliterate a part of my heart because he closes his eyes, looking deterred.

"You shouldn't stay here for me," I say after too long of a pause. That's not what I wanted to say, but it's what came out. Rejecting him right now is scoring parts of me that are still intact, but cutting him loose is the only thing I know to do. Taking a strained breath, I slide off the sofa and walk until I'm face-to-face with the boarded-up display case. Somewhere inside there are the ashes of the shirt I was forced to take off. An act of humiliation by Chase to disarm everyone in the room. Funny how stripping people of simple things weakens them.

As I let these thoughts reel through my brain, I hear George get up and do what he does best—try again. He's going to try and make me feel better or try and make things between us better.

"What if I stayed here for me? What if I stayed because loving you is the only thing that's ever made me feel alive?" he says to my back.

I force myself to turn, to look into his bronze eyes. "You didn't want to be with me when I loved you with half a heart. I don't even have that left anymore. You'll be thoroughly unhappy with what I can offer you."

"Maybe, but at this point, if I can make you better, I'll do it. I'll break my own heart to give you half. To repair yours."

"You think I'd ever let you do that? I care about you too much. I want you to be happy. I want you to stop putting me first. I want you to live your life and stop looking to me to fulfill something in you." I take in a long unsatisfying breath. "I want you to leave."

"Roya," he says in that stern voice I love so much, but can't fully allow myself to appreciate right now, "I know you're trying to save me, but not from this place. You're trying to save me from breaking my heart again. Shouldn't that be my decision?"

"You should go to Dartmouth. If you don't go now, you might never. You and I both know that you need this. I can't give you what you want, especially now. I don't want you to stick around here and give me the selfish distance I'm going to ask from you. Leave." His emotions push across the room, piercing my heart. "Please leave and go and live your life. You deserve to be happy, and I don't think you're going to find that here. You definitely won't find it with me, not like how you deserve."

"The irony is that you won't find happiness with me, which is why I'd never be happy," he says.

"Maybe the truth is, I *will* never be happy," I say.

"I don't think so…more than anything, I hope not." He takes my hand, and I allow it, knowing he'll keep a boundary between us that I need right now. Bringing the back of my hand up, he kisses it once. "I'll always love you. I'll always return for you."

◆

For another week my life progresses into a cylinder of nothingness. George leaves, going away to college. I fold the frequency adjuster into a box with promises to put it back on if he ever returns. I don't regret that I encouraged him to leave. I regret that I couldn't tell him the one thing he deserved to hear. After everything that's happened, expressing my love to someone is like marking them with a curse.

Joseph and I are both lost in a daze and can't find a way to return to the land of the waking. We're our father in almost every single way. We're zombies. Although Joseph and I decided to continue to move through the Institute, we're effectively doing what Trey is doing—we're paralyzed to the future. Joseph and I are afraid to act. We're afraid to live. Very much like our father, we're afraid to do anything because every time we do we cause pain to the people around us and that's too much to bear at this point. Too much pain has occurred. We must have all taken a silent vow in that elevator to stop causing pain, and therefore, on some level, we all three stopped existing.

◆

The submarine has been repaired and a new operator hired. For some reason it signals hope to me, like if things can physically leave and enter the Institute, then there's hope for my own healing process. That's the reason I go to the dry dock. I had no reason to visit it before now, never curious about the way Bob and Steve's packages entered the Institute.

And just when I thought the Institute had no more secrets to reveal, I step into a new dimension of this world. The arched, tunneled room is the size of a warehouse. Underwater lights illuminate the greenish water that half bathes the long, black missile-shaped submarine. I feel like I'm standing next to a whale and I kind of want it to swallow me whole right now. Stairs submerged under the water next to the submarine remind me of how this place transforms when needed. And I'm completely deflated to know that being here, seeing the submarine about to take its maiden voyage after the repairs, doesn't make me feel better. It reminds me that I'm half submerged in a reality. And as much as I'd like to, I can't surface completely from it. Disheartened, I whip around and charge straight into Ren. He's wheeling a suitcase beside him, another one tucked up under his other arm.

"What are you doing here?" he says, the usual disgust not coating his words.

"Not finding what I was looking for," I say dully. "What are *you* doing here?" I eye the bag under his arm, the traveling coat draped over the rolling case.

"I'm leaving," he says with a shrug.

"Oh. For good?"

"Yes, for good. If you're lucky you'll never be graced with another of my handsome sneers."

I almost laugh. Leave it to Ren to almost pull that emotion out of me after everything. The saltwater lingers through the air, a welcome scent. A promising one. "But…"

"I promised a length of service to Trey and I've fulfilled it. It's time I move on."

"So you served the Institute all these years to make up for…for what you did?"

"No, I served your father. He asked me to help secure a certain future. For most, I would have told them to piss off, even after all I'd done. But Trey isn't most people. Maybe one day you'll see that."

"Right now he's hardly a person. How can you leave, when he's in this state?"

Ren gives a knowing smile. "Missy, I'm not going to be the one to wake him up. I can guarantee that."

"But…what is? I mean…how?" I don't know why I keep speaking in abbreviated sentences, like a kid giving a speech in front of a distracted classroom.

Ren's eyes fall on my forearm to the scar left there when he cut me during our first meeting. "You know, Mae could heal that ugly scar. One less blemish on you."

"That's all right. It's a reminder of when I first learned this world was real."

"Aw, you almost sound sentimental."

"And it also reminds me that one day I should return the favor to you."

"No, Roya, I'd say we're finally even." The marks around Ren's throat have mostly faded but are still reminders of the strangulation which almost ended him. The one Chase stopped because of a convoluted plan which didn't work and then did. If I'd acted faster, maybe more wouldn't have died. Maybe Trey wouldn't have been damaged so much.

"Can I offer you some advice?" Ren says, dropping his attention to his fingernails and then staring straight at me.

I brave myself for a diatribe spiked with insults.

"Most people aren't happy. They sing songs like they are. Make up cute little stories. Post pics of the rare times when life wasn't dreadful. Most people are stomaching this whole affair called life. Are these people complainers? Probably. Most are. But they're also just blokes who're too afraid to take a risk. So they live lives in a redundant cycle of complacent apathy. Then these people wallow around day after day in their unhappiness. The more you do that, the more you lose sight of the chances you could take to make things better.

"Here's my advice, missy. Don't let chances slip past you because you're too afraid to take risks. And don't make loss in your life make you a loser. Sure, you're sad now, but if you're willing to gamble a little you might be able to fix things. One thing I know is you don't want to wake up and realize you could have been happy, that the risks would have been worth it, but you dwindled away your chances."

"Okay," I say, considering his strange advice. "So I should take a risk? Hmmm…Because pretending to love a psychopath wasn't enough?"

Ren regards me carefully for a moment, his green eyes hovering almost too long on my bemused face. "That was the risk you took to save the Lucidites. Taking a risk to survive isn't that impressive. Taking a risk to be happy, that takes guts."

"Well, thanks," I say, not meaning it. "If this magical chance to relieve all the trauma from my life skips past me, I'll be sure to stake my life on it."

"One more thing," Ren says, like his words are gold. "Sometimes redemption happens in the past. Time isn't linear, Roya. Use that to your benefit."

I scratch my head, shaking it, my thoughts muddled. "Is that why you're leaving? Are you taking a risk so you can be happy?"

"Are you insinuating that I'm an unhappy person?"

"I think I am," I say, crossing my arms in front of my chest.

"The truth is, I've never liked this place," he says, waving his hand around. "It's too cold and sterile. But I've liked having a second chance to become something less despicable than what I used to be. That isn't happiness but it's improvement. Who knows what the future holds, but yes, by leaving here I'm taking that risk."

"Where will you go now?" I ask.

"Oh, there are many places where a Dream Traveler can start anew. Maybe even I'll make a friend this time." He says this like it's a ridiculous joke.

"So you're not saying goodbye to anyone?"

"Well, I guess you count as someone. Barely though. Goodbye, Roya," he says, stepping onto the grated walkway leading to the submarine. After a few paces he turns and looks at me. "Oh, and thanks for ridding this world of Allouette. I've never slept so well."

The first smile in two weeks graces my lips. "You didn't save Joseph and me seventeen years ago for our sake, and I didn't kill Allouette for yours."

"No, we did it because it the right thing to do. Still…thanks, that bitch made my life hell."

"You're welcome," I say, and walk away.

Chapter Forty-Nine

There's one Lucidite law I never thought I'd break. Messing with Middlings isn't the worst thing in the world. Moving objects in the physical realm while dream traveling also isn't that big of a deal, if done rarely. And spying on the future, well, it can have its dangers, but mostly it just creates a mind game. However, there's one law that was created to protect the Dream Traveler. *No past self-interaction* is considered the most important of our laws. Breaking it, especially repeatedly, can leave a person with a schism in their consciousness. I only plan on breaking this law once, but still that could be enough. Maybe this is what Ren meant by taking a risk. I can think of no bigger gamble than this.

With apprehensive focus I set my attention on a specific time and place. Almost immediately I fall backwards through time, a feeling that took me a while to get used to when I first started dream traveling. As soon as I strike the right time in the past I'm suspended momentarily in the wormhole, and then I race forward. Each turn is followed by a blanket of adrenaline. Each stretch of silver tunnel brings me closer to facing this choice I've made. I close my eyes to collect some courage and don't snap them back open until I'm crouched on the street, the cobblestone under my fingertips.

July 13, 1997. Stockholm, Sweden.

In front of me stands a door as ordinary as all the rest on this narrow street. The buildings stand close together here, casting most of the area in shadows. For this reason I don't spot him until he's less than a block away. If it wasn't for the strained look on his face I might actually say he looks a little boyish. However, the anxious looks he keeps casting over his shoulder cause premature wrinkles to mark his forehead and eyes. It's only when he halts in front of the door and takes a deep breath that the worry lines that will someday be permanent fall away.

I only allow myself a brief glimpse at the bundles he's carrying against his chest. They're wrapped in dirty blankets, and one is squirming a little. The door swings open soon after Ren knocks. Trey looks like he's been expecting someone, but from the look of disgust in his eyes it wasn't Ren. I take this opportunity to move around them, and trespass into the entryway. I know my presence can't be seen, but I still don't want to pass through them for some reason.

Words now spill out of Ren's mouth; his British accent was more pronounced seventeen years ago. I only half listen to him, almost not wanting to witness this part of my history. My attention stays focused on Trey. He swipes his hand across his head of mostly blond hair. Neither man actually looks much younger than they presently are, just certain things have aged on them.

Trey's turquoise eyes, coated in disbelief and growing sorrow, dart from Ren's face to the two poorly swaddled babies in either of his lanky arms. Our father yanks us to him, angry tears already rimming his eyes. And Ren is a host of burden, all regret and remorse.

"I know I can't excuse my behavior," Ren says. "If somehow I could prove to you that I never meant for this to happen then I would. I wish—" Suddenly Ren's eyes skirt to the left, to exactly where I stand beside Trey. Startled he takes a sudden step back. Then catching himself, like he's just seen a ghost, he leans forward carefully, his hand outstretching toward me.

He senses me somehow.

"Get out of my sight," Trey says to Ren, revulsion in his voice.

Ren snaps his attention back on Trey, looking somehow lost. His eyes flick back in my direction as he nods slowly. "Yes, of course," he says, looking from Trey to me, his brow knitted with confusion.

Without another word Trey slams the door in Ren's face. He steps until his back is against the wall and slides to a seated position, cradling two tiny and fragile babies. First his lips tremble, then he pulls us closer into him. The first sob that escapes assaults me in the pit of my stomach. "Noooo," he cries, his tears falling on the blankets just beneath him. "No. No. No. No. No," he says in a traumatized rush, his chest now vibrating up and down. Trey throws his head back until it hits the plaster wall behind him. "Why? Oh my God, why?!" he shouts and there's a real question in his shaky voice, one I'm certain will haunt me for a long time. And for the first time ever I see my father for who he truly is—a man who lost the woman he loved.

After seeing the astonishing look on Ren's face I realize that this visit can hold more than just closure for me. I was hoping to come here to understand Trey. To understand enough that I could find the next direction to navigate in this muddy water I've entered. But maybe…maybe there are more options for me here.

I kneel down, never looking at either baby, and hover in close to Trey. My lips only a few inches from his ear. "Dad…" I say, testing the word. He doesn't startle, only continues to convulse with silent tears. "If you can hear me, then listen. This is Roya. I'm one of the babies in your arms right now and I need you to know a few things. First of all, you've got to stop blaming yourself for her death. Sometimes you don't get to live your life with the ones you've loved. You'll never know what a life with them would have been like. And that wasn't the point in the relationship in the first place. The point is to get you to the next place in your life, a place where you wouldn't have gone otherwise. Secondly, please know that your mistakes won't scar anyone, even you. They will just be mistakes and once again without them no one will progress. One day I'll blame you. I'll hurt you. I'll misjudge you." I've never had this happen in any dream travel, but as I speak a single tear falls from my eye and lands with a splat on the floor. "And one day I'll forgive you for everything. One day it will all work out. But you have to get up now and in the future. You have to protect us. You *have* to send us away." And I can't believe the next words that fall out of my mouth, but they do, as real as water flowing in a river. "You *have* to separate us…because if you don't, then we'll die."

Trey hitches in a breath, holds it and pushes upright. For the first time he pulls the blankets back and stares at the faces of the babies in his arms. His eyes circle around the empty flat, like he's heard a voice he's trying locate. Not finding what he's looking for he returns to the faces of the infants in his arms, and caresses a hand against our cheeks individually. "It's okay, children," he says, through a tattered voice. "I'll take care of you. Forever I'll watch over you."

For several hours I sit with my father and grieve. I picture that he's able to rest his head on my shoulder, to have someone besides two infants to confide his pain in. My tears fall so rapidly that they soak my shirt. And never do I look at my own face, not that I'd know it from Joseph's. Still, that's not the point of the visit. It's to stare into Trey's eyes, to understand his pain and therefore the weight I inherited.

He talks to us. Tells us how much our mother loved us. How much she wanted us. He tells us about their dreams, about the plans that would never come to pass. And I listen, sometimes reluctantly, sometimes unable to understand his words through his grief-stricken tears. But I don't move from his side. For all of that night, I stay with him. I watch him sink into the person that I know now. I watch him evolve from the man who opened that door with anxious eyes to find Eloise, to the man who realized she was never coming home again. I watch my father's heart break over and over again in one night, and that's when I make the decision to love him.

When I know my night is drawing to an end, that I must retreat for my own health, I make as if to rest my hand on Trey's arm. I picture…I wish…I sense he feels me. "One last thing before I go," I say to the man who's finally laid his children down on the bed, to rest without his arms. "You need to trust the man who just delivered us to you. Ren is a good man. For that matter, so are you."

I let my hand fall through him and I disappear, back to my room inside the Institute.

♦

When I enter his room the next morning, I expect him to be staring at the wall like he normally does.

He is.

I expect him to sit motionless while I settle into the chair beside his bed and open my book to the place where I left off.

He does.

I expect him to remain frozen while I sit and read.

Almost, like a machine operating for the first time, a bit rigidly, he turns. Looks at me. "Roya," he says, his voice quiet, unused.

"Trey?!" I say, sitting forward, dropping the book.

"Dad," he corrects, staring at me from his place higher up on his bed.

"You're…what?" I say, disbelief coating every word, every thought.

He brings his chin up, his turquoise eyes holding a strange hope. "You've…you've…finally done it, haven't you?" he says in a ghostly voice.

"What? What have I done?" I say, rushing to his side. I almost grip his hand but hesitate a few inches away.

He reaches forward and seizes my hand, his eyes swelling with tears. "All your life I've been waiting for you to experience that moment but I never knew when it would come to pass. And it has, hasn't it? You visited me?"

Confused and elated I say, "Yes, I've been here every day."

He shakes his head. "Not here. In the past." He gulps, swallowing down tears. "I named you Roya after that."

"After what?" I say, knowing what's coming next, but needing to hear it.

Tugging my hand in closer, he looks at me with earnestness. "I knew you were there. Seventeen years ago I felt you. I felt the messages in the words I didn't hear. And I knew they were yours. They were, weren't they?"

I nod, an ache erupting in my chest, engulfing the space around me.

"You saved me all those years ago. And all these years you've saved me by giving me hope." Sliding his hands across his drenched cheeks, he sucks in a breath. "And I've been waiting, hoping I didn't imagine it because then it meant that at some point in the future you didn't hate me anymore. That one day you forgave me enough to risk your life to save mine. And you did. All these years I would never have been strong enough if you hadn't come to me, inspired me when you were first born." His weak smile is full of pain. "I've been merely surviving, waiting to get to this point. Waiting for you to get to this point. To where you saved us."

I slip my hand from his and fold my arms around his neck, hugging him into me, feeling him convulse with sobs against my chest. "We're there now," I say. "We're there now."

Chapter Fifty

"I am grateful you both will be returning to news reporting," Shuman says, standing with both hands clasped behind her back. "Without your reports we have logged half as many stories as we used to and nothing as significant as the ones you normally report."

"It will be good to be useful," I say, scanning the Panther room. It's always a relief to dwell in a space that doesn't show the damage from Zhuang's attack. To look at Joseph's face and see the light back in his eyes also brings comfort. He was slow to come out of the depression that hit us all after Day Z, but Trey waking up helped. The burden he carries for murdering our grandfather may never leave him, but I will be his secret keeper and help him shoulder its weight.

"May I ask you a question?" Joseph says to Shuman.

"You may ask both of your questions to me."

Joseph gives Shuman a confused look. "Nah, I just got one. Where'd you keep all those rattlers that besieged the battle on Day Z?"

"I keep them in various places around the Institute," Shuman says dispassionately.

Joseph looks at me and raises an eyebrow before turning back to Shuman. "Ugh, is that safe?"

An almost smile flicks in her eyes. "It is," she says, answering his second question. How she does that, I have no clue. Shuman turns without another word and stalks away.

"I think she has a crush on me," Joseph says, looking satisfied.

"You think everyone has a crush on you."

"They do...well, not you. That'd be creepy."

"Speaking of people who have crushes on you," I say.

"He gave me until the end of the year to come out," Joseph says, shaking his head and writhing a bit.

"And if you don't?"

"Then T man is through with me for good."

"So what are you going to do?" I ask, although I already sense his answer.

"Work on a speech to give at the Christmas feast," Joseph says.

"Oh, so you're going to wait until the last possible moment, huh?"

"Oh, sis," he says, draping his arm over my shoulder as we walk. "You know you gotta make them wait with suspense. It makes 'em want you more."

"Well, and also you're scared to death about telling the Institute you're gay."

"I'm tryin' to give you love advice which you desperately need, so don't go changing the subject."

"I'm good actually. I've got the 'impossible-to-get' act down."

"Oh, that you do," Joseph says with a whistle.

Taking a seat in my news reporting recliner I say, "Hey, and why would you think there would be a Christmas celebration at the Institute? None of the Lucidites I know are Christian."

Joseph laughs. "And most of the people I know who celebrate the holiday aren't Christian either. It's a much needed occasion to wear red and lavish your loved ones with gifts."

"Red isn't my color," I say.

"Well, just buy me something really expensive that I don't need."

"You're making money news reporting now, buy yourself something."

"I don't log as many reports as you since mine are so far in the future. I know you're pulling in like thirty thousand a week," he says with a disgruntled huff.

"Have you ever wondered where the money to fund this place comes from?" I ask, kicking my feet back and forth over the side of the chair.

"Gosh, Stark, if I wasn't in your head I'd think you were pretendin' to be that thick."

I give him my usual "what the hell are you talking about" look.

"Sis, what do you think Pops does when you log a news report with tomorrow's lottery numbers for the state of Oregon? You think he just swells with pride that his daughter has such a fun gift?"

"He uses that to make money?"

"As well as other methods. I mean having a gaggle of clairvoyants gives the Institute information about future stocks, worthy ventures, and not to mention the technology we sell to the US government."

"Man, that's genius," I say.

"It's a good thing I'm gonna take over this place and not you, you've got zero business savvy."

"Well, hopefully you'll take pity on me and keep me employed, dear brother."

"Oh yeah, you'll be my bread and butter," he says with a smile. The space grows comfortably quiet. "Does that mean you're sticking around even after your two-year sentence is over?"

"Joseph, wherever you are, that's where I want to be. So yes, I'm sticking around."

Chapter Fifty-One

The following Sunday, as everyone chows down on fresh food, the Head Official for the Lucidite Institute boards the stage in the main hall. My father walks with a new confidence as he makes his way to the center of the platform. Despite the weight he's lost he appears strong. Before he even takes the microphone in his hand I notice the people in the main hall revolve on him, respect in everyone's gaze. Had they always looked at him like this? Was it my perspective that kept it hidden from me? Surely people have a new found respect for the man before us, who everyone knows has sacrificed everything to protect the people he loves.

Every shred of scrutiny that my father ever faced dissipated when the stories began to circulate. The ones about how he'd lost our mother, sent his children away to protect us, and watched over us every single day without fail. And all to shelter us, and to safeguard the fate of the Lucidites. Too many times recently I've overheard people in the main hall or the library speaking about my father like he's a living legend. And it always brings a small smile to my heart, because he truly is. He's the passion and fortitude that writes the stories of unconditional love.

"I know everyone here has been through a long and strenuous ordeal," my father begins in his unemotional tone. "And I'm here to reassure everyone that we will recover from this. I will make sure of it."

Trey lets his eyes drift to where Joseph and I sit and I find it difficult to maintain eye contact with him. We aren't back to normal because before this we had no normal. After hours of sitting with him while he lay in a hospital robe I feel past normal with the man who stands on the stage before me. He isn't just my father, he's a leader of a place I've realized is my home.

Trey clears his throat and just when I expect him to run his fingers through his silver hair he keeps his hands firmly planted on the microphone. "All of our enemies are gone. We have survived, although I know we have suffered. We will rebuild. We will heal. We will get past this. I will make it my mission to ensure that every person at this Institute, every Lucidite, has the resources to rise from this challenge. We're a family. And we will stand together stronger because of what we've experienced. If there's anything that any of you need to do these things that pushes us forward, please come to me personally. Thank you."

The brevity in his speech is what ignites the silence that follows. I love that he knows long speeches are not the way to loyal hearts. Lowering the microphone he stares out at the sea of faces, making eye contact with all of the residents. Applause erupts around the hall, but my father quickly quiets it, not looking for the endorsement of his people. His intention was to bolster confidence, not receive it. He pulls the microphone to his chin again. "Dr. Livingston has a couple of logistical reminders for you all, so at this point I'll hand the microphone off to him."

Aiden takes the microphone, his casual nature exuding across the main hall. It might just be me, but he lights up spaces, spreads an energy of passion wherever he is. "Here's the deal, people," he begins with a melodramatic sigh. "Even if you've used the GAD-C a trillion times, I want you to review the new procedures for how to operate the devices. I have to make this demand of all of you, because A) some of you long-time users are getting a little sloppy and that's not going to bode well for you." Laughter explodes from various tables.

"I'd like to see my nose in a new place for a fun change," a guy says from the back corner.

"Yeah, yeah. Not on my watch," Aiden replies with a chuckle. "And B) I haven't just been working on my Pac-Man gaming skills while our esteemed leader was recovering, as some of my employees like to joke. I've made critical upgrades to the devices and you'll only be aware of them if you read the new instructions. The specifics on the new functionality are posted beside the machines." Aiden pauses. His eyes fall to the floor of the stage. The pause lengthens, making people in the room stir.

Finally, Aiden brings his eyes up and looks at Trey and then out to the rest of the crowd. He pulls the microphone back to his mouth. "Oh, and there's one more thing. It's of great importance and something I want to make everyone aware of." He scans the room as everyone focuses on him, waiting for this specific information. Aiden clears his throat. Fidgets with the microphone. His eyes find me. "I'm relentlessly and inescapably in love with Roya Stark."

My eyes widen in shock. Aiden stares out past the prairie of faces, his gaze pinned on only mine. People make noises around me but I don't pay attention to them. Aiden and I stand alone in the main hall, the only two souls on Earth connected by our gazes. Entangled by a love so pure it erases everything around it.

I chance a look at my father. His stare bounces between Aiden and me several times. Astonishment writes a new expression on his face, one I've never seen before. I guess my father's intuition doesn't inform him of everything. I lose the opportunity to take in his next reaction because my attention is assaulted by Aiden as he leaps off the front of the stage and hurries through the cheery Institute residents. Too fast he stands before me. I push out of my chair and walk directly to him, magnetized by a force.

"That was quite the announcement," I say, chewing on my lip.

"Long. Over. Due," he says, scratching the back of his head. "You wouldn't believe how many people keep botching up the GAD-C procedures. It's just a matter of time before someone auto generated with their parts all wrong."

I slap him playfully on the chest. We laugh, both of relief and nervousness. People move out of the main hall now, some lurking, watching us. Aiden isn't the least bit aware of them, his eyes fastened on me.

"Well..." he finally says. "Now there's no keeping this thing between you and me under wraps. The secret is out."

"Indeed," I say.

"So I hope you'll have me even if I'm unemployed."

"Aiden, I will have you any way I can get you."

A brilliant smile lights up his face. "Really?"

"Yes, really. It's always been you, Aiden. Always. No one else owns my hear—"

My dad's sudden appearance by our sides interrupts me. He looks at me and then Aiden, his mouth and eyes pinched. I'm prepared to say whatever I need to defend us. To lay down every excuse to protect this guy I love and the job he loves.

Trey turns to Aiden. "You know—"

"Dad, this is—"

My father holds up a hand, shakes his head at me. "This isn't something I want your opinion on, Roya. This is an issue between

Aiden and me, as he is an employee of the Institute. I would ask that you kindly back out of this conversation," he says.

I have no intention of backing out, but I shut my mouth just this once. It's something about the meaningful expression in my father's eyes. We've come so far and the last thing I want is for us to regress.

He turns and focuses on Aiden, looks to be calculating something. "Aiden, I believe you've taken a big risk to do what you've just done. A sacrifice of sorts. You knew that, didn't you?" my father says, peering at Aiden with a measured glare.

"Yes, Trey, I did."

"How long has this been going on?" Trey asks, his eyes only on Aiden.

Aiden looks at me and dares to smile. "Since the moment I saw her."

"Hmmm," my father says like a disgruntled sheep. "I see."

"Dad—" I interject.

"Again, Roya, this is not a matter I want your input on." He steps sideways, his back to me, and half whispers in Aiden's ear. "Well, I only have one last thing to say to you on the matter and then we will be done. No arguments. Is that clear?"

Aiden doesn't say a word, just nods, eyes dripping with tension.

"After a declaration like that I think you owe my daughter a kiss." My dad hitches his head sideways, chancing a glance at me over his shoulder.

"Yes sir," Aiden says.

The smile that flits to my father's face takes a gentle pressure off my heart. He claps a hand on Aiden's shoulder and leaves.

Aiden's eyes land on me at once. "Your father is a wise man," he says, a giant smile on his handsome face. The main hall is almost empty, but when Aiden steps forward and slides his hand along my cheek I lose sight for anyone but him.

"I love you," I whisper. He kisses me. A kiss so brilliant and pure I'm transported. If anyone is still in the main hall watching this expression of love then I believe they are inspired too. Love like this…love like ours, is the kind to dream about. Pray for. Slaughter demons to protect. The love I have for the guy holding me now is more than enough to sustain me always, it's enough to heal and flourish my heart, set it free to finally allow bliss into my life.

Epilogue

Through the years my correspondence with George stayed steady. He knew of my life and happiness. Although at times I sensed his disappointment that it wasn't with him I think our friendship meant more. It was difficult to convince him to attend the wedding though.

"George, you're one of my dearest friends. Please. It won't be the same without you there." I knew what I was asking of him was a lot, but many years had passed. Our friendship had deepened, never with a hint of romance. Still, I always knew he was in love with me, always felt it like fabric against my skin.

"Roya, you'll ruin your wedding dress by wearing the frequency adjuster."

"Oh, there's no way I'm wearing a wedding dress," I said, sitting on the dewy grass and enjoying the misty hills of Laos before us.

"But it's your wedding day," he said, taking the seat next to me, legs crossed.

"Exactly. It's *my* day. And I'll look absolutely ridiculous on top of Mount Kilimanjaro in a fluffy dress. Let Samara wear one for me."

"Mount Kilimanjaro, huh?" he said, raising an impressed eyebrow at me. "So Samara will be there?" George inquired casually. He hadn't returned to the Institute since he left. He once told me that returning would be like going backwards, and it had been so difficult for him to move forward. Now he was in his graduate program at Dartmouth. He stayed closed off from the rest of the Lucidite society, keeping mostly to himself. This was one of the reasons I wanted him at the wedding. I wanted the event to feel complete, and George was a part of the love that had led to my union with Aiden.

"Of course Samara will be there. Everyone will be there," I said.

"Is she your maid of honor?"

"Do you think for a second Joseph would allow that?!" I laughed. "Joseph elected himself into that role. Trent is Aiden's best man."

George was slow to cover his grimace at the mention of Aiden's name. "How is Samara? I haven't seen her since I left."

"Good. She married a telepath," I say, enjoying the brilliant gold sunrise as it kissed the tops of the mountains.

"What a perfect match," George said.

"Maybe we can find you an empath."

He lowered his chin. Gave me his trademark punishing stare. "You're the last person I want trying to make a match for me."

"I'm sorry, George. That was insensitive. I only meant—"

"You don't have to worry about me," he interrupted.

"But I do," I said, reaching over and grabbing his hand, squeezing it once. "Are you happy?"

"Roya, I don't need someone in my life to make me happy. I'm certain I will love again, not like I love you, but I will. Still, I don't want to search for someone hoping they'll fulfill a part in me. That's what you told me, right, before I left?"

"I told you to stop looking to me to make you happy."

"Right, and that goes for everyone else too."

We sat quietly listening to the birds. Watching the sun shift, creating new patterns on the mountains. After several minutes of silence George said, "You feel guilty for how things turned out between us."

There was no arguing with him and we both knew it. I pressed my lips together and regarded him for a long moment.

Finally he said, "Everything I wanted was pinned on you, like you were the bulletin board for my dreams. Do you realize how wrong that is? Don't feel guilty, because if we would have ended up together, neither of us would have been happy. Love like that is too unstable, it's destined for disappointment."

His hand was still in mine. I squeezed it and leaned my head on his shoulder, letting out a gentle sigh. "Oh, George..." I said, all my words falling away into the delicate mist.

♦

The wedding didn't end up being on Mount Kilimanjaro. It had been a lofty idea of mine, but I finally decided I wanted to be married in the flesh. The wedding was held in the only place fitting, the main hall. Garlands of hydrangeas in blues and greens hung

305

around the space. A gazebo was erected in the center of the hall so that our guests sat around it in a circle. And real grass was brought in so that Trey led me down an aisle that felt like it was inside a garden.

Aiden wore the same tuxedo he had when we danced during the party after the Day of the Duel. And I was somehow persuaded by an unrelenting Joseph to wear an actual wedding dress. It was simple, strapless, and light, since I had the train chopped off.

My something blue was the sash I wore around my waist which matched Aiden's eyes. The something borrowed was a set of diamond combs from Samara that she arranged in my pinned up curls. The something new was a necklace of pearls my father had given me that draped in rows around my neck. And the something old was the frequency adjuster which I'd had a pocket sewn into the dress to hold. Even though George said he wouldn't come, I had put it into the dress anyway. And when I marched down the aisle, my father's arm almost vibrating around mine, I was relieved to find George staring at me from the second row. Then my eyes found Aiden's and everyone in the room disappeared from my attention.

"Aiden is a lucky man," George had said as we danced through the crowd of happy Lucidites after the ceremony. "I knew he loved you since the moment the frequency adjuster fired up for the first time. I knew you loved him then too."

Traumatic relief at his disclosure constricted my chest. When the dance neared the end, he kissed my hand. Suddenly the words I struggled with so many times came out unrehearsed and as natural as the sound of wind. "I love you, George. I always will."

He didn't say another word, just offered me a rare smile, one that made his deep brown eyes light up.

♦

I didn't knock, just strolled on in. He was so engrossed in his work that he didn't see me until I was a couple feet away.

"Oh, no you don't. I've got too much work to do to have you prancing around my lab teasing me with distractions," Aiden said, backing up several feet.

"I think I'm going to choose to be offended by that," I said, continuing to stroll in his direction.

"If you choose, but I'm still going to politely request you take your pretty mouth out of my lab." I reached for him, but he slipped away with a sideways smile. "I promise to give you audience later."

I huffed. Hopped up on the high table currently cluttered with gadgets. "And I promise to be quick, but there's something I need to discuss."

Aiden leaned against the opposite table, giving me a skeptical look. "All right, go on with it."

"*Well,* you know the Head Strategist's living quarters across from ours are bigger. And...I was thinking that before Trent is promoted to the position, that we make the case to my father that we move into the place."

The Institute had been through half a dozen Head Strategists since Ren had left. The position had opened up again and since Trent had been working successfully in the department for a few years it was strongly rumored he'd be promoted.

"Yes, but if it's a space issue then it's a moot point. There are two of them and two of us."

"That's where you're wrong. We need more space. There's soon to be three of us," I said, motioning between him and me.

His eyes were clear and blue and wide. In two movements he was in front of me, hands cupping my face. "Roya, you're...?"

"I am."

If happiness has a sound then it's the chuckle that fell out of Aiden's mouth. His breath was warm as he neared my lips. I wrapped my legs around him, tugging him in closer as he kissed me more delicately than ever before, each a moment captured and frozen.

"Oh Jesus," Joseph said when he entered the lab. "Do y'all always have to be making out?"

We parted enough so just our noses were touching. Without taking my eyes off Aiden I said, "Yes, we do."

"Well, Stark, you told me to meet you down here. What's this about?"

"Mr. Jordan, the future you foretold to me on Day Z is about to come to pass," Aiden said, eyes still pinned on me.

"What?!" Joseph bellowed, moving forward. I looked away from Aiden to catch the gleeful look in my brother's eyes. "Li'l Joseph is on his way?!"

"Wait!" I said, staring between Aiden and Joseph. "That's what you told Aiden on Day Z? That's why you released us?" I asked Aiden in astonishment. "He told you we were going to have a child together?"

He smirked and nodded.

"Why didn't either one of you tell me?" I said in a high-pitched screech.

Aiden kissed me softly on the cheek. "We wanted it to be a surprise."

"Surprise!" Joseph said, wrapping his arms around the two of us giving us a group hug. "Man, this boy is gonna be so lucky to have me as his uncle."

"And you know it's a boy?" I asked, still reeling from disbelief.

"Without a single doubt." Joseph half skipped to the exit. "Well, I've got my work cut out for me telling everyone this news."

"Uh…" Aiden began, "shouldn't that be our job?"

"Nope, y'all stay here and do what you do best," he said, sending the door shut after him.

"Well, that's all I wanted to discuss," I said, pinning my hands on either side of the workstation. "As promised I won't take any more of your precious work time." I tried to push him to the side so I could spring off the table.

"Oh, no you don't," Aiden said, locking me in place with his body. "I believe this calls for a celebration."

He planted a soft kiss on my mouth that quickly turned into a series of harder ones. The music overhead was ironically the first song I ever heard in his lab, *Plans and Reverie*. The emotions, his hands, the music, the feel of a room coated in his energies transferred me to a plane of reality without ever having to dream travel. Entangled in his arms and his world, I collided with something new.

◆

I left their place boarded up for the first year. Although I'd inherited it, as well as everything they owned, I thought that going there would make their absence unbearable.

I was wrong.

308

When I walked through Bob and Steve's home for the first time after their death, their energy returned to me. Being in their home made me feel they'd never be gone from my life, that there'd always be a way to reconnect with them. And even after their death, they continued to have a positive influence on my life. People who are innately good, as Bob and Steve were, don't lose their ability to inspire when they leave this world.

After our son was born, Aiden and I made the decision to live half the year at the Institute and the other half at the lake house. It was important to us that Max was able to play in the sand, run through the grass, and swim in the water. But we also wanted to continue our work at the Institute, and expose our child to the lives that had shaped *both* of our childhoods. It wasn't that we wanted our son to have a normal life, we wanted him to have a life that was meaningful. And that meant knowing both the world above and below the surface of the water. These were choices we made to suit our lives, which is why I was surprised when my immediate family assumed the new living arrangements included them.

"It's called working remotely," Joseph had said. "And the lake house is plenty big for all of us."

He'd shown up last night as I rocked Max on the porch, listening to the crickets in the bushes and watching the lightning bugs swarm around the sloping lawn.

"But how did you get here so fast?" I asked, remembering the long trip by submarine, plane, and then car.

"Well, I don't have an infant, so dream traveling to the nearest GAD-C isn't too difficult. It's only a few hours away. Although, I would sweet talk your hubby into building one closer. What's the point in sleeping with the guy if you can't get favors?"

"There are many reasons," I said, with a wide smile.

"Gross," my brother said, slipping Max out of my arms. "Give me my boy. Soon the others will be here and they'll be tryin' to steal him from me."

"Others?"

Joseph winked at me before taking off with Max. "She's so thick to think we'd let her steal off with you for a whole six months. I'm gonna teach you how to fish and catch tadpoles and—"

"He's only six months old," I said with a sigh.

"Shhh. Don't you limit this child with those low expectations."

♦

The next morning I awake to the sound of laughter. It's unsurprisingly Aiden's. What surprises me is to find him drinking coffee and playing chess with my father.

"Hey, Dad," I say through a long yawn. "I didn't know you were visiting." I kiss his cheek and check on Max, who's scooting himself across the rug.

"Visiting? Hmmm…yes, that's what I'm doing," he says, giving Aiden a sly smile.

"Have you moved into the room next to Joseph?" I ask, through another yawn. Joseph and I spent the whole night catching up. We'd only been apart a few weeks, but still with limited opportunities to dream travel due to the demands of late-night feedings, it was difficult to see him.

"I have," my father says, looking a little sheepish. "Is that all right?"

"Just no late-night parties," I say, taking Max in my lap.

"All right, go ahead and finish your story, Trey," Aiden urges.

"Oh, yeah…where was I?" he says, scratching his head. "Well, she must have been around eight. After two weeks the principal called her into his office and said that he was concerned because her hair was so unkempt."

"What are you doing?" I ask, suddenly standing with Max tucked under one arm.

"Telling him about the time you refused to brush your hair because you thought you were creating a hairdo masterpiece."

Aiden doubles over with uncontrollable laughter.

"They actually sent her home and told her not to return until she brushed it because her hair was becoming a distraction to other children," my father says, tears in his eyes from laughter.

"Max," I say, pinching his chin which is pointy like his father's. "I'll never do that to you; embarrass you with stories about your childhood."

Joseph sweeps around the corner, plucking the chubby baby from my arms. "Well, of course you won't because my nephew is perfect and will never do anything embarrassing." He leans down

310

and whispers in his ear, still loud enough for me to hear. "That's because you take after me."

A laugh falls from my mouth. "Oh, is that where he got that dark brown mop?" I ask, tousling my son's hair.

"He may have gotten Livingston's hair but he got my eyes," Joseph says, staring fondly at his nephew.

"My eyes," I correct.

"Ours," Joseph says with a wink. "Max, even if you're all arms and legs like your father then you'll still be perfect."

"All little Maxie has to do is an ounce of exercise and he won't be all lanky looking like Aiden," Trent says, coming into the room.

"I exercise," Aiden says, stuffing the rest of a croissant in his mouth.

"Playing with wires doesn't count as proper exercise," Joseph says.

I wrap my arms around Aiden's shoulders from behind and kiss his cheek. "Don't listen to them, they're just jealous. If Joseph ate like you he'd be fat."

Joseph takes in a sudden breath, gasping. "Don't say the 'f' word in connection with my name," he scolds.

Max sticks his fist in his mouth. Drool slides down his chin.

"Hey look, Maxie does take after you, Joe," Trent says, turning to me with a conspiratorial look. "He drools so much at night that every morning he's got to change his pillowcase."

"Yeah, he never outgrew that," Trey says, swallowing down the last of his coffee.

We all laugh at Joseph's expense. Trey turns around, taking a break from his chess game with Aiden. "Trent, when Joseph was a kid he used to think there was a right and left sock, the same way as there is with shoes."

"Pops," Joseph says, rolling his eyes. "I always knew when you were there. I did that stuff to entertain you."

"It worked," my father says, smiling like he's seeing the memory in his mind.

"Oh, Joe, you can't know when a Dream Traveler's visiting you when you're awake," Trent says, softly punching Joseph on the arm.

My father lifts his gaze to mine. "Oh, I disagree."

I return his delicate smile with my own. Then I turn my attention to Aiden. "Well, Dr. Livingston, while we have babysitters I offer you the opportunity for a rematch."

"Okay, but I want a head start," he says.

"Are you really going to feel good if you win that way?" I say.

"I don't plan to win," he says, like the idea is preposterous. "I just don't want to lose too badly. It's not really a fair match since you grew up swimming." Aiden turns to Joseph with a crooked grin. "We've raced every afternoon since we got here. Haven't even come close to beating her yet."

"Hey, Livingston gives me an excellent idea," Joseph says, a sudden light in his eyes. "Pops, can we have a pool at the Institute?"

My father's laughter isn't rare anymore like it used to be, but still I notice it always gives me pause. "I think the logistics of how to do that successfully are beyond me, Joseph," he says in response.

"That's a nice way of saying that's the worst idea ever," Trent says, laughing.

I kiss Max on the forehead. "You keep an eye on these three, all right?" I say to my son, who coos back to me.

"How about a driving range?" Joseph says, his eyes brightening with new ideas.

"No," Dad says.

"Bumper cars?"

Our father pretends to think for a few seconds. "No."

"When are you going to grow up, Joe?" Trent says, laughing harder now.

"Did I ever give the impression that I was gonna? How about a petting zoo for your grandson?"

My father picks Max up from the play mat and holds him in the air over his head like he's an airplane. "Well, I was thinking about building an aquarium in the lobby," he says. "Would you like to see some fish, little guy?" Max giggles. "I think that was a yes," my father says, bringing Max to his chest.

I turn to Aiden, a look of unabashed glee on my face. "Are you ready to lose again?"

"Almost," he says. "Let me just go get my trunks on."

"K, I'll meet you outside."

"No warming up. That wouldn't be fair."

"You don't need fair, you need a miracle to beat me," I sing as I push the sliding door closed.

Once I'm outside, the Texas sun warms my shoulders immediately. The lake gently rocks against the retaining wall, making my thoughts recede. When I first dream traveled into the Institute I almost drowned. Aiden saved me. Shuman said she didn't tell me to auto-generate my body because that created a series of events that secured a future for millions. All I know for certain is when I awoke on that GAD-C, shivering and half dead, I fell instantly for the guy who saved my life. It's my love for Aiden that propelled me in the fight against Zhuang, that carried me through the Grotte and inspired me countless other times. It's strange to think how the love I have for one guy encouraged my actions so in the end I saved so many. When I submerged into the murky lake waters the night I entered the Institute for the first time, I had no idea where I was going, what I'd face and that on the other side would be the guy of my dreams. And if I would have known I'm certain things wouldn't have turned out the way they did.

"All right," Aiden says, joining me in the yard. "I'm ready to be schooled."

I turn to him with a devilish smile. "You know I have no intention of swimming with you?"

"Oh?" he says, arching an eyebrow.

"Yes, but we're still getting in the lake."

"Mrs. Livingston," he says in pleased tone.

I strip down to my bathing suit, which I mostly live in while at the lake house. "I know a private place," I say, taking Aiden's glasses off his face and tossing them on my stack of clothes in the grass.

"I think I need help with my shirt too," Aiden says, pouting his lips.

"Then I'm your girl," I say, lifting his shirt up until he grabs it at his shoulders and tosses it behind him. I trace the scars on his chest, the ones he received while at the Grotte. Under my fingertips the raised marks are soft, only distant reminders of something from a different life. Standing up to my tiptoes I wrap my arms around his neck and lean in to kiss him. He reaches down and sweeps my body into his arms, cradling me against his chest. I don't have a second to react before he races to the dock. Laughter spills out of my mouth, even as I bury my face in his shoulder.

"Aiden Livingston, you better not throw me in!" I scream.

"I wouldn't dream of it. I'm taking you down with me." And then he jumps off the end of the dock, his legs kicking like he's trying to run over air. We're briefly suspended between the sky and the earth before we plunge into the tepid water. He releases me once we're fully submerged, but within seconds I swim back into his arms. Under the water Aiden's hands find my face. He draws me into him. His lips sink into mine. My heart fills beyond capacity. Ascends through the waters of the lake and into the heavens. And when our bodies break the surface I'm breathless.

The End

Acknowledgements

I called the second book a monster. But this one was actually a raging beast. There are a lot of people who helped me corral this book, strap a muzzle on it and make it into a civilized creature. To those people I owe my heart and many words of gratitude. Writing a three book series is one of the hardest things I've ever done. Still I am grateful that in the cosmos or wherever these assignments are made I was the one chosen to write these books. My first thank you goes to God or the Source or whoever opened me up enough to write these stories. I've never for an instant thought this was my story or that I was the creative genius behind this all. I know better. These books came through me and I've had too many awe-inspiring moments not to fully believe that. Much like Roya, I don't know what I believe, but I know I came from somewhere and I know that's where this book came from too. So thank you.

Thank you to Christine LePorte, my editor. Writing this book was easier than the other two because I knew I could rely on you to make me look good. Thank you for always being prompt to answer my questions and being wonderful to work with.

Thank you to Andrei Bat, my cover designer. I'm infinitely grateful you won that contest. And I'm inspired by your work. Hope I didn't wear you out too much with revisions, because you probably haven't seen the last of me yet.

Thank you to the musicians who inspired the playlist for this book: Imagine Dragons, Greg Laswell, Glen Hansard, Snow Patrol, Foo Fighters, and Lana Del Rey.

Thank you to my friends and family. It's really hard to express how much you're overwhelming support has meant to me. Thank you to Heidi. You're endorsements keeps me reaching higher. Thank you to my father and Kathy for your support and encouragement. Thank you to Edie and Randy. I'm very blessed to have you all.

Thank you to Dane Maliski, Meghan Toledo and Colleen Maliski. Your brilliance made this book better.

Thank you to Lydia, my daughter. One day someone will steal your heart and make you want to do something incredible just to show them how much their love inspired you. On that day you'll know why I wrote these books. For you, my muse. Thank you.

Thank you to Luke Noffke. I'm a writer who doesn't have the words to express how grateful I am to you for listening, supporting and being amazing through this all. It isn't easy to be the partner to an overly anxious and compulsive writer, but you make the role look downright glamourous. You astound me with your patience and thoughtfulness. I love you!

Thank you to my readers. You absolutely make this a bundle of fun. I love hearing your feedback. I'm infinitely grateful to have the opportunity to share my books with you. And I'm equally grateful that you read them. Thank you!

I have so many people to thank and it's impossible for me to list everyone here. I'm so grateful to every writing teacher who encouraged me. Every person who pushed me. My first bosses who believed in me. It all created a place in me that had the confidence to sit down and write. Honestly, I'm just a small town girl from Texas. I used to spend my evenings writing poetry in the woods and day dreaming about one day doing something bigger. I guess dreams do come true. Maybe they're more real than I ever imagined. Thank you to everyone. I love you.

Sincerely,

Sarah

About the Author:

Sarah is the author of the Lucidites and the Reverians series. She's been everything from a corporate manager to a hippie. Her taste for adventure has taken her all over the world. If you can't find her at the gym, then she's probably at the frozen yogurt shop. If you can't find her there then she probably doesn't want to be found. She is a self-proclaimed hermit, with spontaneous urges to socialize during full moons and when Mercury is in retrograde. Sarah lives in Central California with her family. To learn more about Sarah please visit: http://www.sarahnoffke.com

Check out other work by this author:

The Reverians Series:
Defects, #1:
    In the happy, clean community of Austin Valley, everything appears to be perfect. Seventeen-year-old Em Fuller, however, fears something is askew. Em is one of the new generation of Dream Travelers. For some reason, the gods have not seen fit to gift all of them with their expected special abilities. Em is a Defect—one of the unfortunate Dream Travelers not gifted with a psychic power. Desperate to do whatever it takes to earn her gift, she endures painful daily injections along with commands from her overbearing, loveless father. One of the few bright spots in her life is the return of a friend she had thought dead—but with his return comes the knowledge of a shocking, unforgivable truth. The society Em thought was protecting her has actually been betraying her, but she has no idea how to break away from its authority without hurting everyone she loves.

Rebels, #2
Warriors, #3

Spanish version of *Awoken*: *Despertada*

www.ingramcontent.com/pod-product-compliance
Lightning Source LLC
Chambersburg PA
CBHW020336180626
46812CB00001B/226